FOR THE HELL OF IT
...AND SOUVENIRS!

JOHN T. MALTESE

FOR THE HELL OF IT

...AND SOUVENIRS!

MILL CITY PRESS

Mill City Press, Inc.
212 3rd Avenue North, Suite 290
Minneapolis, MN 55401
612.455.2294
www.millcitypublishing.com

ISBN-13: 978-1-938008-30-6
LCCN: 2012923233

Cover Design and Typeset by Steve Porter

Printed in the United States of America

Thank you to my mother, sisters Jodie and Janet, my wife, Wendy, and our children, Chris, Michael, and Mackenzie, for assisting and allowing me to work on publishing this book in honor of John T. Maltese.

Introduction

"THE STORY BEHIND THIS BOOK"

Our father, John T. Maltese, a former Marine, wrote this book in the late 1950's while he was teaching Journalism at Steubenville High School in Steubenville, Ohio. Our mother, Sophia, tirelessly typed the story using an old manual 1950's typewriter. For the next forty years the manuscript of more than 650 pages sat in a box in the attic of my parents' home.

In 2005, I asked my mother to bring the now yellowing pages up to Michigan on one of her visits to my home. Although barely readable, we made copies adjusting the depth of the toner, attempting to make the copies more legible. I then placed the copies back in a storage box in a closet of my home for the next few years, never reading it. My father had passed away in 1995, and with the exception of my mother reading it while typing the novel, no one else had ever read the book.

In January of 2008, my wife Wendy and I were planning to go on our first vacation without our children in over fifteen years. She asked if I was going to bring a book to read on the trip since we would not have our kids to keep us busy over the five days. I decided to take the two loose-leaf binders containing the 681 pages of my dad's book. I planned on giving the book a chance to see if it was "readable" from start to finish. An avid reader of newspapers, sports magazines, civil war stories, and medical journals, I am not a "novel reader." The last book I had completely read was "Killer Angels," a novel about the civil war, and that was over fifteen years ago. I started reading my dad's book while on our cruise get-away and could not put it down. Therefore, upon returning home, I asked my mom why my dad had never had the book published.

She informed me there were many reasons. These included the labor involved and the difficulty in the 1950's of having a book published, especially on a teacher's salary. She went on to say their main priorities were to provide for and raise their children; therefore, the pages of the book were placed in that box and stowed away in the attic. I told her I felt we should have a few copies of the book published for the family's sake as a legacy to my father and her, especially so that their grandchildren would have copies of his book. She thought it over and gave me permission to publish the book. Unfortunately, my mother passed away in January 2010, prior to publishing.

Initially I thought of retyping the book, but with the large amount of pages, a friend recommended scanning the pages to a computer. This sounded easy enough and would keep the pages as close to original as possible. However, I discovered scanning pages typed from a manual typewriter used in the 1950's do not reproduce well, resulting in many errors. Therefore, I spent the next two years during my limited free time scanning and correcting the scanning errors, trying to leave the pages as close to the originals as possible. I also tried to check some of the facts in the book. Unfortunately, I was unable to review the scanning errors or verify the facts with the author, my dad. However, through these many hours of work, it became a labor of love for me.

Is this book fact or fiction? Are the characters in this book real? Unfortunately, due to my dad's death in 1995, and no one reading the book until myself in 2008, these questions cannot be answered. I believe it is a story based on facts as well as fiction. This book was written by John T. Maltese who served in the United States Marine Corps during World War II. He was a rifleman, a private who fought on many island "rocks" in the Pacific, including Peleliu and Okinawa. I believe my father used his experiences during his time in the corps to write this novel, times that he spoke of often with such pride and honor.

He always stressed and let it be known to all who knew him that he was a Marine who served in WWII. He was a "former Marine," a fact he would remind everyone since there is no such thing as an ex-Marine. "Once a Marine, always a Marine!" If parts of this book have true characters or names, please let it be known that he respected and honored all Marines that served in the corps with him. He spoke and wrote of nothing but honor and respect for these Marines, and for the others, he would say, "Semper Fi, mac!"

Over the past few years when I have had the opportunity to discuss with others the possibility of having this book published, I have realized there are many others who may wish to read and enjoy this story by a Marine who served in WWII. These individuals include not only my dad's family members, but I also received encouragement from other former Marines, including those who served in WWII, as well as others from that generation. Family members, sons and daughters, and grandchildren of those who served in the war or lived during this period have expressed interest in reading this book. I hope they and others will find the story interesting and possibly informative about the events their family members experienced during WWII.

Or maybe you were one of my father's students. You probably remember the days when students who did not want to hear the class lecture on the subject of the day would coerce my father into getting off the class subject by asking him, "So, Mr. Maltese, how did you win the war?" Then an hour later, the bell would ring signaling the end of the class period, no class lecture taught, but what a great "war story" you had just heard.

Although this book may be a "wartime romance" novel, please remember while reading, from beginning to end, this is a book about Marines in WWII, written by a Marine, and the final story is about Marines. It was written, and now published for all to read the stories of those who honorably served in the United States Marine Corps during World War II.

God Bless you Mom and Dad!

John T. Maltese, Jr., M.D.

The rain fell, the bodies shivered,
but life had long since departed.

<u>Prologue</u>

The rain was falling in torrents, one dreary, damnable, November day in 1945 over Camp Pendleton, California. Some 80 soaked human objects squatted or stood on the muddy parade ground as the rain beat unmercifully down. All about them Quonset huts stood invitingly, but the Marines had their orders. They were to stay put and wait.

Apart from the main body of troops sprawled a small group of battered intimates. Seemingly unaware of the rain, they sat or lay amidst their gear. Sea bags and packs, caked with California mud, served as opportune seats or sacks for the hard bitten crew. Strangely missing were the rifles – the men seemed naked without them!

There were six of them - some tall, some short, all with a look of fear and death about them. They were close friends, an observer could tell, but they were unlike each other as God could make them. A weird crew, they sat staring at nothing visible to the naked eye.

"Wonder when we'll get discharged?" McPherson was speaking. He really didn't care! No one answered – not Alex Blue, the old man of the crowd, a foot-sore Oklahoman who had cursed the day he had deceived the recruiting station doctor many times during the past two years; not the college boy who had learned more about human nature than any author would dare put in text books – no one answered. They were all deep in thought, except Malton. He watched them and saw in their eyes the years of hell they had put in the far off Pacific. There were six left, but there had been more, many more – alive, sensitive human beings who had lived full lives since joining the Marines a few years before. Malton looked from one war-scarred face to another, etching deep into his brain the part each played in the theater of life that had been theirs since 1941. He fumbled in his breast pocket for a waterproof pouch, felt it safe within. Here he had pieced their and his stories, and someday he would write it.

He has! Those stories follow. Believe them or disallow them if you will – but, they won't be easily forgotten.

He was just a boy,
but manhood arrives
quickly during war!

A WARTIME ROMANCE

Chapter One

The Hollywood early morning sun beat warmly down upon a peaceful Sunday's deserted streets. Church bells sounded in the distance, calling all denominations to services. The serene quiet which hung heavenly over Southern California belied the fact that elsewhere men were dying in this war year of 1943.

Frank Brabern rubbed the sleep from his eyes and in the process brushed Chuck Taylor who was also groggily making his way dutifully to the Sunday church services.

"Wow, what a hangover!" Taylor gingerly rubbed his head, "What time did we sack out?"

"Bout three," Brabern, slim and square shouldered, had shaken off the effects of the previous night's drinking bout as only a 19 year old can. "Where's the church?"

"It's on the next street, down that way!" Taylor pointed with his chin toward a steeple that pointed its nose into the spring mist. "We'll cut through the alley up there."

The two Marines, one slim and tall, the other short and stocky, unconsciously walked in step down the deserted street. A clock above the door of a closed jewelry shop indicated that it was 7:45 am. Simultaneously glancing at the clock, the pair quickened their pace. Brabern brought his eyes from the clock to the street ahead. A 1941 Plymouth convertible was at the curb fifty yards ahead, and from all indications intended to stay there. An Air

Force emblem on the license bracket brought an automatic sneer to Brabern's lips. Breaking the morning stillness, the car's starter stuttered and stopped, the growl producing no reaction from the motor. Taylor nudged Brabern and whistled through his teeth.

Brabern took his gaze from the Air Force emblem and for the first time noticed the frustrated driver. The long blonde hair shone fiercely in the sun as a girl's head bent over the steering wheel. The Marines moved to the side of the car. The girl stopped depressing the starter. A long slim leg withdrew from the distant starter pedal. Brabern stopped looking at the foot and his eyes made their way up the girl's leg until the bronzed skin was suddenly hidden above the knee by the sky blue material of a dress.

"Help?" His eyes found hers, set deeply in a bronzed but smooth face even lovely in anger. Their blueness matched the paleness of the dress. Beneath the tan, a tinge of red formed as she tugged at her dress.

"I can't seem to get the darn thing started!" Tears began to well in her eyes and she brusquely drew well-manicured fingers across her eyes.

"Move over!" Brabern walked around the front of the car and opened the driver's door. She scooted across the seat, finally succeeding in her attempt to draw her skirt over her knees. Taylor was leaning on the door, a smile on his face. Her eyes met his and again the red tinge came through the tan.

"Think it's flooded!" Brabern turned on the key, depressed the gas pedal to the floor, stepped on the starter and held it for a few seconds. The roar of the motor greeted his efforts, and he turned and smiled at the girl. "That does it." He opened the door and stood there as she slid beneath the wheel.

"Thank you. I was frantic." She returned his smile, looked across to Taylor who hadn't moved, hesitated a moment, and then quickly reached a decision. "Maybe I can drop you somewhere?"

"We're just going to church," Taylor nodded toward the steeple, and then quickly threw a look at the Jeweler's clock 7:57 am. "Hey, we're late! Maybe you could drive us."

Brabern glanced at the clock and without waiting for a second invitation gently pushed the back of the driver's seat with its beautiful cargo forward and climbed into the rear seat. Taylor had already seated himself in the front seat. "Set", he said.

Brabern watched the girl through the rear view mirror as she pulled the car from the curb. About 22, he figured. Sure a beauty. High type too. A guy could always tell. Married, he had seen the ring on her left hand. Had looked for it, as a matter of fact. Probably to the air force guy who owned the car. Sure a beauty! His eyes met hers in the mirror. An embarrassed smile crossed his lips. The expression on her face indicated she knew he had been studying her.

He leaned forward on the seat. "What are you doing up so early on a Sunday morning?" The church loomed in the distance.

"Frankly, I didn't know it was so early. I didn't sleep much last night." A frowned creased her lovely face.

"Neither did we! Owww!" Taylor held his head.

She laughed. "My headache is different. I've got to find an apartment. That's where I'm going now, to check on few listings I saw in the paper last night." The frown deepened on her face as she slowed the car before the church. People were climbing the stairs quickly to get settled before the services started. Taylor opened the door, pushed the seat back forward and waited for Brabern to move. Brabern was still staring at the girl in the rear view mirror. "Let's go, Frank!"

Brabern started, and then moved out of the car. He turned to the girl, "Thanks! Good luck!" He slammed the door and started up the steps.

Taylor touched the brim of his cap and smiled at the girl whose eyes and thoughts were on the back of the Marine entering the church, "We appreciate it."

She looked at him, the embarrassed look again evident! "You're welcome!" She put the car in gear and without gazing back, drove down the street.

Taylor stood a moment at the curb watching the car disappear. What a doll! There was a circuit connected there. Those two could start a fire. His eyes fell on the Air Force ensigna on the receding car's license plate. Trouble, too!

The services lasted an hour. Taylor shot an occasional look at Brabern. His eyes followed the religious ceremony, but his thoughts were in an open convertible. Taylor shook his head. The kid had been hit hard by that blue-eyed doll. He'd have to talk to him after the services were over.

Brabern scarcely knew what was going on in the interior of the church. Blue eyes, bronze skin and the smile he saw in the rear view mirror filled his mind. He was known to be timid and shy by his buddies at the base at Pendleton. Out of boot camp six weeks, he was about ready to be shipped overseas. Not the mommy's boy type, he nevertheless resented not receiving a furlough to go back to Ohio.

Not that he had a steady girl back home. Oh, he had dates, but no girl had ever meant too much to him. He would have liked to see his folks again before being shipped. He thought about the girl. She's married! Wonder if her husband's stationed nearby. Wise up guy. You're not the type.

The movement of the congregation toward the doors shook Brabern out of his lethargy. Taylor was staring at him, then he picked up their caps from the pew, handed Brabern his and moved up the aisle.

Brabern stopped at the foot of the steps, looked slowly up and down the street.

"Ease up, buddy! You're heading for trouble!" Taylor softly said, his steel gray eyes clouded with concern. A veteran of six months in the Corps, Taylor in his 25th year, was a leaning tower for the younger men in the transient outfit. "That gal could be poison! Don't forget that ring on her finger!"

Frank Brabern had made up his mind. "Chuck, I'll see you back at the base tonight, O.K.?" His voice revealed his difficulty in reaching the decision. The two paths he could take were clouded by the beauty and unknown quality of the blonde. He needed help in his course.

Taylor studied his buddy for a minute, then quickly made up his mind, "O.K. but watch out for booby traps. If the action gets heavy, clear out." Taylor watched his words' effect on Brabern. Their meaning was clear. He smartly turned and headed toward the parish room at the rear of the church where he knew coffee and donuts were being served. The boy had a play! He'd do a lot of growing up today.

Brabern watched Taylor disappear into the crowd, then turned to the street. He didn't know exactly what his next step would be. He watched the increasing traffic on the busy street.

She said she was going to check on some apartments. She'd be gone for a while - yet it had been an hour since she had left them off at the church. The walk back to the jewelry store took ten minutes and the antique clock registered 9:30 A.M. as he stood under it. He looked at the houses on the street, the three story type common to the older residential sections of downtown Hollywood, each with tiers of porches. The glamour of Hollywood was in the outlying districts. In the area around Hollywood Blvd. and Vine, only cartoon studios and short subject departments of the major studios remained. Which house did she live in? The car was not parked in the block. He studied the houses.

During the next hour Brabern's thoughts traced the gnawing years of his life to this moment. A natural athlete, he had always been a leader in any crowd. Admired by both males and females, he nevertheless had never forced his attentions on anyone. He had entered the Corps free from home ties. No special girl back home, parents who lived in an upper middle class home in one of exclusive villages outside Cleveland, and who were proud that their only son had distinguished himself as a civilian and now promised even greater accomplishments as a U. S. Marine.

He smiled as he thought of his mother sitting at her bridge club. "Yes, Frank, is doing rather well in the Marines, shot expert with the rifle you know!" Her proud head erect as she dealt the cards for bridge. A wonderful woman and mother, but he had long ago decided his wife would not be like her. He envisioned his father. A highly successful lumber broker who came from a small Ohio River town. A brilliant business man, but content to lead a peaceful home life, but his mother had other ideas. Contented enough while Tom Brabern was struggling with success, but now that the battle had been won, she was no longer satisfied with remaining quietly in the background. Along with business success she wanted social prominence, and so she pushed her husband into community leadership. A prominent member of the Lakeside Country Club, Tom Brabern was active in the Y.M.C.A., the Chamber of Commerce, and many other civic organizations. Tom condescendingly smiled at his wife's pushing. She had earned her years of social prominence. She suffered patiently enough during the building years. Frank snapped from his reminiscing as a yellow convertible turned the far corner, and a flash of golden hair caught the glint of the sun. He watched the car pull to the curb in the same proximity as it had been before. Frank didn't move - he still didn't know what his next step would be. A touch of panic gripped him. Instinctively, he reached for a cigarette.

Opening the door of the car the girl stepped into the street. The flash of legs drew Frank's attention. His eyes were on the legs and it took seconds before he realized that they had suddenly stopped. He raised his gaze to the girl's face. She was looking across the street at him, a puzzled look in her eyes. Neither moved for a minute and then she crossed the street to the jewelry store against whose door he was leaning. Every step was a motion of beauty. He hadn't realized she was so tall. The long legs pushed the silky material of her dress in graceful patterns as she moved toward him. Brabern blushed as the thought that this was the most beautiful girl he had ever seen raced through his mind.

She stopped three steps away from him, a smile on her face. She was a head shorter than he and the tilt of her head as she looked up at him drew her well-formed breasts taut against her dress.

"Well, I didn't have any luck with the apartments." She easily went into the conversation. Not a word about him waiting for her, as if it had to be. "Tomorrow I'll have to look again."

"Hope you have better luck." Frank realized these word were hollow, just filling the void as each looked into the heart of the other, frightened over this strange magnet which had drawn them together. He smiled! Softly, he said. "Look, I've got until midnight to start back to Pendleton. Couldn't we go someplace?" He saw the expression on her face and quickly added, "Damn it, I haven't spent any time with a woman since I left my mother at the station three months ---" He stopped, dropped his head "I'm sorry."

"I understand." The words gently and quietly spoken. When he raised his eyes, he saw that she did.

She had moved closer to him. "I have nothing I have to do the rest of the day. You wait in the car. I want to change these apartment hunting clothes," she laughed softly and turning quickly, started back across the street, pacing her steps so he could walk alongside her. She stopped at the side of the car. "I won't be a minute." She again looked into his eyes to confirm her decision, then turned and ran up the steps of a house.

Brabern opened the car door and sat down. He suddenly realized that he hadn't lighted his cigarette. He looked for the car lighter, pushed it in and then leaned back in the seat. Well, Brabern, he thought, you've done it. So this is what it is like, first time in his life to pick up a girl. The thought angered him. The girl was not the type that fitted the time worn expression. He reached for the lighter and fired his cigarette. He found himself trying to fit the pieces of the jig-saw puzzle together. How did he know that her husband wasn't waiting for her in the apartment? What made a beautiful girl like her even take the time to talk to him? He couldn't figure the puzzle out. Well, he finally decided, let's let the pieces fall together themselves.

The closing of a door made him turn again to the house. Racing down the steps was the girl. The dress had been replaced with a pale green blouse which was cut to fit the contour of her body. She wore a pair of white shorts and her bronze legs testified to the fact that she wore shorts often.

She reached the street side of the car and he reached over and opened the door. Looking up into her eyes he was surprised to see that now they appeared green matching the blouse.

She slid behind the wheel and reached for the key. "That didn't take long, did it?"

"It was worth waiting" He was surprised to hear the words coming from his lips.

She laughed musically. "I feel comfortable in shorts. This will do if we decide to go someplace more formal." She added as she placed a matching skirt to the blouse on the back seat. The motion outlined her perfect form against the blouse and shorts. Brabern self-consciously, but not able to stop himself, examined each outline of her body.

She turned, unaware of the hunger that raged deep inside the Marine beside her.

"Where to?" she started the motor easily this time. She tilted her beautiful face to him. "How about driving up to Griffith Park? I like it there." She spoke matter of factly as if she had privately reached that decision previously.

"Suits me. I'm not familiar with this part of the country."

A need to tell this girl something of himself came over Brabern. He watched her drive, the effortless way she moved the car through the heavily trafficked streets. She held her eyes to the road, her cheeks high with a smile which beautified more, if possible, her lovely face.

She took the cue gracefully, her eyes still on the highway, "You're not from the West? I didn't think so. Let's see if I can pick out the state." She turned to him, the smile even deeper on her face. "I'm quite an expert on placing dialects. Pennsylvania?"

The game went on for several minutes, laughter following each incorrect guess. The guessing had taken on an added objective. The pattern of conversation helping to overcome the uneasiness which both felt. A magnetism hung heavily over the few scant feet that separated them in the car. If asked to define it, neither would be able to explain the strange feeling that existed between them - a young Marine from the Midwest and the girl from where? The guessing game soon reversed and it was established that her home had been in Boulder, Colorado!

The inevitable question was due and Brabern overcame his qualms over it long enough to pose the one thought which hung over him. "Where's your husband?" The words sounded strained as he said it. The look on her face clearly indicated that the one thought which kept forcing its way to the fore in him was the one being pushed to the rear of her mind.

"Jerry's somewhere in the Pacific. He's been gone for three months." Her voice was low now, "He's with the air force, a fighter pilot."

Brabern studied her face as she went on telling the story that was being duplicated many times in many cities throughout the country. The war, which no one wanted, (was that entirely true) had laid the plot heavily on the women of the nation. It followed a strange pattern - the feeling that no one, but no one, could tear a marriage apart. And so, youngsters everywhere, denying, but nevertheless fearing the uncertainness of the times, rushed to the ever present justice of the peace, and became one for all time. When the hand of the God of War beckoned the men overseas to fight for a better world, the thought was sickening, the vacuum left was hard to fill. It was much more difficult for the new wife left behind - the warrior had the companionship of others immediately, and in the not too distant future, an enemy who was determined to forever keep him away from his bride, to preoccupy him, but the girl, especially those who had followed their men as close to the point of embarkation as possible, found the world suddenly devoid of the one thing that mattered. When she wiped the tears of departure from her reddened eyes she found herself alone in a strange town, usually with no friends and faced with a decision of whether to return home or to stay close and await the return of the warrior.

Brabern read the story well. An intelligent student of human nature, he had matured early intellectually, if not emotionally. The girl, her name was Candy Trabert, the questioning had disclosed, was reliving the moment of departure. He hated to break in on this reverie but he found himself asking. "What are you going to do now?" He was surprised at the sound of his own voice.

The question had surprised her also, for the very thought had been so long in her own mind. She stopped the car for a red light and turned to him, a near panic in her eyes.

"Want me to drive?" He already had the door open and was racing to the other side. She had moved over to the middle of the seat. The sound of horns told him that the light had changed. He put the car in gear and smoothly moved forward.

"Thanks!" Her voice was heavy with swallowed tears. She could feel his rough green blouse sleeve against her bare arm. Strength seeped through the coarseness and she drew heavily upon it. She was about to move but the loneliness that had been with her for three months forced her to stay close. She looked at him through the rear view mirror. His face was square cut, as if chiseled from a piece of granite. Deep brown, or were they black eyes, bore straight ahead in the valley created by the high lean cheek bones. His nose was straight except at the bridge where a football injury had broken the perfect line of it. The overseas cap he wore set jauntily on the right side of his head. His hair, what she could see of it, was a rich brown. She studied his mouth - it was the most distinctive feature of his face. The set of the strange lips held a firmness that revealed his character. Sensitive and firm, they seldom seemed to move, even when he smiled. Quiet by nature, she guessed, but one who reached decisions quickly and then followed them through. Like waiting for her - a fear tugged at her heart. She was being drawn to this boy - she knew he wasn't yet twenty - she sensed rather than knew it.

Suddenly she realized he too was looking into the mirror. She blushed and he impulsively took his right hand from the wheel and placed it over hers. Their eyes held in the mirror, and his pulse matched hers. A blast of a horn shattered their moment. He had gone through a red light.

He sheepishly put his hand back on the wheel. "How about some directions, little lady. I'm lost." He emphasized the lady, and the fear that she had felt earlier slowly receded.

She laughed as she got her bearings. "Turn left at the next block. We'll go up to the Observatory."

"Aye, Captain." He concentrated on the traffic and soon they had arrived at the peak of Griffith Park where the beautiful observatory sat. They spent an hour on the arched porch that surrounded the observatory from which an unparalleled view of the city of Los Angeles lay unfolded below. They talked of many things - non-entities which created a comradeship. Both were hungry for companionship. Gradually they talked of Jerry Trabert, as they knew they must. It had been one of those war time marriages. Both had been at the University of Colorado, he a senior, she a sophomore, when the war had broken out. Pinned, their companionship on a college romance level had bloomed into a much more serious note with their impending separation. It was not a sudden marriage. They had almost six months to think the entire matter out. Graduation day for Jerry became wedding day for the two of them. Their parents had given their blessings. They hadn't been separated more than three days after their marriage - she had managed to go with him to the numerous fields to which he had been sent. The past year and a half had been happy. Their folks had been financially able to help out. Then came the inevitable orders - Jerry had been ordered overseas. Suddenly their happiness had been shattered.

"The first weeks were the hardest." Candy said, her right eye glued to the metered telescope. "We had no friends here. We were entirely too happy together. Then," she sighed, "I began to get over feeling sorry for myself and became uneasy with my uselessness. Dad wanted me to come home, but this is where he left from, and," she stopped.

He nodded. He had already completed the picture before she began again.

"That was about 10 weeks ago. I offered my services to the U.S.O. downtown. Don't laugh."

He didn't.

"I became busy and a little of the hurt left. I've a little desk down there where during the week, I do little things, like writing letters home, sewing on stripes. It's pretty quiet during the week. On week-ends the traffic gets heavy. Week-end passes brings sailors, soldiers, Marines - oh, I should have said Marines first, shouldn't I?" Her eyes lighted teasingly, "Marines, sailors and soldiers come in looking for places to spend the night. We have a listing of homes which take in service men. They're usually people who have boys in the service themselves. It gives them a feeling that they have someone of their own home again." She finished with a softening of the voice.

He had recognized the comparison of their being together. He smiled kindly and put his arm through hers. They walked toward the car. He admired this girl - admired the thousands of others who like her were not quite able to cope with the emptiness which had been cast upon them. He felt he had to say something.

"Playing hooky today?" He opened the car door for her. She climbed in gracefully. The sun was sinking over the observatory dome as he got behind the wheel.

"Sundays it slows down until the U.S.O. is almost deserted. It's my day off." She again had arranged in the middle of the seat.

Her position had not gone unnoticed. He felt his pulse - beat increase and a surprising thought came into his mind - he disgustedly thrust it aside. He wanted her!

"How about some dinner?" He was hungry. Their lunch back at the Observatory had consisted of hot-dogs purchased from a side-walk vendor.

"Fine, I know just the place for the way I'm dressed. Head up Wilshire Boulevard to Santa Monica." She reached into the rear seat and still on her knees placed the skirt around her full hips. Pulling herself snuggly into the skirt she returned to a sitting position beside Brabern. She looked up at his sun-hardened skin and suddenly felt a pang as she realized that he too would soon be on his way overseas. She had grasped at the opportunity to be with someone, to feel the strength of a man. It hadn't resolved the problem which had plagued her and indirectly had resulted in their meeting. The quietness, save for the cool breeze which hummed musically into the open car, was beginning, once more to be explosive. He, too felt it, but he knew that it was she who must break the silence.

"You asked me this morning what I was going to do now," she said pursuing a safe conversational course. The decision was an important one, and the answer was still lacking, it was obvious by her hesitancy. Brabern waited.

"Frankly, I'm not sure." A small frown had creased her face. It seemed out of place amidst all the beauty. "My lease on the apartment expires next week. The land-lady has a nephew from back east stationed at El-Toro, and naturally she promised him the apartment. His wife is still home and he's anxious to have her with him." Her eyes now wore an understanding look. "So the problem's mine, I've been looking for another apartment, but I'm not sure I want to find one - ." She stopped. Once again the unspoken words stood clearly between them. Both knew that in a prolonged friendship between them danger lurked. "Turn left at the beach. It's the third restaurant on the right."

He slowly but expertly pulled the car into the parking lot. The sound of an orchestra filled the deepening dusk. He looked down at the beach and the white sand now gray in the darkness.

He took her arm and they walked toward the beach club. Surrounded by the lush tropical vegetation of Southern California, the imposing single story structure spread in semi-circular fashion toward the sea. The voice of dinnerware drew his attention to the gaily swinged patio-porch surrounding the protruding half-moon which faced the ocean. In the flickering light of protected candles, he could see couples sitting at white table clothed tables.

"Like it?" She asked as they walked toward the front entrance. "I've been here before." she stopped, then quickly added. "With a girl from the U.S.0."

A smiling doorman opened the door and they entered a large thickly carpeted room where a hat check girl took his cap and handed him a ticket. Frank spoke to a bowing headwaiter who lead them through a huge crescent shaped dining room nearly filled with young servicemen and their wives, girlfriends - or other men's wives - the thought forced its way into his mind They were led to the patio-porch and seated at a railing table overlooking the ocean and handed large menu's bearing the name "Torcio's".

"Real nice." The awe that he felt at the "motion picture" setting clearly was noticeable in his voice. "This is the kind of place serviceman try to find, but never with any luck, unless they happen to meet people like you."

A waitress took their order, and while waiting they followed the sound of music to an open air dance-floor immediately beneath the other side of the porch-patio where they were seated. He took her in his arms, and smoothly they glided over the floor. Never much of a dancer, he nevertheless had no difficulty leading this wisp of a girl to the accompaniment of the music. He held her close, the scent of her perfume, clouding his thoughts. Once she pulled her head back and only then did he realize he was crushing her. She smiled into his eyes and settled into his arms. He could feel her trembling and knew that she too felt as he did. When the music stopped he took her hand and they walked slowly back to their table.

Small talk during the delicious meal led to his duties in the corps.

"I'm an infantryman." He said it softly as if in reverence. The intense pride he took in the Marines revealed itself forcibly with every word he spoke. "Not much of one at that, I guess." He brushed the one stripe he wore on his blouse sleeve. "Right now I'm in a transient group at Camp Pendleton." He paused and then looked directly into her attentive face. "I'm due to be shipped at any time. Right now we're just marking time."

She looked at her plate where an almost untouched portion of pie rested. Once again the overwhelming feeling that had come over her before began to rise in her breast. She almost unperceivably shook her head. She hardly knew this Marine. She was married - had no right to feel this way. Jerry, I'm sorry - I do love you. She raised her face and calmly asked "You don't know where, do you? Perhaps you might run across Jerry."

The words smacked him in the face. He had almost forgotten her husband. Damn fool. Then he understood that she had said what she did to break this mad race to heartbreak toward which they had been heading. He smiled and spoke self-assuredly.

"Marines don't associate with dog-faces." His serious face broke into a wider grin as he added, "but I'm hoping I do meet the lucky stiff." She joined his joking manner.

"Thank you, King Marine." The tension had been shattered and soon they were talking of the beauty of the ocean and the activity which war had brought the Los Angeles area. Both expressed the prophecy that this war, if it had done nothing more, would lead to the rapid development of the west.

Time flew all too quickly. He had to be at Union Station at 12 to catch the train that would get to Pendleton early in the morning. He called for the check and they got back to the car. Candy insisted that she drive him to the station. He didn't argue too much - he hated to leave the companionship of this girl.

Union Station was packed with long queues of sailors and Marines waiting for the south bound train which would take them to the bases that dotted the coast from Los Angeles to San Diego. The clock in the tower showed 11:30 as Candy slid into a parking space. She turned off the ignition and slowly turned to Frank.

"I have a few minutes. Mind if I wait here?" The inner struggle he felt was discernible in his actions, the fumbling with the cap he held in his hands.

She turned more toward him, one leg doubled beneath her on the seat. She didn't smile. Her eyes looked again at his nose, his determined jaw. He was watching the servicemen rushing into the station. She felt a sorrow for this Marine that lessened her own loss. Her fears that she had made a mistake that morning had long since gone. She saw him for what he was. A lonesome serviceman, far from home and the small world over which he reigned. A good kid, not the wolves on the make she had to fight off every night at the U.S.O. Yet she knew that he wanted her, and as she faced the fact squarely, that she wanted him. The thought shocked her, and she tried to thrust it from her. As she watched him she knew she had nothing to fear from this man. He would not force her - she also knew that she had only herself to fear.

"Will I see you again?" He hadn't looked toward her. He still watched the men file into the station.

The words brought her back to the present. She heard herself saying "I don't know!" She didn't recognize her own voice. "Everything's so uncertain. You may be shipped out tomorrow. I might go home! Oh, Frank!" Tears were in her eyes.

He moved toward her in the seat. "Look, Candy, maybe today wasn't such a good idea, but I'm glad it turned out the way it did." His voice was clear, decisive."I've never met anyone like you before. Maybe, I won't be shipped out this week. Maybe you'll find another apartment, but regardless, I'm glad that today happened."

He took her hands in his. A tear rolled down her cheek. He watched it fall from her cheek onto her blouse.

"So am I, and I'm sorry, too!" she turned toward the emptying station. "You'd better go."

He squeezed her hand and got out the door. She slid to the passenger's side of the seat.

"Frank, if I don't go home, and you're still here, I'm at the Main Street U.S.O." She hesitated, "I'd like to see you again."

Leaning against the car, he looked deeply into her eyes, and seeing consent there, gently kissed her on the lips. A hunger sprang up that quickly stopped the kiss. "Goodbye Candy!" He quickly turned and she watched his swaying step as he moved across the lobby. A figure emerged from the shadows and fell in beside him. She recognized the other Marine, Chuck Taylor who had been with him that morning. Had it been only that morning? She watched them disappear and then moving to the driver's seat, backed the car out into the traffic.

The two Marines had stopped and turned back to the street. Chuck watched the car disappear into the night and noticing no movement on Frank's part said, "Come on, boy, we'll miss the train!"

They turned and fought the crowd into the train. It was typically crowded and they found no seat. The three hour ride was long and the cramped coach irritated the tired, sleepy Marines.

The two buddies hunched on the arms of seats and didn't speak. Occasionally Frank's thoughts of Candy were broken as his eyes met Chuck's who stared unselfconsciously at him.

The train crawled into Oceanside, California, and three quarters of the Marines sleepily got off. A long, line of cabs waited at the station to haul the Marines into the huge Camp Pendleton which spread far into the hills. It was impossible to walk to the remote sections of the camp which was laid out in areas. 13 area, where the transient group to which Chuck and Frank were assigned, was ten miles from the gate. The scramble for cabs was a battle and the two Marines headed for an all night hamburger shop.

They sat on the counter stools and ordered a hamburger and coffee each. When they were served, Chuck turned to Frank. He studied his buddy. They hadn't spoken the entire trip.

"That was a pretty scene at the station." He knew that it was a cruel thing to say but he wanted to draw the other from his melancholy.

Brabern's face hardened and he looked sharply at his friend. Then the set of his jaw relaxed. Taylor tried again. "What's the scoop Frank? Tell old dad." The tone of his voice was different, more understanding.

Frank turned again to his coffee, slowly took a sip, "She's married. Probably going back to Colorado this week." He twirled the seat toward Taylor. "And she's a damn good kid!"

Taylor nodded. He got the picture and he knew it would all come out. He remained silent and let the boy talk. They finished their sandwiches and finding empty cabs outside, headed back to camp. Brabern told of the day's events slowly, Taylor nodding occasionally. As the cab pulled into the area Frank was wearily telling of the scene in the station. "Well, what do you think?" He didn't want an answer, Taylor told himself.

They climbed the steps into the barracks. "It will all work out. Just play it out." Taylor punched his friend on the shoulder and headed for his bunk. The barracks was alive with the snoring of Marines. Brabern slowly undressed, went to the head and then climbed into his upper bunk. Taylor was already sleeping below, but sleep did not come to Brabern. His mind was too busy. His eyes were still open when reveille sounded.

The next few days were filled with the many odd duties the services find to keep waiting men busy. Time to sit and think is one of the banes of service life. Homesickness and trouble brew from idleness and so the 149th replacement battalion was kept busy. Long hikes over the hilly terrain of the old Santa Margarita Ranch not only kept the troops occupied but also retained the fighting edge that weeks of vigorous training had put on the men.

Scuttlebutt had the battalion sailing nightly but as the days slipped by and the heavy equipment remained unmoved on the parade ground it was obvious that departure would be some days off. Taylor had kept a close eye on Brabern. The tall youth was drawn into a tight shell and his periods of carefree conversation were few. Even at nights in the area slop-shoot he just sat listening to the escapades related by the other Marines. They were always plentiful after a liberty weekend. The battalion's lovers were always encouraged to tell of their conquests and they always obliged. As the days passed the stories became more fiction than fact as the imagination soared into what might have been.

On Wednesday, Brabern did not stay at the slop-shoot until closing time as the ritual of the group had become. Instead he returned to his barracks and there Taylor found him an hour later bent over a blank sheet of paper. Taylor sat on the edge of the bunk and watched his friend.

"Frank, you'd better drop this. You'll drive yourself nuts." He looked over the edge of his pipe as he held a match to it. "She's married and intends to stay that way, you told me that yourself! What can come of it? Hell, man, you're going over any day now! You'll never see her again. What's eatin' you anyway?"

Brabern impulsively crumbled the paper on which he hadn't been able to write a word and violently threw it in the corner. Heads turned from around the room in his direction. "Let's take a walk." He rose and Taylor followed him from the barracks.

They walked slowly in the darkness, past the motor pool and climbed the small hill behind it and sat on the reverse side where the empty pits of the rifle range could be seen outlined in the dull moonlight below them.

Frank picked up a small stick and slowly traced a senseless pattern in the dirt. "Look, Chuck, I'm on a merry-go-round and I know the brass ring is out of reach, but," he fiercely threw the stick, "I can't help grabbing for it." He stopped but he was only searching for the right words. Taylor waited. "I've never been in love before." The words came embarrassingly and slowly. The darkness hid the tinge of red that Taylor knew was on Brabern's face. "Fact is, I've never really cared for anyone up to now. Life has been a big game and so far I've won without too great an effort. Oh I've gone out on dates, my share of them, anyway. But I've never cared for any of the girls - they were just kids, but Candy!" He paused and the vision of her was clear in his mind. "She's something! I know that it's no use. I could tell that it was no use from the beginning, but - hell, what's the difference." He turned to Taylor. "When do you think we'll ship out?"

Chuck recognized that his buddy had resolved himself. Things were going to be alright - the boy was young! It would be a wonderful memory for him. He wished that his answer was correct, "Probably this weekend."

They sat quietly until lights out sounded over the hills and then they made their way back to the barracks and their sacks. Twenty minutes later Taylor went to the head. When he returned he glanced into the top bunk. For the first time that week, Frank was sleeping restfully. Taylor smiled and climbed in his sack.

Taylor had been wrong. Friday morning, a notice on the bulletin board declared that 62 hour passes would be issued to those desiring them starting at 1800. A whoop of cursing and laughter went up as the word spread through the barracks.

Men made hurried plans to go to L.A. and San Diego. Married men rushed to the pay phones at the Post Exchange to call their wives. The day proved to be one of joyous activity at the thought of a weekend away from the rigors and boredom of camp life.

Taylor had been sent on a working part to another area early in the morning. He returned late in the afternoon and hurried to the barracks to get ready for the liberty. He was digging into his locker box when he heard the spring of the bunk bed shift. He turned and saw Brabern lying on his back, his hands behind his head, staring at the ceiling. Taylor went back to his gathering of his liberty equipment. He closed the locker box, sat on it and began to shine his already glistening liberty shoes. He didn't stop as he spoke.

"Going on liberty, Frank?" He spit on the toe of the double soled right shoe and whipped the shinning cloth brusquely over the glossy surface. He already knew the answer.

"No!" the voice was determined. "Think I'll stay here and write some letters home. It'll be quiet with all you characters gone." He hadn't moved.

Taylor went into the shower room, alive with the playful talk of men who are looking forward to a good time. He found an empty shower and lathered his body. His thoughts were on Brabern. He had to admire the kid. He knew that every fiber of his body ached to head for Los Angeles and the girl, but his sense of righteousness held out. Christ, what a guy! He didn't think the kid had it in him, but then, he'd proven that he was a hell of a man before. Perhaps that was what made them the friends that they were. They were altogether different in character and appearance. He, Taylor, was known as an operator. From the east side of New York City, he had taken his knocks early. His mother had died when he was born and his old man, a subway motorman, had always, but not openly, blamed him for her death. Having been left pretty much alone he had been in and out of tough spots all his life. His one pride was that he had somehow gotten through high school. As for dames, he had been on the make since the time when the older guys at the candy store had egged him on a bitch who spent most of her evenings and some days on her back. He had accepted the challenge and had spent a suffering period thereafter with a bad case of gonorrhea.

"Hey Taylor, you're going to scrub that skin off." A pimple faced Marine stood outside the shower, bare assed with a towel over his right shoulder, waiting his turn impatiently.

"A lot of soap wouldn't hurt you, pimples!" Taylor shot back as he rinsed the soap from his body. He quickly stepped out of the stall and toweled himself. Wrapping the towel about him he walked down the rows of bunks to his own. Brabern was still in the same position.

Taylor put his watch on, noticing that it was 1700. Well, he'd catch the 1720 bus which left Fridays direct from the area to L.A. He'd grab a sandwich at the P.X. and eat it on the bus. He hurriedly dressed carrying on a one way conversation telling Brabern of the work detail he had been on. The replacement battalion in area 10 was loading for the docks in Dago. It looked as if they would be next.

He finished dressing and walked up to the bunk. "Tie a Windsor, will you Frank." He placed the tie on the bunk. Brabern swung his legs over the side and began tying the knot.

"When you going to learn to tie this yourself?" He finished and arranged the tie in the collar, giving it a slight tug.

Taylor smiled and pulled on his blouse, arranged his Buster Brown belt with its shining buckle, squared his cap on his head and sharply saluted. "How do I look?"

Frank looked him over and removed a speck of lint from the well brushed blouse. "As good as possible, and that's not good." He playfully kicked at his friend.

Taylor laughed "See you Monday!" And turned toward the open door beyond the row of double bunks. He walked erectly down the aisle.

"Chuck - " Taylor stopped and half turned. Brabern was sitting on the edge of the double bunk leaning forward. Taylor waited. Frank fidgeted then "Have a good time." He swung his legs back on the bunk.

Taylor swiftly went out the door. He knew what the kid had been ready to say. Hell, he'd find out if she was still there - he wished she wasn't.

The weekend was the longest of Brabern's life. The loneliness of the barracks, almost everyone had taken advantage of this last liberty, did not help him write the letters as he had planned. His whole being ached to see Candy again, but he had made up his mind and he set the remembrance of her into a corner of his mind, but she continuously kept returning to his thoughts. On Saturday he borrowed a jeep from the duty sergeant at the motor pool and spent the day touring the sights of the historical Rancho Santa Margarita. The old Spanish land grant covered hundreds of thousands of acres of land from the seashore deep into the mountains behind. The original ranch house itself was kept as a historical site on the base and it was there that he learned of the glorious history of the Rancho which was now the largest Marine Base in the world. At the ranch house his thoughts were turned again to Candy as he saw Marines pointing out sights to their girl friends. He found himself comparing the girls to Candy.

He ate dinner at the visitors restaurant near the main gate, then went back to his own area. That evening he went to the movie with a Marine whose wife was back in Chicago. The movie was a musical and the hour was a peaceful one. The slop-shoot was almost deserted after the movie, and some of the pain Brabern felt left as he listened to the loneliness the married Marine felt as he told of his wife and home back in the mid-west.

Sunday was easier. The comfort and strength Frank received from the church services primed him for the letters he must write home. He wrote individual letters to his parents and to a high school friend. The letters were full of chatter and pride of the Corps. He read the letters to his parents over again to see if any of his feelings for the girl had crept in. Satisfied that they hadn't, he wrote other letters to people he had promised he would write but never had. Chow call surprised him. He hadn't realized he had been writing all afternoon. The cold cuts that made up evening chow on Sundays didn't sit too well, but he didn't feel like going to the visitors' restaurant again. He was dull from the two days of leisure and spent the evening reading a book his parents had sent. It was typical of the higher type of literature he read while in school, but he found it boring now that he was living a full life in the Corps. Putting the book aside he was asleep long before taps sounded.

Reveille sounded in the early dawn's light and Brabern jumped from his bunk. He reached automatically and tugged at Taylor who grunted and rolled over. Brabern pulled the green blanket from his buddy and smiled at the sight of the forest green uniform which Taylor had not removed before climbing into the sack. The reek of cheap whiskey cringed Frank's nostrils. He again shook his friend and headed for the head which was already filled with heavy lidded Marines. The laughter that pushed the walls back Friday was absent as another week of uncertainty again prevailed.

Roll call sounded and a freshly shaved Brabern joined the ranks in front of the barracks. The troops lined up sluggishly amid the shouts from the sergeants poised in front of the lines of disheveled and weary troops. Calling of the roll revealed that several of the replacements had not made connections. The orders for the day were read and an audible rumble met the announcement that an infantry field problem was scheduled. The order to fall out and prepare packs prior to chow was followed by the griping that rose from the rumble. Cursing and slamming of equipment rang out in the barracks as the liberty tired Marines prepared their packs.

Brabern swiftly fixed his own gear and then turned to help Taylor whose whisker heavy face sagged with too much whiskey and too little sleep. He sat on the edge of the bunk and slowly pushed his canteen into the cloth cover. Frank took it from him and with his own went to the drinking fountain at the near end of the barracks. When he returned Taylor was snoring soundly in his sack.

"Chuck!" He pulled him to a sitting position and slapped him firmly, but gently on the face.

"Get the hell out!" Chuck mumbled but with his eyes still closed began to change from his rumpled greens to his dungarees that Brabern handed him. "What a liberty! Must have drunk a gallon of white lightning." He opened his eyes and smiled with an effort at Frank. "How'd you do here? Man you should have been with me".

His wallet tumbled from his greens onto the floor. Brabern picked it up and looked into the money compartment. A lone single lay crumpled there. Frank tossed it on the sack.

"Holy Hell! We just got paid. You must have set up the bar!" The announcement brought a shrug to Taylor's shoulders.

"Can't buy anything where we're goin', they tell me." He gingerly pulled the dollar from the wallet. "Must have missed that one."

Chow call sounded and the tired Marines suddenly came to life and headed across the dusty ground to the mess hall. The customary S.O.S. was served, dried beef in gravy on toast. The meal went quickly and the battalion was soon on the march to its designated maneuver area. Once there, the various platoon leaders outlined the problem. They were to take a high setting ridge which had been lined with demolition charges.

At the command of the battalion commanding officer, the troops simulated battle conditions. The battalion command post was deployed in a clump of trees. Wire crews carrying thin rolls of combat wire laid communications lines between headquarters and the various platoons. The make-believe began. Brabern and Taylor's squad were to knock out a pillbox that commanded the hill's right flank. Moving automatically, the squad moved into position dropping periodically into protective cover. Fire was directed into the well battered pillbox by the troops. Live ammunition was being used by the soon to be in actual combat Marines. The sham battle was realistic even to the mortar shells simulated by dummy charges, which went off from time-to-time. A flame thrower moved into position and its experienced operator played a stream of liquid fire into the pillbox. The referee flashed the knocked out signal and the squad moved on to its next objectives. After two hours of battle, the troops were deployed in a holding position, where the front line was consolidated. The signal for a break was called and the Marines sank into hastily dug foxholes pulling from their packs the tasteless K-Rations which had been issued.

Brabern and Taylor crouched in the shade of a bullet pocketed tree and munched on the canned dried egg from their ration. Their faces were lined with grime and sweat and it was difficult to see a dry spot on their dungarees.

"I'm losing all that good booze through those damn sweat glands." Taylor was wearing a sink expression that was not feigned. "Those bastards plan these things after a liberty on purpose." He was joking but there was a lot of truth to his words. Brabern knew. He finished his tasteless egg and drew a stale cigarette from the small pack contained in the ration. Lighting it he turned to Taylor, the question that had been on his lips all morning finding expression.

"What did you do in L.A.?" He had meant it to sound different from the way it came out. He immediately saw Taylor grasp the meaning of the question.

Taylor bit on a piece of the chocolate that usually gave him the runs. "Same crap! Spent most of the time in the Biltmore bar." He took another bite on the bar, looked at the mold already covering the chocolate. "Went to the Main Street U.S.O. to get a room for Saturday."

Brabern waited. He didn't know what he wanted to hear. He looked at Taylor. His expression gave no indication of what was to come.

"Saw your friend." There it was. A relieved sensation followed by one of disappointment swept Brabern.

"Then she did find an apartment." The words were mumbled.

"No, she didn't." Taylor threw the rest of the chocolate to the ground and covered it slowly with the tip of his combat boot with dirt. "Didn't talk to her too long. She had some trouble finding me a place to sleep. A lot of swabbies were in from the fleet at Long Beach." He filled and lighted his pipe. "Said she had looked all week with no luck. Said her lease expires today." He blew out the match with a finality that Brabern recognized as the end of the subject.

Brabern nodded and busied himself with the shoulder straps of the pack. Taylor watched him sadly. That's not all of it my friend, but the rest would not help any. The look in the girl's eyes as she recognized him was one of joy which turned to sadness as her searching eyes did not find Brabern in the room. She hadn't asked about him directly, but her voice caught as she asked if there was one cot needed. She looked down when Taylor had said yes and then feeling sorry for the girl had added that Brabern had stayed at camp to write some letters. Her smile without laughter indicated that she had understood. As she gave him the address of the home that had a cot for him, she hesitated a moment. He looked into her eyes.

"Take care of him, Chuck. He'll make some girl awfully happy." He squeezed her hand and left the U.S.O. What a woman! God, he didn't blame Frank! He stopped at the corner, slowly tore up the card. He needed a bed like a sailor needed land.

Tuesday came and went with work details taking care of the men's time. On Wednesday morning an expectancy could be detected as the Battalion commander himself stood before the ranks at roll call. In his hands he held a bundle of papers. The troops waited!

"Men!" He cleared the excitement from his voice. "We start loading today. Get your gear squared away."

It had been ready for two weeks. "The following work details will --". He read a long list of details ammunition, truck loaders, sentries, and a group to Dago to check in the gear for loading. He concluded. "Exact date of embarkation is classified." He instructed the platoon leaders to dismiss the troops for chow.

As the men fell out, a subdued murmur arose, the day they had waited for so long had arrived, but they were unprepared for the actual departure. The shock soon passed as the troops began the task of loading the equipment. As the day went on and the slow decline in the stacked equipment discounted the scuttlebutt that they would sail with the tide the next evening. Further proof was evident at the noon break when a bulletin-board notice listed a limited number 24 hour passes would start that night with married men whose wives were close getting priorities. A rush started for the duty officer's room where the passes were available. Frank and Chuck joined the group - the former suddenly deciding that he would like to see the civilian life once more, since no complications were possible, for surely Candy had gone back to Colorado. The line dwindled as single men were shunted off, griping about the unfairness of it all. Frank was at the door behind Chuck when the O.D. shouted.

"All the married men taken care of?" No comment followed. "O.K. You guys that didn't go on the last 62 line up." More cursing and grumbling followed. Frank felt himself being pushed to the desk by Chuck. The O.D. checked the liberty sheet and made out a 24 hour pass for Frank. He smiled at the popular Brabern as he handed him the pass. "Make it a good one, son," he softly said.

The afternoon went quickly and four thirty found Frank shaving for the second time that day. He slowly dressed, enjoying the envy of the dungaree clad gyrenes who were not fortunate enough to get passes. He took their jibes good-naturedly. Taylor watched him quietly. The kid was more at ease than he had been for a week. He handed Brabern the Buster Brown belt whose buckle he had been cleaning with a blitz cloth.

No busses ran from camp during the week, but the local camp bus went to the gate every hour. Returning the jeers of the group, he winked at Taylor and boarded the 5:00 o'clock bus. At the main gate he got off the bus, showed his pass and stood at the side of route 101 for several minutes. He was undecided on going south to Dago or north to L.A. The highway was lined with about 30 Marines with thumbs extended. Motorists screeched to a stop and picked the green clad Marines up. There was a war on!

Brabern watched the cars stop and then began walking north alongside the highway. He was going to L.A. The most pleasant memories of his sojourn on the west coast were there and he would enjoy his remaining free days in the U.S. there.

He took his place at the far end of the line and within ten minutes found himself flying smoothly along the concrete carpet. He was always amazed at the smoothness and speed of cars along the highway after bouncing along on camp roads in the military trucks. His driver was a Los Angeles bookie who had spent the day at Aqua Caliente in Tijuana, Mexico. The middle-aged man was boisterously conversational. In rapid succession he spoke of his admiration for Marines, the good luck he had that day at the track, and the black book of phone numbers he'd gladly let the Marine use. Brabern politely declined. As the car neared Long Beach the bookie declared he was hungry and suggested dinner on him of course. Frank was hungry himself and felt no qualms on accepting a meal from the man. They ate at the dining room of the Wilton Hotel. The room was crowded with sailors, and from the windows of the Sky Room which was at the top of the hotel, they could see the fleet at anchor in the harbor. The bookie talked on and on, Frank scarcely listening, immensely enjoying the steak that the tout had insisted he order. It was quite a difference from the food - they called it food - he ate in camp.

Pushing his napkin away from him, Frank saw that it was 7:30. The bookie noticing the movement, said they better be going, adding that he'd bet, and he was gambling man, that Frank had a hot one scheduled for that night. Frank unfeelingly joined the man's laughter.

It took an hour to get to downtown L. A. because of the traffic. The bookie let Brabern off at Pershing Square, winkingly telling him to beware of the chippies. Frank sincerely thanked him for the lift and watched the big car disappear into the darkness. He stood at the curb, watching the lights flickering on the Marquee of the Pontages Theatre. He decided on his next move. He'd go to a bar and get a drink - it was the accepted first step of a liberty. He stepped into a small dark cafe and climbed onto a high bar stool and ordered a bourbon and water, The bartender looked at him, sizing him up, then decided he was 21 and went to pour the drink. Frank smiled, he had Chuck's I.D. card on him, if he were questioned concerning his age. Taylor had slipped it to him as he boarded the bus.

He again looked at his watch. What now! The Palladium - he hadn't been there for a while - maybe he'd better get a sack for the night first. The thought brought to his mind the vision that had lurked there since that Sunday, ten days before. He smiled and thought of her back home in Colorado. Someday he would meet someone like her and she wouldn't be married. He slapped 50 cents on the bar and walked out. Getting his bearing he headed down the street to where Main intersected. He glanced up and down and saw the U.S.O. sign on the wall of a building in the next block to the right. He quickly walked there and saw an arrow pointing to the second floor embossed with the letters USO. He took the steps two at a time, a feeling he didn't understand rising in the pit of the stomach. At the top of the stairs he found himself in a large room that took the entire 2nd floor of the building.

He looked around. Two soldiers were playing ping-pong at the far end of the room, others, sailors, were cheerfully banging away at billiard balls. His eyes turned to the right where about 20 sailors, soldiers and marines were sitting leafing through magazines. His eyes caught a sign above them on the wall in the shape of an arrow reading "Rooms" pointing to the front of the building. He turned in that direction and looked straight into the eyes of Candy.

The young Marine and the beautiful girl looked deep into each others' eyes. Brabern didn't remember walking to the desk, nor taking her hands in his. Eyes throughout the U.S.O. had chanced to catch the reaction of the pair and now a growing audience watched the scene.

Unaware of the audience and oblivious to everything but Candy Frank said, "I thought you had gone back to Colorado? Did you find an apartment?"

A chuckle emerged from the girl's lovely mouth. "Not exactly, but I'm still here. Scuttlebutt had it your outfit had already left." Her eyes shone as she spoke and nudging throughout the room brought an increased audience to the scene. From the interior of an enclosed office came the U.S.O. Director, a frown on her lined face. This sort of thing was not exactly looked upon with favor. She leaned against the casing of the frame and intently watched. The silence that had fallen over the room brought Candy the realization that privacy was lacking. She looked toward the office and seeing the frowning director, hastily began shuffling through papers on her desk.

She lowered her voice. "I'm through at 10. I'll meet you at the bus station next door in the waiting room." She smiled up at him and then took up a pencil and began writing illegible lines on a form.

He turned and erectly walked through the smiling faces of the service men to the stairs. He knew that they had not been able to hear the conversation between Candy and him, yet he knew that they had all grasped that there had been more to the scene than the mere routine of obtaining a room for the night. Looks of admiration from several who had tried to make time with the girl and failed followed him down the stairs.

Glancing at his watch, he saw that he had 30 minutes before she would come out of the U.S.O. Across from the U.S.O. was a Newsreel Theatre, and he cautiously crossed the street against the traffic. He entered the darkened theatre, alive with the flashing of big gun fire from a naval action scene on the screen. He settled into a seat and watched the action on the screen. The Navy, according to the narrator, had regained control of the sea in the South Pacific. The defeat at Pearl Harbor had wiped out most units of the Pacific fleet but now, two years later, the fleet was again operating and the new carriers were sending out planes that controlled the air. The action on

Guadalcanal had been confined and scenes were shown of the busy new won base in the Pacific.

As Frank watched he wondered which division he would be assigned to. He knew that they were being sent over because of impending battles that were forthcoming. It had been 8 months since the 1st Division had landed on Guadalcanal and he knew that three Marine Divisions in the Pacific were soon to be sent into battle.

After fifteen minutes of more news events throughout the country and the world, Brabern emerged from the theatre and made his way to the bus-train station from where the unusual street-car trains to North Hollywood and outlying districts of the sprawling city departed. He entered the waiting room and sat on a wicket bench facing the front door. Surprisingly, there were more civilians in the waiting room than servicemen. The sight was an unusual one, for the coast cities had practically been overrun with servicemen. He recalled one night in San Diego when during the entire evening, he had not seen a single male civilian save those who were working behind the bars and in other such jobs.

Candy came through the door. She wore a soft yellow trench coat against the dry coolness of the Los Angeles night. She hastened toward him smiling, and stopped close to him when he rose from the bench.

"Waited long?" she didn't wait for an answer but taking his arm began walking to the side exit of the station. "I've my car parked in the lot next door." She explained. The half hour alone had been enough to recover from the shock of seeing him. She knew that he was going overseas within the next few days. Marines from Camp Pendleton didn't get liberties in the middle of the week for any other reason, she had come to know. She held his arm tightly, gaining strength from it. Briskly they walked, talking of the U.S.O. and Chuck's appearance there Saturday, she chuckling at his obvious imbibing.

They found her car and he held the door open for her. She slid behind the wheel and he found his way to the other side. He hesitated as he climbed in, "Hungry?" he asked.

She smiled and said, "Uh Huh, and I know just the place." She wheeled the car into the traffic. "So you're leaving." She glanced sideways at the Marine leaning against the door.

"Yes, don't know exactly when, but I've got a 24 hour pass. Have to be back at Camp at midnight Thursday. The rest of the outfit back at camp is loading gear now," he paused laughing, "Man, do they envy me!"

She had the car moving quickly along Santa Monica Boulevard. Noticing the landmarks, he smiled, knowing where they were heading. He had formed a question in his mind when she spoke.

"I've decided to stay. Sunday I had my clothes already packed. Had to be out by Monday, you know."

He nodded in the darkness. He moved the handle closing the open window, thankful the top was up on the car. It was cold, or was it just he? She was speaking, "I went to the Hollywood bus station to inquire about the connections to Denver. The place was jammed and there was a long line at the information window. So, not feeling like standing in line I bought a paper and went to the lunch counter. I checked the classified section, wanting to find a used car dealer to sell the car to, and there I found it!" she laughed.

"I thought you said you hadn't found an apartment." He said not understanding.

"You'll see later," she was still laughing. Ahead loomed Torcio's.

Silence except for the music in the distance, surrounded the night spot. Few cars were in the parking lot. Week-days were quiet in the cities near service stations and camps.

He whispered to the headwaiter and he knowingly nodded. Possessed of the memory that is inherent to his select profession he recognized the tall Marine and the strikingly beautiful girl. He unerringly led them to the same table on the patio-porch which was almost empty save for a few civilians and unmistakenly their wives.

Frank tipped the man five dollars, smiling as he recalled Chuck's comment on the inability to spend money overseas.

He ordered for her and the evening took on a different aspect of their previous meeting. Both had had time to evaluate the situation and both had resolved the not unique, during wartime, problem. No longer was there an urgency about their relationship. The panic and uncertainty of their association had disappeared. The young Marine had had his first experience with an unknown quantity. The beautiful but unattainable Candy had swept his keen mind into utter confusion. Her beauty and earthy maturity had brought to him the first feeling of love in his life. He knew now that time would take care of the longing he felt. Loving this girl was not something that would ever disappear entirely, but the inevitable parting, would soon come and his life would be fuller for having met and known her.

Candy, too, had realized the futility of the situation. She had sobbed into her pillow that Sunday, condemning herself for the way her heart and body had responded to this quiet young man from Ohio. Her love for Jerry was deep and firmly entrenched in her heart and she could not understand the ease in which the Marine had shut out that love. Then with the days elapsing she had come to recognize that the loneliness, the utter loneliness that she had felt at the loss of her husband to the Gods of war had led her to actually look for the companionship of the opposite sex. And when this unmistakenly gentle and immature, but strangely masculine and determined Marine had come into her life, she had grasped that opportunity to share once again the feeling of companionship. She didn't discount the fact that her heart had a place for him in it, for never before, except for Jerry, had she longed for anyone as she had since that Sunday. She looked at him now, sitting across from her, thoroughly enjoying the creamy dessert, handsome in his Marine uniform, with his close cropped hair glistening in the moonlight, his strong hands uncomfortably wielding the small dessert spoon.

He caught her staring and embarrassment swept his face. "Never could use these things," he awkwardly placed the spoon on the small platter.

She watched him and wanting desperately to know more about this stranger who would soon be gone asked, "I don't know too much about you. What do your plans call for after the war?"

The solid ground that the trend of the conversation had fallen on encouraged him to speak enthusiastically.

He leaned forward, his green clad arm on the table. "I've always planned to be a doctor." He promptly dropped his eyes to the table, realizing the commonness of the desire. His fingers pushed a crumb of bread over the table cloth. "But maybe I'll be too old to start after this mess is over. I entered the Corps after graduation and haven't even started college." Again he blushed not realizing this aging of himself had already been known by the girl. "If the war's over in a couple of years, I'm still going to take a crack at it. Believe it or not," he held up his hands, "I want to be a surgeon." He laughed.

She smiled and felt that he would be good at the profession. Though large and marked by the tough training he had undergone, the hands, nevertheless, were gentle and sensitive. She took one of them and stroked it gently. "You'll make a great surgeon."

The action brought back the uneasiness that came at each contact. There was a fire burning within them, one that could come to a flame easily with an indifference to the consequences. "Let's dance!" she held his hand gently as they rose and went to the near empty dance floor. They danced to the tunes of the time and lost themselves into an uneasy acceptance to the feeling of being one. The orchestra after several numbers left the stand for a break and the couple strolled to the beach's edge.

The Pacific pounded against the breakwater off shore and cut down the size of the waves as they hit the beach. The night was crisp and clear. Out to sea they could see the outlines of patrol boats protecting against any Japanese submarine that might try to sneak into the huge naval installations along the coast. The threat of an enemy landing which has caused a black-out of the coastal cities has long since been erased and life on the beaches in typical Southern California style had been resumed.

Candy leaned against a palm tree and looked to sea. Brabern offered her a cigarette and when she refused, lighted it for himself. "So you're going to stay here for the duration." His voice sounded strange against the slashing of the waves in the sea close by.

She half-turned to where he stood, three paces closer to the sea. "No, I don't think so! Maybe a month or two more. Air Force men sometime get home occasionally for brief leaves, you know."

Yes, he knew. Those pilots fortunate enough to stay alive were often rotated home when transportation was available for a sojourn before being fed to the Nipponese lions again. A month or two, he smiled. She would stay here till Jerry came home for good, which was evident.

"Say, just where are you going to stay? You didn't tell me." She laughed and took his hand.

"Come on! I'll show you." On the way out of the night club, they passed the smiling headwaiter who, reflected to himself that the handsome marine sure had a beautiful wife.

Candy drove down the ocean highway, mysteriously keeping silent. Frank snapped on the car radio and they rode in silence listening to the music coming from the Palladium. The highway was almost deserted and it came as a surprise to him until he looked at the dashboard clock which hands pointed to 12:30.

Candy suddenly swung the car off the highway. In the dim light of the moon Frank strained to see where they were. Dim objects loomed before them.

"Trailers!" He exclaimed. "You've rented a trailer." He laughed.

Candy joined in the laughter as she slowly vended her way through streets that didn't appear as such to the Marine. She pulled up beside one and stopped. It, like most of the others in the trailer park, was completely dark. "Home," she announced.

They got out of the car and Candy unlocked the door. "Watch your step." she announced switching on a light.

Frank climbed into the trailer amazed. He looked around the compact room - a combination living room, dining area with a small galley in what, evidently, was the center of the trailer. Beyond to the left he could see a bedspread in the small after-end of the trailer, partially obscured by a half-opened sliding door. He had never before been in a trailer and was surprised at the comfort afforded by the built in pieces of furniture. At the right of the entrance door was the living room, complete with carpeting, a modern sofa across the width of the front of the trailer, built-in book shelves, and end tables with secured lamps. All were closed from the eyes of those outside by colorful drapes over the windows which covered the entire and of the trailer.

"Sit down. I'll fix some coffee." Candy had been watching him, enjoying the surprise that was evident in his face. He sat on the sofa, sinking into its deep comfort. He picked a magazine out of the built-in rack and scanned it, periodically glancing at the girl, who, having donned an apron was busy in the galley. She kept up chatter as she worked. The ad she had seen in the paper was stuck in a corner, buried beneath used car advertisements. She called the park from the bus station and had driven right out that morning. She had liked the trailer, its previous occupants had gone east after the husband had been shipped overseas, and had taken it. The rent was high, but, she shrugged her shoulders, as she put a serving tray with coffee and cookies before him on a small table.

"Be back in a minute." she smiled and disappeared into the bedroom, closing the partition behind her. Frank put a teaspoonful of sugar into hot cup and lighted a cigarette.

The door opened and Candy came out. She had changed the dress she had worn to the U.S.O. and was wearing a cotton print that couldn't have looked good on anyone but her. She looked beautiful with her brilliant golden hair brushed back from her temples. She dropped to the couch, one slippered foot beneath her. "There, I feel better."

Frank put down the magazine and turned to her. His insides ached with desire. He longed to hold her in his arms and kiss the loveliness of her lips, eyes, and nose. He shifted his position on the couch. "Candy, I'd better shove! It's late and you've got to be at the U.S.O." Holy cow, if the guys could only hear him.

She calmly looked at him. She had already made up her mind. "Where will you go?" Without waiting for an answer, she added, "You're staying right here, right here," patting the couch. "It's silly for you to look for a place for tonight. Don't argue, I'd already decided that before I brought you here."

He looked at her, studying her eyes as he listened to her words. Burning there was the same desire he felt. He knew that she had fought a battle within herself and knew that he could take her if he wished. Her love for him was not that which she felt for her husband but one which at that moment longed for satisfaction. He tried to reason with himself, the distaste that would come later to them both was brushed aside for the desire of two young bodies. Cursing himself, he took her in his arms. She willingly accepted his kisses and caresses, losing herself in the desire which she had fought against but which had cast out all reason. He lowered her to the couch, the awkwardness of the confines adding to his inexperienced fumbling. He pulled his lips from hers long enough to throw a glance to the bed visible in the other room. His eyes met hers and her head nodded ever so slightly. He picked her from the couch and cautiously carried her to the bed. He stood over her for a moment; his awkwardness had raised her dress above her lovely knees to the pure whiteness of her thighs where the sun had not reached beneath her bathing suit. Gasping, he lowered himself beside her and tenderly kissed her closed eyes and moved to her lips, his hands gently but firmly sliding over her smooth body removing her clothes. The pure whiteness of her skin beneath was in dark contrast to the bronze face and legs. He reached over the bed and snapped off the light. Passionately their lips met and he moved over her. Her lips were next to his right ear and they became one. Her lips silently formed the words, "Oh, Jerry - Jerry, I'm sorry."

The sleek convertible moved through the main gates of Camp Pendleton. The drive from L. A. had been mostly in silence, as they had been silent for most of the day. Their eyes had met often and the understanding had discounted any need for words. The inevitable had happened and the memory of it would never be forgotten. But now that it had happened their need for each other had diminished.

Whistles met the car in front of 13 Area. Taylor was sitting on the steps of the P.X., his pipe dangling from his mouth. Candy stopped the car and turned to Frank.

"Don't be sorry, Frank. Believe it wasn't your fault. I knew it was going to happen. The conscious pains are mine." She took his hand, "I'll never forget you!"

He tightened the grip on her soft hand. "Never." He hesitated. "Would you mind if I wrote to you?" he loved this girl.

"Please, mail the letters to the U.S.O." Tears welled in her eyes. "I'll answer."

He raised her hand to his lips, kissed it gently, opened the car door and was gone.

The troop laden ship moved like an overweight tub through the ground swells. Point Loma slipped farther and farther and farther astern. Taylor and Brabern leaned over the rail along with hundreds of other Marines. Taylor hadn't spoken to Frank about Candy since he returned. He watched the U.S. disappearing over the horizon.

He didn't look at his buddy as he said. "You're lucky to have known her."

Frank was surprised by his voice. He looked at his wise friend and slowly nodded, and then he flipped his cigarette over the side, watching it too disappear in the wake of the ship.

Chapter 2

The ocean was acting up - the blue green of the calm Pacific had changed to gray under a whipping wind and heavily over cast sky. San Diego lay two days behind the heaving fantail of the pot-bellied freighter.

"Going to get rough," the voice came out of the semidarkness of late afternoon. J. C. Malton's lips had scarcely moved around the stem of the pipe. Frank Brabern nodded as he turned to the stranger beside him. Most of the deck had been deserted save for a few hardy men who were playing cards on a hatch cover - the pitch of the ship in the boiling water had begun to take its toll on the troops.

Brabern turned his eyes to the sky. The gray, rain laden clouds were pressing lower - he turned the collar of his dungaree jacket higher. "A real blow coming up not much like home." His voice was raised against the wail of the wind.

"Where's home?" the stocky Marine asked the required question - not much caring for an answer.

Frank Brabern had half turned from the rail, and was studying the man who stood beside him. Malton was not tall, in fact, he stood a good three inches shorter than he, but he was compactly built inside the dungarees. He was deeply tanned - and seemed all the darker in the light.

An onlooker would have noticed that the only similarity between the two were the black eyes. Malton's face was not handsome, but unusual - not handsome, not ugly, but attractive with his high cheekbones and hard chin joined by slim jawbones ran from a broad smooth forehead.

Brabern suddenly realized that he had not answered the question, "Ohio - Cleveland."

Malton smiled. "Been there often - I live in West Virginia, just over the Ohio River," he held out his hand and Brabern was aware of the firm grip. "My name's J.C. Malton."

"Brabern, Frank - What's the J.C. stand for?" Brabern's face wore a grin also - a friendship in the building was acknowledged unspeakingly between the two.

"Just J.C. - initials - they don't mean anything," the smile broadened. "Guess my parents thought the initials were enough."

The pair stood at the rail looking at the sea, their stomachs began to unsettle under the strain.

"Hey, Frank," a husky voice called from an open hatchway which led to Marines quarters three decks below, "I'm going below. God, I'm sick."

Brabern and Malton laughed at the sight of the Marine ducking hurriedly down the ladder to the nearest head, but the laughter was strained, without full relish, for they two felt the hitch and roll of the ship beneath the belts.

"Buddy - Chuck Taylor," Brabern offered. "Came through boot together and have been lucky enough to stay together since."

"Got a light?" the two Marines had not heard the owner of the voice approach, were unaware of the presence of a lean, lithe, Marine wearing a peacetime campaign hat. Tall, he must have stood 6' 2", his face was expressionless below the wide brim of the campaign hat. His eyes, set wide apart were deep in their pits shadowed by thick eyebrows. His cheeks were hollow and subservient to the peaked hooked nose which dominated his face. He wore khakis and in the months to follow they were to realize his dislike for the dungarees, preferring the tight, cut down khaki shirt and clinging trousers. To his right leg was strapped a long sheath, from whose top protruded the handle of an obviously murderous jungle knife. The cigarette hung low from the thin lips. J. C. held a match to the cigarette, and Brabern opened a spot, unconsciously, for the slim Marine to occupy. The third member of a close team had arrived.

"Thanks," the voice tinged with a New England accent said as he accepted the spot by the rail, but instead of hanging over it he leaned his back to its roundness and peered at the super structure of the ship. He explained, "It's easier on the stomach when you get fresh air, but it doesn't help when you look at the pitching waves." His voice sounded with authority, as if travel on the High Seas were not a new or unknown experience to him. Malton and Brabern, their faces reflecting their embarrassment at not knowing this truism of the sea, followed the Marine's example. He hadn't seemed to look at either of the two since joining them and save for the thanks offered for the lighting of his cigarette had not shown any emotion either with his voice or with his face, which had not changed expression once. The three stood, braced themselves against the roll of the ship, watched the ship's activities. At intervals their eyes landed on the knot of Marines playing cards on the weather protected hatch cover.

"I swear that old guy hasn't been below decks since we boarded this tub." Malton said. It was obvious to the two which of the group of four card players he was referring. A fat, balding man in his middle thirties seemed to be the houseman in the playing circle. His sallow skin had a three days stubble of gray hairs on it, and his clothes showed constant contact with the grease coated cables of the ship.

"That's the Commodore." The knife bearing Marine said, flipping the cigarette from his lips and over the side of the ship. His voice was emotionless as the others waited for him to continue. "Name's James McNalton - he's quite a character - trained with us at Pendleton."

"How come you call him Commodore - what the hell is your name?" Brabern suddenly realized that they hadn't exchanged names.

The slim Marine smiled for the first time. "Fagan", he said and almost was interrupted by Malton.

"Cold Steel Fagan?"

Fagan nodded and his face continued to smile. Both Brabern and Malton looked at the tall Maine with added respect. Cold Steel had become a stateside legend among the Marine Corps stations. Nerveless and heartless some said, he had won the awe of the Corps by action in combat at Guadalcanal - heroics, some called it, but others said it was out of pure desire for action. Regardless, he had single-handedly, after other elements of a machine gun nest on the Tenaru River had been wiped out, continued firing until his ammunition had been expended and then had had crawled to another nest a hundred yards away, meshing in hand to hand combat with at least six of the enemy, the official citation read, and then after hanging bandoliers of machine gun bullets around his neck, had again fought his way to his own position which he held until relief came the following morning.

"I thought the papers said you had been excused from ever going back, along with receiving the Congressional Medal of Honor." Malton said as he put his pipe back in his mouth.

"Got awful tiresome back in the states," Fagan said as he watched the card game. "Asked for and got permission to rejoin the outfit. It feels good to be away from those damn newspapermen. Now if they wanted a good story, McNalton over there would make a good subject."

Brabern smiled, realizing the way Cold Steel had turned the subject of conversation from himself - that fit in with the other tales he had heard about the quiet, but ferocious fighter. He caught Malton's eyes and realized that he too had understood the maneuver.

"Well," Fagan continued as the trio watched McNalton draw another pot towards himself. "McNalton's been in the Corps a long time, quite an old salt. During that time he has acquired three things, a passion for women, a passion for playing poker, and a wife!" Malton and Brabern chuckled as Fagan paused, then continued. "Now McNalton loves his wife, or so he says, but he can't resist the temptation of chasing strange tail as often as he can. That's the way it was at Pendleton - he had placed his wife securely in San Diego, had rented a small cottage near the sub base - I was there for dinner once. But soon after he arrived at Pendleton from duty at the base in Dago, he began to wander. It didn't take him long to latch on to hungry females and his turned out to be a beast in Long Beach. She was really a hag - damn close to 50, but she had one thing that McNalton lived on! A wild streak in the sack." Fagan stopped and lighted a cigarette from Malton's pipe before he continued.

"The Commodore said that when the lights were out he couldn't see the face but the body sure worked like hell. This went on for a couple of months - the hag's husband was a Commodore at sea and there was no danger there and McNalton kept telling his wife that he had the duty on weekends and then hightailed it for Long Beach."

Fagan paused and watched the card players get up from the hatch and move with dispatch to the open ladder below. McNalton brought up the rear, his sloping shoulders trailing so low there seemed to be nothing there from the thin neck to the fat ass. Beneath his stubble of beard, he too had turned the color of scattered ashes, yet he still felt strong enough to count the wad of green backs he held between his grimy fingers. So intense was he in his preoccupation that he almost fell over the lip of the hatchway. Fagan's smile joined the robust laughter of Brabern and Malton.

"He'd sell his ass for a dollar and before this cruise is over he'll probably get plenty of offers." Fagan spoke reflectively, then continued his story. "The old boy really had it made. Of course he'd take a weekend in Dago once in a while to make things look on the up and up, but the trips to Long Beach were much more frequent than those to Dago.

"The guys used to lay it on him pretty thick, but the Commodore just smiled and asked them if they had tail in both ports. The climax came on the last liberty before we shoved off. Guess the old man's conscience began to bother him - so he made off for San Diego - he told me that the passion for the sailor's wife had simmered from its earlier roaring blaze - no conquest he said. He slicked up in his best greens and even borrowed some hair tonic for his hair - what there was left of it. The guys just watched the "Master lover" in astonishment - they even sent him off on the Dago bus with words of encouragement and even lent him money when he "confessed" he was broke as a result of the bitch, his own words, in Long Beach."

"So fortified, he entered Dago, and using the suckers' money, he had plenty of his own, made his way to the little white cottage near the submarine base to repent and swear eternal devotion to his true and faithful wife." Fagan came away from the rail, with a sudden heavy roll of the ship. With expert eyes he saw that his two new found friends were beginning to feel the effects of the wild ride.

"You guys want to go below?" his voice was non-committal, but his eyes showed amusement.

"Finish the story!" Malton said thickly, a steadying hand tightly clasping the rail. Brabern nodded - the desire to hear the conclusion of the story fighting the desire to hold tight to a bunk.

"Well, as I said, McNalton went to Dago and saw his wife, but he came back to Pendleton a defeated man." Fagan smiled his mirthless smile, his thin lips just faintly raised towards the protruding Lincolnian cheekbones. "We didn't get it out of him till we were on the 6 x 6's on the way to the docks. He was almost in tears - seems when he had entered the house, his arms outstretched to take the lucky woman into his arms, she ducked away. He was naturally stunned and thought she was teasing him and it added to the fire in his lower quarters which had started to glow as the bus had moved ever closer to the white cottage. This was like old times, a little struggle before the submission. But, he couldn't catch her and finally the words she threw at him began to sink in. He had been secured from his life, she was trying to tell him - she no longer wanted him."

"What the hell was she saying? Naturally he couldn't and wouldn't believe her. He stopped chasing her and dropped exhausted onto the couch. She had stood across the room leaning over the back of an overstuffed chair, her ample breasts heaving with her heavy breathing. The commodore said he could think of only two things - she didn't want him anymore and Christ, he wanted her so badly he could rip the cloth from those breasts and bury his face in them."

"Finally the room stopped shimmering before his eyes and he had meekly asked for an explanation, and he got one that knocked the egotistical wind right from his sails. She had become bored with being alone and had begun to frequent the week-end dances at the Submarine Base. As was inevitable, she, an attractive and well-stacked girl in her early thirties, was given a big play by the submariners and, not so inevitable, had been swept from her feet by a Commodore. He had been looking for her all his life, and now that he had her, he wanted her for his wife."

Fagan puffed on another cigarette, enjoying the reverent silence the tale had received from the two Marines. "And, McNalton couldn't believe his ears - she wanted to marry him - and she wanted a divorce right away. Well, the old boy was stunned but he finally consented."

"You can imagine the scene in the truck. Those gyrenes almost died laughing - one guy almost fell off the truck."

Malton and Brabern were laughing now, a forced laugh because of their condition, but laughter anyway. Malton found his voice somewhere in his coated throat and asked "Did she get the divorce?"

Fagan smiled and shook his head. "Nope. It seems that McNalton talked her into one more session in the sack, so he'd have something to remember her by." The smile broadened. "I guess the old boy threw every trick of Americans' favorite indoor game at her because by the time the night was over she was swearing undying love for him once more."

Brabern gulped down a rising feeling in his stomach and asked, "Then why the hell was he so down about then?"

Fagan flipped the cigarette over the side and started toward the open hatchway. The two unsteady men followed him straining to catch the knife-wearing man's words in the whipping mind. "Well, as the Commodore puts it - it's going to be a long time before he's headed back stateside and the thing which is preying on his mind is that if the wife got lonesome once - she might get lonesome and bored again - and the latter was the thing that was worrying him."

Cold Steel disappeared down the ladder and two sick but laughing Marines followed him below.

The storm lasted three days and practically every Maine on board, save the old salts was seasick. If they withstood the rolling and pitching of the ship, the odor, sound, and sight of sick men in the cramped holds broke through their resistance until they too joined the retching men, some who made it to the heads, others to the 50 gallon G.I. cans which had been strategically placed throughout the ship, others just couldn't move and relieved themselves on the deck.

The bunks were stacked seven high, and there was little room for a man to move, and none to roll over without lifting the canvass sack and its occupant above him. Malton had stuck close to his bunk, leaving only to stagger to the nearest G.I. can. On one trip his thin lips had curled into a smile as he could read the embossed name of the industrial firm on the freshly situated can. It had been made in his hometown.

On the second day he had tried to make the mess hall on the deck above. The trip had been interrupted by dry retching G.I. cans. He was tearing his insides out and felt that some food, though the thought of solids only brought more heaving, would relieve him. It had taken him two hours to make the mess hall crawling and climbing over prostrated fellow sufferers. But there had been no line in the mess hall and he passed quickly down the chow line with the stainless steel tray in his hands. The mess men were smiling broadly as they intentionally threw the food aimlessly in the tray. The creamed, beef landed in the mashed potatoes and was quickly followed by the Navy beans and ice cream.

Carrying the tray precariously across the tilting deck, Malton had no difficulty finding a spot on the usually packed tables - more like narrow platforms, which stood waist high in neat rows in the huge galley. Placing the tray on the table he uncomfortably watched the food slip from one end of the tin slab to the other, depositing some mashed potatoes, beef and ice cream on the table with each trip.

"Looks appetizing, doesn't it?" Fagan had approached unheard in the clattering of tin upon tin. He placed his tray beside that of Malton's. His face was calm, his eyes steady as Fagan watched his friend whose face was pale, whose eyes swam in their wide spaced sockets.

J. C. managed a grin and tried to steady his swaying body. He watched Cold Steel gingerly separate his beef from the vanilla ice cream and followed the course of the fork to the thin line of a mouth. His stomach churned as Fagan savored the meat, chewing each bite carefully seeming to thoroughly enjoy the food.

Malton didn't touch his food; instead he seemed to turn paler with each bite that Fagan took. Suddenly he clutched at his mouth and ran for the hatchway. Fagan watched him go, a smile on his face and the fork midway to his mouth, and then he shrugged his shoulders and continued the fork on its trip to the mouth. As he chewed he smiled. Outside Malton hung over the rail, retching dryly. He felt he was going to die, and then suddenly a terrible thought passed through his brain - he was hoping he'd die, anything was better than this.

"Pass me that book, J.C." Chuck Taylor called from the top bunk of a six tier bank of iron cots in the hold.

"Catch!"- Malton answered from across the narrow aisle. He too had the top cot, a luxury that was much sought by the troops on the transport. They had swapped bunks with other Marines so they - Fagan, Brabern, Malton, and Taylor could be together. Now as taps neared they were lying on the bunks reading the paper bound books which had been furnished the departing Marines at San Diego by the Salvation Army. The selection was meager, but somehow the group had managed to come into possession of "God's Little Acre" and Caldwell's sensual treatment of his characters had become the steady reading material of the group.

The storm area had been left three days before and the calm Pacific had soothed the sea-sickness from the Marines.

"God! This is living." Taylor said as he stretched his frame on the cot, digging his tail into the midsection of Brabern who occupied the bunk beneath him. Taylor continued, "Just like home."

Fagan sniffed the foul, stale air which oppressed the compartment, "Yeh, if you lived in a slaughter house or a whore house."

Malton cautiously savored the air, his nostrils cringing at the foul air of the compartment which still carried traces of the sea-sickness of this and many other cruises. He smiled at the gray steel overhead above him. What a mess that had been - he'd never been so sick in his life. The vision of the hold full of sea-sick men now seemed funny, and the sight of the old gunny sergeant and Fagan forcing their way through the prostrate men carrying 5 gallon casks of dill, sour pickles, only added to the fantasy. His ears could still hear the screams of the sick men as their mouths were forced open, they were too weak to resist, and the sour, but settling large dill pickles were forced in. And the mouths were held closed until the last piece of pickle had been consumed. He, himself, had struggled violently, only to discover that he did feel better as the sourness seemed to sooth his stomach.

"Lights out!" The voice came over the small boxes at both ends of the hold. Immediately the sleeping compartment was pitched into darkness with but dim night lights marking the hatchways. The usual curses filled the room as some had been caught in the middle of writing a letter home, others like the Commodore holding 3 Queens in the poker game, and still others, like Taylor who were in the middle of a good passage of the book they were reading.

The grumblings stopped as the penetrating strains of taps came over the public address system. As the last tones settled over the compartment, silence joined them, broken only by the whisperings of those who had been in the middle of a recounting of their conquests back in the states. Conquests, like the novels being read, mostly imagination.

Frank Brabern pulled the small locket from his pocket, and felt every inch of it. He never took it out during the day, never opened it to see the beautifully face of the girl whose likeness was framed within. He didn't need to look at the picture here in the dark, he knew every detail of the tanned face surrounded by the lush blonde hair. He didn't need to look at the picture - Candy was always close here in the darkness of the ship, her face smiling as it had been when he had last looked at her, and as it would be when he returned. He shuddered - would she be there when he returned? What would become of their love when he returned - if he returned?

The frequent tossing of bodies heralded the approach of sleep, each man fighting the thoughts of home - the doubts which somehow became amplified with distance. Sleep, fitful and uncomfortable came to the troops of A.P.A. 604.

Whoom! Whoom! The sturdy ship rolled distraughtly. Whoom! Whoom! Every hand on board the freighter was now awake - each fighting to rationalize, get his bearings. Commotion and voiced struggling in the darkness.

"Now Hear This! Now Hear This!" the calm voice came out over the loudspeaker and the noise quieted in the hold. "Marines in the holds! Man your abandon ship stations! Man your abandon ship stations!"

The words cut deep and each man in his turn reacted differently as they prepared to go topside to their pre-assigned stations. They knew exactly where they were, had indeed practiced enough times. Many men fumbled, cursing into their life jackets, although strict orders had been to wear them at all times.

No panic developed as the men proceeded up the ladder, although some men hurried more than others. J.C. Malton found himself in front of Fagan as they seemingly moved slowly toward the exit ladders.

"Depth Charges," Fagan said calmly into his ear. "Must have spotted a sub."

Malton realized the truthfulness and logic of the statement. There had been no explosions or rocking of the ship since those first four reports. However, he could tell that the ship had begun its submarine evasion run, first in one direction and then the other.

A blast of cool, salty air struck Malton's face as he reached the top step of the ladder. Then his hand came in contact with the blackout curtain which covered each passageway opening. The double hung heavy black curtains were stretched about 5 feet apart, enough to permit a man to close the rear ones off to the running lights in the interior of the ship before pushing his way through the outside curtains into the open. As Malton crouched into the open, the brightness of the exterior shocked him.

The night was almost as bright as daylight. Malton realized as he easily made his way to his assigned boat station. A full moon surrounded by a heaven full of stars illuminated the sea for miles around.

"Nice night for a sub." Fagan said more to himself than to any particular person. But his voice was clearly heard by the other members of the boat station who also were adjusting their eyes to the night.

"Look at those ships." Chuck Taylor said. His suggestion was not needed for practically all eyes aboard the ship were straining to see the dark hulks about them. They were in the rear portion of the convoy and destroyers and destroyer escorts were racing about them covering the area in search of the sub which was lurking for clear shot at the large, heavily laden ships.

"Christ," a low whistle followed the word from Brabern's mouth. "I feel like a sitting duck." He cupped his hands over his eyes. "I wonder where the hell that sub is?"

"Don't worry," Fagan said calmly, wishing it was safe to light a cigarette, "he can see you - or maybe it would be better to say they can see you."

A frightened voice from the rear of the group spoke up for the first time "You mean there's more than one sub out there?"

The Marines leaning over the rail turned and faced the voice. "Well, I'll be a son-of-a-bitch!" Taylor said and began a controlled laugh. As the others took in the scene they too joined the laughter for there in the shadows cast by the large whale boat was McNalton, dressed only in his Mae West life jacket. He wore no clothes whatsoever save for the Mae West, and he shivered as the cool night breeze brushed by him.

"Where the hell's your clothes?" Fagan asked superiorly. He was fully clothed, complete even to the ever present jungle knife lashed to his leg. On his head, his campaign cap was solidly perched in position. Most of the others had some clothing on them, even if they were barefooted with but skivvy shirts covering the upper parts of their bodies.

The Commodore tried to pull the Mae West lower on his body but failed in the attempt, the blue jacket adamant in its position on his body. "I always sleep nude! The body rests better that way."

"Don't hand me that crap," Taylor said, having heard of the escapades of the older man. "You're just always ready for action."

A flash of flames across the sea cut short the laughter. All eyes were held spell bound as explosion and flashes repeatedly burst through the night. One of the supply ships had caught a torpedo. The night suddenly brightened even more with the flames of the dying ship, and in the reflection the small destroyers raced in to surround the sub. Explosions ripped the area as the depth charges dropped by the destroyers sought out the underwater attacker. All hands watched fascinated by the deadly cat and mouse game. Suddenly, as unexpectedly as it had come, the light disappeared as the hit ship extinguished its own flames as it sank beneath the surface of the sea. The explosions and bubbling water continued.

"Think the crew got off?" Brabern broke the silence with the words which were going through each man's thoughts.

Fagan was beating a steady tattoo on the rail of the ship with the handle of his knife. "Some of them - but not most of them." He said slowly and then continued, "She was an oil tanker - hot as hell."

"Now hear this - Now hear this! Troops secure from boat stations. Troops secure from boat stations. All troops go below. All troops go below. Ships company remain at battle stations. Ships company remain at battle stations."

The men looked at each other in the brightness of the night and then began to follow Fagan to the open hatchway. NcNalton didn't move from his position beneath the whale boat.

"Come on Commodore. The man said to go below." Taylor had noticed that the older Marine had not joined the jostling men.

McNalton shook his head vigorously from side to side. "Not me. I'm staying topside. I'm not going to be caught below if one of those torpedoes pick this tub out."

When Taylor spread the word below, the tension of the submarine attack was broken. Every one added to the story as it made the rounds of the hold. Everyone enjoyed McNalton's terror save Fagan, who just crawled in his sack and lay with his eyes closed.

He was still not asleep as quietness spread once again over the ship, and cot by cot responded to the need for sleep. Fagan did not like weakness in any man, himself included, but weakness was fear, and he could understand. Fear. It was not something to be laughed at - it was a gnawing, painful reaction to the unknown.

Silently he swung from his bunk and lowered himself to the cluttered deck, with eyes which seemed to thrive in the dark, he made his way to the Commodore's cot, and groping over its unruliness, he gathered an arm full of clothing.

Fagan found McNalton huddled beneath the whale boat, shivering convulsively, He held the clothes out to the man. "Put these on before you shake yourself apart."

The Commodore awkwardly, with shaking hand put the dungarees and combat boots on his goose-pimpled laden body. When he finished he still was trembling but not so convulsively. He sat on the deck and pulled the life-jacket about his upper body, carefully securing each lace. Finally, he looked up at Fagan who was leaning over the rail, staring at the Southern Cross far above the horizon.

"Thanks." he mumbled, his teeth chattering with the word.

Fagan turned and looked down at the huddled man. He didn't answer but his eyes, if the Commodore could have seen them, were soft.

"I didn't expect you to bring me anything." The Commodore emphasized the pronoun as he spoke deliberately. "Why did you?"

Fagan once again had turned to the rail, his eyes picking out five other lumbering ships on the sea. High above, the A.P.A.'s ship's horn sounded. Once, echoed by the other members of the convoy, and as Fagan watched, all ships turned to the left slightly in the pre-determined plan to deliberately confound following submarines. It added many miles to a voyage but it also preserved many ships. He hadn't answered the Commodore immediately, but his thoughts were on his words. Finally as he shifted from his right to his left foot resting on the lower rail he said, "I know what fear is like - it's not a laughing matter. So you're scared - it's no crime."

The commodore rose from the cramped quarters he had occupied since he had come on deck, his throat full of his heart, over an hour before. He stood beside Fagan and put his foot on the rail. Sheepishly he said "Hell, I don't know what's got into me." He shook his head in disbelief of his own actions. "I'm just fed up to here," he indicated his neck, "with this tub. Ever since I boarded her, I've had a feeling of disaster. Now, by God, I'm going to stay topside. I don't give a damn what the other guys think of me or what they say. I'm not going below to be trapped below decks."

Fagan smiled condolingly, secure that the Commodore could not see the action. Taking all levity from his voice he said, "You've a right to stay up here. Don't worry about the guys. They may laugh at you now - and ridicule your fear, but soon," he paused and his voice came even more soberly, "they will know the meaning of fear themselves. Everyone who goes into combat experiences it, of course, some deny it, but the man who says he doesn't feel fear, or who isn't afraid of death is a liar."

McNalton tried to see the face of the New Englander. At first he had been surprised at the fluency with which he spoke, and then he had been further astounded with the philosophy which he poured from his lips. This crude person, who had seemed so fearless, had a sageness which was not evident, he somehow felt close to the man, as if they both shared a secret - the secret of fear.

"Keep out of the wind", Fagan offered as he turned and headed for the hatchway. McNalton watched him go; a look of thanks and relaxation, the latter had not been there before on his face.

The trip from San Diego to Noumea, New Caledonia took 17 days. Seventeen days of leisure and pleasure, save for the three days when the A.P.A. tossed about the usually calm Pacific like a cork in a washing machine; 17 days where friendships were formed and others broken - the latter as a result of card game squabbles.

One day the ship stopped its course momentarily, but its huge screw still turned propelling the boat. They, the troops on board the ship were astride the equator and the traditional King Neptune Ceremony took place. Each man was initiated into the order of the shellback in hilarious ceremonies included being hosed down. Some of the less fortunate were even turned loose on the vengeance of the ship barber who unmercifully went rampant with his shears and cut rough courses through what little hair the men had. King Rex, in all his finery held court with his huge pitched fork and high crown. At his side sat his "wife" complete with golden locks fashioned from a dyed yellow mop. Unfortunates who committed no more crime than to be alive were hauled before His Majesty's throne and upon them were bestowed punishments, which added delight to the all-male witnesses. The day was full of entertainment, with a few of the ship's crew manning privately owned instruments for a jam session, with partners doing all the jitter-bugging to the applause of the spectators.

Officers and men alike were subjected to the whims of the shellbacks, and when their enthusiasm was finally spent, each Polywog was awarded a certificate attesting to their now being properly invested into the Royal Order of Neptune.

Even the ships cooks went all out and prepared a delicious meal of fresh meat, potatoes and ice cream. It was a tired bunch of men who went to their sacks that night. But most of the days were spent in doing nothing more strenuous but lying on the flat hatch covers, with the hot sun burning already dark bodies darker, talking, playing cards and learning the backgrounds of the men.

Before many days had passed, groups, or cliques, as they would be called in civilian life, had been formed. And these groups more or less gathered together to pass the hours of the day. One such group was composed of Cold Steel Fagan and his followers, for followers they had become.

Cold Steel Fagan accepted his role of old salt gracefully and with indifference. He did not impose his knowledge or experience on the men, but offered advice willingly and without condescendence. He was a New Englander and naturally sage and withdrawn. He didn't disclose his age but he was older than most of the men.

J. C. Malton, from West Virginia, that peculiar breed which belonged neither to the south nor to the north. Educated, he with Brabern, was often called upon to settle disputes. Stocky and dark, his face was rounded yet lean about the straight hard jaw line.

Frank Brabern, was the Hollywood Marine of the group. Sandy haired, he was handsome, but not pretty-boy handsome. Educated also, he was not boisterous but well-spoken. Tall, he carried 185 lbs of solid muscle on his frame.

Chuck Taylor aged Fagan and was wise in the ways of the world. He hailed from New York City and had knocked around with the tough elements of that underworld city. Tough, coarse, nevertheless, he was fatherly and kind to the younger marines. His favorite subject was Doug McPherson, affectionately known as Liverlip. He was short, with a huge protruding upper lip which earned him his nickname. A show-off, high strung and loud-mouthed know-it-all, he was always embroiled in an argument which Taylor always managed to halt before blood was let.

The silent one of the group was Bill Lasher who hailed from Malton's home town and who hated to be away from home and his girl. He never said much, never entered into discussions, but still lent himself well in with the comradeship which formed.

Rounding out the crew were Chick Young, Arizonian who was but sixteen; Frank Robinson, a knot-muscled Californian; Alex Blue, a flat-footed Oklahoman; Cordyn Wagner III, a flat-stomached muscleman from the state of Washington; and Ross Miller, a slow talking Indianan whose only comment to a story was a long drawn out, "Shiiiit!"

And of course, the Commodore, who, true to his words, spent the remaining days and nights after the submarine scare, securely on deck. After the first round of humor at his actions, the others had followed Fagan's lead and began to look after him, bringing him food and drink, never referring again to his fear.

The 17 days passed slowly, even boringly at the conclusion, as all awaited land fall in the French islands of Noumea which had first been the staging post of the Pacific. Now it had been relegated to a back area, a chain in logistics, and the action had moved up the line toward Japan. Guadalcanal, bloody Guadalcanal of such a short time before, now secure and free from the Japanese save for those who still roamed the hills in the interior scrounging to keep alive, was the main staging area. It was to Guadalcanal that the Marines aboard the A.P.A. would soon be headed, but first there was Noumea, where the Marine Corps replacement battalions, at least those which fed troops to the lst Marine Division, the Old Breed, were encamped.

As landfall drew nearer, the men spent more and more time on deck, watching the horizon for any sign of land. It first came with the arrival of sea gulls who never strayed too far from shore. Their arrival was heralded by the men and the gulls were followed. One night soon after by the spotting of subdued lights - the A.P.A. had reached Noumea, New Caledonia.

It took most of the morning for the rubbery-legged Marines to get ashore, but the time passed quickly as they were picked for work parties helping to unload the stores needed to supply the men up north.

The A.P.A. had drawn right into the magnificent harbor of Noumea and had been skillfully maneuvered alongside a spra dock. Marine 6 x 6's stood lined bumper to bumper, their drivers lounging against the running board waiting for their human cargo.

In the flat lands beyond the dock harbor lay the two story buildings of the city, only the roofs visible over the piled high cases which had been dumped skillfully there awaiting transport, perhaps on this same A.P.A. Rising majestically over the white, glistening rooftops, stood the lush green mountain ranges of New Caledonia.

"Bet your ass we'll be stuck up in those hills, somewhere." Liverlip said dejectedly as he passed a heavy carton to Fagan in the human chain lined along the deck.

Fagan didn't look up at the hills, he knew they were there, although he had never been on New Caledonia before - these Pacific Islands all looked the same. "Don't let it worry you Liverlip. You won't be here long enough to care." McPherson stopped, weighing the words.

"Come on Liverlip! You're holding up the war." Brabern poked a case into Liverlip's ribs.

The sun, scorching hot above, raced across the skies, and as it reached directly overhead, the sweating Marines, their sea-bags light on their backs in comparison to the heavy cases they had tossed around all morning, walked down the gangplank and boarded the buses.

The drivers watched them nonchalantly, a knowing look on their faces. The words which had been flung so profusely by the old salts of three weeks at boot camp at every batch of new arrivals. "You'll be sorry!" were not said. At this area of war they were not needed, but the eyes of the motor-transport men wordlessly conveyed the message.

They sat on the hard, wooden benches built into the sides of the truck beds for an hour, waiting - the endless, damnable waiting, which was so much a part of military life. Gums were beat fiercely, and once again the Corps, the President, and even the Japs, in their turn were damned. Stomachs, not nourished since chow at 0600 began to growl, calling for food.

Finally the trucks pulled out and the men ate the dust of the harbor streets. When the hard surfaced streets of the city were reached, the men once more began to breathe and as they did, they raised their faces from the lapels of their grimy dungarees to look at, what was to most of them, their first tropical city.

Noumea was French, and its architect reminded the southerners among the trucks' passengers of New Orleans. Most of the false fronted buildings on the narrow streets through which they passed had second story balconies, laced with the exquisite decorative iron railings. The streets were busy, busier in the past year than they had ever been before, and the French language signs advertising the wares of the business houses had been joined by newer signs in English for the benefit of the American personnel who had brought solid American dollars with them. The convoy met U.S. jeeps and trucks traveling in the opposite direction bearing the insignia of all branches of the services, but there seemed to be only civilians walking the narrow sidewalks.

Hanging over the balconies, waving prettily at the Marines were French girls. Beautiful girls who wore flashing skirts and low cut white blouses. The troops waved back and added calls to the movement, trying to form in their minds the location of the houses and the girls in case they were able to make a liberty and perhaps something more while they awaited their call North. But as the tracks moved on the men noticed that for every lovely mademoiselle waving friendly, there was a fat dowager standing behind her with a stern and distasteful look on her face. The realization that these girls weren't available for the troops came on slowly but it became a rare sight not to see mommy standing like a mother hen behind the chick.

The houses which lined the second floors soon took over the whole building as the tracks rolled noisily on through the city. And the further the trucks bore into the town the more dilapidated became the structure.

"Hey, look!" Brabern called as he pointed out a huge clapboard house which stood on the corner. Two shore patrol jeeps were parked at the curb, their occupants relaxing with one leg dangling over the sides, and with the S.P. arm bands obvious to the long line of men which led from the single door of the house around the corner and out of sight. Between the first and second floor windows was a large white sign with red letters shimmering like flames - two words almost fit the sign - "Cat House".

"That's for me!" The commodore shouted. Making as if to climb over the side of the truck. Helping hands almost accomplished the exit, and only by grasping firmly the wooden slats of the bench was McNalton able to remain in the truck. Laughter and bawdy remarks flew back and forth.

"You'll never catch me lined up like that." Malton said disgustedly. "What the hell gets into men to line up like that to sleep with dames who've been worked on a dozen times in the past hour."

Fagan watched the West Virginian's hands working on his knees. He smiled inwardly, "You'll find out in about six months." he said softly. "You think you can do without sex? Out here, sex becomes the most important thing in your life - even more important than staying alive." He knew J.C. was watching him, but he didn't raise his eyes. "When you get away from here, you won't see any women at all, not even dark ones. There'll only be men - most of them like yourself - ordinary guys, decent guys, but guys nevertheless. And soon you'll be aching to see a curved body, tits bulging out of a sweater or a blouse. Softness, that's what you'll be aching for, and then you'll start talking - we'll all start talking of women."

Fagan's smile broke to his face "Conquests will be the first step, all the others will listen hungrily - their own minds reliving experiences, innocent experiences of casual necking with a gal back home and those experiences will begin to amplify until they weren't mere petting, but torrid love scenes, and then the men will begin believing they actually happened and proudly join the story telling. Sex! That will constitute 99 percent of the conversation until each man will die a thousand deaths waiting to get back to where he can be with a woman." Fagan lighted a cigarette and looked into Malton's eyes. "Then, you too will wait in line like that if you ever get the chance!"

Malton felt his knees paining him where he held them tightly and let them go, his mind wondering of the truth of Fagan's words.

He looked up over the heads of the Marines facing him. The convoy had left the city and were moving rapidly abound the face of the mountains.

Liverlip had been right. Their camp would be in the boon docks.

A "rose" no matter
what you call it
still stinks

Chapter 3

He didn't look like a Marine, he didn't act like a Marine, but he was a Marine, a damn good one! His name is Liverlip McPherson - remember the name?

New Caledonia in February, 1944, was losing prestige as a supply base. Admiral Nimitz had long since advanced the lines of communication to Guadalcanal and French New Caledonia had come to be but a first step up the ladder of islands to the front which by now were the Marshalls.

Nevertheless, replacement battalions were still set up on New Caledonia feeding the divisions who made the South Pacific their theatre of war. The replacement camp was a pleasant one established a safe distance from Nouema, the capital city. A tent area had been built on the slopes of a small hill overlooking a lagoon and the troops, who stayed on the island but a few days waiting for the processing of their orders, enjoyed themselves when working parties were not needed.

Liverlip McPherson was a replacement as were several friends he had left the states with. He shared a tent with Malton, the West Virginian, "Miss" Blue, the Oklahoman, Miller, the Indianian, and Bob Kee, also an Indianian. All had the same spec number - infantry. Specialists - shoulder a rifle and walk.

It was the day after the green troops had arrived on a stinking Dutch ship and they were all getting in some steady sack time after the rough crossing.

"What outfit they goin' to send us too?" Liverlip lay on his bunk, his arm hanging over the side, dirty fingers toying with an ant on the floor.

"Hope it's the lst Division." Miss Blue wanted the best.

There was some grab-assin, going on in the next tent. The side flaps of the tent were rolled up and several guys could be seen wrestling on the deck.

"Gung-Ho" McPherson said beneath his overhanging lip. The grab-assing stopped. The two guys stared meaningly at Liverlip, then drooped on their bunks.

"Ease up, Liverlip," Malton said quietly. He was lying on his back, eyes closed. "Those guys are Raiders. They'd slit your throat without blinking an eye." He thought of the Raiders - the elite of the Corps, especially trained for quick hit and skip assault. Hand-picked for their ferocity, they were perfect physical, if not mental specimens. One thought had been drilled into their heads - kill!

"They're just corps happy bastards." Liverlip said loud enough for the occupants of the next tent to hear.

A fearless runt, Malton thought. Not more than 18, McPherson had a crop of bushy hair ruled over a fat round face whose predominant feature was a full upper lip which earned him his nickname. Stockily built, his young but hard body scarcely stood more than 5'3" over the ground. Malton shifted his body, opened his eyes and looked into the next tent, where the Raiders lay on their bunks. God, he'd hate to have to tangle with them.

The tropical night was humid and there was a promise of rain in the sky. Quietness reined over the tent area. Most hands were turned into the bunks as midnight neared. Malton lay heavily beneath his mosquito net dripping perspiration on the straw mattress of his bunk. Sleep would not come. Pushing the net aside, he reached for his pipe on the empty K-ration crate at the head of his bunk. His hand came in contact with his wallet. He smiled at its thickness. Pay call had sounded that day - money and no place to spend it. The replacements were restricted to the camp - their orders might come any moment. Noumea was alive this time of the night - Noumea where cheap whiskey and cheaper women were available for the taking - but not for replacements. Suddenly he heard drunken laughter followed by cursing. The sound was coming down the company street. The Raiders! They had gone over the hill and gone into Noumea. It figured - nothing, nobody could stop that cut-throat crew from having their kicks.

The noise increased as the Raiders finished off the whiskey. They were getting mean, Malton knew. Suddenly the noise stopped and he could hear them talking in low tones. Footsteps sounded on the packed earth and his tent flap parted. A swish and his mosquito net was cut open and the tip of a jungle knife pricked his throat. The smell of rotgut whiskey filled the tent. A rough face hovered over him. Not daring to move, Malton waited. The face moved closer.

"You're not the one," the whiskey thick voice said, "where's the little bastard?" the knife dug deeper and the blood began to flow.

A quick movement distracted the Raider and cursingly he ran after the short clad figure who had slipped out the corner of the tent. McPherson was running for his life.

Yelling and cursing once again pierced the night as the Raiders hunted down their tormentor. Tents fell as the pursuers tore the enlisted men's area apart. Not an officer was seen - no one dared to try to stop the Madmen. Long into the night the Raiders searched until at last, giving up their fruitless search, they fell exhausted on their bunks, sleeping off the drunken stupor.

In the morning light, the area was a weird sight. Tents were down, cots overturned. Sheepish Marines went about the task of setting things right. The Raiders slept on, their tents, too, showing the results of the previous nights' onslaught.

Non-commissioned officers quietly went about their duties, readying the area for the inevitable arrival of the officers now that the madness of the night had been replaced by the brightness of the day.

A murmur arose from the troops and Malton looked up from his work of patching the torn mosquito netting, a patch over the wound in his neck. He looked down the company street.

The sight brought a smile to his lips and uncontrolled laughter from the rest of the observers. McPherson was walking erect down the street, his upper lip protruding more than ever. He looked like a schoolboy who had undeservedly been called to task by his teacher. His body was covered, stinkly covered, with a coating of splattered fecal matter. His white trunks were now a wet brown and his legs dripped with the excrediment.

It was obvious where he had taken refuge from the Raiders, the head down in the lagoon area. A six-seater affair enclosed against the elements, the depths of the crappers was the one place where the mad pursuers had not looked.

Down the company street came fat Platoon Sergeant Carver, a first class bastard. Beside him casually strode 2nd Lt. Overtone, fresh out of officer's candidate school and flush with his impatience. Looking at the damage caused by the marauding Raiders the night before the young lieutenant wisely shook his head and tapped his swagger stick against his khaki covered leg.

"Whose responsible for this mess, Sergeant?" An injured tone belied his full knowledge of the previous evenings episode.

"I don't know, sir, but I know where we can find out," the sergeant too lied, but Malton could sense trouble brewing.

The Sergeant stalked to the tent opening where Malton stood. He glared at him, anticipating what would follow. This young wise punk knew all the answers - always making like a professor. So what if he was in college when the war broke out - wise guy - he'd pay.

"Malton," he sneered, "what happened here last night?" The Lieutenant had come up beside him and the stripes on Carver's sleeve grew larger.

Malton didn't retreat an inch. He stood leaning against the flap brace, his pipe unlighted in his mouth. "It's pretty obvious, isn't it?" he took his lighter slowly from his pocket and deliberately watched the fire burn into the tobacco and in the eyes of Carver.

"Don't get wise with me, Who did it? I want names, Mac, names!" Carver's face was flush with anger. The Lieutenant watched with concealed amusement.

Malton puffed gently on his pipe, the smoke curling from his nose. He understood the spot the Sergeant was placing him in. Carver knew who was responsible, but if he told, he would be in for a bad time from the Raiders. If he didn't the shit detail would be his lot.

Carver took a step closer. Out of the corner of his eyes, he could see the Raiders, now fully awake, watching the scene closely. He spoke through his teeth "'Who did it Malton? That's an order."

Malton too was aware of the audience in the next tent. He looked at the lieutenant - no out there. Slowly he looked back at the sergeant. He slowly shrugged his shoulders.

Carver fumed. He turned to the lieutenant. He saw that his show had been ruined - the lieutenant now clearly indicated amusement at his failure.

"All right, Malton. Stay put, I'll get back to you!" Carver turned abruptly and resumed his inspection of the area. Overtone stood tapping his swagger stick, bored with the situation. What the hell, these poor bastards were soon going into combat. The bull-headed Sergeant was making an ass of himself. He slowly turned and walked back down the company street. Wonder if he'd get a letter from Ruth today.

"O.K. Malton, get out of that sack!" Carver stood above Malton's cot, his eyes still burning with anger. Malton stared up at him - the bastard, the Corps happy bastard. Slowly he sat on the bunk, his eyes finding the Raider tent as he got to the feet. Four pairs of eyes in the tent were on him, they didn't indicate a thing. He stood before Carver, an inch shorter and thirty pounds lighter.

"Get your pail and follow me." Carver swung ungracefully on his heel and left the tent. Malton dumped his dirty laundry from the pail and followed. The area was silent with all hands sitting in their tents following the action.

Carver stopped at a fifty gallon oil drum filled with water, a glint in his eyes. "Empty all the drums in the area, and refill them from the lagoon. Don't secure until they are all finished. Get me?" He looked into the empty eyes of Malton, waiting for a complaint. There must have been over thirty such drums in the area, a precaution against fires.

Malton didn't answer. He silently put the pail down and laboriously turned over the drum, the water sloshing in the sandy soil. Carver, looking for trouble, unhappily walked away at his failure once more to arouse this damn hillbilly.

The area came alive with Carver's departure. The Marines, save for the Raiders, cursed the three striped bastard. Some offered to help, but Malton shook them off. He was satisfied with his decision and would follow through. The Raiders were sitting in their tent, playing poker. They were seemingly indifferent to the entire matter.

The morning dragged on with Malton silently and efficiently performing his penance. His thoughts were not idle, however. The defiant victory had been hollow - his mastery over the brutal sergeant had long been established in his own mind. He smiled as he thought how stupid human beings were. Three stripes on the sergeant's arm didn't change the ignorance of their wearer. The one stripe he wore had been put there after boot carp two months before - he doubted if they would ever be added to.

The sergeant's opinion of Malton was not shared by his friends, and he had many. West Virginia bred, he had joined the Marines in his third year at Fordham University. He had weighed his decision long before he had volunteered for the Marines. A journalism major, he had repulsed the sudden urge to join the battle at the outbreak of war. He wanted to be a writer and the war was an interfering element. Powerfully built despite his 5'10" frame, he was subject to the draft nearing his 20th birthday. He didn't fear death, rather it fascinated him. A determined student he had made the most of his education and was wise in all fields he doggedly studied. Quite suddenly in the spring of 1943 he made his move. It was time to put aside the books and enter the service. He had progressed far enough in his education to realize that he would resume his studies after the war, if he got back. The selection of the service was not difficult having studied the different branches with the same scrutiny he studied his college subject matter. Going all out in whatever he did, he knew the Marines was the outfit for him.

His parents had been shocked at his decision, his mother trying every devise to dissuade him. His father didn't interfere, although his eyes showed the concern he felt. Respecting his son's intelligence he knew the decision had been preceded with full exploration of all possible consequences.

Malton's hands were beginning to blister. He heaved a weary sigh as he knelt on the sandy beach, his pail resting in the shallow salty water. A lot had happened since that day in June when he and another to-be Marine crossed the bridge spanning the Ohio River on a train heading for boot camp at San Diego.

Glancing at his watch's hands pointing to 1400 he refilled the bucket, gingerly grasping the handle. His hands, darkened by the hot sun matched his oval shaped face. His dark hair was wet beneath his cap. Tiredness slowed his step as he returned to the area.

The hours passed, Malton's weary bones aching with every step. The tropical sun sank over the lagoon as a last bucketful of water filled the last 50 gallon drum in the replacement camp. Malton dropped the pail, his stomach aching from the lack of food. He hadn't eaten since 0600. Tiredly he made his way among the silent tent city, sympathy filled eyes following his route. He turned into the tent where fat Sergeant Carver lay upon his bunk. He stood in the middle of the tent flap, his hatred clearly visible in his eyes, Carver stirred, saw the private first class, sweaty and grimed, waiting.

"Finished turd-bird?" he sneered, swinging his barrel shaped legs onto the tent deck.

"Now turd-bird, coat the top of the drums with oil." Carver stopped Malton with his voice. His eyes were bright with self-satisfaction. The victory was his.

Malton slowly turned, his empty stomach making audible sounds. He felt the anger climbing up his body. His face reddened. Clenching his raw hands into fists he softly said through tight lips. "Kiss my ass!"

Carver sat stunned for a moment, then clumsily pulled himself to his feet. He stood there legs apart, aware that every eye in the vicinity was watching the episode.

"What did you say, turd-bird?" He had clearly heard the remark the first time.

Malton stared into the eyes of Carver, his own black with the anger he felt. He spoke clearly and loudly. "Kiss my ass!"

Carver took a step forward. He hadn't bargained for this. "That'll cost you, mac. I'm putting you on report."

Snickers sounded in the adjoining tents. "Bastard" came from one voice, safe in the obscurity of many men. Carver felt a need to assert himself. He felt once again that he had been made the fool.

"You cheap hillbilly. I ought to stomp you and forget the report." Carver drew himself to his full 6 feet and drew his stomach up into his chest.

Malton didn't react immediately. At his best he wasn't a match against this mountain, but he was beat with the exertion of his punishment. He sensed the anticipation in the tents. The respect his buddies held for him was at stake. A beating was coming his way, but he knew what he had to do. He shrugged.

"Anytime you're ready." He had said it, and the tents reacted immediately. Before either combatant could retract, Marines poured from the tents and an area behind the sergeant's tent was marked off by a circle of Marines.

Carver made a show of taking off his shirt. Now, the tide had turned. Once again he was in command. He led the way through the circle of Marines and stood in the middle, hands on hips. Malton followed, the weariness slipping off as his body reacted to the excitement. He faced the sergeant, small beside the hairy non-com. One of the raiders had taken command and stood between the men.

"No holds barred!" the Raider was giving the instructions. "Ready? Go, you bastards."

With a bull-like rush, the sergeant was on Malton, flailing with his fists, with clumsy but telling blows. Malton ducked and weaved, taking the blows on the arms. He drew upon his college physical education training. Waiting for an opening, he saw the fat stomach rolling, before him. Drawing upon what little strength he had left, he swung with all his body, sinking his fist deep into the sergeant's stomach. Carver turned green, and doubled up, leaving his face unprotected. Malton swung from the heels. His fist smashed into Carver's face, the sound of crunching bones preceded the crash as the sergeant fell to the dirt. The encouragement of the crowd grew as Malton stood over the puffing sergeant.

"Now, shorty, now," a raider shouted, demonstrating, "one in the nuts."

Malton hesitated, his sense of fair play strong. The hesitation was costly as the sergeant grabbed him by the legs and sent him sprawling. Like a whale Carver was on top of the smaller man; gouging, slugging and choking. Malton felt his strength dissipating, darkness began to close in. Dimly he heard words of encouragement aimed in his direction. Sensing rather than seeing the opening, he raised his right knee and lunged upward. With a cry of pain Carver fell from his victim, helpless and writhing. Malton slowly pushed himself to his knees, started to crawl toward the cruel sergeant, and then fell flat, unconscious.

When he regained consciousness, Malton was lying on his cot. His eyes tried to focus on the Coleman lantern hanging on the tent post, its unnatural light shutting out the darkness outside. Shadows in the tent turned out to be Marines, some sitting on bunks, others standing in small groups, whispering. A wet compress was over his left eye, which he knew was swollen closed. His body ached, every fiber and muscle screamed with pain.

"How do you feel, shorty?" he shifted his one good eye to the foot of the cot, where the referee raider was sitting, his face empty as usual. Malton tried to speak, but his swollen lips wouldn't cooperate. Instead he forced the split lips into what could be passed for a smile. The raider's immobile face unfroze for an instant. A half-smile which didn't know how to act crossed his face. He slowly rose, patted Malton's leg and without a sound, slid out into the night.

Hardly had the tent flap stopped its waving when again it opened and Carver came in, still bent with the knee in the groin. His face was ugly and his jaw was swollen, obviously broken. The whispering stopped abruptly. Carver painfully came into the light!

"On your feet Malton. We're going to see the man." His voice was ugly, all the hate he felt creeping in.

A murmur arose in the tent, Marines began to move in. Carver spoke in the voice of authority the three stripes gave him. "Any bastard interferes and he goes too. I mean it." The shuffling stopped, no one wanted a court-martial on his record.

Malton knew it was coming. He knew Carver's type. The Marine Corps was not proud of his mold, but he was also a vital cog in the plan of command. The prostrate Marine painfully gained his feet and followed Carver through the flap. The street was dark, the Pacific moon obscured by rain clouds. The pair slowly made their way up the hill to the officer's quarters, every step one of agony for both. Here lights shined brightly, laughter and music coming from the wine mess set up for the transient officers.

Lt. Overtone sat in the duty tent, a three-quarters empty fifth of whiskey before him on the table. He was drunk and dammed glad of it. No mail from Ruth today. What the hell kind of a wife was she? No mail - couldn't she just take time out from her whirl of activities to write. He dropped his head on his arms. Maybe he'd get a letter tomorrow. Maybe?

His thoughts were interrupted by the slamming of the screen door of the wood framed tent. He cautiously picked his head up and looked at the two enlisted men, relieved by their rank.

"What the hell is it, sergeant?" his tongue was thick, his eyes watery.

"Sir, I want to put this man on report. Insubordination. Direct refusal to obey an order." Carver was all marine now, standing as stiff and straight as his pain permitted. Malton, too, stood at attention, reconciled to his fate.

Overtone looked at the two. Christ, what a fight. He hoped the Pfc. had won the scrap. Paperwork. He looked at the bottle. He wasn't going to do any paperwork tonight. No mail from Ruth, the slut. "Tomorrow, sergeant, tomorrow." He picked up the bottle, poured the golden fluid into an already half-filled cup. He raised the cup to lips, dismissing the two with a wave.

Carver hesitated. This was against all standard procedure. Then he did an ungraceful about face and went through the screen. Malton too, hesitated, sympathy in his eyes as he watched the young lieutenant. It's a woman, he thought. It always is. He turned un-militarily and left the tent. Carver was waiting.

"You're under tent arrest, boot. Fall out to my tent after chow, tomorrow." He stared at Malton in the dim light then was gone - to sick bay, his jaw ached.

Malton made his way down the hill, gingerly placing each foot to ease the pain. The tent area was waiting, anxious for details.

"I get the book thrown at me, tomorrow." He said as he went into his tent. Carefully he removed his dungarees, gently feeling his swollen body. No bones seemed to be broken.

He stretched out on the bunk, pulling the mosquito net in place. He lay there, reviewing the day's events. He couldn't see any other action he would have taken. The looming deck court-martial worried him. Not anxious for promotion, he nevertheless didn't want the black mark on his record. He heard the other occupants of the tent enter and prepare for the night. He smiled as he sensed Liverlip trying to say something. The kid remorsely gave up and crawled into his sack. Sleep easily came to him. Malton lay on his back, his body slowly losing its soreness. He heard the flap crumble and he felt the presence of movement in the tent. The moon came from behind a cloud and creeped into the tent. In the soft light he made out the four raiders, knives strapped to their legs. He felt a feeling of apprehension.

"We'll take care of Carver, short stuff." the voice was harsh. The others grunted agreement.

Malton forced himself upward, resting on his elbows. He feared what would happen.

"Thanks. But he's mine. It's not the same. He's mine!" Malton was surprised at the authority in his voice. He knew he had made his point. The raiders stood there a moment then they were not there. He hadn't seen or heard them leave. He smiled - so the raiders weren't human! He fell asleep with a smile on his lips.

The white light of the Coleman lantern awoke him. He had been sleeping soundly, the others were sitting on the edge of their bunks. A corporal,

Malton recognized as being a clerk in the base office stood in the middle of the tent, a sheet of papers in his hands.

"You guys get ready. Trucks will be here in," he looked at his watch, "in thirty minutes." He left the tent.

Three men scrambled for their gear. Malton remained in his bunk. Just his luck - the transient group was moving up and he had to get in trouble.

Ten minutes passed. A captain entered the tent, saw the man getting their gear packed. He turned to Malton.

"What the hell you waiting for?" the packing stopped.

Malton stood up in his skivvy shorts. His face reddened. "I'm on report, sir!"

"What's your name?" Malton supplied the information. "You're names on this list." He found it on the orders. "Get packed! That's an order." He turned and left the tent.

Laughter and good natured cursing accompanied the smiling Malton stow his gear. A break and he was going to take advantage of it. The raiders entered, heard the news and thumped Malton on the back as they too pitched in with the packing.

Malton stopped stuffing gear into his sea bag. The others followed suit, staring at the slight Marine.

Malton headed for the tent flap, then half-turned and faced the watchers. His face was hard. "I've got to see a guy!" The raiders studied his eyes. They knew.

Malton went down the company street, his aching bones forgotten. The turmoil of packing hindered any audience to his passing. He left the replacement area and found the tent where the nemesis slept. Making his way from cot to cot he found Carver, sleeping. He looked down at the fat sergeant, his face encased in bandages. Malton slowly pushed away the netting. Reaching down he put his hands gently around the sleeping mans throat. He whispered "Carver."

The sergeant stirred, moaned, and opened his eyes. He was half-asleep.

Malton tightened his grip - Carver's eyes bulged with fear, unable to move. The small Marine bent his face near the trembling face.

"Carver, if we meet up the line in combat, I'm going to kill you. Remember, I'm going to kill you!" He pushed the head back into the pillow, carefully placed the mosquito netting back into position and deliberately moved from the tent into the night.

Chapter 4

Lt. Chet Overtone was unhappy - and drunk!. The clear moonlit Guadalcanal night heavily carried the pleasant scent of jungle wild flowers and the depressing sound of melancholy music. The spring of 1944 found Guadalcanal a teaming staging area where supplies and replacements were stockpiled for the push north. Off Guadalcanal lay Pavuvu in the Russells, where the famed lst Marine Division was training for the hell that was Peleliu, but on the canal replacements were biding their time, many destined for that same 1st Marine Division.

2nd Lt. Overtone was a replacement two months out of the states, and just eight months graduated from Officers Candidate School. "90 day wonders" they had called them in the first World War and the name stuck through the second global conflict. A handsome, slim, New Englander, he looked four years younger than 21. Sandy hair was kept in a constant crew-cut and he appeared always to have just stepped from a shower. Brilliant, his professors had called him at the University of Connecticut. Devastating was the word most used to describe him by the University co-eds. Snob was the true definition of Overtone, the son of a wealthy shoe manufacturer. He had never wanted for anything in his entire life - his doting mother had seen to that. His character had been etched clearly and indelibly by the life he led. He was spoiled, arrogant and emotionally unstable. With this background he was indescribably unsuited for the Marine Corps. But a Marine he was, and a sad one at the moment.

He never could hold whiskey, even in college the overconsumption of alcohol had been mainly responsible for the trouble in which he constantly found himself. Even Ruth was first seen through the maze of a drunken stupor. Ruth, why the hell didn't she write. He hadn't received a letter since he left the states. He took another long drink from the bottle sitting on a make-shift table.

"Better go easy on that, Chet." the voice carried authority. 2nd Lt. Hal Davis sat on his bunk, carefully cleaning his sidearm. He was worried about this kid! He had known him back at Quantico - had been awed by the easy manner in which he grasped the technical aspect of every classroom problem. He knew what was responsible for the heavy drinking bout which Overtone had been on since the day they arrived on New Caledonia a month before. He had met Ruth on a liberty he and Overtone had made in Washington.

He sadly shook his head - why do men marry women like that?

"Mail Call", an enlisted man entered the tent, a pack of letters in his hand. Overtone looked up and watched the corporal shift through the letters. The Orderly looked at the drunken lieutenant and moved hesitatingly to him, his arm extended, two letters in his hand.

Overtone grabbed the mail, oblivious to the sneer of contempt the corporal wore. Lt. Davis motioned the non-com from the tent.

Davis studied the drunken officer who was trying to focus his eyes on the writing. Slowly he steadied his hand and dropped the first letter to the table. A smile spread over his face as he recognized the feminine scroll of his wife. Davis relaxed, and lowered his body flat on the bunk, a smile brightening his features.

Drunkenness slipped from Overtone's face as he anxiously tore open the air mail letter. He rose and went unsteadily to his bunk, sitting on the edge as he began to read.

The smile slowly disappeared, a deep frown taking its place. He thrust the letter onto the bunk, stumbled to the table and took a stiff drink, then another. He staggered back to his cot, fell on it and read the letter again, not feeling the concerned eyes of Davis on him.

Dear Chet,

I've tried to write this letter for weeks, but you know me, no courage. I could make all kinds of excuses but they would be lies, and somehow I just can't lie to you. Chet, I'm leaving you, I'm sorry, but that's all there is to it. I'm getting a divorce. The papers are being sent to you. Why? I think you know, have known all along. I can't be alone, never. I tried, believe me, I tried, but the days are long alone, and the evenings even worse. I nearly went crazy sitting alone, and then I went out with Bill Tyler's wife, you remember her. Well, I met someone! He's with the Office of Price Control here. Chet, I fought it, honest I did but it happened anyway. I've been seeing him ever since. He wants to marry me, and I've said yes .Can you believe this - I think I still love you - but you're so far away! I'm mixed up, but I know that right now I need someone - you're so far away.

Forgive me!

Love,

Ruth

Davis heard muffled sobs at the far side of the tent. The lantern had long been turned off. He listened carefully -the poor kid! Overtone hadn't said anything after he had once again thrown the letter to the floor, but had controllably finished the whiskey and then drunkenly fallen asleep. Raising himself on his elbow, Davis could see the letter, its whiteness reflected in the moonlight. He didn't have to read it - he knew what it was - a "Dear John" letter. It wasn't the first ever received by men far from home nor would it be the last! The bitch - how could women do this to men! Separated by thousands of miles of water, servicemen were helpless to cope with the situation. The constant strain of impending death was enough for anyone, how could a man deal with this unmerciful problem. Davis turned over and fought with the thoughts that were plaguing him. Sleep came with difficulty.

Davis was worried about Overtone. The young lieutenant had been silent for a week. He had stopped drinking! He just sat on his bunk, his hands holding his head. He did his job, what little the waiting period demanded, well enough, but he seemed to be in a daze. When Davis talked to him, he merely stared, saying nothing. The tent tonight was quiet, Overtone lying still on his bunk staring at the canvas roof. Davis sat at the table writing a letter, but he was just marking time. He had gone to the Catholic Chaplain that day, and asked his aid.

Father Kelly sadly nodded his head. "It's a mess Lieutenant - a darn mess." Davis smiled at the near slip. "This makes four since I've been here." He rose from his camp chair. "What's the answer? God only knows. What can you tell them? How can you reason with them when there's no reason to the sordid mess?"

Davis waited! The khaki clad priest looked out of place amid this mass assemblage for war.

Father Kelly sat down again, lighted a cigarette and looked into Davis' eyes, "What can you tell me about this man's wife?" He saw the hesitancy that appeared to the other man. "Don't worry. No matter how sordid it is, I've heard worse."

Davis moved to the tent flap, his back to the chaplain. He couldn't look at the priest while he talked of Overtone's wife.

"She's really not a bad sort," he realized he was apologizing, "but she was not ready for marriage. I don't think she'll ever be. I met her only once in Washington about a year ago. It was at a night club there." He hesitated. "Sir, she's a sexual tramp!" His voice rose. Now that he had started he warmed to the task. "You know the type. She needs sex as some people need food. It glowed about her."

The priest sat in his chair, his eyes closed as if he were in a confessional. "She's a beautiful woman." Lt. Davis continued, "ripe and in full bloom. She stood out in the room as if she were the only girl there," Again he stopped, self-consciously digging his boot into the sand. "Any man was a challenge to her - and any man would want to have her - I did." He whirled and faced the chaplain. "I could have - she made it plain. Not just me, but any man, could have her." he sat on the edge of the bunk, exhausted by the emotion he felt.

The chaplain opened his eyes and softly said, "Did your friend sense this also?"

Davis pulled a cigarette from his pocket, tapped it on his nail, and accepted the light the priest offered him.

"Yes sir, He knew." he frowned at the recollection, "But it didn't seem to matter to Overtone. He seemed to know that he could control her if he kept a close rein on her - but, how can you do that when you're out here in the middle of the Pacific and she's back in Washington."

Father Kelly smashed his cigarette in the ash tray. "The boy needs help - desperate help. He's no good here in the condition he's in. I'll talk to the commanding general of this depot", he rose, marking the end of the interview.

"Thank you sir," he turned to leave and then hesitated. "It had better be done fast, sir. He's not the type to go on much longer like this."

The chaplain nodded and reached for the field telephone.

Davis looked up from the blank paper, he hadn't written a word. Overtone hadn't stirred, and it seemed to Davis that he never blinked his eyes. Man is a strange creature, Davis thought. He'll go along for years, carefree, efficient, capable of loving and hating, all the while presenting a perfect picture of serenity. But it only takes one blow to the heart to change the picture from that of a beautifully functioning being to one that is but an empty shell. It hadn't been many months before, even weeks that Overtone had been the envy of nearly every man with whom he came in contact. He was intelligent, had a beautiful wife and a wealthy father who saw that he would never want for anything. Not respected, true, but nevertheless accepted by his colleagues in recognition of his abilities, which were very well developed by the best training which money could buy.

Looking at Overtone now, Davis thought that perhaps he had unconsciously come upon the one element in the youthful lieutenant which had caused his present mental state. Money, the money which had bought everything he had ever wanted, had taken away - or subdued, his ability to face any situation where money was not the deciding factor. Even his father's vast wealth could not resolve this situation.

The tent flap opened and Father Kelly entered. "Greetings men!" He waved Davis back to the chair from which he had arose. He glanced at Overtone who hadn't stirred.

"Sit down, sir," Davis indicated a chair from which the priest could face the reclining Overtone. Tension mounted in Davis' face. Had the Chaplain succeeded in getting special orders to relieve Overtone.

"Son," the voice was gentle, out of place in this atmosphere of war. Overtone turned his head and for the first time saw the Chaplain. A look of recognition turned to one of defiance. "Son, you're going to have to snap out of this. You're destroying yourself. Face the problem. Don't thrust it from you. What's the answer? What can you do? Make the decision! Other's have. You've got a job to do."

Davis listened to the voice softly pleading. He knew the transfer had not gone through. It couldn't. The precedent could not be established. There were too damn many "Dear John's" in the service. He listened to the gentle voice of the priest and watched Overtone. He hadn't moved, his eyes fixed on the chaplain, not blinking - no motion what-so-ever.

"---perhaps if I could write - perhaps she would listen!" The priest stopped, his voice drifting off into silence. It was no use. Nothing he could say or do would change the expression in those blank eyes staring into his.

The silence grew oppressive. Davis moved his legs. Overtone's immobile face cracked as his lips moved.

"Get the hell out!" The words were clear and sharp! Spoken without emotion. They hung on the humid air.

Chaplain Kelly sat motionless for a moment, startled by the empty voice. Impulsively he rose, started compassionately for the heartbroken man, then stopped. "I'm sorry". The words were barely audible. The stopped priest walked out into the Pacific night.

Davis had sat stunned and unbelieving through the scene. His eyes followed the unsuccessful chaplain through the tent flap, then swung to Overtone. Once again the unblinking eyes were fixed on the top of the tent.

Davis rose, turned down the light on the Coleman lantern and adjusting his mosquito netting, resignedly prepared for sleep.

The jungle night had turned cool and Davis awoke shivering. He reached for the green blanket at the foot of the cot, his eyes sleepily closed. The soft glow of the Coleman lantern on his closed lids caused him to open his eyes. Overtone hadn't turned off the light, he thought, as he pushed his way out of the netting groping half consciously for the center table. He opened his eyes and reached for the lever of the lantern. His eyes leisurely adjusted themselves to the half darkness. Overtone's cot was barely visible in the corner of the tent. Rubbing his eyes to focus them better he softly swore, turned up the light and went to the cot. Overtone wasn't there!

Davis looked about the tent - no sign of the troubled Marine was evident. The crude ashtray on the table caught the lieutenant's attention. He reached down into the charred paper there, still crumbling under his touch. A fragment remained and holding it to his nostrils the scent took him back over a year to the night club in Washington. Dropping the burnt paper Davis rushed from the tent, apprehension roaring through his body. The entire officers area was asleep, only the rustle of jungle vegetation disturbing the quietness of the night. The tropical moon was full and an eerie light played tricks with the coconut trees. The Pacific was calm and the outlines of ships anchored off shore met the glistening reflection of the moon on the water. Davis was unaware of the beauty of the night as he paused in his course, undecided what he should do. A thought brought a smile to his lips and he turned past the long straight rows of coconut trees to the fringe of the jungle and the officer's head. He pushed open a screened door and relaxed as the form of a man sat hunched on one of the seats.

"Chet," he softly called. The form moved, and the face became distinguishable in the softness of the moonlight.

"Is that you, Davis?" The harsh voice of the Commissary officer rang in the night. Davis felt the fear rising in the pit of his stomach.

"Sorry, Cotlin." Davis said disappointingly. "I thought you were Overtone," the other man grunted, and went back to his necessity.

Davis retracted his steps, once again indecision slackening his steps. The lights of the duty officers tent twinkled ahead. He hesitated, he couldn't inquire there. His steps took him past the tent, his eyes searching the interior. The office was empty. He glanced at his watch 0400 - time for the changing of the watch. His feet impulsively led him to the Chaplains tent. Quietly entering, he was surprised at what he saw. There on his knees before a small cross, lighted by a red vigil light was Father Kelly. The Chaplain looked up at Davis, smiled and rose to his feet, placing the rosary he held into his pocket.

"Always pray this time of night. It's quiet – just right for meditation." the priest needlessly explained. The smile left his face, a look of concern replacing it.

"What's the matter?"

Davis felt he was intruding on this man and his God, but he was in need of comfort and support. "It's Overtone, sir, He's not in the tent." he stopped, realizing the stupidity of his statement. He offered apologetically, "I've looked everywhere. I can't find him." His voice broke with the feeling he felt.

The chaplain stepped toward him. "We'll look together." His hand went to the shoulder of the Marine, all the pity and understanding he felt heavy in this touch.

They left the tent and quietly scoured the officers' quarters and then the enlisted men's area. The search was fruitless and the two dejectedly walked to the edge of the line of coconut trees where the white sand met the rich dirt of the jungle. They stopped and looked out to sea. A small patrol boat a mile off shore plowed its course past the anchored ships, on guard against any Japanese submarine which might attempt to prey on the valuable ships.

"I don't know, son, I just don't know." Chaplain Kelly leaned against a tree, his voice no louder than a whisper.

Davis faced the beach - its whiteness stretched out 30 yards before him before it was lost in the blackness of the salty sea. "He's not responsible, Father. He's liable to do anything." His eyes followed the slight breaking of the water on the sand. His gaze moved along the shore line.

Suddenly he squinted, focusing his eyes. "Father", he pointed a little to the left of where they stood. The priest followed his finger about 15 yards from them, a black spot was prominent against the sands whiteness.

The two struggled through the sands softness to the spot. They lowered themselves on their haunches.

"God help us!" the Chaplain whispered through his pursed lips.

Before them lay two regulation shoes, neatly lined up. In each was a carefully placed sock. The toes of the shoes were pointed unmistakably toward the sea.

Chaplain Kelly rose and looked out over the ocean, his lips moving in a silent prayer.

Tears rolled uncontrollably down Davis' cheeks. Gently he felt the rough leather of the combat shoes, his eyes watching the ocean breaking over the reef off shore. He spoke softly.

"It's a long swim."

Plans made at War
For Future Peace
More Often Then Not
End In a Shallow Grave

SEE YOU AT THE HURRICANE

Chapter 5

"Now the Hurricane in New York," Taylor was saying, as the work detail bumped along the airfield with heavy ammunition from one camouflaged depot along Munda air strip to another, "Man! What chicks hang out there - show gals struggling to get along on Broadway - waiting for a break and hungry for a shoulder to cry on."

Fagan sat on the roof of the cab. He was studying his jungle knife for any signs of corrosion which the damp jungle might have caused. "I've been there," he said simply, "sits on Broadway, on the corner of 49th Street - second floor."

"That's it." Taylor exclaimed, his eyes flashing as he remembered the luxuriously appointed bar and night club with its flashing neon light. "I think I was there once." Brabern said speculatively. "Does it have a windblown palm tree swaying in neon lights outside hanging out over Broadway?"

"That's it, That's it!" Taylor now stood in the bed of the 6 x 6, his sun burned face shining moistly in the hot March sun. His eyes were on Fagan's head seemingly, but his gaze played far over campaign hot - all the way back to New York, New York, United States of America, Northern Hemisphere. His ears could almost hear the music of the Hawaiian band on its bamboo hut platform, with the matted roof held aloft by four corners of coconut tree trunks and settled in a typical rain forest with the sea in the background. And couples dancing in the dimly lighted room with its postage stamp tables and wicker chairs, each with a candle held firm in a cocoanut. The entire room seemed to be transplanted out of New York to the Pacific and constantly in the background, almost imperceptible was a recording of waves washing ashore on the distant beach. Scent of tropical vegetation, fresh from a drenching rain hung heavily over the interior. Taylor sighed mightily, "Man, it's a tropical paradise. Just like you see in the movies."

The members of the work detail grinned but only Malton spoke, "You're cracking up already, Chuck." His hard eyes carried a smile partially hidden beneath hidden lids. "You've only been out of the states for two months and already you going rock happy." He paused to form his next words which he spoke cuttingly. "Whoever heard of a guy homesick for a nightclub that was fixed up to be a tropical paradise. Hell! Man! You're at the real thing. The South Pacific. Look about you. Can't you see the swaying palms, the pounding surf?"

Taylor's curse was lost in the laughter of the troops. "You call this paradise. Christ, there ain't even a tree standing enough to admit it." He sneeringly repeated, "Look at this place." Taylor's waving arms prompted some of the troops to look at the jutting strip of island which was Munda, but others, Cold Steel Fagan, didn't flicker an eye. Fagan knew what it looked like. It was no better nor worse, than any other rock he had seen in the Pacific. They all looked the same after the Navy's big shells and smaller but still smashing bombs, had taken their toll. Nothing remained unharmed. The trees, most of them coconut, and not the swaying palms as prewar travel posters had shown, were shattered; those with the fronds still on were bent and twisted. Rock marks, huge craters were in evidence everywhere, save for the air strip which they were now so smoothly riding upon. The Sea-Bees, master craftsmen had ironed out the holes with coral and the strip was gleaming white, a pair of straight even landing fields and would stay that way until the next flight of Tojo's boys came over to drop their greetings again. Thus the necessity of moving the caches of ammo after each raid.

"Say! I've got an idea!" Taylor's voice was again excited and jovial, "Let's all meet after this bitchin' war at the Hurricane and have a reunion!"

The idea quickly grew in proportion, with the thought of fun and relaxation firing the imagination of the men.

Brabern spoke up, "Sounds good to me." He smiled at Taylor.

"We can retell old sea stories and relive these happy days out here! What do you think, Cold Steel?"

Fagan for the first time looked up from his jungle knife, now content that the steel had not become pitted in the salt air. He looked at the eager faces in the truck, pausing as his eyes picked out his closer buddies, Brabern, Blue, Miller, Young, McPherson, Malton and Wagner. These and others whom he had come so close to in the past two months. Eager faces, young faces, unsuspecting faces. They had not yet been forced to face war as it really was. He had had buddies before, good buddies who wore, as he had, this same expression prior to August, 1942. Now those earlier buddies, most of them lay somewhere on Guadalcanal. Again he looked at the eager faces, now questioning his silence. He wondered just how many of them would ever get to the Hurricane again.

He sighed inwardly, "Count me in!" Just that - three words, spoken evenly and quietly. None of the men could sense any feeling in the three words, but it was there. Lack of conviction! Hell, he didn't know if he'd get back to the states - frankly he didn't care too much. He was in his element, so he thought. He didn't want to die, at least he felt fear at the thought or presence of imminent death, but he was born for combat, and he knew it. Some strange exultation came over him when a fire fight broke out. If the truth were to be known - he was happy when he was firing at someone, or someone was firing at him.

"When will we set it for?" Taylor was all wound up now, plans flinging themselves through his head. He answered himself, "How about a month after the war's over?"

Fagan shuddered as he spoke. "Too soon! If you're still over here, and alive," he immediately regretted saying the latter as he saw the cloud pass over the faces of the men. He quickly continued. "It will take you longer than a month to get back stateside and mustered out."

The heads in the truck nodded. Brabern raised his voice as the track pulled up hill at the landward side of the airstrip its motor groaning at the load- "How about 6 months to the day after the war is over."

Again the heads nodded. Taylor once again took the floor.

"Then it's set. Six months to the day after the war is over. 8 P.M. at the Hurricane. Let's shake on it!" He almost fell as the truck suddenly reached its destination.

Jovially, they all shook hands with each other. Malton joined the others as they climbed from the truck, grasping hands firmly under the astonished stare of the Sea-Bee truck driver. The Marines! He thought. What crazy bastards they are!

Malton came up before Fagan and stuck out his hand to the taller man. Fagan took it and shook it firmly, but some of the excitement went from J.C.'s face as he was unable to read the feeling which was in Cold Steel's eyes.

"Third Platoon: Fall in!" Sgt. Myron Konkright sang out. From crudely constructed lean-coos and tents, the Third Platoon, First Marine Division, stumbled into the glaring sun. Mostly new men, replacements from the states, they had been dispatched from Guadalcanal to New Georgia without even joining the Division on Pavuvu. Fagan had been bewildered by the move, had indeed wondered why an infantry platoon had been formed at the Canal from the transient battalion and then sent to Munda on New Georgia for what had been simply a work detail for the Sea-Bees.

They weren't the only Marines on New Georgia, true. But the only others were a Defense Battalion which had set up their Long - Toms and anti-aircraft guns after the assault troops comprised mainly of Marine Raiders, had secured the island group.

"Attention!" Konkright shouted, but the word did not come out in that fashion - it sounded more like "Tent-sunt" The Marines braced and stood stiffly as 2nd Lt. Bruce Capet long-strided his way before them.

Bruce Capet was fresh from Quantico and the officers' training school there. He was a poster-Marine. Tall, muscular and clean-cut good looking with sandy crew-cut hair and a lean bronzed face with sky blue eyes.

"Stand easy." he said and the men before him unnerved and relaxed, all questioning this early falling out for a Sunday morning muster. The sun was barely rising over the horizon of Ondonga, another island in the New Georgia group to the East, "We've got a job," the lieutenant began and smiled at the disgust which crossed the men's faces. "No, not another work detail - a real job," the faces once again showed interest. "We're being sent over to Kolombangera."

The faces remained blank before Capet, still not grasping the assignment, none had ever heard of the place, and definitely not deceived by the flowing multi-syllable name.

Capet's grin broadened, "Kolombangara is an island - it sits off there somewheres", he pointed to the north, "up until a short time ago, D.3 estimated there were 15,000 Japs there." The Marines strained to hear the words, instantly attentive at the number, of the enemy rolled from the platoon leader's lips. "Were there, I said. Now our job is to see how many are still there and to eliminate them."

Malton wasn't sure he had heard correctly. 15,000 Japs on the island and, he glanced about him 28 men in the Third Platoon. The odds didn't seem to be quite even. Beside him Fagan's eyes were glistening, his right hand opening and closing on the hilt of the jungle knife.

The lieutenant was still stalking, "Here's the whole scoop. It seems our troops by-passed Kolombangara and secured Vella LaVella, still further north but also a little west. The nips were then pocketed - except there was still an island north and to the east, Choiseul, which stretched up almost to Bouganville. The next move was obvious. The Japs had to evacuate Kolombangara and try for Choiseul. But the Navy had foreseen this and just played a waiting game. They didn't have to wait long. One night a Black Widow (PBY Flying Boat) spotted the convoy of small craft coming down the slot and reported to the Command Posts, both here on Munda and on the

Canal. The bombers waited until the boats, they consisted of the equivalent of our Higgins Boats and LST's had loaded the troops and were on their way across the slot to Choiseul and then hit them with everything they had. According to the story the Navy pilots tell, they sunk everything on the water. By the time dawn came there wasn't a single boat afloat." He paused, enjoying the awe which was evident in the faces of the troops.

"Our scouting planes have kept pretty close tabs on Kolombangara for several months and haven't been able to detect a sign of life." The grin faded from his face. "That's where we come in - why we were sent directly here instead of joining the division at Pavuvu. Our job is to land on Kolombangara and check the place out for any Japs who happened to swim back. It's a difficult assignment and a risky one, but the Navy assures us that we won't find anyone there and they'll have patrol planes keeping tabs on us. We shove off in one hour. Any questions?" none of the men opened their mouths. Lt. Capet grinned. "You wanted some excitement - been beating you're gums now for a week. Maybe you'll get some. Sergeant! Give the word on equipment." He turned on his heel and disappeared toward the Command Post up at the water's edge, hidden beneath well camouflaged jungle vegetation.

"O.K. you guys," Sgt. Konkright said. "Pack both packs with changes of skivvies and socks, mess gear. You'll be issued a day's supply of K Rations. We'll carry other supplies in the boats. Each man will draw 8 clips of ammo and two hand grenades." He glanced at his watch. "Be ready to move at 0630." He turned and started to leave, then remembering some more information, turned again to face the men, some of whom had moved from the ranks. "Stand easy! And you'd better check your weapons. Field strip'em and clean every part. We just might get a reception on the beach. Fall out."

Fagan was already checking his pack as Malton, Brabern and Taylor moved to their gear. Cold Steel fumbled around in his sea-bag, which was covered by his poncho, raised from the ground by means of a wooden, empty ammo case. Finally he withdrew his hand, holding in his hand a fresh whetstone which he put with another one already in his pack. He also had one in his dungaree pants pocket.

Brabern was busily thrusting his mess gear into his upper pack. "Ever heard of Kolombangera before, Cold Steel?" he asked as he worked.

Cold Steel checked his watch, they still had forty-five minutes before they were to fall out. "Yeh! I heard about it from some guys back at the San Diego Naval Hospital at Balboa." He lowered his head and began to sharpen the glistening blade in his hand, his back propped comfortably against his full pack. "It must be about 15 miles from here. across a narrow slit. It's actually surrounded by New Georgia, Rendova, Villa Lavelle, and Choiseul. The Slot the Lieutenant was talking about is a natural passage running straight from Bougainville to Guadalcanal. These guys in the hospital were on the cruiser Helena. She got into a fight with a Jap fleet in the slot. Caught some pretty heavy shells and sank. The survivors made their way ashore at Choiseul and Kolombangara. Most of them were flushed out by the nips but some were rescued by P.B.Y.'s from the Canal."

"What's this Kolombangara like?" Taylor said completing his packing by stuffing some stationery into his peak.

Fagan looked north. "They say it was just like in the movies - what you, Taylor imagined the Pacific was like at the Hurricane."

A smile spread over Taylor's face as he too looked north.

The Higgins boat roared through the calm waters of the sheltered slot. Overhead the hot noonday sun beat down upon the small speck which pounded through the placid green sea. The blue of the sky turned the scene into one of different shadings of color with its offsetting the blue in the ocean and turning the water green - but not as dark a green as the islands which loomed on all sides.

"What a day?" Liverlip lounged, dungaree shirt off, atop stacked boxes of supplies in the after part of the landing craft. Fagan and Malton, had also managed to seize the observation level cartons, and were reclining, their eyes looking over the beautiful scenery of the Pacific.

"Man, this is more like it!" Taylor stood with his arms hanging over the side of the craft with Brabern and Peterson on either side. "Look at that island ahead." He indicated a large island directly ahead.

"You'll see enough of that for a long time! That's Kolombangara" Lt. Capet shouted through cupped hands from his position besides the coxman.

His words brought the troops sitting on the steel deck of the landing craft to their feet and squeezing through the men lined at the sides of the Higgins boats for a look at their destination.

From two miles off the beaches, Kolombangara was truly a tropical paradise. The straining eyes could see that it was a circular island, lined with white sandy beaches. Rising above a plantation of carefully lined coconut trees was a majestic mountain, its cone top testifying to its claim as a volcano. It had actually been centuries since the volcano had last erupted and the lush vegetation had reaped the benefit of the revived earth. Visible were tropical plants and flowers whose fragrance waifed even to the barge.

But it was the mountain which intrigued Malton. It seemed to begin immediately behind the beaches in a gentle slope and then gracefully climb to its cone far up in the sky. Somehow he felt that if he could see a map, he'd be certain to discover that the island was almost perfectly round and that the volcano rose as if the dome of a dunce's cap whose brims were the beaches.

"O.K. men, down." Let Capet called. "Check your weapons." The troops quickly donned their dungaree shirts, re-hung their bulky packs and checked their rifles to make certain they were able to go into immediate action if the occasion demanded. "Heads downs!" The Lt. called.

The coxman revved down the Higgins boat and the upside down bathtub looking craft drifted closer to the shore - Ceremoni Cove, their prescribed destination lay dead ahead. Slowly the barge entered the 200 yard wide mouth of the Cove and then its cargo of 28 Marines could see from their positions crouched on the deck, the tops of the coconut trees to their left, right and immediately in front.

"Ramp down in five seconds," the coxman called as he spun the wheel of the craft and once again gunned the motor for a driving landing. The sound of the flat bottom hitting the coral floor of the cove was immediately followed by the grinding of chains as the landing ramp was released and fell with a splashing crash on the sandy beach.

"Make for the trees!" the lieutenant shouted. "Keep low and separated," he added as his feet hit the sand almost the same moment the ramp did. The Marines followed rapidly, each with a gnawing fear of the unknown deep in their bellies. Sgt. Konkright dashed to the left and Malton and Fagan crouchingly followed. The other men with Brabern and Taylor leading the way dashed headlong for the trees keeping well separated. Every man's skin was drawn tight against the expected crash of a bullet, but only the wild chattering of the tropical birds mingled with the coughing sputter of the landing barge to break the silence of the day. Inaudible sighs joined the heavy breathing as the troops hit the sandy loam of the beginning of the rows of coconut trees.

"Sgt. Konkright," the Lt. called and looked to the left where Konkright lay, his carbine, slung over the top of a fallen coconut tree. The Sgt. raised his left hand in answer and as previously arranged signaled Brabern, Young, and McPherson to follow him.

Cautiously the quartet made their way through the heavy vegetation which had invaded the neglected lanes through the symmetrically placed coconut trees. The troops covered them until they disappeared from view - then waited, eyes and ears strained for any movement or sound which might indicate the presence of the enemy. The alert men could follow the process of the patrol by the flying skyward of birds as the Marines approached their roosting places in the vegetation.

"How the hell did those coconut trees get in such straight rows?" Peterson called from his position ten yards to the right of Malton.

J.C. laughed quietly. "They just grew that way," he whispered. "They were planted."

"Who the hell would plant coconut trees way out here!" Peterson replied indignantly, certain that Malton was perpetrating a snow job at his expense.

"The British!" Malton answered seriously. "All these islands were controlled by the British and the plantations planted by soap companies from the Copra which comes from the coconuts."

Further information was stopped by the spoofing of birds to the front of the perimeter line. Instantly the Marines covered the area with their weapons, their eyes flicking to Lt. Capet who had his right hand raised in a signal to hold fire. The men, whoever they were, were not trying to hide their approach and as quickly as they had disappeared earlier the patrol headed by Konkright reappeared, walking erect and with smiles bathed on their faces.

Konkright strolled assuredly to the Lieutenant. "No sign of life sir," he smiled, "and from all indications there hasn't been anyone here for months."

Lt. Capet rose gracefully to his feet, his carbine small in the huge hands and arms. "Good, but stay alert, this is a pretty big island, a battalion could be hidden anywhere. O.K. men. On your feet. Let's go, but don't relax for a minute."

And for the first three days the troops were on the island there was little relaxing of the alert which the Lieutenant had ordered. From the moment the troops had followed the Lieutenant's orders to rise, constant activity which was necessitated in establishing a bivouac area. Two perimeter machine gun nests were set up facing the mountain at strategic positions at the edge of the fringe of the 18 rows of coconut trees where it was quickly met by the encroaching jungle.

Several hours were used in unloading the equipment from the landing craft, the first of which were the two heavy caliber machine guns which were immediately set up and dug in. This was to be a reconnaissance of unknown length and the platoon had been handsomely supplied from the unending stores of the base at Munda. Five pyramid tents were set up in the coconut grove along the beach near the mouth of the cove on the right bank of the beautiful lagoon. From the camps position a sweeping view of the open slot was possible and the staggered tents were not more than 20 yards from the gleaming white sand which ran sloping downward not more than a hundred feet to the water's edge. Even cots had been thoughtfully provided to the platoon and an atmosphere of carefree camping overcame the troops as they spent the daylight hours trying to bring the comforts of home to the jungle.

A patrol sent out by the Lieutenant under the command of Corporal Peterson had covered more than three miles on either side of the hastily erected camp and had returned with the word that they found no sign of the enemies presence although positions had been dug around the white beaches. Their words were listened to with awe by the Marines back at the camp.

"You wouldn't believe it" Young said. "They dug slit trenches all along the beach in the coconut grove's fringes." He paused, marvel in his eyes. "You guys know that this damn plantation must go all around the island? Well, these trenches are everywhere and just loaded with machine guns! Yeh, machine guns. When the Nips pulled out they just left all their heavy weapons lay. They're all corroded and the jungle vines are all over them. Christ - it's eerie!"

Lt. Capet smiled, "Guess they were in a hurry." The troops laughed remembering the story of the hasty departure and hastier demise of the Japs once at sea.

"Did ya find any sign of them havin' women?" The commodore was speaking, of course. "I hear the nip officer's carried their own women with them on campaigns."

Young reddened, dropping his eyes from the lieutenant who was still smiling. "Nah, but there were some women on this island."

The Third Platoon, up till now making comments on the sexual drive of McNalton. Young, his modesty forgotten at the rapt attention his last words had commanded continued. "Yeh, women! Up the beach," his hand pointed to the left "about 300 yards there's a house – a big one what's left of it. Must have been the plantation manager's home, and inside we found some women's clothes - no kidding."

"Well, I'll be a son-of-a-bitch?" The Commodore whistled through his teeth. "Wonder if the Jap's got hold of them."

"I doubt it," Capet said, catching swiftly the angry looks spreading over the Platoon's faces. "The British pulled out even before the war started. They knew it was coming and evacuated all their civilian personnel".

"That's more than we did." Fagan said softly remembering the massacre at Pearl Harbor.

Lt. Capet studied the lean Fagan's face. He'd have to watch this man closely. "O.K. break it up. Let's get back to work."

The Marines dispersed to their task of policing the area, wielding machetes to clear the vegetation from the camp area but their minds were on the house and its former occupants.

"Hey, Cold Steel." the voice came from Brabern's tent, it's sides rolled up and strapped to permit the breeze of early evening to carry both cool air and the fragrance of tropical flowers to the occupants who were stretched out on the green blanketed cots.

Fagan ducked his head and entered the tent. Soft shadows cast by the setting sun filtering through the fronds of the tall coconut trees threw patterns of finger like panels inside the tent. Brabern was now sitting on the edge of his bunk and indicated that he had made room for Fagan, but the lanky Marine chose to drop onto his own bunk, the only empty one in the tent. Beside it, resting comfortably on his back was Young, his eyes gazing unseeingly across the plantation, his thoughts many miles away. He barely shifted his eyes as Fagan passed him.

J.C. Malton was on his stomach, his hands busily holding and writing - Fagan knew not what, but it seemed the West Virginian always was writing - mostly into a weather-beaten black book of loose-leaf sheets. Chuck Taylor was reading, it had finally come around to his turn to read Caldwell's "God's Little Acre" and he seemed to be relishing it, despite the efforts of McPherson, who kept up a steady stream of conversation as he lay crosswise on his cot, feet dangling outside the cover of the tent.

Only Sgt. Konkright's eyes were closed, but Fagan was not certain he was asleep - the Sgt. had a habit of closing his eyes when he wanted to work out what to him seemed to be insurmountable problems.

"Where you goin?" McPherson stopped his diversionary tactics aimed at Taylor long enough to ask Fagan.

"I'm sittin', ain't I." Fagan snarled, his usual tone when he was addressing the lippy one - though beneath his attitude he really did not dislike the kid, even though he did talk too much and was too noisy.

"Christ man! I mean before - you were walkin' right by the tent." The upper lip protruded even further as a hurt expression clouded his face.

"Heard you popping off. Figured this was no place for me." Fagan said, his body stretched over the bunk, almost completely covering the length of the cot. "Thought I'd go over to the C.P. Whose got the watch?"

"Miller!" Konkright said his eyes still closed. When the others looked over to the Sergeant's cot, his face was still in repose and the body seemingly relaxed in sleep.

Fagan closed his eyes, a smile on his lips, his brain shutting out the sound of McPherson's voice which had again begun to project a steady stream of unimportant frivolities at Taylor whose lips formed the words as he read silently.

This outfit sure has fallen quickly enough into a peace-time routine, Fagan thought, the smile thin upon his lips. It was true, the five days since the coughing Higgins boat had deposited the Platoon on the island had seen the camp erected, watches formed, and patrols dispatched over the island. Work details were few, barely necessary in fact. The only real excitement came when the daily boat arrived from Munda with supplies, even mail, to those it brought. But the main purpose of the daily boat was to bring back Capet's written report of the Platoon's findings on the island.

The tent had somehow become quieter, Fagan opened his eyes and quickly scanned the tent. The lippy one was gone - his bunk empty, and the others were quietly continuing their various activities in the peace and quiet of the tent. It was fast becoming night, and Taylor's lips were moving, more quickly now trying to finish the chapter, before all the light was gone. Total black-out was in force in the camp.

Sgt. Konkright groaned once and swung his legs over the cot. "Better check the perimeter. You guys straight on your patrol areas for tomorrow?" He asked as he slid his feet into a well worn pair of Indian moccasins.

Grants and nods answered him as he walked through the tent opening. Stooping as he walked, he picked up a coconut and heaved it across the company street into a 50 gallon drum which had been employed as a refuse can. He peered up at the coconuts high up in the fronds of the trees. "One of those damn things is gonna drop on someone's head someday and kill him. Well, the men had better look alive" - he smiled in the twilight gloom - they were a good platoon - bitchers of course, but they were learning fast on this reconnaissance assignment. They would be all right when they actually got into combat.

This was a hell of an island Sgt. Myron Konkright thought. Christ, if some of the guys who had landed on Guadalcanal back in 1942 could see it! They thought that the whole Pacific was like the Canal with its stinking rivers and land crabs and rats and lizards and mosquitoes. They should see Kolombangara - hell! They wouldn't believe him when he told them about it when he finally got back to Pavuvu, or whatever the hell the divisions rest camp was called. He'd never been there but had heard enough about it back on Guadalcanal, the second time around, that is. He'd spent the last year, plus several months, back in the states. Gingerly he placed his hand on his right shoulder where a machine gun bullet had shattered the bone there on the canal and had given him a passport back to the states and the Naval Hospital at Oakland.

He sniffed the fragrance of the dew laden, wild tropical flowers - so different from the mold laden stench of the canal, as he walked.

Kolombangara was a virtual paradise, huge coconut trees, tall, and straight with blossoming palm fronts in the upper reaches. And fruit, here indeed, they had found breadfruit, the staple of the island natives, coconuts, of course, bananas and one patrol had even brought some delicious pineapple which it had found deep in the mountain. The patrols, it was on the patrols that the beauties and mysteries of the lovely atoll were best studied close up. Truly a model which would thrill a novelist or a Hollywood producers heart, it was completely surrounded by white sandy beaches of the purest debris free type, gently caressed by soft leisurely waves, straightened out on the reef which protected the island. The plantation, and the men found strong evidence that it was run by a Britisher, working for one of the leading American soap producers, who also had with him his wife and 10 or 11 year old daughter, rimmed the entire island on the flat bottomland which led to the mountain. A well worn road traversed the plantation, crude, but well-constructed bridges spanning the fresh water creeks which ran down the sides of the volcano. One such creek, the maps of Kolombangara called them rivers, ran within a mile of the third Platoon's bivouac area around the side of the island bordering Ceremoni Cove.

The creek itself was no more than 30 yards wide, but its bottom was almost 20 feet deep where it ran beneath the planks of the bridge, and the troops spent much time during the daylight hours diving bare-assed from the bridge into the refreshing icy, black waters. And the water was black, black in comparison to the blue-green waters of the ocean which were visible from the bridge. Standing there, looking downstream, the sharp dividing line where the black, cold, fresh water of the stream, met the blue, warm, salt water of the ocean created a beautiful sight and what's more made for an ideal swimming situation. The troops swam in the cold, refreshing water until the heat of their bodies had been dissipated, along with the perspiration, and then, they would swim into the warmness of the ocean's water, immediately noticing the temperate change.

"Halt: Who goes there?" the voice came from the machine gun nest on the northern flank.

"Sgt. Konkright!" The sergeant said, "Everything all set for the night here?"

"All set!" McPherson said curling up in the pit, his steel helmet slipping over his eyes. Peterson smiled in the darkness.

"Keep awake! Liverlip." Konkright snarled. "If I catch you sleeping on your watch, I'll have your ass hanging from one of these coconut trees. "The sergeant moved on leaving the grinning Peterson and the fake snoring McPherson in the machine gun pit. Good men, he thought. McPherson's a loud mouthed bastard, but he'd be all right. He'd proven himself as had the others on the patrol.

The patrols themselves had not turned out to be the easy time which they had been expected to be when no signs of Japs had been found. The pattern of combing the island had been set back at Munda by higher authority. Basically it called for four patrols to go out each day. Four patrols of two men each combing a specified section of the island. The four patrols operated independently of each other. The two extreme patrols started by fanning out to the extreme limits of the island from the camp area, the first day meeting each other on the opposite end of the island, then the return trip was made slightly inland. Each subsequent patrol on following days moved inland more.

Two center patrols started across the center of the island the first day parallel to each other about 200 yards apart and returned fanned out toward the seaward part of the island. The entire coverage of the island would take about two weeks. Two weeks, that is, if no concentration of Japs were found which seemed likely.

But the patrols had found plenty of evidence of Japs in their patrols, patrols which had turned out to be back-breaking. The patrol which was lucky to find a path or foot-trail over their assigned area was indeed fortunate for the island was a virtual mass of vegetation, fed by the century old fertilization of the volcano's strewn lava. The only way through was by hacking a clearing through by means of machete, and the going was tough, back breaking work. And the vegetation seemed to grow just as quickly as it was cut down. In this mass of jungle the Japs had lived, selecting as their major camps, swampy areas in the ridges, ravines and gullies which spread out in the foothills of the volcano. One of the biggest encampments discovered was deep in a marshy swamp, hidden from the eyes of cruising airplanes by a heavy covering of high bushy tree which trunks were thick and scaled with sodden mold. In this hastily deserted camp was found enough supplies, heavy machine-guns, flame throwers and ammunition to outfit a regiment. Crude huts mounted on stilts formed the living quarters for the troops and the depots for the supplies. And the Commodore was happy that he was on the patrol that day which stumbled onto the camp for he found feminine clothing, cosmetics, in one long straw matted building which evidently had been the brothel for the occupation troops.

"See!" he had gushed."What'd I tell you. These bastards know how to live. Women, they carry their own women with them. Who says they're uncivilized - Christ, they're smarter than we are. Damn it. I'm on the wrong side in this friggin' war." The mystery of how they moved the supplies through the swampy terrain in the camp area and the heavy jungle without benefit of roads was answered when the Jap equivalent of American weasels, at home both on land and in the water, were found hidden in caves. These contractions were small, no larger than Marine jeeps, but with a thick armor nose coming to a narrow point in front and a small but powerful motor which drove the wide treads of the tank like chain. In all some 200 of these jeasels, as the Marines called them were found, the first to be captured in the war. It was a happy day when a large cache of gasoline was found for the jeasels for the Marines then employed the jeasels for both patrolling and pleasure.

Sgt. Konkright checked the last outpost and went quickly back to his tent. Yes, it wasn't too bad duty, much better than getting your ass shot at on some other rock. Four patrols a day - eight men - it worked out that the men went out on patrol every third day with perhaps a watch in the C.P. or in one of the out posts thrown in. He reached the tent and the light snoring of his tent mates beneath their mosquito nets attesting to their peaceful sleeping. It wasn't too bad duty, he thought as he stripped and stepped under his own mosquito netting.

J. C. Malton felt a weakness beneath his knees as he answered the call of the duty N.C.O. He sat on the edge of his bunk, his hands holding his head, as the others dressed.

"What's the matter, J.C.?" Fagan had stopped strapping his knife sheath to his leg as his eyes caught Malton. He moved over to the stocky Marine's bunk.

Malton lifted his head and smiled, "Nothing, just a little tired." The effort of raising his head was sheer labor.

"Want me to take your patrol?" The offer came easily to the New Englander and the words held no feeling whatsoever.

J. C. shook his head. Fagan had been on patrol the day before and the terrain had turned rough in the area he had covered making the weasel almost useless. Finally, he had learned, they had abandoned it and scaled the mountainous terrain on foot. "No, I'm all right - I'm hungry - be fine as soon as get some chow in me."

As if in answer, the triangle someone had found sounded in front of the odd tent which had been turned into a mess and which each took his turn manning.

"Come and get it," Alex Blue called, "before I toss it to the sharks."

The troops, most in a state of undress rather than dress filtered from their tents in the bright morning sunlight and entered the mess tent where two 50 gallon drums and a G.I. can were bubbling over the crude fire pits sunk into the soft, rich soil and banked with coral. In the two 50 gallon drums had been tossed individual cans of dried eggs and Vienna sausage and the dark concoction in the G.I. can was coffee – real coffee.

"What's for chow, Miss Blue?" asked Young as he moved to the head of the line amidst the mumbles of good natured cat calls from those who were moved back one place.

Alex Blue, his nickname coming from the Amos and Andy program's secretary "Buzz me, Miss Blue." smiled broadly, his flabby faced puffed with sleep and wet with perspiration from the head of the pits. "Special today - eggs and vienna sausage."

"For Christ sake - ain't they ever goin to send us some fresh food." The Commodore said as he slammed his mess gear against his side.

"Vienna sausage is a luxury - don't you know that McNalton." Lt. Capet stood at the tent flap - a grin on his face - no one had heard or seen him enter. "Civilians can't buy vienna sausage - it's a delicacy like caviar."

McNalton regained his composure, "They're just dried up hot dogs to me, sir," he said and both he and the lieutenant joined in with the others' laughter. Malton took the two cans, steaming and scalding, and then dipped his canteen cup in the bubbling brew of coffee. He followed Cold Steel outside and propped his pack against a coconut tree. Appetite less he pried loose the key from the egg can and began to unwind it slowly.

Fagan watched him. "You got the bug, kid?" he asked as he pried a piece of mashed egg from its tin and plopped it in his mouth.

"No - it's just a touch of cat fever." Malton laughed and forced himself to take a bite of the tasteless egg.

"Men!" Lt. Capet stood in the midst of the setting Marines, his mess gear held chest high. "The supply boat yesterday brought orders for us. It seems we were too high on our findings at Vella airstrip."

He was referring to the slim fighter strip which had been cut into the rows of coconut trees half way around the island. "Munda wants us to tear the place apart and see if we can find any Jap reports in those shacks in the woods. Seem to think we might also find an intact plane hidden there. Some fly-boy reports seeing something which reflected light on a sweep over the area. Any of you guys on that segment of patrol find anything that looked like a plane."

"The bastard's nuts," Miller said disgustedly. "Jackson and I scoured that area damned carefully. There ain't nothing bigger than a wash tub left in one piece over there."

Lt. Capet nodded. "That's what I reported but intelligence seems to think we might have overlooked something, so we are to cover every inch of ground." He paused and then found Sgt. Konkright sitting with Brabern and Taylor. "Sergeant, we'll take 12 men - the regular patrols will cover their area and leave the men who were out yesterday here to keep an eye on the camp and man the TBX. We'll shove off at" he checked his watch "0830." Looking at the men for a sign of any objection, he found none. All wanted to get a look at the strip. Only Miller and Jackson showed disgust on their faces.

He heard Jackson mumble as he found a spot and sat down to his now cold eggs and vienna sausage. "Those bastards at Munda don't know a plane from a shit trench. We ain't goin' to find anything."

The patrols took off on schedule, Malton pale and perspiring as he clasped two hand grenades to his cartridge belt.

Brabern, his patrol buddy stood with Fagan waiting. "Don't push it, J.C."
Fagan said softly, "if you can't make it, don't push it."

"I'm ok, damn it!" J.C. snapped curtly, then repenting smiled at Fagan.
"You keep your ear glued to that TBX – you might hear the war's over."

"Yeh! Or that the nips have landed in Frisco Bay." Brabern added as he
shoved off in the direction of the jungle. J.C. followed, feeling Fagan's eyes
digging into his back.

For 2000 yards they followed the larger patrol's jeasels dust as it
wound down the plantation road. At the other side of the bridge which
crossed the swimming spot they checked heir target map and then took off
into the jungle.

"Wish the hell we could have brought that jeasel." Brabern said as the
sweat began to burn his eyes.

Malton merely nodded, the weakness under his knees more pronounced
and the jungle waving before his eyes. He had the bug, Malaria he knew, but
he could make it, he was certain.

He plodded on, content to let Brabern lead the way. Brabern had slowed
his pace and kept glancing over his shoulder to see how J.C. was making out
- the sight was not too reassuring.

"Let's take a break," J.C. gasped as he leaned against a willowy jungle tree.
They hadn't come a mile from the bridge, but already J.C. was completely wet
from perspiration. Slowly he slid down the sloping trunk of the tree, his well-
cared for rifle tumbling from his grasp.

Brabern quickly knelt beside him and taking his canteen from its cover,
poured some tepid water through J.C.'s parted lips.

"Christ, J.C. you're burning up with fever." Brabern's hand holding
Malton's head turned hot from the malaria racked brow. "You've got the bug!
You can't make this patrol like this." He rose, his brow lined and wrinkled
as he tried to find a solution. J.C. didn't try to object this time. He was too
weak to protest. Brabern looked down the swath he had cut through the
brush, pondered a minute and then spoke, his mind made up. "Look J.C. You
think you can make it back to camp. It's all downhill and a path is pretty well

cut." He turned to the jungle before him. "I'll go on. If this patrol isn't made today, it will throw the whole friggin' schedule off, and those bastards over on Munda will have a shit hemorrhage." He looked down at Malton "How about it, J.C. Think you can make it. "

J. C. struggled to his feet, more than happy to accept the assist offered by Brabern. He pulled a dry tongue over dryer lips, "I can make it, O.k." he tried to focus foggy eyes on Brabern. "What about you? Can you make it alone?"

Brabern laughed and walked several strides back down the trail with the staggering Marine. "Sure - and the privacy will be great, after being with you bastards so long." He clapped J.C. on the back and watched him go down the trail. He'll make it, he thought, as he shifted his pack on his back and turned back to the foliage which blocked his path up the side of the volcano.

J. C. didn't remember much of his journey down the path, his eyes watery and almost shut from the burning fever which swept over his body. He realized he had fallen several times, and knew he had lain each time for quite some time, but had somehow managed to force his way to his feet and go on. He didn't know how long it had taken him to cover that mile - he had lost all sense of time. He had fallen once, at least, he knew objectively, because his fuzzy brain had registered the fact that his right hand was aching - grimly he had forced his eyes to focus and had almost cried aloud when he saw his fingers closed about the barrel of his rifle, which was wedged in a fork in a tree trunk. He had been automatically pulling, his knuckles scrapping the rough bark of the tree.

It had taken hours to free the rifle, it seemed to him. The simple procedure of releasing the rifle and picking it up after it fell had finally occurred to him but he was afraid he wouldn't be able to pick the weapon up again, and the first principle of the corps "don't lose your rifle - it's your best friend" kept hammering at his tired brain.

And he had fallen again, he remembered falling when he had started running - at least he thought he was running - when he heard voices - or thought he heard voices somewhere through the midst which had fallen before in his eyes. Yes, he was down, he knew, but he had to keep going - so he forced his body to move – crawling along the foul jungle floor. Then night came - it must be night - everything turned. black - so it must be night - then it was all right to sleep! Not for long, just a little while - then he would feel better and could get back to camp easily.

"Hey, Cold Steel! Come on in! The water's great – just like ice." Chick Young blowed water like a whale and treaded water, refreshing himself after the night's watch in the machine gun nest. He feigned fright. "But take that damn knife off first, before you cut someone's balls off." The two other Marines in the water, Barger and Garber, laughed, as did Miss Blue who stood next to Fagan ,who did not laugh, on the timber rail of the bridge.

Miss Blue watched the swimmers for a short time, then studied the finesse with which Fagan honed his knife on the whetstone. Tiring of that, he let his eyes travel aimlessly over the area, gazing now and then at the palm fronds motionless at the top of the coconut trees. He took a big red and white railroad man's handkerchief from his pocket, squirming precariously around as he did so, and wiped the perspiration from his pudgy face.

"It's hotter than Oklahoma - even under those trees - there's not a breath of air blow....What the hell's that?" He interrupted himself as he saw a movement in the jungle beyond the rows of coconut trees. He pointed his finger.

Fagan swung off the bridge and slitting his eyes against the treacherous rays of sun filtering through the coconut trees, followed the direction indicated by the arm. He saw nothing at first -then the brush moved and he could see a form - a man's form crouched in the bushes. "Scatter" he called grabbing his rifle from where it rested beside him against the bridge's railing. He raced from the bridge and ducked behind a cocoanut tree, ramming a bullet into the chamber with one quick flick of the M-1's bolt. He could hear Blue doing the same to his left and the subdued splashing water related that the swimmers were heading for shore and their weapons.

"What do you make it out?" Blue whispered and he peered from one side of a coconut tree.

"Can't see yet" Fagan whispered back and signaled the other Marines who came up to take cover. A silence fell over the jungle, interrupted only by the full throated calls of large tropical mika birds who sat high in the leafy palm fronds, their colorful heads held low between their wings and called, in a language more screeching than sedate, to each other. They seemed to be given a play by report of the action below to each other, all of them calling at one time. The clatter grew louder as the figure crept farther out of the protective thickness of the jungle into the comparative bareness of the lanes between the rows of majestic coconut trees.

"Looks like only one of them." Chick Young whispered as he sighted down the long, slim and deadly barrel of the M-1. "I think I can pick him off from here." Cautiouslessly he braced his side to the tree and snapped the safety from the trigger guard. A slender finger enclosed the hair trigger, and began to close slowly as the figure came painfully slower toward them. The sights of all the rifles were trained between the green clad shoulders, all but obscuring the head covered with the steel helmet - the helmet which now raised upward, disclosing the sweat strained face which was pale beneath it.

"Hold your fire! For Christ's sake, it's J.C." Fagan sprang forward as he uttered the words and raced through the high brush which barred his way. Young and the others followed, covering the lanky Marine as he dashed upright, headlong, without caution toward the crawling figure. He fell beside the trembling Marine, now shivering with the cold which follows the fever of malarial attacks, only to give way a second, third, and sometimes fourth time to the blistering fever. Tearing his thin shirt from his back, he wrapped it around the semi-conscious Malton .

"He's bad off." Chick said softly, with the knowing tone of one who had lain helpless in the throes of the jungle sickness. "We better get him back to the camp and get some quinine into him."

"J.C. - can you hear me? " Fagan's voice was emotionless. "Where's Brabern?" He was once again the traditional Marine "Is he O.K.?"

Malton opened his eyes, his face quivering from the chill, his teeth chattering, uncontrollably in his half open mouth. A moment of rationality seemed to sweep him and he understood the words which Fagan had spoken "O.Kkkk". He went on, "mmmm!"

He said no more and once again the eyes closed, his weak malaria racked body sliding back into merciful unconsciousness.

"Let's get a stretcher made." Fagan said evenly as he got to his feet, the long gleaming knife sliding effortless from its sheath. Picking out two straight trees 15 or 20 feet high he began chipping with his knife, the chips flying as the razor sharp blade cut into the wood. Miss Blue had attacked the other tree which Fagan had indicated with his own jungle knife, but could not match the speed and effectiveness of Fagan and his cold steel. Young had raced back to the river and tore down the shelter half of a pup tent, which each Marine carried around his bedroll, he had rigged as back rest on the sandy beach.

By the time Chick had returned Fagan had stripped the small branches from the moist thick tree trunk and had trimmed it to a little over J.C.'s length, placing it along the unconscious Malton, now trying unknowingly to tear off his clothing in another siege of the malarial fever. Tossing the trunk to Blue, he attached the other tree which Miss Blue had not yet succeeded in felling. The fat, overage Marine took the now smooth pole and began to secure the shelter-half to it, ordering Young and the other two Marines to take the laces from their boon dockers . Fastening the laces to the eyelets, he expertly bound them to the pole. In several more minutes Fagan had the other pole ready and the stretcher was completed. The whole operation had taken but a little over five minutes. The lessons which had been taught in self -preservation back in the states had been learned well.

Gingerly the body of the stocky Marine was lifted to the stretcher which had been placed alongside. Then without a word being spoken Fagan and Young knelt at the front of the makeshift stretcher, Fagan grasping the pole with his left hand and Young the opposite pole with his right. Garber and Badger repeated the action at the rear and then Blue who knelt beside the stretcher to his left, said quietly. "Up," and Malton was lifted from the deck in a swift motion, Blue steadying the twisting form slung in the shelter half, then quickly checking all the ties, to ascertain if they were going to hold. Satisfying himself that the knots were evenly distributed and taut, he said "Let's go," to the litter-bearers and in the prescribed manner, Fagan led off with his right foot and Young with his left. At the rear, and in unison, Garber and Badger joined in. In several moments Blue had caught the cadence set by Fagan, the lead man on the right and in a crisp voice conned cadence "Hup-hup-hup-hup."

The going was easier once they made the openness of the road and Blue upped the count. Soon the litter-bearers were dark with sweat and once, Blue interrupted his count to offer, "Anyone want spelled." No answer was given as the bearers kept their eyes straight ahead as they concentrated on keeping the count going. Blue then resumed his "hup-hup-hup -"

The right arm of Young had feeling in it no longer, but he knew the others had also lost their sense of owning the arm which bent to the task of carrying the sick buddy. But, they, like he, would never admit they were pooped for two reasons, the primary one being that they were doing something for one of their own, one who had shared their laughter, had consoled their sorrow, and now needed help and they wanted to give it to him without wanting anything in return.

The other reason was the unspoken Espirit-de-corps which had made them this unit of oneness. They were never to complain, unless it was for trivial things - beating their gums they called it, like the lousy food, the lousy mail service, the lousy inspections, and the countless other gripes men beat their gums about without actually caring too much about it. But when it came to doing what they were Marines for - the suffering of combat, the enduring of all hardships connected with it, they would not give up until they themselves dropped. It had been driven, literally and figuratively, into their brains that they could do anything, better and longer, than anyone else, and they would drop before they would admit, to anyone else, but to themselves, first of all, that anyone be he a soldier, sailor, or another Marine, was braver, stronger or more enduring.

Their appearance from the road south of the camp was witnessed by the land crabs, lizards, tropical birds, and McPherson and Peterson, who were pitching horseshoes - relieved from the patrol because of their stint in the outpost the night before. Liverlip saw them first, just as he swung his right hand back to let fly a shoe.

"Christ!" he said dropping the shoe and causing a surprised Peterson to jump from its downward path. "What the hell happened?"

Peterson had also caught sight of the four sweat-stained men lugging the litter quickly down the path trampled down between the rows of coconut trees. Miss Blue was in the vanguard, running now at the sight of the camp area.

"Lend a hand there, you guys," he called as he raced past the two opened mouthed men, counting, unconsciously, the tents to make sure he went into the right one - the lieutenants. As he found the square medicine chest, and rummaged through look for the bottle marked quinine, he heard the litter-bearers in the next tent transferring Malton from the shelter-half stretcher to his own bunk. The bottle was full, he saw, as he finally found the square jar with the huge white A on its lid.

"Got it?" Fagan asked as Blue, still panting heavily from his dash through the hot sun, entered the tent. The big Oklahoman nodded in answer and handed Fagan the bottle, his eyes resting on Malton in the bunk.

The malaria suffering Marine lay still on the bunk, blankets quickly confiscated from the neighboring bunks covering him. His face was wet with perspiration and his wide lips, were puffered and cracked with fever. He didn't move, his body quiet again, after the last attack of the chills.

"How many?" Fagan asked as he tilted the open end of the bottle onto the palm of his right hand. He looked at the others around the bunk, saw their blank stares and said brusquely, "How many, Chick?"

The baby Marine shifted uncomfortably and scratched the back of his close cropped head, his long, ragged fingernails sounding like sandpaper as they came into contact with the short bristles of the short hair. "Let's see!" he drawled in his Arizona twang. "Better give him two, yeh, give him two.

He's got a pretty bad case. But give him some water, for Christ's sake -" He added as he saw Fagan forcing the pills into the unconscious Marine's mouth - "those things are lousy."

Many hands pulled canteens from their carriers, but it was Miss Blue - gentle, old Miss Blue, who raised the still head and held the canteen to the burning lips of Malton.

"That'll kill the fever." Young said as Blue lowered the head to the cot. "He'll be out for a while, but the quinine will do the trick. Arthurs will do the rest when he gets back from patrol." He spoke of the corpsman who was assigned to the platoon for venture on Kolombangera. Fagan nodded and tightened the blankets around the prostrated Marine, then rising, followed the others from the tent into the mid-day sun. "Come on!" Fagan tossed over his shoulder as he made his way to the last tent in the company street. "Let's get some chow - the patrols won't be back for several hours yet."

All but Fagan slowly made their way after Miss Blue, and disappeared into the tent. Fagan sat with his back against a tree, Malton visible in his bunk, the tent flaps rolled up and secured to permit what little breeze there was blowing, to cool the inside. Cold Steel Fagan's thoughts turned to Frank Brabern and his passage through the jungle. He wondered how he was making out.

Frank Brabern at that moment was hacking his way through a patch of fan shaped elephant ear sized plants. Sweat poured from every pore of his body and in its saltiness ran into his eyes, mouth and into his ankle high boon-dockers. Brabern's thoughts too had been occupied - the lonely sojourn through the segment of his patrol had allowed plenty of time for thought. Already he had dwelled on Malton's condition, his good fortune not to have become a victim of the bug, and the platoon's good fortune that no Jap had deemed it wise to remain and enjoy the marvels of Kolombangera.

But for the past hour his thoughts had dwelt on Candy - lovely, beautiful, desirable Candy. She had come alive to him in his solitude - the long-legged beauty of her magnificent body, her soft golden hair enveloping the soft face which held within it the green eyes, petite nose and sensuous soft lips. She was waiting for him - he knew! Waiting, the letters had not said so, but he knew, had known since the day months before when she had become his in the trailer along the ocean in Southern California. No words had said that she was his, but he had known then - and knew now from the tone of her letters. But, when he thought of her, as he did now, which was often he had a feeling, an anguish able feeling, that their love - their oneness for eternity, was not to be. And always there came into his thoughts at these moments, a simple insignia, an air force insignia, mounted jauntedly on the rear of a small convertible.

No word had been spoken of the airman after the sheer delight they had shared in the trailer. The long ride to Camp Pendleton had not been interrupted by words of promise, of waiting, of divorce. She had been his, was still his, his heart spoke fiercely, but she was another man's wife. Somehow he knew, had known during that long ride, that if he had said "Get a divorce, Candy" she would have nodded and that would have settled the matter. But he hadn't and not known then why he hadn't.

Brabern swung viciously at the brush. The realization of why he had not suggested a divorce had come to him slowly -painfully, during long awake hours on board the Pacific spanning transport. She would have said yes, and there lay the reason. He hadn't the right to ask her to get a divorce and wait for him. She had loved the airman - and her love was not easily given he had discovered. She had given it to him - and herself as well, but there had been a terrible need of someone to fill the gap left by the airman which had prompted her to let herself be attracted to him. She still loved the pilot, he knew, and that did not detract for her love from him.

Sighing, he paused and sat down on a small depression on the underside of a knoll, shaded from the blistering sun. Pulling from his dungarees his green, government issue handkerchief, he wiped the perspiration from his face. "Where did this triangle lead to?" he thought. The pilot must know by now of their tryst, or did he? She had not spoken to Brabern of writing to him of their meeting - and now that he had gone there had been no need to write but what of the future - when this damn mess that the proceeding generation had created for him to unravel, had been settled? He could not quietly disappear into the sunset. He loved her, needed her, and intended to go back, but what if it were not being shuffled that way? - what if the script had been written differently? That is if he wasn't going back home?

He placed his rifle beside him and drawing his bayonet from the seaboard, drew her name in the soft yielding brown dirt. What then? He shrugged his shoulders! Then he hoped she hadn't written the airman! Not that he thought for a moment that she wouldn't tell him about the Marine someday -he knew her too well, but it would do no good now. It would only cause heartache and frustration in the pilot's mind and heart. She would go on and wait, but for the airman - that's what she would do, he knew and he was glad! She deserved happiness, and she could find it with the Air Force. He smiled, and the vision of Candy became clearer, and the insignia on the car flickered in the background, a sign of security which she could lean against.

But what if they both cheated the odds and returned. What then? A frown crossed his face. She loved him - loved him strongly, but she also loved the pilot. The frown increased as the vision of Candy, with her face distorted in confusion and pain welled in his brain. He sat there like that for several minutes and then he shrugged - time and fate would have to take care of that. He sheathed the bayonet and reached for his rifle.

His hand never reached it as the small wiry body hurtled down from atop the hill, the butt of a Japanese 31 caliber rifle crashing into the exposed head of the Marine. Brabern fell forward, oblivious to the excited jabbering of four Japanese soldiers, in tattered clothing, who appeared from the brush to join the attacker in tearing the pack from the limp shoulders of the Marine in search of food.

Candy sat at the tiny table in the trailer, her small right hand holding a pen over a piece of dainty stationery. Her face was clouded as she looked at the words she had written. She couldn't find the right words though she had thought of what she had to say to her husband for more than six months. Six months in which her letters had been gay, unimportant yet she had not felt gay - her heart ached at its division - How could you tell your husband that you loved another - had given what was morally and lawfully his to another - had given eagerly - with love. Tears welled in her eyes. She took the pen to paper again and laboriously made it write the pain giving words.

"He should be back by now." Lt. Capet looked at his watch.

The platoon sat and stood around. The big patrol three of the smaller patrols among them. One face was missing - Brabern! "He's out there, alone." Sgt. Konkright said as he looked where the coconut cove disappeared into the jungle. "It would take him longer to cover the area."

Fagan was honing his knife. Without looking up he said, "He should be back." The words were full of meaning which escaped none of the men.

Malton moaned inside his tent. The sound turned the men's attention to the interior where the corpsman, Arthurs, worked over the feverish unconscious Malton. "He'd be all right in a day or so," Arthurs had said. "They just have to keep him filled with quinine."

"I want 7 volunteers." Lt. Capet said as he took his revolver from his holster and checked the clip. Immediately every man moved forward. A smile crossed the young lieutenant's lips.

"Sergeant, you stay in charge here. Fagan, Blue, Young, Garber, McPherson, Peterson, Badger. You come with me." He had signaled out the men who had not made the earlier patrol. "If we're not back by dark, Sergeant, prepare the platoon for an organized platoon diversion at dawn."

"Aye, sir" Sgt. Konkright attempted to disguise his disappointment at not being selected for the patrol. He conferred with Capet, both pouring over an overlap of the island, confirming the route of the patrols for the day.

"Let's go!" Capet started across the coconut grove. "Stay in squad marching rank. Fagan, you take the point, Garber, you bring up the rear." He slowed and allowed Fagan to pass him. The platoon watched the backs of the patrol disappear into the brush.

Frank Brabern slowly regained consciousness, his head ringing. He tried to move, but his arms were pinned behind him, circling a tree. His legs ached and he tried to lean the weight of his body against the tree. Rationality came before vision and his throbbing brain realized that he had been tied upright against the tree. Dimly his eyes saw light and he tried to focus them on the area before him – the sound of Japanese voices penetrating the ringing in his ears.

Gradually his vision returned - he could make out the outline of four bodies scattered about him, each jabbering excitedly in turn. One body was larger than the others - it must be standing closer.

I've had it - he thought - the realization penetrating his consciousness. Damn his carelessness! He had been taken without being aware of the nips presence. Incredibly he could still see the image of Candy - a Candy whose back was now turned toward him - whose long blonde hair hung loosely over the collar of her dress.

The Japs were laughing and he sensed rather than saw the Japs moving closer. He blinked his eyes - trying to focus on the twin objects protruding from the body. Searing pain crashed into his head as the nips fingers dug into his eyeballs - he screamed, the sound of his voice mingling with bells which had now become shriller in his eardrums. From somewhere he sensed hands on his hips and blackness came as his manhood dropped bloodily onto the ground as the knife in the hands of the Jap sliced across his groin.

It's my fault if anything happens to that kid. Capet spit fiercely as he moved behind Fagan who was almost double-timing as he followed the crushed vegetation which marked the path Brabern had made. I should have sent another man in Malton's place - I knew he was sick - saw it clearly at the morning chow. What the hell could have happened to him? There had been absolutely no trace of any other human being on the island. But where the hell was the kid?

They had been on the trail for an hour now and were nearing the high ground of the area. They should have met Brabern by now if he were coming back. The poor kid - he cursed almost aloud as he realized he knew so little about him. Where was he from - did he have a wife back home like he did? Immediately, as he did on every other patrol, he thought of Carolyn - his Carolyn. Carolyn of the coal black hair, and green eyes back home in Staunton, Virginia. And of Joie, the son she had borne him and which he had never seen. Poor Brabern! Wonder if he had a son or daughter he had never seen. Damn it! This friggin' war – the widows it made.

He stopped and dropped to one knee at the upraised hand of Fagan in front of him. Slowly he moved forward to the side of Fagan and then heard it. It sounded like moans coming from in front of them. The brush was thick and he couldn't make out from where the sound had come. Half turning, in his crouched position, he motioned to the squad to deploy in skirmishes and watched as the well-trained men disappeared on both sides of him. He crawled past Fagan and moved quietly up the path. He could hear the others in the brush to the sides and before him. The moans became louder as he pushed aside a large elephant bush and stopped, his mouth a gasp at the horror his eyes beheld.

"The dirty sons-of-bitches," Fagan cried. He stood upright and with his rifle at the ready crashed through the small clearing.

"Jesus Christ!" Young softly said beyond the clearing as he emerged into the thinness of the brush. He turned his head and vomited violently.

Fagan moved beside Brabern, his face contorted in anger as his brain tried to formulate a plan of action. He dropped his rifle and extended his hands and then held them motionless. He didn't know what to do. The other members of the patrol crouched at the edges of the clearing, their faces white with shock at the remains of the marine strapped to the tree.

Brabern was pinioned to the tree by his rifle - its bayonet passing through him and sticking deep in the tree. His head was dropped on his chest - blood covering his once handsome face, saturating his dungaree jacket and joining the flood from the stomach wound in painting the bare legs red.

"Brabern!" Lt. Capet said gently as he bent his head to the macerated man's ear.

"What the hell we going to do? " McPherson sobbed, "He's bleeding to death. Do something for God's sake - Do something!" he cried hysterically.

"Shut your god dam mouth." Alex Blue hurled at him - his own frustration evident in his voice.

"Please, please, no more! No more," the weak voice of Brabern was heard by every man.

"It's OK, Frank. " Capet struggled as he tried to remember the man's first name. "They're gone. We'll get you back."

With some unknown ounce of strength, Brabern lifted his head an inch, and with sightless eyes tried to comprehend what had been said. His blood red face slowly twisted into a smile - a smile that was gruesome and crooked. His lips moved and Fagan bent to hear the words - then as if even the smile had taken what remaining life the body had left, the head slumped onto the chest.

Fagan put his hand inside the bloody dungaree jacket, held it there a moment -and then withdrew it and held it before him, his eyes glued to the blood already beginning to dry in his palm. "He's dead." he said.

"Those dirty bastards," McPherson cried jumping to his feet and swinging his rifle into the brush.

"Easy!" Capet said sternly. "Fagan, pull that damn thing out." He ordered, his voice hard.

Fagan looked at Capet for a second, then grasping the stock of the rifle, jerked it from the tree. He threw it into the brush, fragments of the dead marines entrails dropping from the blade in its flight.

"Let's get him down." Capet said with finality as the men tenderly cut the body from the tree, oblivious to the blood which came into contact with their hands.

"Blue, Young - make a stretcher! Garber, Badger wrap Brabern in your ponchos." Capet turned from the activity - Blue and Young making a litter for the second time that day and Badger wrenching as he struggled to get the poncho from his back. Capet walked slowly to the edge of the clearing where Fagan stood motionless, his eyes seeing the jungle for signs of the Japs.

Capet took a cigarette from its sweat wet pack – offered one to Fagan and then put the pack back in his dungaree breast pocket as Fagan had not moved. "What did he say at the end Cold Steel?" Capet spoke almost in a whisper.

Fagan didn't move for a moment and then turned his head to the lieutenant, his gray eyes blazing with hate, anger and revenge.

"See you guys at the Hurricane!" he said his thin line of a mouth almost motionless.

Candy sighed, put down the pen and picked the letter from the table. The frown deepened as she read the inadequate words. The pen had not glided over the paper easily – the words had come with difficulty and now that she had the wounding explanation down on paper, it sounded callous, cruel - but there wasn't an easy way to write a "dear John" letter, as she had heard servicemen call them. She had tried to explain what had driven her into another's arms, but just how do you explain lonesomeness to a person who, despite being completely surrounded by people, was infinitely more lonely. It was no good Candy realized - it was cold, merciless, and inadequate.

Slowly she crumpled the paper between her hands. Then fiercely she tore the feminine stationery into pieces and rising, dumped them into the sink garbage can. She stood looking at the moon reflecting itself on the Pacific, her mind reaching the decision that she would always remember.

She had to tell Jerry - she couldn't deceive him or herself but there was no point to do it now. She would not tear his heart out on some desolate rock in the Pacific. There was time, plenty of time when he returned to explain all the details - details for which she felt no remorse. Jerry would be back before Frank - she was surprised at the certainty of the thought. Then she would tell him - tell him that she longed for a Marine - loved a Marine - Oh, loved him in a terrifying way. She raised her right hand to her eyes to stop a tear which threatened to break loose from the valley of her soft eyes and rain down her face. Suddenly it was joined by others and she covered her face with her hands - crying desperately for Jerry, for Frank - and unknowingly for the agony which was in her own heart.

"We make out about 8 in the party" Lt. Capet said to the hard faces which stared up at him from their positions on the ground. Each member of the platoon held his rifle, a full clip ready for instant use. The lieutenant talked, more than one eye turned to a small white cross made from a 10 in 1 ration box which gleamed in the sun near the mouth of Ceremony Cove. The earth which covered the grave was still fresh as were the words of the Commodore who spoke over the body as it was laid to rest the evening before as a startling red sun set over Choiseul across a fire red sea.

"God placed him upon this earth but a few years ago, and God saw fit to take him now. He didn't live a long life, nor an eventful life until a few hours ago. He was a young man, full of fire for the good things which the Almighty put upon this earth. He hated little - nothing which we, his constant companions knew about. He didn't want to die – but he did die!" A pause as the voice grew harder "die at the hands of an enemy he had been ordered to fight like a man, but that body which was a man, to which all here will attest, was desecrated by that enemy. Revenge, dear Lord, is but thine, but we ask you, Almighty, let us here, his friends, be the tool of your revenge. Rest in Peace."

The words still hung over the thick air of Kolombangara - a Kolombangara which no longer was a peaceful, beautiful, tropical paradise remote from the war which raged all about it, but a Kolombangara which by the death, the merciless death of Frank Brabern changed into a thick jungle of but another island which hid the enemy. An enemy who had killed, and most certainly would not live to remember, the angry human hands it had perpetrated.

"O.K. Let's go!" Capet said softly, adjusting the sling of his carbine loosely on his shoulder for rapid usage. He watched the patrol moving determinedly into position. The whole platoon had naturally enough volunteered to seek out the murderers, but he had selected only 10 - the ten who were closest to the slain Brabern. They stood waiting - Fagan, Taylor, Young, Blue, Badger, Peterson, McPherson, Commodore and Sgt. Konkright. He knew that behind his back Malton lay in his bunk staring at the preparations - still too weak from the raking attack of the day before to get to his feet.

He looked at the men, staring impatiently at him waiting for the raised forward movement of his hand which would signal the patrol on. "I just want to say this one thing - we are not bringing back any prisoners." The words were not needed by the men, the determination to settle the score was evident in their eyes. "Shove off, Sergeant."

Mike Konkright plunged into the brush, the early morning sun bright against the blue skies. Behind him followed the patrol, silent as they moved with the experience gained from constant practice and training. Each had his own thoughts but they all reached a focal point on their purpose.

Tropical birds, surprised by the silent advance of the patrol, moved into the clear, moist Pacific air at the careful, hunting approach of Marines. The lessons, tiresome, senseless at the time, of stealth were being put to good usage now. Doggedly, unhalting the patrol fanned over every inch of terrain surrounding the path of the last ill-fated patrol. Pierced, taut lips, tightened further as the word was passed when the spot of the fanatical murder of Brabern was reached. But Lt. Capet kept the troops moving, signaling to the men to double their alert.

If possible, the advance became more furtive, the discerning, steady eyes of the Marines scathing in their search for the enemy. Several times Peterson, who was on the point of the patrol signaled for a halt, and as the men of the patrol dropped to the dark, smelly soil of Kolombangara with their rifles at the ready, Capet and Konkright knelt beside occupied Peterson, who was studying the tell-tale marks the passage of human beings through the jungle leaves.

"What do you read?" Capet asked, his eyes darting from left to right, ascertaining whether his men had deployed correctly to cover all fronts. Assured, he turned his face to the bent head of Peterson, who was fingering a broken branch from an elephant bush.

Peterson shook his head "Broken in the wrong direction." Then indicating the almost invisible depression of a split toe shoe, "they came this way yesterday when they trapped Brabern. But they didn't pass back through here."

"Shit!" Konkright ejaculated spewing tobacco juice over the elephant bush. "Where the hell did they go - they couldn't just disappear?"

"Lieutenant," Peterson said. "I'd fan the men out a little more, and have them check the deck for any signs."

Capet nodded and Konkright spread through the ranks passing the word. As Peterson took off again the order was carried out with the eleven men spread thinner.

In the next hour four false-alarms were examined and discarded by the observant Peterson, but the fifth discovery by Miss Blue brought excitement to Peterson's eyes.

"Fresh, within two hours," he announced to Capet as he crouched close to the deck and studied the area. "I count eight. They stopped here, then moved out in that direction." He pointed to the right, where a low ravine dipped from the side of the volcano.

"Hey, Lieutenant," Fagan called through his teeth as he knelt in a clump of bougaville bushes. He held up a discarded K-Ration carton which had formerly held three Camels. Cold Steel's face was unreadable, his gray eyes mere slits beneath bushy eyebrows. His jaw was set and his mouth a slender line of lips which held color. "These are the guys we want!" he said softly as he put the spent carton into his dungaree jacket.

Capet nodded and then turned away, his face red with renewed anger at the memory of the violated body of Brabern. He pushed his right hand forward and once again they moved out. The tiredness which had made itself known in the limbs of the men disappeared at the realization of the nearness of their prey. The terrain became more densely covered with vegetation and pitted with step offs as the ground fell away into the ravine.

Every few minutes Peterson would bend closer to the deck, examining the signs left by the Japs. Sometimes he nodded, other times his right hand merely tightened on the stock of his M-1, but the men behind him knew instinctively from each reaction that they were nearing their objective.

Suddenly Peterson dropped to the deck, and as one the patrol followed. Capet crawled to Peterson's side and started to speak, but the scout held his right finger to his ear. Capet strained his ears but all he could hear was the sounds of the jungle but then he heard what the specially trained ears of Peterson had heard first - voices in the distance, the high screeching jabbering voices of Japanese. He turned to warn the men, but they had already heard. Warily, he tested the slight breeze to ascertain the distance which separated the two alien groups. "200 yards?" he whispered to Peterson.

Peterson had already made the observation and he nodded. Cupping the safety of his rifle with his hands to muffle the sound, he pressed the safety off and placed his finger on the trigger guard, a smile on his face.

Capet spread his hands over his head and then moved them in an encircling movement and then moved his right hand forward. He and Peterson waited until the flanks had moved out and around into position and they too crept forward:

Minutes passed and with their passing the voices became louder. Carefree voices, sometimes loud and boisterous – other times a lone voice rushing on in solitude followed by laughter.

The Japs were unaware that they were being trapped in a vise. Capet stooped and listened. He nodded approval. The approach of his men was noiseless and undetected. He strained his eyes to search between the brush to see if the enemy was within sight but the vegetation was too thick, but he was close, not more than 50 yards away. Fifteen feet to the right of Lt. Capet, Cold Steel Fagan lay stretched out flat, his right hand lightly curling around the trigger of his M-1. His head lay against the stock of his piece and the right gray eye was gently pressed to the sights of the steadily held weapon. Lined squarely in the scope was the Jap who was holding forth amongst his friends, keeping them laughing. His left side was turned to Fagan - a thinness of the foliage in front of Fagan's hidden vantage point permitted him to make out at least 100 Japs through the slightly rustling leaves of the tropical bushes.

Fagan waited, his mouth dry from the tension. The orders had indicated that the Lieutenant would fire first, and then the others would follow suit. But every shot must count as a wild bullet might catch one of the encircling group. Fagan's eyes were half-smiling - he had his boy all picked out -

just don't anybody pick him off before he did. Suddenly, the Japs stopped talking and Fagan could see that a sound had attracted the Nip's attention. Instinctively yellow hands began reaching for weapons which had been laid aside. Fagan held his breath, remembering the rest of the attack plan - if the enemy seemed to be aware of the attack, pick out a target and fire. The Jap had moved from his upright position in the center of the clearing but he had not passed from the sight of Fagan's weapon. An almost imperceptible squeezing of the hair-thin trigger and the boom of the heavy throated M-1 was joined by the splattering of the Jap's head as the 30 caliber bullet plunged through the best target Fagan had, the ear lobe, and pounded the now inept brain into nothingness.

Quickly Fagan picked out another target amongst the wildly scampering Japs, but before he could squeeze off a second round other rifles from the surrounding jungle spoke and the screaming Jap spun twice as two bullets eagerly entered into his body. Now the entire jungle was alive with the crackling of rifles and the thinner voice of Lt. Capet's carbine joined in the deadly fire as the trapped Japs dashed first in one direction and then another as they realized there was no escape. One Jap, small, thin, and emaciated, stopped suddenly in his wild scrambling and rising to his full height in the center of the clearing, raised both hands above his head - and then melodramatically lowered them as bullet after bullet eagerly fought their way into the perfect target. A look of disbelief covered his face as he joined the other corpses on the ground.

"Hold your fire!" Capet yelled from a kneeling position. "Blue, Garver, check the area." The two Marines scampered into the area, their approach covered by the nine other men. Garver signaled the others on. Cautiously the patrol entered the clearing, which had evidently been merely a rendezvous area for the Japs.

"Make sure they're all dead." Sgt. Konkright called to the troops as they began to inspect the bodies curiously - it being the first enemy most of them had ever seen. McPherson held his M-1 to the head of a Jap and unloaded four bullets into the corpse.

"Don't waste ammo!" Fagan growled between his teeth as he grasped the small one's arm. Then walking to the next body he placed his bayonet attached rifle to the left side of the Nip's back - leaned on it and squashingly pushed it into the man's back. He looked at Liverlip whose face was now ashen, "Be careful, you don't hit a rib, though, you might break your blade."

"Knock it off." Lt. Capet yelled, his eyes questioningly studying the hard faced Fagan. "Check the bodies for any information which might be helpful to intelligence and then stack the bodies. Let's get moving - it's getting late."

The patrol wearily filed back along the plantation road. The hot sun was dipping fast behind the extinct volcano casting beautiful, long, and mysterious shadows across the rows of coconut trees and white glistening sand. But the beauty of the site was lost to the men of the patrol. They marched, seemingly effortless with their rifles slung over their shoulders with their thumb of the right hand tucked beneath the sweat stained leather straps. Their heads were held high beneath the steel helmets and their eyes were cast straight ahead - but not focusing on anything. The eyes were unseeing - or perhaps seeing visions which were not there - visions of home, of familiar faces - of one familiar face which they would never see again.

In rout step the legs, automatically thrusting themselves forward, carried sweaty, begrimed bodies - the bodies of strangely unlike but like human beings. The two men at the end of the column emphasized the unlikeness - Fagan and Blue - the former, young, slim, hard, a professional Marine - the latter, pouchy, older, soft, a civilian at heart - but alike in one thing, the inward satisfaction of achievement the encounter of the day had brought to them. The tracking, trapping, and merciless murder they had participated, relished in. The grim but pleasant satisfaction they had received at the sight of blood, life-giving blood, escaping from the fatal holes brought about by the bullets from guns their trigger fingers had triggered. Both these men had been well-reared-taught the wrongness of bringing harm to another - that killing was wrong - who grimaced at the recounting in the daily papers of one person having taken the life of another.

Lt. Capet slowed his step as he rounded the deep curve of the island shore of Ceremoni Cove and turned his head to the grave of Frank Brabern, still fresh with the newness of not forgotten sorrow. The Lieutenant gently touched his helmet in salute as he went by, each man in turn looked at the grave as they passed – some mouthing silent prayers, others crossing themselves, and Fagan, bringing up the rear, smiled as he looked at the grave – seeming to be talking directly to the dead Brabern.

"We got the no good son-of-a-bitchin' bastards, Frank!" Then dropping to one knee, he put a hand on the damp brown, soil which covered the corpse of his friend he crossed himself - the first time in two years and patting the grave softly said.

"We'll all meet at the Hurricane, buddy."

Slowly, he rose, put his hand into his dungaree pocket, pulled out the small Camel carton, and placed it beneath the cross. Then smartly saluting, he turned and double-timed to the rear of the distant column.

Chapter 6

"God watch over you." Chaplain Jerome Barnes intoned the words almost silently as he stood beside the rail of the A.P.A., his right hand raised in a reverent salute to the men who climbed down the netting to the bouncing landing craft below. The darkness in the Pacific night battled to hang on but the horizon was becoming light beyond the small island which heaved with every shell burst. That island was Peleliu.

Cold Steel Fagan waited beside J.C. Malton, Liverlip McPherson, Jim Richardson and Ross Miller for the signal to go over the side. Carefully slung over their backs were the weapons upon which their lives depended, rifles, and strapped to each leg was a jungle knife, the most imposing belonging to Cold Steel. It measured ten inches and its blade was honed to razor sharpness by its owner. Hugging the Marines backs were single packs holding a change of socks and little else. Crisscrossed over the pack straps clung the wide band which secured the gas mask case; it would be discarded as soon as the beach was reached. It had only proved to be a cumbersome nuisance in previous campaigns.

"We're next!" Cold Steel flung the words out of the side of his mouth as he shifted the weight of the rifle on his slim right shoulder.

"Up and over," the small boats officer waved the line over. Beneath his breath he added, "good luck."

The sea was acting up and the boys in the boats had a difficult time holding the nets in the boats. A loose net and the dangling men would be crushed against the ship as the small boat pitched in the swells.

"Watch my fingers! Damn it!" the painful cry came from a man below Malton as the latter gingerly felt for the next rung.

"Hold onto the side strands, you guys." the coxman yelled up. "Come on, you boots, we ain't got all day!"

Dropping heavily into the half-loaded landing craft, J.C. rearranged his binding gear, already loosening the gasmask case for quick disposal. Taking his rifle from his shoulder, he gingerly cradled it as he moved to the back of the boat where Cold Steel already sat, his knife in one hand, whetstone in the other.

"Salt air is going to rust that." J. C. grinned as he dropped beside the lanky Marine, his stomach tossing a bit from a combination of the pitching boat and the nearness of fear.

Cold Steel pushed his steel helmet back from his forehead. "Scared, Malty?" he tested the blade without looking at the Marine beside him.

Malton pulled his knees up before him and cradled the M-1 across his lap. He was perspiring heavily - the day would be hot! "Scared to death," he spoke the words slowly, without embarrassment.

For the first time Cold Steel turned his head toward Malton. He looked straight into his eyes and quietly he said, "You got company."

The words sank into Malton's head slowly as he realized their truthfulness. His eyes, accustomed to the grayness of dawn, played about the landing craft. The coxman gunned the motor behind him and the small boat shot from beside the lumbering assault ship. Sitting against the bulkheads of the boat, the Marines stared straight ahead, their eyes unseeing, their mouths silent. Fear was each man's companion, a fear which bit deep into the innards of recruit and seasoned veteran alike. For the man going into combat for the first time, the fear was one of ignorance, of not knowing what the next minutes would bring. For the veteran of other landings the fear was one of knowledge of knowing what the next few minutes held - but the fear was not stronger in one than in the other, both groups felt the gnawing spreading, becoming all consuming.

The silence was broken by the slap of the waves on the flat ramp of the boat as the coxman jockeyed the clumsy boat into the small circle of landing craft some two miles off shore. Cold Steel raised himself to his feet, his head crouched beneath the outline of the bulkheads of the open boat. His eyes watched the two wakes of white foam which raced toward the beach. He shuddered inwardly, the first two waves were rushing for the beach, they would be next. He turned his eyes toward the huge ship they had just left. His mouth dropped open.

"Well, I'll be a son of a bitch." his mouth curved into a huge grin. Other Marines scrambled to their feet.

"What's up, Cold Steel?" Malton stood full length, his stature not forcing him to crouch. He followed the direction of Cold Steel's finger to where a sailor was sitting astride one of the ships whaleboats, a paint brush in hand as he added a thirteenth battle flag to the twelve already there. Thirteen combats. The Marines roared as they watched. The ship sat two miles off shore and soon would be leaving but the crew claimed a combat star for the operation.

"Damn you guys! Here we go." The coxman gunned the motor and the small landing craft shot through the choppy waters toward burning Peleliu.

J.C. crouched beside Cold Steel. Silently the lanky Marine reached out and shook hands with those about him. He turned the hand to Malton last and squeezed his hand, "Stay close, buddy!"

Malton nodded and turned his attention to making sure his rifle was set. He clicked the magazine into place and gently pushed the safety button. His heart pounded so loudly that it was difficult for him to breathe. Suddenly the sound of small arms fire, American, could be heard, followed by the whining cry of answering Japanese fire. Soon a throaty heavy caliber U.S. machine gun joined in a fire fight with a screeching Jap Mambu. Malton pulled his head down lower - the beach was hot.

Whoosh! A giant mortar shell landed close beside the beach bound small boat and it rocked as the concussion wave tossed against the side.

"Here we go!" the coxman sat hunched at his controls, his face wet with the salty spray. "You've got about 25 yards of water - brace." The grinding of the boat's bottom on the coral floor of the ocean was followed almost immediately by the metallic lowering of the ramp.

"Let's go!" 2nd Lt. Hal Davis called as he darted toward the ramp and his first combat. The men followed their leader who jumped feet first into the shallow water. 2nd Lt. Davis had not yet reached the coral floor of the beach when he had fought his last battle. A small hole directly between surprised eyes snuffed out a future which had taken 22 years to build. Beside the prostrate body of the Lt. fell other bodies. A mambu perched high above the beach, strapped in a cluster of fronds atop a coconut tree, played a stream of death giving fire across the gasping mouth of the landing craft on Beach Red, its fanatical operator frothing at the mouth in wild ecstasy.

"Over the side!" Malton didn't even recognize his own voice, as he shed his pack and gas mask as his eyes followed the tracers tearing apart flesh and bone of those in front of him. The warm water of the Pacific felt clean as he let it close over him. Desperately he tried to swim away from the shore but the rifle dragged his progress. Making a split-second decision, he shed his trusty rifle just as the water about him was kicked up by the hot lead from the machine gun. Quickly, he surface dived to the bottom, his fingers grasping the cutting edges of coral. He swam away from the beach, fear urging him on.

Malton's eyes smarted from the brine of the sea water and lungs cried for air as he pushed himself beneath the surface of the water to the protective open sea. Gasping for desperately needed air, he bounced to the surface, his eyes wide with apprehension. Floating deep in the water he scanned the beach.

Everywhere he looked, men were lying on their stomachs in the sand in hastily scooped foxholes. Some were firing into the trees, but most just drew themselves in as close to the sand as possible to escape the withering fire which pelted from the trees. Flaming landing craft bobbled helplessly in the shallow water off the beach, their coxman hanging lifelessly over the dead controls.

The Japs had really tricked the assault troops and the Navy, especially the latter. For three days the heavy Navy warships had belted the shore with their big guns and for the past twenty-four hours the island had burned so heavily that it was impossible to see the atoll for the smoke. There had been some doubt among the Navy men that there would be any enemy alive - some joke! They weren't ghosts behind those light weapons and certainly not controlling the mortars which so effectively were pattering the beach with shells.

Malton treaded water, the weird sight before him almost unbelievable. Quickly he spun his body in the water until it faced the sea - there in the distance the ships sat, all eyes of the crews and troops watching the massacre taking place on the beach. Another wave of small boats were bearing in toward the beach. A moment of indecision almost strangled Malton and then he spun around again and slowly treading water moved back toward the beach. He kept his head low in the water as he made toward a drifting landing barge. Coming along side he edged his way toward its gaping mouth, his stomach revolted as he pulled his head over the ramp and almost bumped into a head whose sightless eyes were open in death. A dozen other dead Marines lay in the barge.

Pitching violent, J.C. pushed himself - away from the barge and struck out with a slapping water-logged stroke toward the beach. Bullets kicked up before him and effortlessly he slipped once again beneath the water until he was well away from the spot where he had submerged. Slowly he let his head rise above the water and then gulping deeply of the air he pushed down once again until he felt the side of a barge which lay stuck on the coral bottom of the beach. He inched his way forward, his feet slipping on the coral floor. Playing his eyes on the line of trees 75 yards inland he waited. One minute passed, then two, three - his keen eyes caught no glint of a rifle barrel in any of the trees and no flash of fire. Bracing himself for an expectorant burst of bullets he dashed up the beach, his heavy clothing slowing his speed. He ran 15 yards and then dived into a shallow mortar shell hole which already had an occupant.

Panting heavily, he buried his head between his hands, his heart pounding with fatigue and his dry tongue thick in his mouth.

"Been for a swim?" the voice was cool, relaxed. Malton pulled away his right hand, never raising his head. Focusing his right eye he saw Cold Steel smiling at him!

"Cold Steel! Christ, I thought you were dead!" Malton scooted over in the sand, careful not to expose himself to the small arm fire which had once again picked up its tempo.

"Pretty damn close to it right now, buddy." The smile had left Fagan's face as he looked behind them. Dead Marines lay scattered over the beach - the war over for them. Slowly he fastened the strap on his helmet and braced himself for movement.

"Where the hell you going?" Malton whispered between his teeth.

"Be back in a minute!" Cold Steel snapped and squirmed down toward the water line, his rifle cradled expertly in the crook of his arms to keep the mechanism out of the sand.Malton followed him with his eyes until he disappeared into a shell hole.

"Company A! Get ready to move!" The voice rose over the firing as Lt. Fred Carney tried to consolidate his troops,

Malton felt helpless and naked as he hugged the sand with no weapon, not even a hand grenade. The noise of loosened sand made Malton quickly go for his jungle knife. He relaxed as Cold Steel dropped back into the hole.

"You'll need these," Fagan pushed a rifle and helmet toward Malton. The squat Marine grunted his thanks and disregarded the drying blood on the helmet liner as he put it on his head, grateful for its protection. Quickly his hands went over the rifle, dislodging some of the sand which had entered the breach when its previous owner had fallen to the earth for the last time.

For the first time since the ramp of the landing craft had dropped down on the coral rock of Peleliu, J.C. Malton relaxed - perhaps that's not the word for it, as taut nerves unwound from their twisted, tortured anxiety , more aptly fit the description. The feel of the M-1 in his hands accounted for the easoning of the tension. No longer was he naked, now he had a powerful speaking weapon of his own, his life expectancy seemed prolonged.

Turning carefully over on his back he took his pipe and tobacco from their waterproof container and slowly fingered the tobacco into the well-burned bowl. He smiled as he recalled the months that had passed since he first received it.

"Don't get too comfortable!" Cold Steel peered over the top of the foxhole, his eyes glistening from the action. "Carney's gettin' ready to push. Sit tight!

I'm going to get the scoop." With a shower of sand left by his scrambling feet, Cold Steel was gone.

Malton climbed carefully to the lip of the hole. The damn fool! Fagan dodged and ran, crawled and squirmed flat on the deck. Every shell and mortar hole was reached amidst flying bullets. It seemed to Malton the lanky Marine didn't have a prayer but a prayer he offered and smiled as Cold Steel made his last dive into the hole where Lt. Carney had set up his company command post.

Malton's eyes slowly played across the terrain around him. The beach was white and clean - it had been before the blood of dying Marines had tinged it - now it was cluttered with Marines, both living and dead, and the discarded equipment of the four waves which had made the beach. Several thousand men were on the beaches - several thousand men who but minutes before had crouched as he had in the belly of a landing craft knowing that some would be dead while others would live, with all feeling that the decision of their fate was not theirs but all feeling that death would come to the others and not to them. It had been exemplified quite clearly he thought as he recalled the old story of the 11 men who lined up for a dangerous patrol into the Jap infested jungle of Guadalcanal.

"This is one hell of mission, men," the officer in charge had told them as he stood eyeing each one carefully. "A hell of a mission! Believe me! In my opinion probably only one of you will get back alive." The words had sunk in slowly and each Marine had then sadly looked at his buddies in line. Through all their thoughts sifted but one thought. "I'm sure going to miss those guys."

He smiled at the memory, a humorless smile that tugged deeply and melancholy at his heart. Many of his close buddies, intimates for months had felt that way, felt the sorrow that came with the knowledge that close ties would soon be snapped and now, they lay dead on the hot sands and warm salty shore side of a hell-hole called Peleliu. The increased sound of small arm fire jerked him from his thoughts. He wiggled his way to the top of the shell hole. Cold Steel was on his zigzagging way back to the hole. Covering him as best he could, J. C filled a clip of 30 caliber bullets into the trees that lined the jungle edge.

Cold Steel landed face first in the shell hole, his dungarees blackened by perspiration. It was hot and the coral of the island reflected the rays of the heat like giant movie reflectors.

"Move out at 0950," Fagan panted as he lighted a cigarette. Malton glanced at his watch. Had they been on this rock only two hours? "Casualties are heavy all along the beach. Lt. says we're operating at half strength. You seen any of the guys?"

Malton shook his head and the perspiration splattered about him. He wiped a grimy sleeve across his face leaving a smudge of dirt on his cheek. He nodded to the coral reef five hundred yards from the beach where many landing barges had hung up and where the Japs with their mortars, anti-boat, and mountain guns had taken a heavy toll of life and equipment. "We'll never reach our phase line today." Malton said quietly.

The island of Peleliu was an essential obstacle in the war for the Central Pacific. It was the last great Japanese naval base and more important, contained a hard surface runway where planes could operate against General Douglas Macarthur's troops in his assault on the Philippines which was expected in the not-too-distant future.

The operation was to last but three days according to the commanding general - only three phase lines were on the operational map. Somebody fouled up and bad. The scene around Malton and Fagan was one of chaos and no relief in sight. Their objective - the Fifth Marines, was to cross the two mile wide island over the airstrip - that objective wouldn't be reached if they didn't get off the beach.

"Here we go," Fagan flicked the safety off his rifle and winked at Malton. Suddenly the area was alive with small arms and machine gun fire as the men of the Fifth charged up the beach. The lead was flying at them thick and heavy as each man desperately tried for a crevice to fall into. Malton rolled down a shell hole and grunted as Fagan landed atop him.

"Holy Hell!" Fagan whistled through his teeth. "There must be millions of them." The perspiration rolled down his nose and he flicked it off with his forefinger.

"We didn't move 45 yards," Malton wheezed as he looked toward the fringe of trees which were another 40 yards away. He pulled his head in as a bullet kicked up the sand several feet away. Suddenly shells began blasting on the beach. Systematically they played over the area. Malton cringed in his hole with every blast. The Japs had every inch of the beach zeroed in and were methodically blasting the life of the troops on the beaches. Light machine guns and rifles were still firing steadily from the trees and some of the Japs had been sent to their ancestors, their bodies hanging limply by the ropes which had held them in the trees.

The hours of hell passed, the men of the 1st, 5th and 7th Marines crushed against the sand, unable to move. More men died, many more wounded. The total casualties the first day would reach 2,000. At noon the crescendo increased, heralding a counter-attack by the Japanese. For the first time the pinned down men of the First Marine Division could see their enemies as they repulsed the little yellow men who were determined to throw the invaders back into the sea. But the men of the Corps, true to their tradition, held fast. They weren't advancing, but damn if they would retreat

Twice more before 1600, the regiments repulsed the counter attacks, each time advancing a little on their own until they had penetrated the fringe of the jungle, a bare hundred yards from the slapping waves of the water-line.

Malton crouched behind the shattered hulk of a coconut tree, Fagan 10 yards farther inland behind a huge boulder of coral. For the first time they didn't feel naked as they had on the beach, where it had seemed that every jap in the Imperial Empire was sighting down a rifle at them.

"J.C.!" Fagan called to his buddy. "Over here," the lanky Marine was waving Malton toward him. J. C. zigzagged to his friend crouching low to the ground. When he reached the coral he followed Fagan's finger.

From the of the comparatively treeless coral, a view through the less than 50 yards of the jungle disclosed the open airport. Malton was surprised at the hard packed runways which looked like concrete. Then he saw an object moving. He squinted his eyes - Jap medium tanks were moving toward them across the field.

"Tanks!" Fagan shouted. The cry passed swiftly down the line and the Marines drew tightly into position to thwart the attack. Riding on the tanks were the Japanese Infantry, perched precariously against the superstructure. The word was passed to hold fire until each man could draw a sure shot at the riders.

Malton squinted his eyes against the piercing sun and watched unbelievingly. The tanks rattled and coughed as they came across the field. They looked like toys in comparison to the U.S.'s tanks. Slowly they drew near the small fringe of jungle. Above the din came the signal - "Fire!"

Carefully J. C. picked out his target, a body clinging to the side of one of the lead tanks. Slowly he squeezed the trigger - the body lurched and fell to the coral. Malton cringed as a following tank rumbled over the still form. It was like a day in the shooting gallery - the concealed Marines picking off the Japanese infantrymen. Strangely enough, the tanks did not once fire the cannon which protruded from their armor. The tanks suddenly, their backs shorn of troops, turned to the right, toward the ridge and groaned away. A shout of relief rose from the troops only to die away as another and larger wave of tanks was spotted crossing the field. A deeper throated growl was heard behind Malton and Fagan, and J.C. crawled back toward the beach. His eyes brightened as he saw a dozen Sherman tanks being unloaded from large landing crafts. As he watched one was hit by a 150mm Jap mortar and it turned turtle. The Japs, entrenched in the hills, were letting go with every weapon at their command.

Stubbornly, the tanks formed their attack position and throatily growled their way to the beach. Their heavier fire power was cheered by the Marines in the jungle as the heavily armed tanks moved on to the airfield. It was strictly no contest as the toy tanks withered and burned from the smashing fire attack. The battle lasted but a few minutes and then the Shermans withdrew to the comparative safety of the jungle leaving the burning Jap tanks before the Marine lines.

Darkness was falling fast and the word was passed to dig in for the night - the word held a dreadful meaning for Marines who had been in combat before. The comparatively few hours of tropical darkness held a terror that would linger through the long days. Sleep was impossible under the combat conditions. It was a time for harassment - of whining bullets, whizzing mortar, whomping artillery shells - and silent infiltrators.

Malton and Fagan took turns digging the foxholes, one digging, the other standing watch, eyes carefully moving from one tree to another, from one crag to another looking for the snipers who held in his rifle life or death. Two foxholes were dug facing the airfield, both joined at the beach ward side and forming a letter V. A better field of fire was covered in this manner. The slits were sloped a little upward at the airfield end and at the connecting point a small hole, the size of a grapefruit, was dug about 4 feet deep. In theory, if a hand grenade was lobbed into the foxhole, it could be kicked into the hole at the bottom and the depth surrounded by dirt would absorb most of the shrapnel, the only problem was getting the grenade down the slope into the hole before it exploded.

It was already dark when the two had finished their foxhole - the task had been made more difficult by the coral which had mixed with the part dirt, part sand island surface. All about them, other perspiring Marines were completing their holes. A runner crouched, running from one fox-hole to the other giving the password for the night. The small arms fire had almost stopped and the big shells were not being dropped by the Japs for the time being, but far out to sea the big naval guns spoke occasionally and they could be heard wheezing overhead on their way inland.

J. C. dropped into his foxhole, his body settling against the hard ground, his rifle pointing toward the airfield, a portion of which was lighted by a burning hangar at the far end. Cold Steel sat in the lower part of his foxhole - to J.C.'s right and opened a K-Ration. He cursed as he opened a small round can of egg salad - at least that's what the manufacturer of the slop called it.

"You gonna chow down?" Fagan asked, his mouth full of the dry, foul food.

"Not hungry." Malton wiped his hand. across his perspiring face. He pulled his canteen from his belt, shook it gently to determine the amount of life giving liquid there and then cautiously raised the canteen to his lips and poured the tepid water into his parched mouth. He allowed himself but one swallow. Slowly and carefully he replaced the canteen into its holder "Got much water left, Cold Steel?"

Fagan shook his canteen on his belt. "Nope! Ain't seen a water carrier, either, have you?"

Malton thought. Slowly he shook his head, then added aloud, "Ain't any on the beach!" He thought a moment, his hands sifting the coral sand. "Can't be much water on this rock, either."

"Tighten up on the drinking." Fagan offered as he made sure his canteen cap was tightly secured. "It may be a long dry spell." He dropped into his fox hole and settled for the long night.

The minutes seemed like hours as total and complete darkness settled over Peleliu. The small arm fire completely ceased in the 5th Marines area. Occasionally to their left and closer to the ridge which was to come to be known as Bloody Nose, a small fire fight would break out between a whining Jap 31 Mambu and a throaty 30 caliber machine gun. But the heavy 150 mm Japanese mortars followed their deadly composing of the small beachhead. They came whizzling almost silently and then whommp! Every 20 seconds another would fall at another target of the beachhead. They left suffering and death in their wake. The corpsmen had a busy night.

J. C. couldn't sleep - even if he had dared to, he couldn't have! He braced his body every time another mortar announced its arrival. Death was certainly coming a calling, but it was not death that he was afraid of - he had been too close to it before. He didn't want to die, but he wasn't going to fear death. A smile half-crossed his lips in the darkness, then what was he afraid? The smile froze unconsciously on his face - was it the uncertainty of death? Was it how he would face death? Was it - ? Slowly he shook his head -

Whatever it was - there was no question about it! He was afraid.

"J.C." the sound came from Fagan's foxhole. Malton answered softly. "I'm going down to the beach. I'm thirsty." The words struck Malton right between the eyes!

"You crazy bastard!" He almost shouted in his anger. "You'll get killed!" He shook with fury.

"See you!" Fagan was gone.

J. C. trembled with anger. His best buddy was a maniac. He knew it only too well! He looked for trouble if it didn't come his way. Cold Steel Fagan! Damn him!

Minutes passed and Malton anxiously awaited the return of Fagan. Minutes which seemed like hours passed frightfully slowly. The occasional whine of a Japanese sniper's bullet was followed by the sharp crack of a Marine's M-1. The eerie light of a flare cast the shattered terrain of Peleliu into a marinade of gruesome crags and valleys.

The ridge was ghostly to his left as the wavering light descended fitfully to earth. Stripped bare of vegetation its crevices were amplified by shadows. Tracer bullets beat a path on the incline of the hill, only to be answered by another line of orange red tracers racing down. The First Marine Regiment, known in the corps only as the First Marines, had their work cut out for them. The securing of the ridge would not come as easy as the high command had carefully calculated. The spine of the island which ran down the center of the coral rock was pockmarked with caves, each a deathtrap to attacking Marines. Malton sighed and brushed a grimy hand across his tired eyes. Where the hell was Cold Steel?

A noise to his right drew the prostrate Marine's attention. Malton half relaxed sensing the return of Cold Steel. Dimly he could see the crouching figure approaching his arms close to the ground. Suddenly, a flare died behind the figure, outlying the silhouette. Malton strained his eyes, something not exactly reacting according to normalcy. Suddenly the glint of an object in the right hand of the man confirmed his growing suspicion. He rolled quickly over on his back as the figure came hurtling through the air. Instinctively

J. C. raised his hands to fend off the infiltration and as he did so he felt a sharp pain in the inside of his right wrist as the Jap's knife pierced the skin. Fumbling in the darkness J. C. grasped the small wrist and applied all his pressure to take away the knife. The twobodies merged as they twisted in the confines of the foxhole. The smell of the Jap flooded J.C.'s nostrils as he slipped his right arm around the enemy's head and dug his fingers into the throat of the attacker. Malton heard the Jap gasp and struggle for freedom. Panic overcame the small, wiry man and it too became his adversary. J.C. could feel the man's grasp on the knife loosen and sensed rather than felt the knife slip to the bottom of the foxhole. In an instant he released the wrist and applied both hands to the Nips throat.

Fiercely the Jap withered, but each twisting motion enabled J. C. to get better position until he had the Jap pinned beneath him. Almost unconsciously he tightened his grip on the thin throat, his fingers digging deeper and deeper into the windpipe. A flare burst open above and Malton was shocked back into sanity. He stopped shaking the head upward and downward and gently let it come to rest in the foxhole. A 31 mm bullet whined close to the hole and he pressed his body down closer to the corpse, his face almost against the sallow yellow one of the Jap. Intently he stared into the bulging unseeing eyes, revulsion and nausea overcoming him. Throwing himself out of the hole he retched, tearing his empty stomach apart. He lay flat on the sharp coral, his stomach unable to answer the demand of his sensitivity. Painfully the retching eased and Malton lay still, his head turned toward the corpse lying still in the foxhole. He rubbed his hands against his dungarees as if to cleanse them of the act which they had just accomplished.

He had just killed a man - a living, breathing human being! His heart tried to repulse the thought. It was not the first enemy he had killed - of that he was certain, but it was the first he had actually been keenly aware of. Jungle fighting was a blessing, a chaplain had once told him because the dense undergrowth hid the enemies from each other and bullets were aimed merely at movements and though men died - and died violently as a result of those bullets, the men behind the rifles which fired the bullets didn't know for sure if they or someone else had actually done the deed. But this had been different, his two hands, now consciously oversize, had grasped a man's throat, and surely and deliberately had stopped the flow of air into the lungs - and, he shut his eyes at the thought, he had kept exerting the pressure long after life had left. In the eerie light of the flare he looked upon the man's face - it was a young face, unlike the posters of Japanese he had seen with protruding teeth and slanting eyes. The boy must have been his age, with parents back in Japan somewhere, as anxious as were his for their sons well-being. Maybe he had a girl - or, Malton uncontrollably shuddered, a wife or family - and - now he was dead, dead on a Pacific hunk of coral. J. C. buried his head in his hands and tears came into his eyes. He lay there for a minute, then two and slowly, he regained control and rationality.

The Jap had come to kill him - had watched from a concealed place the departure of Cold Steel and then had quietly sneaked into his foxhole with a deadly knife ready to kill him. The choice had not been Malton's - it was his life or the Jap's and God had been on his side - and now the Jap was dead in his foxhole. The thought struck home more clearly as a fire fight broke out. He grinned as he thought of the dead Jap in the protective shelter of the foxhole, while he lay here exposed to the Jap fire and that of his own men.

Gingerly he slid into the foxhole, squeezing in beside the Jap. The body was still warm, but the foxhole was too small for the both of them. A fiendish thought raced through his mind and he fairly burst into laughter. Cold Steel was a joker - and a sadist at that, reveling in the agony of others, as he pulled trick after trick. Now it was his turn to be the butt end of the joke. Silently, he reached under the Jap and lifted the body, rolling it over the lip of the foxhole and down into the crater of Cold Steel's indention in the coral. Then Malton lowered himself as comfortable as possible into his hole and awaited the return of his friend.

Cold Steel Fagan gingerly picked his way along the equipment laden beach. The stench of death pinched his nostrils. Dragging in the island sand as he dashed from one protective cover to another were four canteens, dangling from shoulder strap length as Fagan carried them in one hand, the other preoccupied with his ready rifle.

The thin, drawn face was immobile now, as it had been when he removed the canteens from the dead bodies of fellow Marines. The mouth was drawn in a straight line, the cold gray eyes unblinking and unwavering as they tried to pierce the night looking for any danger which lurked in abundance about him whether from the enemy or his own comrades who were edgy with the uneasiness that comes with the first night of a landing.

Picking out familiar landmarks, Fagan moved quickly, dodging heavy concentration of his own troops. Silently he passed through the sparse stretch of coconut trees and vegetation which constituted the jungle between the beach and the airfield. Dropping to his stomach he carefully surveyed the ground before him and a flash of a smile crossed his face as he recognized the front that he and Malton had faced as they dug their foxhole. His eyes traveled to a shattered coconut tree, half of its trunk hanging off to the right, silhouetted in the flares from the ridge to the left. He counted foxholes - one, two, three, four - there was his. Cautiously he made his way to the edge of the foxhole his nose twitching as it did when he smelled Japs. Putting the canteens on the lip of the dark hole, he jumped in and came in contact with the body of the Jap. Cursing softly he grabbed the nip by the face with his left hand, meanwhile whipping out his scalpel sharp jungle knife. The battle was on!

Cold Steel groaned, grunted, gasped for breath as he sought to will the attack of the invader. The action lasted a minute at the most - a short minute to Malton, suppressing laughter in the other half of the two pronged foxhole - a long minute to the struggling Cold Steel, his life supposedly in peril. Then all was still - the battle had been "fought" and won and Cold Steel now composed himself, perspiration rolling from his pointed chin from the exertion of the "combat."

"J.C." Cold Steel's voice was breathless.

Malton tried to control the desire to burst out laughing. On the third attempt, he managed to utter a sober "Yeh!"

"I think I got me a Jap!" the voice of Cold Steel Fagan was tinged with pride as he intoned the words.

Malton waited a second as if awed by the announcement and then slowly, clearly, but softly whispered across the coral to his buddy. "You mean the dead one I rolled into your foxhole awhile ago?"

The darkness seemed to deepen and even the noise of battle could not break the silence which fell over the area. Malton could not even hear Cold Steel breathe and then like a steaming locomotive, the air came hissing through the lanky Marine's teeth. "Why, you dirty low blowing bastard!"

Malton broke into subdued laughter, uncontrollably louder as Fagan rolled the corpse from the foxhole and resumed his position facing the airstrip.

As the night deepened and the longness of the minutes lengthened, the incident of the corpse was all but forgotten. The word had been passed down the line to be on the lookout for an expected counter attack during the night. Both Malton and Fagan lay face down in the foxholes, their rifles pointing over the lips of the holes, pointing, with safety's off, toward the direction of any forthcoming attack. Neither of the Marines had slept for almost 24 hours, but the eyelids, though heavy with fatigue, never dropped drowsily - sleep never bothered the troops in the front lines!

The night was periodically brightened with a burning flare, whose eerie shadow casting light wavered over the airport searching for attacking Japanese, or by the bursting of heavy naval shells on the ridge to the left of them. The word passed unofficially along was that the line was running pretty straight on the fringe of the airstrip. Scuttlebutt had it that the First Marines, on the left flank and closest to the ridge had taken a heavy pasting suffering heavy casualties during the hours since the landing. The original plan for taking the island had been quickly discarded and a more realistic one substituted.

Heavy firing broke out occasionally but it was only a one-sided fire fight with nervous Marines shooting at shadows that appeared to move when the wavering, shifting light of falling flares hit high spots on the terrain.

Malton and Fagan, too, were sure that they saw movement before them and had expended a slip of bullets each on nothing more than coral formations lining the air strip. The night slowly passed, the minutes dragging painfully on. The firing tapered off with the acquisition of experience in the line.

"Die, you Malines, die!" the high pitched voice seemed to come from the right of Malton's and Fagan's foxhole. The area was quickly traversed with more than two dozen rifles and machine guns. Then silence resumed and with it the feeling of self-satisfied action which comes with having wiped out an enemy.

"Die! you Malines, die!" the voice seemed to come from the same spot and bewildered Marines again flung lead to the spot, this time accompanied by earth shaking hand grenades. A white flare burst noisily in the sky and as it fell the troops strained their eyes looking for the blasted body of their tormentor. The light seemed to duck and dodge its own smoke as it fell, pointing out one spot momentarily and then searching out another spot on the near smooth terrain. As the flare settled to the ground and burned itself out, the Marines waited!

"Die, you Malines, die!" the voice was mockingly shrill. Again the rifles barked, and the grenades pounded the terrain.

"Hold your fire!" The word was shouted down the line. Morosely the men, now troops, realized the logic of the words. Thousands of rounds could be expended on a ghost of a voice as it pierced the night - from where, no one could tell in the echo-carrying openness of the strip.

Malton and Fagan waited, their eyes watering from the strain of trying to penetrate the blackness. They tensed every 15 minutes or so when the voice again audibly voiced his epithet. The night was the longest in the lines to the two Marines.

The first lighting of the new day was greeted with disbelief by the men of the First Marine Division. The disbelief stemmed from the prolonged agony of the endless hours of darkness which seemed never to end. Cupped hands over barred luminous dials of watches had shown the time every thirty seconds during the night. Disbelief of the accuracy had been shown clearly by the tapping of the watches by their owners. But now - across the narrow strip of flat island, the sky on the horizon was beginning to lighten - slowly but surely - heralding the beginning of a new day! - Day - the tired bodies of the Marines seemed to revive with the thought. True, the new day might bring death - surely, would bring death - but the daylight brought sharply into focus the land on which they must fight. The nights held the terror - the fear of the unknown enhanced by the knowledge of the night fighting ability of the enemy. But now daylight was once again the order - not the mere huddling in foxholes awaiting the whim of the Japanese.

Malton watched the sky brighten, watched the early dawn creep across the skies toward him. The tropic dawn as well as sunset is accomplished quickly, and within five minutes the airstrip before him and the ridge to the left were clearly and sharply defined in the light of the sun as it came over the horizon. A smile crossed his lips as his eyes sought out coral banks and discarded Japanese oil drums which during the night had taken on the appearance of Japanese.

The scene on the airstrip was one of complete inactivity. Nothing moved the landing field itself with its X'ed runways of packed coral - not unlike concrete - were devoid of any activity. Pock marks along the strips' length, testified to blasting from the ships of the fleet and bombings of both Navy and Marine Carrier based planes. The remains of Zero's were strewn about the field, but Malton was surprised as to the few there were. No heavy planes were visible - he surmised correctly that they had been flown elsewhere in the shrinking empire, before the full force of American air and sea power had been brought to the task.

Far across the island J.C. could see what was left of hangers and operations buildings nestled between the landing strips and the ridge. Even now, the burning materials of the structures still smoldered casting off towers of smoke.

The stillness of the entire picture before him finally dawned on the stocky Marine as he lay in his foxhole. Only an occasional shell from the sea interrupted the quietness as harassing fire played high on the ridge now devoid of all vegetation. Squinting his eyes against the bright sun which now rose from the sea. J.C. could make out what appeared to be openings everywhere on the side of the cliff. Caves, hundreds of caves, the reality struck home with a thud - and there was but one way to get them out and that was by infantry action with flame throwers, hand grenades and concussion bombs.

"Cold Steel!" Malton called to his buddy. Receiving no answer he called again. Still no answer was forthcoming. Cautiously Malton raised his body and peered into the joined foxhole. Fagan was on his back, his mouth open, sound asleep. Dropping back into the shallow depth of his own hole, Malton smiled at the ability of his fearless friend who though alert during the night, probably had fallen asleep with the coming of the first light of day.

For the first time Malton was aware of his own fatigue. His lids were heavy with lack of sleep. He closed them, just for a second and he too dropped off into sleep.

"Pass the word," the voice came from the foxhole at the left, Malton starting back into consciousness. "Cold chow! Easy on the water. Move out at 0630. Keep close to the deck. We're goin' all the way across." The voice had awakened Cold Steel, who gruntingly was relieving himself over the edge of the foxhole.

"Cold Steel," Malton called as he fumbled in his pack for breakfast K-Ration, "check that ridge. Look at the caves - it's going to be rough. We'll be damn good targets crossing the open strip."

Cold Steel looked steadily at the ridge with its caves honeycombed nearly every place the eye stopped. He wiped his hand across his cracked, thirsty lips. "72 hours, the man said. Just Standard Operating Procedure. All fouled up!. We got no bitch coming. The first Marines have to take that ridge."

His last words were drowned out by a heavy barrage of shell fire from the ships out to sea. The whistling overhead was deafening, and Bloody Nose Ridge seemed to explode. Shell after shell, large and small, smacked into the coral rock, rupturing the already disfigured face. Smoke rose quickly as the

Marines crouched in foxholes watched the entire ridge become enveloped in the haze.

"That'll help," Cold Steel said, voicing the sentiment of those within earshot. A feeling of released tension swept across the Marines. They had been acutely aware that their positions had been clearly visible to the Japs in those caves. Now they were shielded by the rain of shells and subsequent smoke. Here and there men cautiously sat up in their holes stretching muscles which had did little moving all night. Danger still lay in the treetops and spider traps, true, but in the moment of apparent relief, they were lesser evils.

Fagan sat up in his foxhole, one of the first to do so, his eyes examining the body which lay outside his shelter. All along the line, voices called, pointing out the corpse to others. All had heard the two tussles of the night before, but had waited the dawn to see the results. Relief was visible in the men's eyes as they saw Fagan and Malton alive, and the body of the dead Jap.

J. C. rolled the short distance to Fagan's hole in one turn and sat beside his friend looking at the body. In the light of day, the body lay still in its gray green uniform, surprisingly long and heavy. The Jap lay on his stomach where Fagan had rolled him, blood clotted on the many wounds where Fagan's knife had pierced him. Fagan climbed from the foxhole, and coldly went-through the pockets, one-by one. Malton watched him, his throat tight.

The pockets contained little, but what a man ordinarily carries, a surprisingly clean handkerchief, a few minor denomination Japanese coins and a wallet, bare save for a few pictures. Malton cringed as he watched Fagan flip through the pictures in the wallet. One was a picture of a thin, plain looking girl with a flat, expressionless face, another was a family portrait of an elderly man and woman and four children. Fagan scanned the picture then coolly turned the body over. The face was distorted in pain, the thin, colorless lips parted slightly, the eyes half opened.

"That's him with his family," Fagan said, then rolled him back again on his stomach. Carefully he put the pictures back in the Japanese's pocket and nonchalantly placed the coins in his own.

"You guys get the word." It was the headquarters company runner who broke the silence which had fallen over the area as all hands watched the scene of Fagan's explorations. He squatted down beside the pair in the foxhole. Before getting an answer, he continued, "We move out in," quickly he glanced at his watch, "in 12 minutes. You guys better quit messing around with that Jap and get some chow down."

"How about some ammo and water." Malton shook his canteen, the small amount of liquid splashing up against the sides.

"The ammo gang will be here in a minute," he indicated a group of Negroes moving down the line. "There ain't no water. The nips sunk all the water carryin' barges as they came in. Stretch the water out, that's the word." Glancing hurriedly from left to right, the runner moved on to the next foxhole.

"We'll be all right," Fagan placed the extra canteens he had foraged the night before on his ammunition belt. "You gonna eat, Salty?" he asked Malton, already opening a can of hash for himself.

J. C. was surprised that his hands still held the unopened K Ration. His eyes moved to the body of the Jap, "I'm not hungry." He turned his back on the corpse aid watched the ammo carriers approach. While Fagan ate he took five clips of M-1 ammunition from the men, asked for and received six hand grenades. It was a long way across the island.

The ammo group picked up the heavy boxes, their black faces glistening with perspiration from the exertion in the stifling, already hot air. The sun had cleared the horizon and was casting burning heat from the white coral.

Above the din of the exploding shells on the ridge the word was passed to inspect weapons and stand by to move out.

Instinctively, Fagan's hand went first to his knife. Assured that it was safely sheathed, he then inspected his rifle, checking for sand or coral in the breech. Malton pieced together a collapsible ram rod he carried in his pack and passed it through the barrel with an oily rag. He handed the ramrod to Fagan along with the latter's share of ammo and hand grenades.

Tenseness again began to mount as the Marines braced themselves for the assault. Each man's eyes kept returning to the ridge on their left, now completely obliterated by the dense smoke. The firing would stop just prior to the moving out hour - - the First Marines had to move into the area and would be subject to their own ships' fire if it were to continue.

Malton picked over each piece of terrain ahead, looking for low spots which would serve as concealment. He also watched for any movement, knowing that in that very open seemingly empty space, the enemy, not many, but sharpshooters, were awaiting the attack, waiting in their spider traps - four feet deep holes in the ground, covered by a fiendishly contrived natural looking cover.

Malton glanced at his watch. 90 seconds to go. In the sudden stillness of the day as the big guns let up their plastering, he wondered of the safety of his friends, Miller, McPherson, and Richardson. How had they fared the landing? Were they alive or did their bodies lie mangled in the surf or on the beach. Only of Fagan's and Kee's condition he was certain, the latter was lounging uncomfortably back in the Russell's, awaiting word of the fate which had befallen his buddies. 30 seconds to go! Malton smiled as he thought of the cursing and bitching that had gone on when the towheaded Marine from Indiana had learned that he would not be making the assault on Peleliu, but would be left back on Pavuvu with the maintenance troops of the division. 15 seconds to go! The damned fool didn't know how lucky he had been.

"Let's go!" the cry went up and down the line and instantly the troops sprang front their holes and crouchingly ran zig-zaggingly across the field. All hell broke loose as the men hit their feet running. The seemingly immobilized mortars and artillery pieces in the ridge spoke authoritatively and accurately. Shells and mortars patterned the strip, blasting Marines in all directions. The troops had scarcely traveled thirty yards when the signal was given to take cover, the order being entirely unneeded.

Up on the ridge, the Japanese troops methodically sighted their weapons in the mouths of the numerous caves. The barrage of Naval gun fire had succeeded in closing up many of the caves but deep within the bowels of the ridge, the cave passages were joined forming possible escapes. Laid on the floor of the caves were narrow rails, and over these were constantly passing heavy mortars, some 155 MM, and 105 and 75 MM, artillery pieces. Thus, when one opening from which to fire was clogged the usable weapons were merely moved to another opening and put into operations. Every possible target area on the island, the Marines were to find out, was plotted and accessible from the bold narrow, ridge which ran three fourths of the length of the island

The First Marines had left their positions along the fringe of the jungle at the same time the Fifth and Seventh were deployed. The Fifth's area was the airstrip and the elimination of all enemy troops defending the hangar area, while the Seventh Marines were to cross the smaller southern tip of the island to the right of the 5th Marines and then deploy a solid line South, pushing the enemy troops into the sea.

The heavy fire was directed now by the Japs on the 5th and 7th Marines, and the First Marines took advantage of the inability of the artillery to be effective at close range and pushed along the base of the ridge. Here fire fights between the battle wise men of the First and the Japanese infantry took on fierce proportions. Doggedly the Marines moved up the foot of the ridge, until they came to the first level of caves. Grenade teams working with four men, two offering covering fire and two crawling to the sides of the mouths of the cave attacked along the line. Dull explosions within the depths of the caves boomed in competition with the small arms fire. Much noise resulted but little else was accomplished as the Japs had withdrawn through the connecting tunnel passages to the next higher level. Satchel charges were then thrown into the caves in an effort to collapse the openings - many men would be killed if the caves were left open after the Marines had pushed upwards for the Japs would be able to pass back through the lower level of caves and snipe at the advancing Marines from the rear. The coral proved superior to the attack of man and little success was achieved with the satchel charges.

Down on the airstrip, the Fifth continued to move up in short dashes. The call for a corpsman was often in the air as men fell beneath the piercing shrapnel blasts. Snipers, too, took their toll!

Fagan and Malton stayed close together, keeping an eye on each other. After one dash, the fourth since the push had started over two hours before, the two buddies found themselves in the dubious protection of a hole in the coral caused by a bursting 155 mm mortar.

"Damn those bastards," Fagan cursed through parched, cracked lips. Both he and Malton wet-soaked with perspiration, their entire dungarees dark with sweat, "Where the hell are they? What a hell of a way to fight a war."

Malton squinted his eyes. His reaction inwardly was the same. They hadn't seen a Jap, dead or alive since they had attacked. He glanced at his watch and then turned his head toward the beach area. "Christ! We haven't come over two hundred -" he stopped, his eyes catching a movement in the coral about 30 yards behind them. Without moving he watched. Slowly the ground seemed to be rising. The sun caught the barrel of a rifle beginning to poke its nose from the hole. Quickly Malton whirled in the depth of the shell hole and crawled on his elbows to the far side of the protective cover. Cautiously he peered over the lip on the hole. Now the rifle was all the way out of the hole and the spider trap cover held a foot off the ground by the bowl like helmet of a Japanese soldier. The barrel was pointing to the right of Malton - the Jap hadn't seen him! Slowly the sights of J.C. Malton's rifle lined up the head and slowly drawing in his breath, Malton squeezed the trigger.

The rifle protruding from the spider trap fell free to the ground and the top of the trap fell shut with a dull thud. Malton watched for a second, his eyes glued to the limp rifle. Seconds passed and the rifle stood unmoving, then suddenly it squirted in the coral dust, the breech shattered with a bullet.

"How's that for shooting, Mac?" Malton turned. Five yards to the right and rear of the stocky Marine, Cold Steel Fagan was lying on his stomach, his rifle held gently in his hands, his finger still on the trigger.

Malton smiled. "Scratch one!" Suddenly he realized that he did not have the same feeling he had experienced the night before when he had met in hand to hand combat with the infiltrator. His stomach was not quivering with the nausea he had felt last night as he thought of the dead man. His mouth hardened. He wanted to live, and he would kill to live!

1400 found the men of the Fifth Marines, three quarters of the way across the sun baked air strip. Before the assault battalions stood the now clearly visible shells of the hangars which had once held the fighter planes and light bombers stationed on Peleliu. Behind the hangars, standing boldly in defiance were concrete control buildings with four foot reinforced concrete walls. Indestructible fortresses, impregnable to the shells and bombs of the American forces. From the small, thin slits along the walls of the two storied buildings came occasional bursts of flame, the only visual indication that the last ditch defenders inside were still alive.

Behind the assault troops the vast and unbelievable organizational procedure necessary to keep the men in front fighting were already taking the vacated positions of the front line troops. Divisional headquarters had moved from aboard ship and were setting up a Command Post behind a sheltering ledge of coral off the beach where the 7th Marines had landed the day before.

The field hospitals were set up amongst the trees which separated the airstrip from the beach. Huge crosses designated the mercy operation, pitifully asking for the protection decreed by the Geneva applied rules of International Warfare. Even before the tents had been fully raised, the doctors were giving field treatment to the wounded, performing emergency operations and rushing the men down to the beaches where they were shuttled by landing craft to waiting hospital ships standing off shore. On Peleliu, the doctors were being plagued by another enemy, nature. The white coral of the island reflected the burning rays of the sun, and man after man collapsed from heat prostration.

Another detail slowly performed its duties. The men of the Grave Registration Group went about their task with grim solemnity, inspecting every corpse on the beach and in the jungle. Grimly they cut off one of the dog tags each man wore, noted the markings on his equipment to identify his outfit, and then removed all personal belongings. The latter would be shipped back home along with a personal letter from the commanding officer expressing regret, but at the same time pride for the behavior of the man in action. Burial crews were already trying to penetrate the thick coral in order to bury the dead, but the island which had defied the men while alive, now steadfastly refused to receive the dead men in its bowels. Conceding defeat, the burial crew, hastened by the sickening odor of decay which the heat accelerated, scooped out shall graves, wrapped the remains of the Marines in camouflaged ponchos and then covered the graves with coral sand and small mounds of chipped coral. The task was not an easy one, and the hidden Jap guns in the ridge caves continued to harass the beach area. Tightened nerves were stretched to the breaking point and rations of medicinal brandy was passed out in such quantities that soon the burial detail worked in a relief giving alcoholic stupor.

Along the line the battle for the operational area of airfield heightened. The Jap high command had evidently chosen the area as one on which they would make a major stand. The four concrete enforced buildings were angled from the base of the ridge to offer maximum protection to each other. Huge chunks of concrete had been knocked off by the heavy naval fire and the reinforcement still lay grotesquely exposed, but the buildings still stood firmly, a tribute to their builders' engineering ability.

Malton and Fagan had been reunited with their platoon what was left of it, and lay in another of the hundreds of shell holes. The platoon had numbered 28 when they left the assault ship the morning before - now the platoon had a complement of 12. Dead were Platoon Commander Lt. Hal Davis and 8 of the enlisted men, their bodies scattered between the landing area and the present position. Seven other were already evacuated to the field hospital. What had begun as three squads, there now were less than enough for two squads. Platoon Sgt. Myron Konkright had assumed command and now he lay with Malton, Fagan and Richardson in the shell hole.

"J.C.!" Konkright called. The stocky Marine rolled over beside the sergeant, carefully keeping his rifle out of the powdery coral. Konkright looked tired. "J.C.! Take Fagan, Richardson, Findlay and Bowers and try to toss some grenades in that building." He indicated a building which stood approximately 75 yards before them. Malton looked carefully at the fortification, studying every minute detail of the terrain between his cover and the building, searching for possible shelter along the way. Grimly he nodded, his eyes drawn to the small slit openings in the side of the buildings. It was going to be tough. Turning his head he tried to find the positions of the other men of the Fifth. He caught an occasional glimpse of green dungarees in the holes and crevices parallel to his own. They were farther away from the building - the job rightfully belonged to his platoon.

"Cold Steel, Rich, Findlay, Bowers," his calm voice belied the upheaval which was going on within him. The men raised their hands from their rifles in recognition of his call. "Buddy Konk has ordered us to toss some cookies in the building ahead. Every man have at least three grenades?" The men checked, and nodded, their faces masking their feelings. "Okay! Cold Steel, you come with me, we'll start out to the right and work up. Rich - you and Bowers work up from the left. Findlay, you bring up the rear. Got it!" Once again the nods were made. "Check the ground now! Pick out good spots to duck." He was surprised at the command which his voice held. He turned to the platoon Sergeant.

Konkright looked at the six remaining men. "You guys open up on the slits when I give the word. Keep firing until I tell you." He looked at Malton who had finished checking his piece and grenades. His mouth formed "Good Luck."

"Let's go!" Malton yelled and squirmed over the lip of the crater, drawing his feet under him and running low when he hit the top. He sensed rather than saw Fagan about five yards to the right of him. Malton fixed his eyes on another crater 25 yards before him. All along the line the Marines quickly realized the plan and hundreds of rifles spoke as one, pelleting the building openings with rifle and automatic weapon fire. Answering fire kicked up the dirt before Malton and Fagan as they zigged and then zagged. J.C. hit the crater with a flying leap and quickly braced himself for another dash. Fagan was already in the hole and ready to go again. Jap 31 caliber machine gun bullets kicked up the coral about them. Malton felt a piece of coral dig into his cheek.

"Come on!" It was Fagan who cried out, as he disappeared over the edge of the hole. Malton followed, his body almost parallel to the ground, his rifle all but dragging in the dust. The next crater was further away and the panic of fear struck forcibly as he dashed toward it. A sudden scream mingled with the whining of bullets as he flung his outstretched body into a deep hole, his knee suddenly sending painful messages to his brain as it struck a sharp piece of coral. Fagan grunted as his body hit the unexpected depths of the crater.

The crater was deep - the result Malton knew of a 16 inch shell. It afforded deep protection from the building. Malton gulped in deeply of the fresh air, his lungs bursting from the effort of the running. His dungarees clung thickly to his body.

"Bowers got it!" Fagan was pulling a hand grenade from his belt. Malton quickly remembered the scream. Carefully he looked over his shoulder. Bowers lay still to their left. A sudden burst of fire from the building greeted Findlay as he crouchingly ran to replace the dead man. Fagan and Malton tensed as they silently urged on every step. Unconsciously they held their breath as he stumbled, regained his balance and dived into the hole already holding Richardson.

"He made it," Fagan offered, his face red from the exertion. Silently his eyes met Malton's and the two drew strength from each other.

"We're about yards out," Malton said. "Did you see any big openings in the side of the building?" He hadn't but he wanted confirmation from the sharp-eyed Fagan.

Fagan shook his head. "We can't get any closer. We'd be sitting ducks to those guys in the second deck." He breathed deeply. "Only thing to do is get to the building, hug the bulkhead and flip the grenades in - if we get that far."

Malton had already realized that was the only possibility. "There's probably two rooms on each deck." Malton pieced together in his mind the construction of the building. "We'll take the right half of the front - Rich will take the left I hope. You had better take the top deck - sharpie!" He smiled. "but don't miss - I don't want a hand grenade on my head." Fagan smiled, his face barely cracking.

Raising his hand, not visible to the Japs in the concrete building, he signaled back toward his lines, indicating they were ready for the final drive. Slowly he wrapped his fingers tightly about a fragmentation grenade, its 20 ounces, the size of a large deadly lemon. He felt the safety lever which extended almost the length of the grenade digging into his hand as he held it pressed tightly to the side of the grenade. He drew a deep breath and motioned to Fagan.

Malton said a quick prayer and sprang from the crater, his feet moving faster than he had ever moved them ever before in his life. A crazy thought rushed through his mind as he dodged through the fire which came hurtling from the building. No one would have tackled him when he had played football if he had covered ground this way. Bullets struck in front of him as he slid to the right, the bullets followed; he dodged to the left. A searing flame struck his left arm, throwing him further in that direction out of the path of more bullets aimed where he had been. He crashed into the face of the building and plastered himself against it, not two yards from an opening. Fagan thudded beside him, panting.

Malton could hear the Japs screeching orders within the building and his fascinated eyes, looking quickly from the right to the left, watched the rifles and machine gun muzzles turning, trying to get in position. The openings were less than 6 inches wide and not more than a foot high, good for pivoting for firing in front of the building, but impossible to play a path of fire along the side of the wall. Quickly Malton, his body flush against the side of the rough concrete building turned, his back flat against the wall, his left arm aching as it brushed the side. Fagan had already done the same and was looking at Malton's arm where his dungarees were red with blood.

Findlay and Richardson were belatedly making their move and every weapon in the building was firing as they dashed to the building. Findlay lurched and pitched to the ground blood spurting from his face. As he stumbled to the ground more bullets hit him, his body lurching with every bullet.

Malton closed his eyes, nausea creeping up on him. When he opened his eyes he saw Richardson reach the protection of the wall.

Now every weapon in the fortress tried to pick off the three men. Malton's eyes were riveted to the coral three feet before them where bullets splattered. Suddenly he came out of his fixation, the Japs would soon realize that grenades would do the job. Grasping the grenade in his right hand, he grimaced as he pulled the pin out with his left. Holding the lever tightly against the grenade he moved his right hand across his body and held it above his right shoulder alongside the small slit opening. He could reach but a little further and touch the muzzle of a Jap M-1 which nervously was moving slightly. Drawing a deep breath, he released the lever, and counted - "Mississippi 1 - Mississippi 2 - Mississippi 3 -" with his left hand he jammed the Jap rifle down on the ledge of the slit and snapping his wrist flicked the grenade into the room. Almost instantly a muffled explosion trembled the wall. Shrieks of pain were heard as the shrapnel cut its victims. Another explosion, less noticeable, testified that Richardson had tossed his grenade. Another pin was pulled, another agonizing count of three was recorded and Malton's second grenade blasted the room. Quickly a third was tossed, the action repeated by Richardson. The bottom portholes were empty.

Fagan, in the meantime, had concentrated on the top floor openings, watching the slits. As the explosions crushed the first deck, the barrels of the weapons stopped moving, momentarily , then again wagged furiously. Fagan moved alongside Malton and as the third explosion sounded dropped his rifle, pulled the pin and attracted Malton's attention. "Give me a foothold," he yelled. Quickly Malton grasped his meaning and formed his hands into a cup. Fagan put his left foot in Malton's hands and lithely sprang up, the bullets from above flying dangerously close to his head. Turning his right foot sideways, he slipped it into a first deck slit, and hung there perilously, digging his left hand into the concrete, his head almost bumping into the barrel of the rifle above. Sizing up rapidly his next move, he released the safety lever, smashed the Jap weapon against the side of the opening and tossed a grenade inside. Once again the screaming announced the success of the grenade. Holding fantastically to the ledge with his left hand, he grasped another grenade with his right hand, pulled the pin with his teeth and rendered another death dealing blow. Fagan dropped to the ground, his left hand bleeding from the rough concrete. Without hesitating, he inched his way over to where Richardson stood flush against the far edge of the building. The scene was repeated there, with Richardson forming the ladder. First Fagan threw his grenade and then Richardson's remaining. Smoke and flames shot from the interior as Fagan rejoined his buddies on the hard surface of the coral. No longer was there any sound from within. The three men dropped exhausted to the ground.

When they lifted their heads, they saw components of the Fifth moving up in the protection offered by the now harmless concrete building. They waited, not moving a muscle in their tired bodies.

"Let's see that arm." Cold Steel raised to his knees beside Malton, their perspiring forms protected from the probing Japanese fire by the concrete building. Gently his long slim fingers rolled away the shattered dungaree sleeve. "You've lost a lot of blood! Corpsman! Corpsman!" Fagan's voice rose as he summoned a naval medical enlisted man from the approaching troops. No sooner had the lanky Marine called then a small figure detached himself from the Marines and zigzagged his way quickly to the shelter of the building.

He crawled to Malton's side and expertly surveyed the wound, probing with sure but gentle fingers. "You're OK, Mac! Just a flesh wound." Pulling a casualty tag from his pack, he filled it out quickly and attached it to a button. "Can you make it back to the beach?"

Malton's face twisted into normalcy from the grimace of pain it had worn during the corpsman's battle field treatment. "I'm not going off the island?" His eyes clearly indicated that he did not relish the thought. He had dreaded combat again prior to landing but he didn't want to leave now.

"For that scratch!" the corpsman grinned. "Hell No! They'll treat it at the Mobile Hospital back on the beach and probably send you right back to your outfit." He wasn't fooled - he knew this Marine would always crave the thick of the action - would go crazy if he were not in the thick of battle not because he was glory hungry or "Gung Ho" as these crazy, wonderful Marines called it, but because he would tear his heart out worrying about his friends in combat - friends like the insane, long knife carrying Joe who knelt beside the wounded marine now! He had seen them in action, as had almost all the remaining men in the fifth Marines - seen them miraculously tear across the exposed strip in the face of deadly fire - seen them accomplish the impossible - knock out an impregnable fortification. His eyes watching the pair on the deck, were wide with admiration.

"Take it easy, Salty!" Fagan was bending close to the sitting Malton, his big paw of a hand resting lightly on the lone sound arm of the squat Marine. "Sure you can make it O.K.?"

Malton looked up, his eyes reflecting the calming reaction the shot of morphine the corpsman had given him. "I'll make it!" His face hardened. "Take care of yourself until I get back." The corpsman smiled. He had been right.

Malton sat outside the field hospital tent, exhausted from his scrambling back to the beach area, and from the loss of blood he had experienced. He was much weaker than he had thought. He closed his eyes and dropped off into a sleepy unconsciousness.

When he awoke it was dark. With difficulty he tried to adjust his eyes to the darkness. In the distance he could hear the sounds of war, but the constant shattering explosions of shells had been replaced with but an occasional stray mortar shell. His open eyes could make out stars dimly shining through the swaying trees above. Slowly he realized, through the stupor of the drug exactly where he was. A moon nearby startled him and he slowly turned his head to the right.

Accustomed finally to the dark, he could make out the form of a man lying three feet from him on a stretcher, the white bandages which completely covered his head attracting what little light cast by the night. He felt beneath him with his right hand - he too was on a cot. Gently he passed his right hand across his body. The pain was still there, but the wound had been tended to while he was asleep. In the darkness he smiled - while he was unconscious.

"How do you feel, mac?" the voice was soothing, the professional warmth of the tone implied confidence which carried through to the patient. J. C. turned his head. Standing beside the cot, bending over in order that he could speak quietly and still be heard, was a stocky corpsman, his face invisible in the darkness.

J. C. tried to smile reassuringly, his lips spreading further with the realization that his face, also, was imperceptible in the Pacific night. "O.K., I guess." He flexed his arm a little, the pain reaching dully into his fingers. "Hurts some! But you're the expert. How's it look to you?"

"Just a flesh wound." The corpsman said bending over a little more. "The bullet cut through the fleshy part of your upper arm. Messed up suntan a little and you've lost quite a bit of blood. The Doc wants to look at the wound again tomorrow."

J.C. tried to sit up, but he could not lift himself from the bunk - his weakness surged through his body, finally dispatching the futility of his efforts to his brain. Uncomfortably, self-consciously, he realized that his motion had not escaped the corpsman. "How long do I have to stay here?" He spoke the words as unconcernedly as he could, but he heard the tinge of urgency the words carried.

"Relax, Mac, it's going to be a long war. You'll get back into action soon enough -" As he spoke he gently placed his hand on Malton's good arm.

"How long?" J.C.'s voice was insistent.

"O.K! O.K!" Malton could tell by the sound of the corpsman's voice that he was laughing. "Maybe two days, maybe three. You're lucky - or are you?" his voice trailed off. "Some of the guys here won't be going back into combat," his voice dropped lower, "some won't be going anywhere ever."

The corpsman straightened up and moved off into the darkness, Malton following him with his eyes until he disappeared, enveloped into the night's blackness. But the man's final words remained - drumming into his ears over and over again until the doped Marine fell off into fitful sleep.

Dawn was breaking when Malton again woke. In the gathering light, he again recalled slowly where he lay. Gingerly he tested his muscles cramped by lying in one position. The motion surprised him. He felt strength returning to the tired body. Putting his right hand on the stretcher cot, he pushed himself to a sitting position. As he dragged his left arm up, he felt no sharp pain. Encouraged he flexed the muscles of his forearm, cringing somewhat as the pain reminded him of the wound. But he could move the arm and gingerly he ran his right hand over the clean white bandage. It felt good - good and secure.

For the first time he became aware of the sounds of war, a firefight was going on to his left on the southern extremities, the short end of the island and to his right on the damn ridge. Straining his ears to discern the fire behind him he could hear the muffled sputter of rifle and machine gun fire far across the island. Inwardly he smiled, the Fifth Marines had moved on across the strip, must be close to the opposite beach. Feeling tired he began to lie down. As he did his eyes took in the hospital compound. Stretcher cots were neatly laid out in rows of four for about fifty yards, every one holding an inert form. At the head of the rows he saw what he correctly surmised to be the operating tent. At close interval surrounding the cots were armed Marines, each holding his rifle, at the ready, eyes scanning the jungle looking for possible snipers.

He saw corpsmen and doctors working on the wounded - providing medication with swift but unseemingly unhurried motion. Sighing heavily he closed his eyes to the scene of torn flesh, the sun filtering through the trees turning his closed lids red.

"Jack, see if you can rustle up some more tents. These men should have cover." The voice was unfamiliar to J.C. "Christ, there are a lot of them. Sure wish to hell those landing crafts would move quicker."

"The Mercy is filled, sir." J.C. recognized the corpsman who had bent over him during the night. The men were standing over his cot, the wounded Marine could tell by the sound of their voices, but he didn't open his eyes.

"The beach master is shuttling the wounded to the transports with large enough sick bay space." The voice showed the strain of fatigue. "The top brass didn't count on this many casualties."

"How many?" the older voice spoke quietly wanting but still not wanting to hear the answer.

The corpsman hesitated. "As of 0400 the count through the field hospital was over 3,000 - that's not counting the dead."

Malton winced, opening his eyes with a start. 3,000 wounded! His stomach heaved! 3,000! 3,000 men who but two days before had been whole, alive human beings. And his friends, his buddies. How many of them were listed among the casualties? He swung his eyes to the corpsman and then to the man who stood beside him a doctor! In his face he saw the same expression which he, too, was wearing. The Navy Doctor felt his eyes on him and his gaze turned down to him. The painful expression was quickly turned to the professional doctor meeting patient clinical expression.

"Good mornin! How's the pain, Malton?" Gracefully he dropped to his knees and began removing the bandage expertly.

Malton watched the doctor work, his face noting the balding spot atop the grey haired head. The doctor was tall, and slender, his face lined with the many hours spent administering to the dying. J.C. felt secure in the man's hands. "Doesn't hurt at all." he lied, "I'd like to rejoin my outfit, sir."

A smile creased the older man's face. Absently he said quietly, "In time, son, in time." He finished unwrapping the bandage, laying bare the open wound, the two inches of torn flesh. Gently he raised the arm watching the expression on the Marine's face, not missing the slight twitching of pain the youth tried to conceal. He bent lower, prying gently under the arm where the emerging bullet had caused a rough tear in the flesh. The skin was clean, devoid of blood. "We'll sew this up!" he said to the corpsman as he rewrapped the bandage.

"Doc! Are you a doctor there?" The voice was etched in pain and trembling, the voice barely audible in the din of the not too distant firing. It came from the man Malton had seen during the night, the man who, his face covered entirely with bandages, had not moved. Quickly the corpsman moved to the unmoving form. He placed his hand on the arm of the man.

"Are you a doctor?" the mouth, through a narrow slit in the bandages barely moved.

"I am," the doctor had turned to the man. His face was blank, accustomed to situations like this.

"Doc! My face! It's on fire and my eyes - I can't stand it." The plea was accompanied with pain.

The doctor made a motion to the corpsman who quickly prepared a hypodermic and baring the man's arm administered the morphine. The voice continued, the words not forming on the delirious lips.

Gradually the moving lips moved more slowly, until finally they stopped, their master deep in the soothing, unconsciousness afforded by the drug.

"His eyes are gone!" the doctor spoke in a little more than a whisper, "his eyes, nose and most of his face, but he still can muster the energy to speak despite the pain."

Heaving a deep sigh the weary medical man struggled to his feet. He shook his head disbelievingly. "I'll never understand the human body, its endurance, its raw strength, its ability to do its damndest to overcome all odds. By known standards that man should be dead. Corpsman!"

The corpsman stood entranced at the recital of the doctor, never before had he heard the man speak so many words and with such feeling. He fairly jumped at the call "Yes, sir!"

"Put this man on board a barge now. And put him on the Solace! " The voice was now hard, again the professional tone reasserted itself.

The corpsman sputtered "But, sir, the Solace is filled - we've orders to –"

"Damn it man! I said the Solace. Tag him that I personally ordered him aboard the ship." The Lt. Commander turned and walked along the row of wounded, the fixed smile again on his lips.

"The Solace - Christ!" The corpsman bent and attached a new tag to the unconscious man. "Kerns! Tracy!" he called and two Marines who had been sitting on a fallen cocoanut tree at one end of the hospital area, tiredly moved over.

"This guy goes out now! To the Solace! Get it! The Solace! Move out!" The corpsman stood, hands on hips waiting, for the Marines to question, but the Marines were hardened, well disciplined. They simply stared momentarily at the short corpsman and then deployed themselves to the opposite end of the stretcher and gently lifted it. As they moved off in the direction of the beach, the one at the head of the stretcher tossed over his shoulder to his buddy "Wonder who bit off a piece of the doc's ass?"

Malton smiled and looked at the corpsman who stared into the backs of the stretcher-bearers.

"What the hell you going to do?" he said almost soundlessly. "What's that doc?" Malton still smiled, his tongue lingering on the word doc.

The corpsman turned and looked down at Malton, remembering his presence for the first time in minutes. Seeing the smile, his face reddened. "Nothing, nothing!" then his tone softened, "that's what I meant when I said maybe you're lucky." He squatted on his haunches alongside Malton's cot and pulled a cigarette from his pocket offering it to Malton who refused.

The corpsman lighted the cigarette "The doc -" he smiled, "the real doctor, I mean. He's one helluva man. Every one of those guys are special to him - you think they all had a chance to live the way he treats them! That guy," he pointed the cigarette in the direction of the beach, "he'll be dead before noon. The doc knows it, but do you think he'll let up! Hell no! Every ones going to make it - that's what he tells himself." He turned his head to the lines of stretcher bearers depositing the crop of first wounded from the dawn's attack. His eyes searched the ridge and the now almost continuous firing which came from that direction. Violently, he threw the cigarette to the ground and rising crushed it furiously with his foot. He looked down at Malton a line of perspiration or of tears clearing a clean path down his grimy face. "What the hell's the use!"

J. C. watched the corpsman disappear. What the hell was the use? He closed his eyes but the vision of pale bloodless lips moving in a silent plea for help could not be shut out.

Malton was in the hospital compound for two days and then was released for duty to his outfit.

"You dopin' off bastard!" Cold Steel's full teeth obliterated the rest of his face as he pumped Malton's arm, "So you came back! Sure! Now we got the dirty work over! You came back!"

"How's the chow back there?"

"True they got real women nurses?" Richardson and Konkright piped in, their joy in seeing the stocky Marine bright in their eyes. The Fifth was on the eastern edge of the island, deployed in a half-circle facing back across the northern end of the island, the airstrip they had crossed directly in front of them. They had secured their assigned portion of the island, now were awaiting further orders. The men knew what they would be - their eyes and ears could see where the action on the ridge was still fierce. They would soon join the men of the First Marines in the damnable Bloody Nose Ridge.

"Miller got hit!" Konkright voice was low, emotion strong in his voice, "a sniper got him just as we reached the east beach. The bastard pumped one through his left shoulder."

Malton was conscious of the strain the men felt. He forced himself to ask "Is he dead?"

All three Marines shook their heads in unison. Cold Steel had his whetstone out, sharpening his knife. "Not when he left here." He spat on the stone. "Out cold though. Frebee, Kaine, Johnson. They're all dead."

Malton counted mentally, his face blank of the feeling he felt at the roll call. Frebee, Kaine, Johnson - he saw them all in his mind, their smiling faces, alive - alive! And now they were added to the already devastating casualties. 28 men in the platoon and now there were only 8 left.

"Just a squad." Malton failed to recognize his own words, startled by the sound, as he vocally put into words the three words his mind thrust upon his brain. "Just a squad!"

"We're pulling back south!" Konkright said loudly, trying to distract his men's minds. They sat hunched on the deck, 8 crummy Marines, only Malton with more than a snatch of sleep since they had landed on the rock 4 days before.

"Putting us in reserve down the coast about a half mile - rest us up before they put us back in the line!" He nodded toward the ridge. "The Seventh goes up tomorrow - there's not much left to the First."

All eyes turned to the ridge, which rose a little more than 2000 yards from them. Reflected in the weary pupils was the smoking shell shattered knob which had not long ago been completely covered with vegetation. Fear, silent, but soul reaching, sank deep into the bones of the remains of the platoon.

"Remember, if anything starts, you guys get the hell back to the outfit." Sgt. Konkright, the weight of responsibility heavy on his shoulder, stood above the sitting Fagan and Malton, his pack slung by one strap over his shoulder. "The area is on the eastern tip, about 1500 yards that way." He indicated. with his free left hand.

"Got cha," Fagan drew heavily on a cigarette, his back leaning on a water carrier, "don't wait up for us."

Konkright broke through the chorus of laughter, the troops released from their moving out positions, in skirmish formations. "I'm not shittin' you - damn it." His face was red with anger. "Listen, you corps happy bastard - if any heavy fire breaks out in the area, forget about the water carrier and rejoin the troops." He looked straight into Fagan's eyes, "We need the water, bad, but we need men more importantly right now! Guard the damn thing, but don't get killed doing it. Understand?"

Fagan spit on his whetstone. Malton smiled at his friend then got to his feet. "O.K. Sarge." He punched the disturbed non-com's pack meaningfully. "We'll be all right!"

Konkright turned to the waiting remnants of his command. They were a motley crew - the kindest thing that could be said for them was that they were alive. Tired, hungry, with the eyes of men who had seen death first hand, they were walking, obeying dead men. He had tried to turn over the platoon—

squad to the Battalion Command Post after the outfit had reformed after completing the ordered seizure of the strip and the eastern tip of the beach where it joined the landing field, but the commanding officer Major Denim had merely stared at him.

"Sergeant," he had began wearily, holding his head in his hands, "this outfit's operation at less than 30 percent. We've some platoon's right now that are being operated by corporals." He looked up and continued slowly, "and it's not going to get any better. Keep your men going! Any questions?"

Konkright had looked at the Major as he had, shaken his head. The man was almost done. His shoulders sloped wearily, his forehead wrinkled with the responsibility of command. As Konkright left he could hear the Major on the field telephone calling Division C.P. back on the beach pleading for replacements.

"O.K. you guys, let's go - be alert." Konkright's words brought a smile across the already cracked lips of the six men of the Third Platoon, First Battalion of the Fifth Marine Regiment. Shifting their packs, they followed the sergeant down a well worn path through the scrub brush. Alert, it mattered not to them that they were surrounded in their journey by other Marines, well it might be the Japs - a bullet might end the dull pain of fatigue.

Malton watched them down the path, his refreshed eyes offering encouragement with every step. Unconsciously he rubbed his wounded arm.

"Still stings, huh." Fagan spoke quietly. Malton turned and squatted beneath the shelter of the water tank protected both from snipers on the strip, but more important at the moment, from the blazing sun which had begun its downward swing to the west. Fagan was still concentrating on the knife, testing the sharpness of the edge - his eyes never seeming to leave the labor, yet conscious of every movement about him.

"Itches more than anything." For the first time in days he pulled his pipe and tobacco from his pack. Filling the crusted bowl with tobacco, he lighted it and drew deeply on the stale tobacco - letting the smoke trickle from his nose. The pair sat silently keenly aware of the proximity of the war about them. "How does it play to you, Cold Steel?" The question had lain deep in his mind for the past two days.

"How does what play?" Fagan said, his fingers grinding the blade.

"Peleliu - this damn massacre - " Malton answered, exasperation in his voice.

Fagan looked up, shaken by the tone of the stocky Marine. He fired his eyes on the arm of his friend.

"Easy, boy." he said soothingly. "Well, it was bound to happen sooner or later." He lighted a cigarette and blew a well formed smoke ring. "We've had it made the last few operations. Everything's gone by the book. The Marshalls and the Marianas were set ups - we just played according to the script, just outnumbering and outsmarting the little bastards - perfect operations - the strategists called them." He sighed, "But this one didn't go by the script. Hell! With the pounding the Navy gave this rock and the low level bombing of the Air Wings, it figured to be a mere mopping up excursion for the ground troops." He stopped and then said, almost disbelieving his own words. "You know I felt the same way sitting out there on that tub - you couldn't even see this rock for all the smoke."

Malton nodded his head in agreement. "Me, too. Fact is I felt let down that there wouldn't be anything left for us."

Fagan blew another smoke ring. "The man said 72 hours - less than 2 percent casualties." He laughed hollowly. "The Japs didn't get the word!" He pointed over his shoulder toward the ridge. "The only way we'll get the bastards out will be to blast them out of those caves one by one. It's going to be a dirty job."

"Scuttlebutt back at the field hospital was that the army was coming in to help." Malton said the words evenly, without emotion. Fagan threw the cigarette violently from him and spat after it. "Who the hell needs them! We'll do it ourself!" Once again he was at the whetstone with his knife.

J.C. grinned at his buddy's anger. He had heard the same comment from the wounded Marines back at the emergency hospital - men who would not shoulder a rifle for a long time - some never again. They were down - but they still had the Espirit-de-corps which made the Marine Corps the elite fighting force of Uncle Sam.

The afternoon passed and twice during that time they had supervised the loading of water cans from the carrier. The life-sustaining liquid was still at a premium, the supply coming only from aboard the ships standing off the island. No water had been found in their section of the island, and one intelligence man had correctly determined that the only water on the island was in the northern half of the coral rock - behind the enemy lines.

Every half-hour either Fagan or Malton carefully inspected the oval drum for leaks. Small arm fire sporadically signaled the presence of the enemy in the area and one small bullet hole could drain the meager supply which still remained in the drum.

Almost instantly the sun which hung over the Western horizon dipped and the island prepared itself for another long night.

"Fagan - there's a hell of a lot of activity out there." Malton was crouched beneath the belly of the tank, his eyes scanning the strip in the quickly fallen darkness of night. "What do you make of it?"

Fagan crawled beside his friend and carefully studied the bust of fire from small weapons and the course of machine gun tracers. The latter were tearing across the strip in low trajectory. They watched for perhaps 10 minutes and became aware that tracers which had seemed far away were now closer and were intermingling as they traveled in both directions.

"They're counterattacking." Fagan said in an even voice. "Check the pattern of fire. They're coming down the coast."

It was true, Malton could plainly see. A wedge was being driven in the eastern flank and the troops closer to the center of the strip were falling back to keep the line straight in order that they would not be encircled.

"Time for us to leave." Malton said slipping his pack to his shoulders. "It's going to get hot here in a few minutes. We can't control the strip at night, our positions are too vulnerable. Let's go!"

Fagan hadn't moved save to snap the safety from his Ml. "We're O.K." The voice was cool, almost anticipating the fire fight that would be theirs soon. Already elements of the First Marines, for it was they who were being pushed back, were passing southwards, had drawn almost all of them.

Malton could barely see his irresponsible buddy in the darkness, but he bore his eyes heavily in the general direction he had last heard the thin New England accent. "Fagan, I'm getting the hell out of here. Come on!" His voice was hard and he hoped persuasive. Pushing back from under the water carrier he carefully calculated the proper direction. He knelt on one knee and waited - no movement was forthcoming from Fagan and the battle of machine gun chasers was almost upon them. Once more he called "Let's go." Not waiting for a response he crouched the ground as he headed down the darkened path.

After thirty yards it became evident that he was alone, that Fagan had not left his position. Cursing beneath his breath, he strained his eyes trying to determine the course of the path. He stopped on the unfamiliar terrain – the path had become larger, wider in the past few yards. Crouching he awaited the next flare and when it came, he could make out the route ahead. The path had indeed, widened and now was wide enough to permit the passage of a jeep. As far as he could determine, the path was clear. All about him he could hear the sound of movement as the troops continued to fall back to the reserve line which had been established a short distance south. Correctly he determined the safest course would be to skirt the edge of the scrub brush which lined the path.

Suddenly a burst of fire from rifles and carbines sounded to his right. He quickly flattened on the deck and again cursed. Some trigger happy bastard had been spooked and like a forest fire it had spread rapidly as uneasy men had begun to visualize Japs. Malton caught himself wondering how many Marines would be killed this night by Marine rifles discharged by Marine fingers.

"Corpsman! Corpsman! Damn, I'm hit!" the words cut through the mechanic man made sound of fire as only a God made sound of a voice could. It jarred Malton from his lethargy and he began to crawl, he dared not walk down the path. The pace was slower but definitely more secure this way.

He panted, his mouth dry, his stomach angry at the beating it was being subjected to along the cutting coral. He stretched flat on the deck, his lungs calling for air. His rifle rested free beside him, his forefinger curled about the safety. Deeply he sucked in the air, through his opened mouth and nostrils - cringing he stopped and held his breath. He spat trying to discharge the odor which had pierced him. He knew it only too well - the smell of death - of decaying flesh. Somewhere about him were the bodies of dead troops - Japs he knew - yet how, he could not honestly say! Forcing himself to a kneeling position he began to crawl forward, more quickly now, urged on by the foul smell.

The night had completely conquered the Pacific day and it was black, heavy, complete darkness which was so prevalent - at least it seemed to occur often, especially in combat where the fear that darkness brought was more common. The lone figure of the Marine could not be seen more than five yards away and he clung to the brush along the edge of the path. Carefully he moved his arms and legs, gingerly he placed them down, leery of a sharp edge of coral which could inflict a slow healing and extremely painful cut.

His nose twinged with the smell which instead of dissipating, seemed to get stronger. Malton put his full weight of his upper torso on the rifle which he carried in his right hand and raised his left hand and pushed it ahead of him. A squishing sound accompanied by an unbearable deluge of odor caused Malton to vomit. Gently he raised his right hand and continued on, not daring now to pause. Beneath his crawling form he could feel the bloated bodies of dead men with his weight-- They seemed endless as he moved over, gagging as he went. Finally he was clear of the corpses but he went on - on until he could smell only his own left arm, dripping he knew with the smell of death where it had pierced the bloated to the bursting point of a body.

He lay still for several minutes trying as best he could to clear the mess from his dungaree sleeve. His stomach ached from the racking which now produced nothing. Grimly he fought to regain the rationality which had left him on contact with the corpse.

He lay quietly, barely breathing. A movement in front of him and slightly to the right caught his eye. He waited - waited breathlessly for a flare to furnish him enough light to permit his rifle, which he now had pointed in that direction with his finger loosely holding the trigger. A dim glow filled the night behind him - a flare from the ridge area. Before him he could barely make out a pile of rocks - coral rocks, and he felt rather than saw the barrel of a machine gun. He waited not having a clear shot.

"Password?" The words were uttered softly and barely reached Malton's ears. Inwardly a grin began to spread as he hears the American voice. Softly but distinctly he called "Lilies." He waited, his ears reaching for the counter.

"Lola! Come on mac, hurry!" the voice was urgent. Malton got to his feet and ran crouchingly to the gun emplacement, and bounded past just as one of the Machine gunners said to his buddy. "I sure hate to lisp." Mirthless laughter approved the thought - all passwords had a multitude of l's since the Japs could not pronounce the letter clearly.

Within the circle of the defensive area, a sense of security, perhaps false existed. The shattered regiment, now not much larger than one its full strength battalion would be, had spread out egg shape across the slim southern section of the island. Further beyond them on the thin finger of Peleliu, the Seventh Marines rested, awaiting the 'morrow when they were scheduled to move through the Fifth lines and replace the almost depleted First Marines still banging away unsuccessfully at Bloody Nose Ridge. The three battalions, in name only, of the 5th spread heavily on the northern line and in lesser number facing the east and western beaches. South, the line, more a tribute to standing operating procedure than to any great necessity, was thin, settled by the more seriously hit outfits. In the center was a conglomeration of outfits not then needed to form the outposts.

It was in one of these gatherings that J. C. Malton found his buddies, already dug in and tense from the small arm fire that was infiltrating the area.

"Where's Fagan?" Sgt. Konkright asked when Malton had traced him out in the dark and uneasy bivouac area. Konkright hunched in his shallow scooped hole from the coral inviting the Marine in with him. "What the hell stinks?" Konkright spit out of the foxhole, the sudden spray causing unkind remarks from Richardson and McPherson.

"Me!" Malton hissed revolt in his tone. Without any emotion in his voice he related the incident of the bloated bodies. When he was finished he spat, away from the foxhole.

"Christ!" Konkright said his tongue thick in his mouth, his throat dry and coated with the taste of the thick odor which had seemed to increase as Malton developed his story. Swallowing with difficulty he again asked "Where the hell is Fagan?"

Malton dropped from his knees where he had been resting onto his stomach, the firing had intensified. "He wouldn't come!" The words were terse, bitter.

"That figures! The crazy bastard, he'll never learn," McPherson was the one man in the outfit that had not been conquered by the overwhelming Fagan, instead he took advantage of every opportunity to needle the lanky Marine. "Well, at least he won't get any of us killed with him."

"Knock it off!" Malton spoke angrily, the words clipped in staccato fashion as he glared through the darkness at the spot from where McPherson's voice had come. "Knock it off!" the voice carried authority.

Konkright sighed and shifted his weight in the foxhole, trying to get the piece of coral which was stabbing him in the back to nibble at some other portion of his anatomy. "Malton, better get some shelter. It's going to get hot here soon. Damn soon!" To emphasize the words he snapped the safety from his rifle.

Malton scooted along the coral until his fingers found comparatively loose digging, and then lying on his side, he unfastened his shovel from his pack and began to hack noisily away at the unyielding ocean matter. In a matter of moments he was perspiring profusely, the sweat adding unkindly to the already wrenching odor of the human secretion he had obtained from the corpses of the Japs. His fingers ached from the scratching away of the coral when the shovel used more as a machete than as to its maker's purpose had sufficiently loosened the rock like substance. At last he had managed to get enough of the coral loose for him to bury himself within two ridges, but it took the scrapings from the hole to make the sides high enough for him to be even partially protected.

Gingerly Malton settled his weary frame in the hole, his face toward the colorful but death sending tracer bullets which played upon Bloody Nose Ridge. Fascinated he motionlessly watched, his finger resting easily on the trigger plate of his M-l. The sound of gunfire, increasing and decreasing in tempo was unheard by him so accustomed had he become to the constant report of the angry weapons. His eyes, watching the lethal fireworks, were not heavy with the sleep, that the time in the hospital area had given him, but his mind - his thoughts were heavy - thick with thoughts which dwelt unmovingly from the lanky, cocky Marine who was somewhere out there in the direction in which his rifle now pointed. Cold Steel - Cold Steel Fagan - a madman, a fearless madman but deep, beneath the crude, hard surface, a living, miraculously intelligent philosopher. Uncouth, uneducated, yet the Bostonian was, once you scratched the surface, capable of deep reasoning, unerring logic.

The corps had been a haven for Cold Steel Fagan, a place where he could live the animal existence he was constitutionally suited for. He had been out of place in civilian life, cooped up by the conventions which insisted he be a proper Bostonian. He had graduated from high school - rather the fine schools of Boston had graduated him, only too happy to accept his passing on - not that he had caused undue trouble. He lived by the rules - accepted them, but not once did he project himself into the accepted behavior of academics. He had sat in school, seemingly unaware of the classroom about him - of the teachers who had to pry from him some action - only infuriating them when called upon with his flair for a dreadful long moment of silence while the entire class seemed to fix their eyes upon him and then, slowly, without a trace of emotion either in his voice or face, had offered the correct information. He always scored his point to the consternation of the teachers. He knew the answers - the teachers and other students knew it, but what the hell was the sense of it all.

Only once during his tenure in high school, and it was the customary four years, did he show any sign of his true self and that was the first Career Day held in the school. It was during his senior year and the innovation was at first received by him as was all the other events of high school. He had signed up for three sessions - three because that was the minimum required. Two dull hours, by his standards, had been endured listening first to a fat, pimply faced, bulldogged squirt of a man who spoke of the advantages of a New England shoe manufacturer and second by a tall, thin, enthusiastic engineer who oozed confidence as he faced the young students. Only once did the confidence depart him and that was when his eyes met the derision that sat immobile in Fagan's - he didn't look again in that direction.

It was during the third session that the shell had broken. It had been then 1940 and the war clouds had already begun to form and the school administration had thought it wise to invite the local recruiters to participate in the Career Program. Fagan had listened to the Army and Navy recruiters spin their spiel with his usual unhearing attentiveness, but when the tall, husky, green clad Marine had taken the floor and cast his eyes contemptuously over the teen-age boys, his right hand forcefully pummeling his open left with a swagger stick, Fagan recognized the expression as his own. The Marine had stood there for over a minute, basking in the self-conscious uneasiness of the students before he spoke, and then curling his mouth in a sneer he rocked the room with a booming announcement.

"The Marines Want Men!" his eyes swept the room, and then contemptuously his voice added with derision - slowly forming the words, "I doubt if we'll find any here!"

The shocked room was silent! But in one corner, a lanky student smiled for the first time that day. Cold Steel Fagan was beginning to find his career! He listened to the Marine cajole, taunt, and deride the students, speaking of the hell that was the Marine Corps, of the demands it made on body and soul, of the espirit-de-corps that existed. As he concluded he again pummeled his leathery hand with the swagger stick. His voice intoned the words "If any of you punks think you got the stuff it takes to be a Marine, see me after this bull-session!" Glaring he sat down!

Fagan was first in line for an interview after the meeting had been adjourned. The months of school until graduation had seemed interminable to Cold Steel. Still he sat in the classrooms, present in body and the mechanical perfection of doing just enough to get by, but inwardly he had found his mark - it was the Marine Corps for him.

When the time finally came and the diploma had been handed over to him by a puzzled principal who had never succeeded in dissecting and comprehending the workings of the mind of this boy, he had suddenly felt free. He had fulfilled the obligation his parents had demanded and now the future was his.

Martha and Pat Fagan had not been stunned that graduation evening in the large living room of the Fagan's run down rented home when Jerome Fagan, for that was his given name, had calmly announced that he was going to join the Marine Corps. Nothing this strange son could do would surprise them. They had accepted his ways, as long as they didn't interfere with the goings ons of the other seven children in the Fagan brood - and Cold Steel never once did that - rather he was a loving brother to the rest of the children in the family even if he didn't outwardly, unduly show his true feelings. So on this night the father and mother had sat beside each other on the worn overstuffed couch and had merely stared at Jerome who stood leaning against the upright piano against the hallway wall. Finally Pat had gently nodded his head - he realized decisions were always carefully thought out by this, his eldest and favorite son.

"You'll make a good Marine, son," his eyes were misty and he took a big red bandana from his hip pocket, fluffed it out and noisily blew his nose! "A damn good Marine!"

"Pat!" Martha Fagan scolded in a well practiced manner but her eyes watched Jerome, her love for this quietest of her sons evident in her eyes, "You're sure, Jerome?"

Cold Steel had looked from one beloved parent to the other. Gently he nodded and suddenly on an impulse which had seldom before entered his body, had walked over to the couch and taken each's hand. The three were one, consent, pride, and determination fusing into the powerful weapon which had been borne into Jerome Fagan.

From the beginning Fagan had been a good Marine. He had excelled in boot camp, had excelled with the rifle, had been capable of greater endurance and stamina than any other Marine in his platoon. The D.I.'s had pounced upon him at once, and had unmercifully ramrodded him, but he stood firm, straight as a young sapling, weathering, actually thriving on whatever the drill instructors chose to throw at him. It hadn't taken the D.I.'s long to discover that here was the near perfect specimen of a Marine - one who could take order without questioning, who could endure the hardships of war without flinching no matter what would come. He looked the part - hard, fierce eyes, grooved deeply in a thin hawk-like face - high cheek bones arched prominently over flat leathery cheeks. A thin line for a mouth and an unshowing face.

The D.I.'s were aware of his possibilities and potential at once, but they didn't let up on him for a moment. He became an example to the other boys of the platoon - an invincible character who could take all the crap thrown at him and come back for more - He was a symbol and as the D.I.'s had figured, a symbol to which the others would try to pattern themselves. The hopeless Marines of Platoon 468 outdid themselves trying to live up to the actions of Fagan. They drove themselves even more than did the seemingly heartless D.I.'s and molded themselves into a close smooth functioning platoon. They mastered the drill - they could run more laps on the obstacle course - they took more and longer full pack hikes among the boondocks - they killed more sand fleas - they could fieldstrip rifles faster - they could shoot rifles better - in fact they outdid every other recruit platoon in boot camp and ended boot camp with the honor platoon citation. Today there still stands at Paris Island the records Platoon 468 established and the D.I.'s of the platoon still have in their possession the citation they received from the base commander for turning out the best damn recruit platoon in boot camp.

They smile when they think of that platoon - smile with the knowledge that the citation rightfully belongs to Cold Steel Fagan.

Fagan's rise through the ranks should have been phenomenal, but those who predicted officers bars for Cold Steel, truly didn't really understand the lanky Bostonian. He could have become an officer - he was offered Officer's Candidate School no less than four times, but Cold Steel Fagan was a born private - and a private he insisted on staying. No matter how many times he was put up for promotion - and it was frequently - he unsmilingly shook his head. When forced to take Corporal's test he unceremoniously studied the problems on the sheet before him, arrived at the correct answer thoughtfully and then methodically put down the wrong answer. He had infuriated officer after officer - had been threatened and cajoled, but he would take the tongue lashings, standing erectly at attention, and then would, after the officer had run down, do a smart about face and repair to his quarters - a smile on his thin lips.

Fagan was a private - a damn good one he knew - but he did not want to be burdened with command. He had carefully planned his course of action upon entering the Corps. He would take orders - do his damndest to do his job and do it better than anyone else but he did not want, when war came, and he knew it would, to be burdened with the responsibilities of others. He wanted to play it Fagan's way - and not have to worry that his actions would endanger others.

He had succeeded when war came and he found himself overseas he was still a private and proceeded to play his lone hand. In two previous combat operations prior to Peleliu, he had conducted himself according to his plan and had distinguished himself to the point that he was entitled to wear upon his breast two silver stars and another medal was sure to be forthcoming after the episode at the blockhouse.

In his almost four years in the corps he had never really been close to anyone until he had met Malton - a man he felt could understand him - and let him pursue his own way - offering and receiving friendship without asking it or any other commodity. The two had been buddies for over a year and often they sat for hours without a word being exchanged, but those hours were ones of comradeship and closeness which was penetrating.

Malton lay facing the ridge, unconscious to the replay which had crossed his mind concerning his buddy. He had heard the story bit by bit - a little from Fagan himself - more from others who had heard the tale of the indestructible campaign hat wearing Marine. The hat, so like a boy scouts hat and the peacetime wearing apparel of the Corpsmen at overseas stations during the lull between the wars, had become as much as a trademark with Fagan, as had the knife which had earned him the nickname which he accepted as a tribute.

The tracers were drawing closer but J.C. seemed unaware of them as he continued his thoughts of Fagan. He intoned the words almost aloud - Fagan was steel nerved but not without fear or without purpose. He recalled a night on Cape Golouster when the rain had stymied all attempts of American and Jap alike to wage effective war. The griping had been heavy and damning. McPherson had been cursing the rain, the Japs, the Corps and everyone else - offering what was the use of it all anyway. Long after everyone had gone into a half sleep half coma and Fagan and J.C. had sat back to back huddled beneath a lone poncho, Malton had been surprised at the sound of Fagan's voice.

"There is a purpose of the whole thing." he had started and then had remained silent for a full five minutes before he had repeated. "There is a purpose of the whole thing. But it's hard for the little guys like us to figure it out. War's a part of man's reason, for being on earth - there have always been wars - and there will always be wars as long as the Man up there keeps men on the face of the earth. In every generation there will be fanatics who feel that it is their destiny to conquer the world - that the reason they were put there was to forcefully rend all men into his own domain - and," Fagan sighed, "There will always be others, like us, who will have to stop them - to combat the madmen's efforts - to keep freedom alive - the lot of mankind. A lot of men die to prove that freedom should exist but they will make their point whether on some small island - or on a large barren continent. We are those men - and we have to succeed - and will succeed." Fagan dropped his head on his shoulders and was snoring in a moment.

And now J.C. Malton was once again going through the agonizing pain of suspense. Somewhere out there, in that blackness - in the dark tropical night was Cold Steel Fagan - in all probability unaware of the danger in which he was in. Perhaps unaware did not cover the true picture, Malton smiled - Fagan was always aware of danger, yet he was imperious to it.

"The crazy bastard," Malton spat through his teeth, "Someday - someday he's going to take one too many chances." The thought froze in his consciousness and he shook his head trying to dislodge it. In doing so he became increasingly aware of an upbeat in the tempo of the firing about him. He cleared his brain and peered deeply into the night. Someone or something had kicked up a fire fight to his right. Tracers mingled with the flash of small arm fire in a criss-cross pattern. The bullets clung close to the ground and the Marines dug in the coral foxholes tried to withdraw even farther away from the lethal fire. Suddenly Malton heard a sound through the din of gunfire. He strained his ears trying hard to hear again the sound. There it was again - someone whistling - whistling softly, but smoothly without a tremble. Cold Steel - it was Cold Steel.

"J.C. J.C.!" the voice pierced through the night. Malton pushed back his helmet, cupping his eyes in his hands and then releasing them quickly in an effort to better penetrate the darkness.

"Cold Steel Fagan, over here." Malton whispered in the direction from which he voice had come. He listened and watched. Slowly a form began to take shape to his left. Instinctively Malton slipped the safety from his rifle. The man was walking - walking upright amongst the tracer fire. "Fagan, you crazy bastard, Get down."

The knife slipped noiselessly back into the sheath and Fagan sat down beside Malton's foxhole.

The pair remained silent for a moment, an unspoken feeling of relief at the other's safety present between them. J. C. once again put the safety back on his rifle.

"Gotta match?" Fagan quietly asked, an unseen cigarette dangling from his dirt caked lips.

Malton almost burst into a violent shudder at the words. "For Christ's sake, Fagan. You light that cigarette and every damn weapon on this rock will blow it out, and you and me with it." He trembled with fury at the Marine. "Better get your ass in a hole, before you get hit. Come on in here." He braced himself up against the side of the coral.

Fagan got up and nonchalantly shrugged. "Too crowded - I'll find one." He stretched and gave a yawn. For the first time his voice held some feeling "Take care of yourself, Malty"

It was the first time he had used his private nickname for Malton since they had hit the island and a warm surge of comradeship swept through the Marine in the foxhole. Motionless he watched Fagan slip off into the darkness and suddenly he was gone, his every sound attracting fire from fellow Marines. Twice Malton heard the whisper and the second time a smile couldn't help but break his cracked lips. Fagan called, "You dead in there," as he found a foxhole and once received a grunt in return. The second try brought no answer and Malton could feel and hear the lithe Marine roll a corpse from an unneeded foxhole. Within a matter of seconds Malton could hear Fagan peacefully snoring unconscious of the deadly fire which had by now built up into a heavy fire battle.

Malton found his own head dropping heavily on his shoulders as sleep tried to take over the exhausted body. Every time he dozed he was awaken by a heavy snore which emitted from Fagan's open mouth, yet each time he could not determine whether the snoring or the increased mowing which followed it was the cause of his being awakened. Finally Malton picked up a handful of coral chips and tossed them grenade fashion in the direction of Fagan's foxhole. The sleeping Cold Steel gave a startle and immediately had his knife in his hand.

"Fagan - for Christ's sake - turn over! Your snores are going to get us all killed."

The now wide awake Marine swallowed away the taste of sleep that fought the dryness in his mouth - his bloated tongue cruised the cracked lips. He hoarsely said, "Must have fallen asleep. What time is it?"

Malton glanced at his watch, carefully cupping the luminous dial as he slipped back the dungaree sleeve from his wrist. He stared, unbelievingly. "This thing must have snapped its main spring." Again he peered at the face of the watch, his eyes hypnotically glued to the sweep second hand. "I make it 2300."

Fagan laughed humorously and again rolled over on his stomach. "It's running." he snorted. "Better get some sleep - your ass will be dragging tomorrow." Malton could hear Fagan arranging his body to fit the dips and rises of the coral rock.

The night grew comparatively quiet as more of the exhausted Marines drew off to fitful sleep - their dreams full of the death scenes their eyes had seen enacted during the day. Somewhere far to Malton's right, an M-1 methodically clicked its bullets at an unseen target every few minutes. Malton smiled at the sound - it was the same with every man the first few days in combat - every shadow was a Jap - and must be killed. Nothing was expended save ammunition.

J. C. played his eyes across the scrub brush he knew lay before him making certain not to linger on any spot for long. As long as the eyes moved, you could make out any movement in the dark, but the moment your eyes held one spot, everything seemed to move.

Malton didn't know when he fell asleep but suddenly he came wide awake as all hell seemed to burst about them. Heavy Jap mortars were exploding throughout the area. First came the whoosh like a train plunging into a tunnel and then the deafening explosion and concussion sprayed coral and metal chips about seeking out the soft yielding skin of human beings. Malton buried his face in his pack, and hunched his head deeper into the protective cover of his helmet. Barely seconds passed between explosions and cries of pain and for corpsman joined the din of the one sided battle.

Above the noise came the voice of Sgt. Konkright. "Stay put you bastards!

Dig in the coral with your noses and swivel sticks." The words were consoling if not reassuring. "McPherson! Get your fat ass down or I'll shoot it myself."

The barrage tapered off as quickly as it had begun. A flare, shot by one of the destroyers sitting off shore brightened the sky, turning the night into a ghostly day just as a corpsman slid into the protective covering of a foxhole. His final thrust for safety was accompanied by a flair of bullets from a position in a clump of mangled trees to the left center of the line. Malton joined in the crescendo of fire which was thrown across the open space. The fire fight lasted a moment and then tapered off - the whining sound of the Jap 31's silent! As the flare reached the ground Malton surveyed the terrain - the Japs had penetrated the lines in force if those who had shot at the corpsman were any indication.

"Third Platoon! Sing out," the command came from Konkright. "McPherson-yo-alive and aching for a woman," the words did not hide the fear he felt.

"Richardson - yo!" "Young - yo," "Blue, Yo." Peterson - Yo", Malton - yo" - an expectant pause filled the night as every remaining member of the third platoon waited for Cold Steel Fagan to answer.

J.C. felt his lips go dry and his heart a tattoo on the cage of his ribs. "Cold Steel - Fagan ." No answer came from the foxhole and in the light of another ship fired flare, no movement was visible within the shallow foxhole.

Malton grabbed his rifle, drew it to him and softly whispered, "Konkright, I'm going to check - You bastards hold up on your fire." He waited until the flare had bounced into the ground and then, the position of foxhole still etched in his mind from the last flare, wiggled from his hole and crawled across the open area. His movement caused a rash of fire and brought cries of "Hold your fire, you trigger happy sons-of-bitches." from Peterson. The distance was about 40 feet, Malton had judged when he had jumped off from his foxhole, but now every inch seemed a mile. His body itched with perspiration from the exertion and his elbows, cradling the rifle, ached with the bruises of coral rock. He edged closer to the hole, the realization that at any moment another flare would be screaming skyward. He stopped 5 yards from the foxhole where Fagan had taken cover and listened, his ears straining between the metallic smashing of rifle fire for the sound of snoring - any sound which would indicate that Fagan still lived.

"Cold Steel!" Malton whispered and then waited for an answer. None came - and J.C. again inched toward the foxhole. His hands brushed against steel - Fagan's helmet. The barrel of the rifle clicking as it struck the protective cover.

Suddenly, Malton was dragged into the hole, strong wiry arms pinning his to his sides. The form in the foxhole rolled over him and Malton could see glint of the steel blade in the semi-darkness.

"Hold it for Christ sake!" Malton croaked, his voice a mere whisper as Fagan's left thumb pressed on his windpipe.

Fagan released his grip as if stung, and the raised arm with the knife slowly lowered. "You grab-asser!" Fagan's voice was cold - the tension of the near kill at last bringing emotion into his voice. He stuttered, "I could have killed you!" He dropped heavily beside Malton, their two bodies crushed against each other in the foxhole. "You grab-asser!" Fagan repeated. "What the hell you doing? I could have killed you." The words were unbelieving - not yet fully aware of the situation.

Malton felt the deep feeling of comradeship between them which he had discovered just a short time ago. "You didn't answer Konkright's sound off." he explained softly, "I came over to check."

"I was asleep," Cold Steel intoned the words matter-of-factly resorting to his emotionless words.

"Sleeping!" Malton exclaimed. "Didn't you hear the mortars? Christ, man. Don't you hear anything?"

A smile broke unseen in the darkness on Fagan's lips. "I heard you!" he sighed readjusting himself in the hole. "Shells don't bother me - figure if they're going to kill me, might as well be asleep - but anything moving;" he paused, "like you - I hear. Don't want anybody to get me unaware." He yawned, "Now get the hell out of here and let me get some sleep."

Malton grinned and gathered himself for another dash - this one back to his own foxhole "Better keep that helmet on – one piece of shrapnel can part your hair for good."

Fagan grunted his eyes already closed. Malton waited for another flare to burn itself on the deck then called "Coming through," and wiggled his way back to his own foxhole. Breathlessly he called out upon reaching its safety "Fagan O.K.! Just sleeping."

Curses filled the air, each denouncing the stupid New Englander, but not too well hidden in the oaths were notes of relief.

A whooshing sound drove the heads back into the depths of the foxhole. The shell detonated in the midst of the area throwing dirt over the already filthy men. Soon the barrage which had such a short time before ceased was pounding out, inch by inch, the positions of the Marines. Screams and curses rang clear through the smoke filled night. Death joined the confusion as a huge 155 mm landed in a foxhole and forever ended one man's fear of battle.

Cold Steel Fagan had not been able to drop off back to sleep and the noise and acrid smell of exploding shells disturbed his efforts at sleep. He felt a flying piece of coral strike his left shoulder. Cringing at the momentary pain the lanky Marine decided he had better put on the helmet which lay to his left on the lip of the foxhole. Wearily he reached out, groping for the bulky helmet.

It was just at this moment that a trigger happy Marine thought sure he saw some movement in the brush and proceeded to empty a full clip of eight rounds of 30 caliber bullets in that direction. But, fate as it will, stepped in for the movement was not a Jap scurrying in the brush but only Cold Steel's hand fumbling for his helmet.

"Ow - Damn, I'm hit." Cold Steel cried into the night as knife like pains crushed through his hand, up his arm, and through his shoulder. Quickly he withdrew his arm, painfully aware of the rush of blood that surged from his hand. The pain was so severe that it took him several moments to determine just where and to what extent his wounds were. Groping carefully with his solid left hand, he felt his fingers one by one, grimacing each time as he awaited the pain which did not come - did not come that is, until he reached where his right forefinger should have been and found there only a blood soaked stump.

"Corpsman - Corpsman!" Cold Steel yelled, pain evident in his voice.

"Fagan, Fagan! Where you hit?" The voice was barely audible through the sound of arriving and exploding shells and the chatter of machine guns and small weapons which had joined the deadly serenade originated by Cold Steel's "Adversary". "Cold Steel! Where you hit?" Malton was screaming now, anxiety in his cry.

"Ow - it's my god damn friggin' finger. The damn bastards shot it off. Corpsman - Where the hell are you?" Fagan had calmed down as he had taken stock of the situation.

From a distant foxhole a corpsman answered, his booming voice winning the audible contest with the exploding shells. "Wrap it up yourself, mac! Put some sulfa on it and stop the blood." The voice sneered, "I'm not going to get my balls shot off just because you don't know how to take care of your friggin' finger."

Laughter, strangely out of place in the searing battle scene, spread infectiously along the bivouac area as the word was passed by mouth. Malton suppressed a grin as he heard the corpsman's word. "You O.K. Cold Steel. I'm coming over." he cried.

"Keep your ass there, Malty," Cold Steel answered, his hands obeying the instructions of the corpsman, awkwardly but with some degree of success. "I'm O.K." he grunted as he poured the sulfa into the open wound. "I've got a tourniquet rigged - I'll be all right."

Malton tried to see through the deep darkness to where his buddy left knowing full well that the lanky Marine could use some help but wouldn't ever forgive an unwarranted exposure to death on his account. J.C. stayed put, listening attentively to the guttural sounds which waifed through the lulls between the rounds of explosives. Finally, unable to keep his eyes open any longer, he fell into a heavy unnatural sleep, one inner faucet of his brain tuned in for a call for aid from Cold Steel.

"The dirty son of a bitch - he shot my friggin' finger off," the delirious voice of Fagan broke the comparative stillness of the night. The New Englander had strayed off mentally as a result of shock. "I don't give a damn if my whole hand falls off. I'm staying put in this friggin' hole." The words awoke the drawing trigger happy replacements along the beach area and once again the night was filled with small arms fire. "Knock it off." was heard from more experienced and cooler heads. The firing subsided.

"My friggin' finger - wonder where it is - maybe they can sew the friggin' finger on!." The droll, monotonous voice droned on, silent for a while, then as a new stab of pain struck home, impatient, whining once again. The words seemed to relieve the tension of the situation and chuckles could be heard following each outburst.

But Malton was not laughing, his fears for the welfare of his buddy increasing as the endless hours creeped on. He had almost convinced himself on several occasions to crawl over to the wounded Marine's foxhole but each time, the futility of the action outlasted the passion of his heart.

The first rays of light crept over the horizon to Malton's right and the black sky turned to gray and then a pale red in the distance as the new day began to push the night around the face of the earth. Throughout the area objects became visible and the feeling that they no longer shared the ground with the enemy came over the troops. With daylight came to each American the feeling that it was his turn to be the aggressor once more. Somewhere before him J. C. could hear orders being yelled and the sharp crack of gunfire testified that once again the Marines were attacking.

Malton waited five more minutes until the entire area was visible and then he crawled from his foxhole, his muscles aching from the cramped foxhole. About him from the corners of his eyes he saw other men crawling from their sanctuaries of the night and beyond Fagan's hole he saw a corpsman, his bandolier of medical supplies about his shoulders moving toward him.

Fagan was sitting up in his foxhole by the time Malton arrived. He was staring at his hand, actually seeing the wound for the first time. The hand was swollen almost twice its normal size and the blood clotted stump of a finger grotesquely pointed toward the sky. The stunned expression turned to a half smile on the strained blood soaked face. The corpsman arrived and immediately began to apply medication to the wound.

The corpsman stared at the grinning Fagan. "What the hell you grinning at?" he asked.

Fagan's mouth cracked wider. He spoke slowly. "Looks like I'll be going back stateside", he said. "Can't fire a rifle with that stub."

The corpsman looked questioningly at the wounded Marine and then at Malton - both of whom now had faces wide with grins.

Youth is wild,
Youth is passionate,
And age looks on.

Chapter 7

J. C. Malton sat on the edge of the fox-hole, his unshaven face lined with the fatigue of days in the front lines of the hell which was Peleliu. About him other similarly begrimed Marines leaned over tasks of housekeeping which had been neglected for so long. The small island about them roared with the sound of war. Not more than 5,000 yards off, the battle for "5 sister's hill" was raging and smoke from occasional demolition charges hung with a pallor over Bloody Nose Ridge.

The battalion had been pulled out of the line but hours before and joyfully but tiredly they had marched the short distance to the comparative security of the southern tip of Peleliu, out of reach but not out of sound of gunfire.

"Get much mail, J..C.?" Liverlip McPherson stood in his foxhole a short distance away, a piece of brick-stale cake in his coral begrimed hand.

"Plenty! Enough to read for days." J. C. tiredly said as he held up samples of the first mail they'd received since landing on the island weeks before.

He looked at the letters in his hand and carefully sorted them - A smile creased his face as he noticed his mother's inarticulate handwriting. The smile turned to a questioning frown at the pile of small blue envelopes. He held one to his nostrils, the perfume smarting his eyes, his nose and his heart.

Memories rose before his eyes - memories of stateside and the fall of 1943.

"Damn it, no!" Malton cursed violently as he looked down on Liverlip McPherson who sat in the plush chair leisurely. "It's no good! I didn't expect

you to sign us up for a hen party! I just used this place to meet! Damn it!"
Malton dropped onto a sofa, unaware of the eyes on him.

The Main Street U.S.O. was crowded this Saturday night, the latter part of
November, 1943. Los Angeles was jammed packed on weekends. The luster
of the big city's lights drew servicemen from the camps up and down the
coast. It was a liberty haven. The city of L.A. and its suburban communities,
Hollywood included, threw open its arms and pocketbooks to these young
men who were soon gone to the South Pacific battle area.

Malton glared across the lobby at his friend Liverlip McPherson. The
short, blond, and pouting youth sat unconcerned, eyeing up and down the
trim hostesses who shuttled about the room, performing numerous tasks,
none more pleasing to the men than the movement of their feminine bodies
as they passed before the ever observant eyes.

Malton cursed again! This was his first liberty in weeks and this Liverlip
had loused it up good. The protruding lip had left camp the night before on
a 62 hour pass - Malton never knew how the kid swung them - and they had
agreed to meet here the next night at 7:00 p.m. Malton's liberty didn't start
until 1200 Saturday and it was a 100 miles from Camp Pendleton to the big
city.

The young punk had signed them up for a party. He knew the kind well.
The city was loaded with girls, lovely women - there was not enough of them
to go around - even spread thin. They could get a man any day or night of
the week, but there were many plain, dull girls also. Not lookers, they were
left alone by the servicemen so to get a man they would throw parties, all
supervised by the U.S.O. What a set-up and Liverlip had signed them up for
one of the dull sessions.

J. C. Malton was four months out of boot camp and the liberties were few
and far between, and he wanted to make the most of the few. An easterner,
he was from West Virginia, he had looked forward to the West Coast and the
possibilities of Los Angeles. A powerfully built youth in his 20th year, he had
left college to join the service. His college days had been spent mostly in study,
now he wanted some fun and a hen party did not meet those specifications.

He pulled his stocky frame from the chair, put his overseas cap on his close cropped black hair, and moved toward Liverlip again. His eyes were a stormy black in the hard sun-tanned face. "Come on, Liverlip, let's go." His full straight lips drew taught, the muscles bulging in his high cheek bones.

"Hold on, Malty, just till the dame arrives who's going to drive us. We'll size her up." McPherson didn't move, his lip protruding even more and his kinky blond hair forming clefts in his profile.

Malton resignedly dropped on the arm of the chair. His eyes played over the large room and fell on the desk in the front where a serviceman could apply for a room. Now there's a sharp chick - he thought as he watched the blond girl behind the desk. She was talking to a stocky Marine - pretty serious conversation - she must know him.. The name on the name plate on her desk said Candy - the name fit.

A long-legged brunette had emerged from the stairwell leading to the street below. All eyes followed this new entry in the attention getting derby. She gracefully walked to the reception desk, a smile on her suntanned and beautiful features.

"Party number 2, please. Come to the reception desk." The voice on the public address system was efficient, businesslike.

"That's us, J.C." Liverlip said, his eyes never leaving the long-legged girl at the desk. "What'd I tell you. She's a looker. What'd I tell ya?"

"They always send the prettiest to pick up the crew. It's bait to trap the suckers." Malton felt he knew these set-ups only too well.

"Come on." Liverlip rose from the chair, adjusted his blouse and waddled toward the desk, followed by a reluctant Malton. Three air force men and two soldiers were already at the desk when they stopped in front.

"Fellas, this is Elaine Rutter," the girl behind the counter said. "Have a good time."

The long-legged girl smiled at the men and the group followed her down the stairs, Malton bringing up the rear. Liverlip was right there in front, walking beside the girl, playing his line in fast and furious dialogue. Malton almost laughed aloud at sight of the tall girl, striding gracefully down the street, with Liverlip, barely reaching her shoulder, jogging beside her to keep up.

They were led to an ancient station wagon, all piling in with Liverlip drawing the center seat in front. The girl drew the car awkwardly into the busy Saturday traffic. The limited confines of the station wagon released some of the inherent shyness of its cargo, and soon they were all talking and laughing.

Liverlip turned in the seat and winked at Malton, who winked back. Resigned to his fate, J. C. began to enjoy the ride. The Air Force men were from Santa Anna and the soldiers from nearby camp, and the usual exchanges of identification further cleared the remaining restraint.

Elaine drove the station wagon furiously, winding in and out of the traffic at a pace and with such a lack of ability that even Liverlip shuddered. In answer to the inevitable question raised she said, "What's the scoop on the party?" She smiled. "I don't think you've ever been to one like this before." She hesitated. "As a matter of fact it's the first any of us have ever tried."

Her words were received with mixed feelings. Liverlip, of course, thought that for sure they had struck a live one and Malton likewise positive that his old hen theory had been right.

"Well, I'll tell you exactly how it is," the girl was fumbling for words. "It will be all right. One of the girl's mothers will be there." She was stopped by Liverlip's moan. Malton's smile widened. Hastily she went on, "All the girls at the party are engaged." Another moan, this time several others mingled with McPherson. "Our fiancés are all stationed elsewhere back east or overseas. The girls, we all go to U.C.L.A., thought that they'd like to entertain some servicemen, just like they hoped girls near their fiancés camps would do - Do you see?"

The group offered as how they did and each one in his own thoughts tried to think of a way out. Liverlip turned his head. He didn't want to meet Malton's eyes. Corporal Karney, one of the soldiers drew out a bottle of tequila he had wrapped in his coat and downed a healthy slug. Malton smiled - he'd need it.

The station wagon drew to a stop beside a white stucco house, ablaze with lights. They emerged from the car, cramped from the uncomfortable seats.

Drawing Liverlip aside, Malton surveyed the situation. In both directions the street lay in a straight line. As far as they could see in either direction no cross street held busy enough traffic to be a main artery leading back to L.A. Malton doubled his fist and shook it in Liverlip' face. Karney stood beneath a tree in front of the next house, wedging his bottle in the crook of the trunk above his head.

The reluctant servicemen followed the swishing long legs of their escort on the serpentine walk. The home was modest but well kept. Malton noticed the shadow of a feminine form cast upon a wall visible through a second floor window of the Cape Cod style house.

Long legs scarcely paused at the glass paneled door. Opening the screen she led the way into a softly lighted living room where musical feminine voices sounded.

A traffic jam began at the living room door. Malton, who was bringing up the rear heard and felt a stillness come over the troops. Liverlip forced his way from J.C.'s side and stuck his head between two burly soldiers and stopped short. The silence deepened.

"I'll be damned," Liverlip broke the silence and the uncomfortable tension that had arisen. Entering the room, introductions filled the air. J. C. Malton finally was able to stand in the doorway and survey the scene. Inaudibly he whistled through his teeth.

Scattered about the room, already receiving the blunt ends of practiced lines, were six of the most beautiful young women Malton had ever seen. The long legged escort was included in the classification. For the first time J. C. really looked at her. Liverlip had been right - she was a looker.

A smile crossed Malton's lips as he sat on a piano stool in the alcove of the room, his fingers idly striking the keys. The living room was large and tastefully appointed. The walls were decorated with what J. C. recognized as excellent copies of the Masters, each highlighted with its own concealed light.

Sofas and comfortable easy chairs spotted the room, a pair of love seats facing each other before a wood burning fireplace in which a warming fire burned peacefully. It was a pleasant room, well lived in, and homey. J. C. watched the men and girls talking, becoming acquainted. Slowly his eyes traveled the room, cataloging each girl. One impression stood out in his mind, long legs had said they were all engaged, and now their actions confirmed her words. Pleasant, entertaining, talkative, true, but they were acting like engaged girls. Lovely, true, but reserved and taut with the knowledge of their vow.

J. C.'s smile broadened as he watched the servicemen, Liverlip in the vanguard, doing their best to break through the barrier created by the engagement ring each girl wore. This would be an interesting evening.

Malton turned back to the piano, his fingers finding the keys to a song he had heard on the radio several times back at camp. Bing Crosby had recorded it - "I'll be Home for Christmas." J. C.'s fingers experimented with the keys - striking and hesitating. He had become rusty - his ear for music not in practice. A movement in the living room doorway, caught his attention, and his fingers stopped as he focused his eyes in the semi-darkened foyer. Again the inaudible whistle formed but was quickly repulsed. There standing in the doorway dressed in a wispy blue dress was a vision if he ever saw one.

Jodie Franklin stood there, watching the Marine at the piano, her green eyes glistening in the light from the fireplace. She gently shook her head and the soft gold hair fell from her shoulders. An amused smile played on sensuous lips beautifully placed in a tiny face which was in accord with her small perfectly proportioned body. Her high full cheek bones highlighted her eyes which in the dim light seemed depthless.

The stopping of the music on the piano drew Liverlip's attention from the small redhead he was trying unsuccessfully to snow. He followed J. C.'s gaze to the girl and stared. He shared Malton's opinion of the angel in blue. Quickly he rose and went to the doorway.

"Greetings, fair angel," McPherson gallantly bowed, sweeping his hand across his chest, "and what cloud did you come in on?"

The girl reluctantly took her eyes from the Marine at the piano and turned to the small boy before her. He was scarcely two inches taller than she. She laughed at him, more amused by the picture he presented, than by what he had said.

"Greetings to you, Marine," she said in a twinkling active voice. "I'm Jodie Franklin," her eyes were on J. C. as she spoke. Liverlip quickly took charge of the girl, taking her to the dining area at the far end of the room where he poured her a glass of non-intoxicating punch.

Malton followed the pair with his eyes for a moment, then struck the keys harder as he remembered the engagement ring on her finger. Corporal Karney, came in from outside and leaned on the piano, his tequila loaded breath searing Malton's face. His eyes were clouded and his hands unsteady as he lighted a cigarette.

"Better take it easy on the Tequila," Malton smiled. "It's pretty strong stuff."

The corporal winked with difficulty, then slightly staggering, made his way to a small group fiddling with the dials of a radio trying to get some dance music. Succeeding, there was much confusion as the men rolled back the carpet, J.C. moving from his seat to aid in the task.

The couples paired off, J. C. holding his hand out to the red head. Smiling she gracefully slid into his arms, her scent leaving him a little breathless. Her red hair danced along with her body as the embers in the fireplace shimmered on its glossiness as they kept time to the music.

"You dance beautifully," the girl said softly as she pulled her head back from his coarse blouse. "I watched you at the piano, you play well."

Malton smiled at the flattery, not believing it in the least."I don't play," he said laughing, "never took lessons - but I like to fiddle with the keys."

"Cutting in, Salty," the tapping voice could be no one but Liverlip. Reluctantly he withdrew his arm from the slim waist,

Looking into the disappointed eyes of the girl he said, "Thank you."

Malton was thirsty. He fought with the desire to go outside to the soldier's bottle. Instead he headed for the refreshment table, noticing that still another soldier had cut in on the air force cadet who had taken Liverlips's place with Jodie. He smiled inwardly - the girl was being rushed - he admired the others' taste.

Drawing himself a cup, he dipped the glass serving spoon into the pink punch. His eyes saw movement in the kitchen beyond and he strolled casually in the brightly lighted room. The older woman there looked up from her task of making sandwiches and smiled at the Marine.

"I'm Sally's mother - the chaperone." The smile on her lips was joined by a prolonged wink.

"And a good one, too!" J.C. recognized the name of the red head. "They seem to be having a good time," his head ever so lightly tilted toward the dimly lighted living room.

A frown crossed her face "and you - " she stopped, concern in her voice.

"Mind?" he indicated a kitchen stool against the sink and sat when she nodded. Finishing the punch he placed it on the draining board "I'm having a wonderful time," he smiled then continued, "but it's not the girls," he stopped reflecting "though they are all beautiful. It's your home! I miss mine - the decorated walls, the curtains in the windows, the piano, the - " he stopped shrugging his shoulders.

Sally's mother smiled, recognizing home sickness. She handed him a carving knife and placed a huge ham before him. He eagerly started carving, thanking her inwardly for the silence she offered him.

The swinging door which the woman had closed swung open, bringing with its opening the sound of music and subdued laughter - and Jodie. She looked at the Marine, at the ham. Her eyes lingered on the square hard shoulders - uncontrollably drawn to the masculinity of the Marine.

Sally's mother watched the scene, a knowing smile on her lips. Jodie became conscious of the woman's gaze. Blushingly she said "We're almost out of punch, Mrs. Green."

J.C. quickly looked up from his work at the sound of the cultured voice. His eyes stared into the deepness of the girl's. A smile formed on his lips. Jodie's gaze never wavered.

"Aren't you going to dance with me?" There was no smile on Jodie's lips as her full lips formed the words.

J. C. slowly placed the knife on the carving board. "Couldn't fight my way through all the other troops."

All three laughed. Jodie held out her hand. "No obstacles now, Marine."

J.C. turned to Mrs. Green who nodded smilingly. The husky Marine and the wisp of a girl went into the living room and he took her in his arms, aware that he was trembling within. They moved effortlessly, her left hand engulfed in the coarseness of his. They didn't speak, but the contact of their bodies responded to the music with wordless motion.

"Cutting in." Liverlip was pulling at Malton's arm.

Malton looked down on his buddy, anger showing in his dark eyes. He said out of the corner of his mouth, "Get lost, Liverlip." Immediately he regretted the slip of his tongue which brought about the usage of the nickname.

Gently he released the girl and stepped back. Jodie looked up at him silently and her eyes followed him as he made his way through dancing couples to the piano.

The evening wore on quickly. Malton danced with all the girls except Jodie and was impressed by their poise and beauty. Their early restraint had dissolved and with it gone the party had taken on an amusing, to J.C., air. The servicemen's lines were no longer cast off so quickly and several couples had separated from the rest and seated themselves in the corner of the room deep in serious conversation. Malton smiled as he thought of the mixed emotions turbently casting themselves within the engaged girls. One of the air force cadets was making a big play for Jodie much to the unhappiness of Liverlip who was generally making a pest of himself.

Corporal Karney had stopped going to the tree crook long before - his bottle evidently empty. Malton looked at him now - slobbering drunkenly over Sally, who was embarrassed by his one track advances. Sandwiches and punch glasses littered the side tables about the room.

The door to the kitchen opened, the white light of the overhead light brightening the room. Mrs. Green stood there for a minute, her hand holding open the door. Then she was gone - the signal for the conclusion of the party had been given.

"Time to go home," Sally bounced up thankfully from the clutches of the drunken soldier. She rushed about the room speaking briefly to each of the girls and servicemen.

J. C. entered the foyer, looking for his overseas cap. Liverlip joined him, rumbling through the pile of coats lying on a bare old fashioned square table.

"Is this yours, J.C.?" The voice was behind him and Malton turned. Jodie was standing near the living room door, his hat in her hands. Beside her stood the air cadet, a frown on his face. She moved slowly toward J.C. the hat extended. Softly she said, "Will you take me home?" It wasn't a question, more of a statement. The look in her eye was one of determination, of possession.

J. C. felt a resentment at the tone, as he looked at the frail but luscious girl. Then his eyes passed from her to the air force cadet, who waited - a sneer on his handsome face. He started to say that he was sorry but as his eyes found hers, he saw that they were pleading.

"Sure," he took the hat and helped her find her wrap, the fly boy aiding. Finding it, she held it to him and self-consciously he helped her slip into it. The cadet frowned indignantly.

"Be back in a minute," Malton said as he stepped back into the living room. Looking about the cluttered room he felt a sadness at leaving this piece of home. Mrs. Green was picking up the glasses and dishes. He stopped before her.

"Thank you, Mrs. Green - " he stopped, unable to adequately express his true feelings at this return to civilian life for a few hours.

Mrs. Green looked up at him, the same knowing smile she had worn in the kitchen on her lips. "Come back, again, J.C. Anytime!" she took his hand and squeezed it. She liked this Marine - her son, if he had lived - would be like him, she knew with a mother's prejudice.

The crowd was leaving shouting farewells as they moved down the walk as Malton returned to the foyer. Sally stood at the door still repulsing the drunken soldier. Jodie stood before a mirror adjusting her soft white short coat. Beside her stood the cadet and Liverlip, inwardly waged in combat.

Malton went to the door, stood between Sally and the amorous soldier. "Thanks, Sally," he smiled at the redhead who returned the thanks with her eyes. "All set?" he asked.

Jodie stepped from the mirror and moved beside him. Liverlip and the cadet colliding as they hastened to follow her.

Jodie put her small hand in his coated arm and they stepped out into the dry cool night. At the sidewalk J.C. stopped and looked down at the girl, seemingly unaware of the two servicemen.

"No chariot, my lady," he smiled. "You give the orders."

Jodie tightened her hold on his arm, a tremble from the coolness of the night air of Los Angeles on her hand. "We can catch a bus on the corner," she said softly, uncomfortable by the crowd which surrounded them.

Malton followed her step to the right, smiling as he saw the now empty bottle of tequila perched in the crook of the tree. The narrow sidewalk barely held the four as they walked down the dark street toward a semi-busy intersection. Both sides of the corner held laughing girls and their escorts as they awaited buses.

J. C. joined in the good-natured talk as they took their place among the group on the near corner. The cadet had drawn aside his two air force men and was talking quietly to them. Occasionally their eyes turned to where Malton and Jodie stood.

Jodie saw the small group and she looked up at the Marine, apprehension on her face. Malton took her cold hand in his and smiled a reassurance which he did not feel.

"Don't worry, my lady," he said loud enough for only her to hear. "The Marines always have the situation well in hand," he added laughingly, indicating Liverlip who had sensed brewing trouble and put out his upper lip in defiance. "Liverlip will protect us."

She laughed, the musical sound of it bringing self-assurance to J.C. The bright lights of their bus approached and good-byes were called across the street. They boarded the bus, Malton fumbling for change. Disgustedly he opened the top button on his blouse and pulled out his wallet, irritated by his delay. The money he received from the girl bus driver jingled in the fare box as he turned to the interior of the near empty bus. All the others had already found seats as he made his way down the aisle.

Jodie was sitting on the outside seat and scooted over as he approached. The looks of resentment of the air cadet seated across the aisle was not undetected as he sat down. The bus driver expertly took off into the night, the bus alive with the chatter of carefree couples.

"Thanks, my lady," J.C. said as he settled in the matted seat. Impulsively he took the hand of the girl and was affected by the tightness which she responded to his touch.

"Thank you," she whispered. "I didn't know how I was going to handle that cadet. He was serious - he frightens me."

J. C. turned and faced the girl who looked like a magazine ad in her white bunny coat. He was surprised at the fear in her eyes. He studied her carefully. Somehow the pieces didn't fit together. She was not the type he figured to be frightened easily. She had seemed so sure of herself at the party. She was beautiful, well bred and - aware of her effect on men, he was sure of that. He wanted to know more about her - he was more than anxious. Uncontrollably he had found himself watching her at the party embarrassed when his eyes had met hers. Frankly he told himself that his aloofness had been prompted by the unavailability of her. He had been surprised at her request to take her home - now, at her mention of the cadet and the fear he saw in her eyes when she spoke of him - he thought he understood.

Fingering the small diamond ring on her finger he said meaningfully, "Tell me about yourself."

She sighed and turned to the window, the light from homes flickering by, "I shouldn't have gone to the party?" she turned to him, an apology in her eyes. "It had seemed such a good idea. The fact is - it was suggested by our -" she gestured with her free hand toward the girls "mothers one night at a bridge game. You know we all go to U.C.L.A.?"

He nodded. "Well our mothers thought it was a good idea to entertain some servicemen, as they hoped our men might be entertained by some nice girls," she smiled embarrassingly at the comparison, "and I think they thought that we needed some male companionship also."

"I think it was a good idea." J. C. interrupted.

Gently she shook her head, the blond hair falling in place on her shoulders. "I'm not so sure," she pouted, "look what happened." She looked meaningfully at the couple several seats in front of them, the girl's head on a soldier's shoulder.

"Just the loneliness, and a shoulder. It will pass." Malton smiled at the naitivity of the girl.

Again the perky head shook, "I hope so. Thank goodness it's not me!" Self-consciously she began to remove her hand from J.C.'s, then stopped, redness creeping into her face.

She sighed. "About me?" He nodded. "Well, I'm just a college girl waiting for her man to come back. Oh, he's not overseas, not yet anyway. Ed's stationed at San Francisco - in the Navy" she concluded proudly.

"A swabby huh, you could have done better," the Marine teased.

She drew from him, then seeing the smile on his face relaxed. "He's a wonderful guy," she said dreamily. "It's funny. We grew up just blocks apart playing together as kids, then suddenly he entered the Navy and we discovered each other."

J.C. laughed softly, "And how old are you now?"

Jodie turned to him, hurt in her eyes. "18!" she said emphatically, then dropped her eyes. "Well almost 18." She looked quickly out of the window, getting her bearings. "We get off soon - the next stop." The fear returned to her eyes.

He squeezed her hand reassuringly. Rising, he helped her from the seat. Jodie went toward the front of the bus. The cadet moved, getting ready to get up across the aisle. Malton placed his hand emphatically in the cadet's eyes, a hard look in his black eyes as they met the man. "Stay put, Mac!" he said meaningfully.

The cadet looked into the eyes, then quickly turned to his buddies, who were occupied with their own feminine companions. He relaxed in his seat unhappily as J.C. moved toward the open door of the stopped bus. He paused as he passed a sad faced Liverlip whose pouting lip protruded even more, showing his discontentment.

"I'll meet you at the Biltmore Lounge in," J.C. glanced at his watch, "in about two hours." McPherson reluctantly nodded and watched his buddy help the beautiful girl from the bus.

The lights of the downtown headed bus disappeared into the darkness as J.C. and Jodie turned down a deserted side street. Malton surveyed the territory with the naturalness of a trained combatant. The homes on the peaceful street were comparatively new, and set back about seventy-five feet from the sidewalk. Most were two story dwellings but some were the rambling ranch style one storied type which had been built just prior to the beginning of hostilities. As he walked down the street past the middle income homes, J.C. again felt a twinge of homesickness.

"Here we are," Jodie had stopped before one of the ranch homes, a light visible in a large picture window. The home was long - built of stucco and squat to the ground in comparison to the two story houses on adjacent lots.

"Thanks for bringing me home, J.C." Jodie's voice was soft and warm as she moved toward the sheltered front door.

"It was my pleasure," Malton smiled as they stopped, the slim girl turning towards him and looking up into his eyes. "It was fun and I enjoyed being in a home instead of a barracks again," he looked toward the house.

"Perhaps you can come back tomorrow?" the girl stopped, surprised at the invitation which had come from her lips. She was disturbed, both by her involuntary action and the hard, but attractive Marine.

The battle the girl was waging within her did not escape

Malton. He took her hand as he shook his head, "I'll call if I can," he took the girl's soft shoulders into his rough hands, lowered his head till he could feel the coolness of her breath on his cheek, "Don't tempt me, my lady, I'm not too strong-willed - remember that swabby."

Quickly but gently he kissed her lips, stepped back, turned and walked to the pavement, and then was gone down the street, the melody of "I'll be Home for Christmas" whistling through his lips.

Jodie Franklin leaned against the door and watched him pass from under the light of one streetlight to another. She was trembling, but her heart felt warm and vibrant. Her lips still felt the firmness of his. She raised her hand and gently touched them. They were warm! Shaking her golden head firmly she roused herself from her melancholy, angry at herself. What had happened to her - why this quickness of her heart. She thought of Ed - tall and fair - so unlike this shorter and darker Marine. She found herself comparing the two in appearance. At every feature Ed emerged the victor, his good looks, his blond curly hair, his straight nose, perfect teeth - his blue eyes - no! The Marine's eyes! Perhaps that was it! Vividly she remembered the Marine's eyes! They were black - fierce hard eyes - cruel but gentle - piercing but gentle - demanding but offering! She found it difficult to remember his other features. Dimly she saw the high cheekbones - the blunt and flat nose, the straight full lips, the dark close cropped hair, the square, chiseled jaw.

The door groaned and her mother opened it as she pulled away. The older woman was in a housecoat, her eyes bleary with sleep. She looked around, surprised to see her daughter alone.

"I heard you come up," she yawned, "thought perhaps you needed rescuing when you didn't come in." She turned and went to her bedroom, her slippered feet noiseless on the thick carpeting.

Jodie smiled at the retreating back. She turned and went into the living room and reached for the light on the round center table by the picture window. She snapped it off, and went to the still burning embers of the log in the stone faced fireplace. She stood there a moment and then slowly dropped to the floor, her head propped on an elbow, gazing into the fireplace.

She thought of the Marine, distraught at her inability to cast him from her thoughts. She nodded to herself – it must be the eyes. The way they looked at her, sometimes smiling, sometime condescendingly, as if she were a child. Her temper flared - he didn't even seem to notice me at the party. She went to her feet, gathered her coat and quietly entered her room unaware that what had attracted her to J.C. had been lightly skimmed over. He hadn't even seemed to notice her at the party. That was an odd situation in this lovely girl's life. Unconsciously, she had always accepted the tribute paid her by any male, any time. Not conceited, as a matter of fact, she was as popular with her feminine friends as with males, she nevertheless had inwardly come to expect the pursuit of every male. J.C. Malton had not pursued - and that bothered Jodie Franklin - she was attracted, affected by this unhandsome, rough Marine.

Malton sat at the bar in the Biltmore Lounge, a bourbon and water in his hand. His eyes traveled through the smoke filled room to the entrance way. Where the hell was Liverlip? He looked at the illuminated clock over the bar, 3:30. McPherson should have been here 30 minutes ago. His eyes roamed about the room where servicemen sat playing chippie with drinks, their intentions clear to everyone. Malton smiled. They would be lucky if all the night's pleasure would cost them would be money. Purposely his gaze didn't travel down the bar where a bleached, heavily made-up blond kept staring at him, her overworked body bulging in the shiny red evening dress she wore. No thanks. He wasn't having any of her kind. Nevertheless, her stares made him self-conscious. Placing a bill on the bar he slid off the stool and went into the lobby of the hotel, leaving a disappointed girl whose stare quickly latched onto another likely prospect.

The lobby was crowded, mostly with servicemen. The desk was jammed with them trying to get rooms, the clerk tiredly shaking his head and pointing, to the no vacancy sign to which no one paid any attention.

Quickly J.C. eyes scanned the huge lobby unsuccessfully searching for his buddy. Fear that he had run into trouble with the cadets plagued Malton. He cursed himself for leaving him on the bus. Casually his eyes found an empty easy chair against the far wall of the lobby facing the revolving doors of the entrance. Quickly he crossed the padded floors and jostled a sailor who had the same destination as he sank into the plushness of the oversized chair. The sailor started to complain and then saw the eyes which had so confused Jodie earlier and slouched away looking for another chair unsuccessfully. Throughout the lobby servicemen sprawled in chairs, fast asleep. The management had tried months before to prevent the men from sleeping there, but an understanding manager had accented the fact that each weekend there were thousands more servicemen as there were available beds.

Malton watched the doorway for McPherson, his eyes dropping closed from fatigue. When the huge clock tolled four, the Marine was sound asleep.

"Anything else, Mac?" the homely waitress asked brushing her unkempt hair from her eyes with the back of her hand.

Malton shook his head as he drained the last drop of hot coffee. Before him sat an empty plate which had held a generous serving of sausage and wheat cakes. Outside the small eatery, Sunday traffic moved past Pershing Square, its greenness an oasis in the concrete and glass jungle of downtown Los Angeles. Malton picked up the check and stiffly, his body aching from the uncomfortable night he had spent in the hotel lobby, walked to the cashier. Paying the check, he made his way through the ever present servicemen to the street. Up above the sun was already hot and high in the sky. Finding a barber shop open, everyone catered to the servicemen on passes, Sunday or not, he waited his turn, his hand brushing the thickness of the stubble on his face.

Glancing through a Sunday paper crumbled by numerous hands, J.C. again worried about Liverlip. Fighting his concern, he smiled as he thought of the rendezvous they had made for that day. They were to have a home cooked meal at the home of a friend of Liverlip. The family, and that included a girl who had a crush on McPherson, had been from Detroit, the small Marine's home town.

The availability of lucrative positions for engineers had drawn the head of the family to the aircraft plants which surrounded L.A. The two Marines had visited them once before and had willingly accepted the offer of a meal the next time they had liberty. The smile broadened on Malton's face, Liverlip wouldn't pass up a free meal.

Patting his stomach Malton looked at his hostess, "That surely filled a deep cavity here, Mrs. Eberly."

The four of them laughed, Fred Eberly the loudest. "I know what you mean. In the last war ---"

"Oh, Daddy!" Bernice Eberly frowned, cutting off the recitation which was about to engulf the dining room for an hour. She turned to J.C. "I just can't understand it," concern lined her homely face. "Doug said he'd be here. Didn't he?"

The name sounded strange to J.C.'s ears, then he regained his thoughts, nodding "Uh-huh, but you know Doug." The name was strange to his tongue.

"We know Doug, all right," Eberly laughed his coarse laugh Again, pushing his chair from the table. "Let's go out on the patio, son, while the girls clean up the dishes."

J.C. excused himself and followed the squat, fat man through the French doors to the flagstone patio. It was a beautiful spot, the well landscaped enclosed spacious green lot bright with indigenous sub-tropical plants. He gently dropped to a gaily colored chaise lounge, his meat sitting contentedly inside him.

"Cigar?" Fred Eberly asked, drawing two from his beautifully cut sports coat.

"No, thank you." J.C. continued embarrassingly, "I've never smoked."

"A Marine that doesn't smoke. Wait here!" The command drifted behind the man as he waddled into the house.

It was an impressive home, J.C. had noted - an expensive one in an exclusive section of Alhambra. Modernistic in design, it seemed all windows. Engineers came at a premium and Eberly was a good one.

"Here you are! Try this!," The older man held an imported briar pipe in the offered hand and a new leather tobacco pouch in the other. "Got it from a client last week" he winked. "Mark it down as the beginning of a vice, an enjoyable one true, but nevertheless a vice."

J. C. accepted the briar, noted the costly cut of it and inexpertly began to fill it. Taking the lighter from the patio table beside him he held it to the pipe, drawing deeply from the fragrant, tasty tobacco.

He leaned back on the lounge, enjoying the semi-sweet taste of the smoke. Eberly sat on a lawn chair peacefully watching the Marine's enjoyment.

J. C. was thankful for the older man's quiet. His keen mind was again asking. "Where the hell was Liverlip?"

The servicemen's special lumbered through the night toward San Diego. Thoughts of liberty tired sailors and Marines dozed, some sitting, many standing. Malton dozed in the ladies compartment on the plush circular seat which was void of arm rests. He had the entire lavatory section to himself. It was a trick he had discovered on previous liberties. The troop laden train carried no women and it was perhaps the only uncrowded spot on the railroad. Awaiting the time when the lights were dimmed and most of the car's men were asleep, he and Liverlip would slip unnoticed into the lavatory and lock the door. The dressing compartment afforded luxurious appointments - it was their own private compartment. This night Malton was alone. He had looked for his buddy at Union Station but the small one was nowhere to be seen.

J. C. entered the darkened barracks room. Snores around the room. Making his way to his bunk he gazed at the top bunk. Liverlip was soundly sleeping. Resisting the urge to pound the Marine, Malton dropped into his sack, too tired to remove his clothing.

Reveille sounded shrilly over the loud speaker at the far end of the room. Another day was starting at Camp Pendleton, major training area of the Marines on the West Coast. Moans and curses met the repeated bugle call. Wearily men, most still clad in their dress greens, pulled themselves from their sacks.

"Up and at 'im, J.C." Liverlip, clear eyed and fresh rumpled the close crop hair in the bunk beneath him. Malton opened his eyes, they burned from the lack of sleep. He sat on the edge of the bunk, unbuttoning slowly the rumpled blouse. Gradually he became aware of Liverlip, happily whistling as he wrapped a towel about his naked body.

"Where the hell did you go yesterday?" His voice was throaty and dry. "I looked all over for you. You'd better call the Eberly's. They were all for calling the morgue." J.C. had stopped undressing, conscious of the all conquering look on Liverlip's face.

The small Marine walked to the long straight row that led between the tiered bunks. Safely out of reach he triumphantly announced, "Spent the day at Jodie's house." He moved farther away from Malton, whose mouth was hanging limply open. "She's pretty sore that you didn't call her." He ducked the pillow that J.C. violently threw and laughingly went to the shower.

The little bastard - the little bastard. J.C.'s anger turned to amusement. He should have figured it out for himself. He knew Liverlip only too well! He frowned as he remembered that he had promised Jodie he would call her. Shrugging his shoulders, he resumed undressing, inwardly laughing at his own stupidity.

The days passed quickly for J.C. and Liverlip. They were in the midst of intensified combat training. Every morning was a new challenge. Ten mile hikes and combat problems were usually the order of the day. The hikes were most resented. The Platoon leader that was in charge of this training group was an ex-football player from Notre Dame. A giant of a man, he had played end for the fighting Irish. His long legs and stretching stride had made the hikes a living hell. He stressed conditioning above all other things. Walk a mile, double-time a mile was his formula. Each hike found men unable to stand the pace and not willing to concede to their weakness, they struggled on, finally falling unconscious on the trails.

"Don't stop," the platoon leader shouted. "We'll pick them up on the way back." So the platoon just stepped over the prostrate men -- too weary for even sympathy. When the platoon returned the now conscious men fell in ranks, sheepish looks on their faces.

This week was an exceptionally rough one. The lieutenant, Gil Gomer was his name, was in a bad mood. The hikes were longer and faster. "The bastard must have fought with his wife," Liverlip offered during a five minute break on the trail. His green dungarees were completely wet with perspiration.

Malton lay beside him atop a small hill, cursing the lack of a cooling breeze. He drew slowly on his newly acquired pipe watching Gomer sitting straight as a pin on a tree trunk at the head of the platoon, cautiously smoking a cigarette, not even appearing winded.

"Lay off that water!" Lt. Gomer shouted at a Marine who was draining a canteen. Lt. Gomer was angry. Downright damn mad was more proper. Inside his breast pocked beneath the imprinted U.S.M.C.,he could feel his request for transfer to active duty. It was stamped "Denied." His temper again rose. When were they going to put him in the real fight? This was the third denied request for transfer in as many months. Nursemaid to a bunch of kids. He had seen them go off into forming divisions but he stayed on. Too valuable here he had been told. He was needed here to harden these young punks into hardened killers. Tempted to ease up and do such a poor job that he would be transferred, he had failed. His conscience rebelled at the thought of what his flaking off would do when the boys went into combat. They would be weak, unable to withstand the grueling torment of days in the line. Doing a good job, huh, OK, he'd show them.

"Off your asses and on your feet." Gomer ordered as he planted his feet wide spread on the mountain trail. "Doubletime – Ho," a smile lingered on his lips as he jogged down the trail. Fighting men, they wanted, fighting men they'd get.

The slop chute was filled with drinking Marines. The beer was weak and green, but it was cold. It helped irrigate the sweat drained bodies. Liverlip and Malton sat with Bill Lasher at one of the tables, each drinking the last of four allotted beers.

"What do you hear from Judy, Bill?" Lasher was from J.C.'s hometown and they entered the corps together.

Lasher put down his drained glass anxious to talk. "Got a letter today. She says if I don't get a furlough when this course is up, she'll come out here."

J.C. smiled. He felt sorry for his friend. Lasher had been engaged to Judy Francy for seven years. Now they were to be married – married that is, as soon as he got a liberty. The pair had left Wheeling early in May and had not been back since. Malton smiled as he remembered the statement he had made as they crossed the Ohio River. "Take a good look, Bill, we might not see that sight for a long time." His words had proved to be a prophecy.

Now he said, "Good – but she'd better start packing."

The trio laughed. The bar-keeper was ringing a bell – that signal that the hour of closing had arrived. Mail call on Wednesday in Barracks E of Area 14 of Camp Pendleton at 1700 brought mail from home - from parents, sisters, wives, sweethearts and even bills from over-taxed civilian creditors. Mail call was persistently followed each day by a quiet half-hour. Those who received the important missals lingered over the contents. News from far brought back a nostalgia for what had been - made the great distances seem smaller - for those who received no mail it was a sad period, one of concern, worry and longing. It was when the mail clerk didn't call a man's name at mail call that home sickness took the largest toll.

J.C. Malton had a good day. Three times his name had been called, and three times letters had sailed from the hand of the clerk who stood atop a locker box, sailed over the heads of other waiting Marines. Two of the letters were air mail from home, he recognized his mother's handwriting. The third piece of mail was merely a first class letter in a small blue envelope. J.C. waited until all the mail and packages had been distributed, then shouldering his way through Marines who had not received any mail but who waited hoping that perhaps the clerk had left their letter in the folds of the mail sack, he made his way to the privacy of his bunk.

"My faithful, ever-lovin' following," Liverlip was already in his top bunk and he kissed the handful of letters he held, card hand fashion. J.C. laughed. Liverlip wrote to dozens of girls - some he didn't even know whose addresses he got from other Marines.

Malton flopped face down on his bunk facing the aisle of the barracks where the light was better. Lovingly, he held the mail before him, looked at the handwriting again, frowning at the Los Angeles post mark on the blue envelope. He held the letter to his nostrils, the perfumed paper changing his expression to one of wonderment. He had smelled the fragrance before. Placing the letters from home beneath his braced chest, he opened the blue envelope. Turning the one page sheet of stationary over he glanced at the signature "Love, Jodie." He smiled, the same bewildered expression on his features. The handwriting was small, articulate and extremely feminine. As he flipped the paper over again, the fragrance once again reached his nostrils, creating an image of its owner.

"Dear J.C., It's simple. Doug gave me his address ---"

J.C. chuckled aloud at the realization that she would know his thoughts as he opened the letter.

"I'm in class - the professor is boring us all to tears. Why is philosophy so dull! The poor man is about to put himself to sleep - he might as well join the rest of the class. This makes a time to catch up on letter writing! I just finished my daily to Ed and I thought I'd take the time to write you off."

J.C. smiled at her apology. She had managed in their one meeting to never let it be forgotten for one minute that she was engaged and now she was convincing herself - at least trying to - that it was alright to be writing to him since she had already written to the sailor in San Francisco.

"I waited for your call Sunday. You said you would and I was expecting it. When Doug showed up without you, and said you had a date I understood, but I still expected it."

Malton smiled at the awkward repetition.

"Doug is a fine boy, so much fun. He said that you couldn't break the date "the gal's got him hooked" was the term he used, I think. He made a big hit with my sister. She's thirteen and more his type. Don't tell him that, please! Almost time for the bell to ring. Thanks for letting me pass this dreadful period writing to you.

Love,

Jodie.

Malton turned over on the sack, looked up at where Liverlip's form sagged the springs directly above him. Quietly he raised his two feet until they were directly beneath the corpulent portion of the little Marine and then, drawing all his strength in his legs thrust upward. His feet hit the springs so hard it almost knocked the top bunk off its braces. Liverlip's body flew through the air and crashed to the deck between Malton's bunk and the next bunk. J.C.

leisurely turned over on his elbow, looking down at the stunned McPherson. Liverlip opened his eyes and shook his head, meanwhile feeling to see if any bones had been broken.

"What the hell you doin'?" A new resentment filled the little Marine's eyes as he pulled himself to a sitting position. From the barracks other Marines had dropped their letters and rushed to the scene of the bombing, wonder in their eyes.

J.C. kept staring at McPherson, slowly his right hand went to the bunk and gently between his thumb and his forefinger he dangled the blue letter.

"Jodie says I had a date Sunday." His voice was harsh, but his eyes were not angry. "She also says that a gal's got me hooked - rather she said she got that information from you. How about that?"

Understanding came into Liverlip's face. Slowly he recoiled leaning on the far bunk, his mouth fell open. "Wait a minute, J.C. ---" McPherson stammered as Malton got to his feet and leaned over the little Marine. The spectators tensed - sensing a brawl. Malton hands shot out - grasping under Liverlip's armpits. Quickly he lifted the stunned McPherson to his feet, then refastening his grip, he hoisted the surprised Marine to the top bunk. Liverlip looked down at Malton who had started laughing. Realizing that it was not a taunting laugh he joined in, though not so convincing. The Marines crowding the aisles stood not understanding, some laughed, others shrugged. Slowly they moved to their own bunk muttering about what service did to some guys minds.

"You little bastard." Malton smiled as he said the words. "Cuttin' me out, huh. I look all over for you and you're cuttin' me out. Some buddy."

Liverlip dropped down from the top bunk and sat on the bunk across from Malton's when the older Marine had again dropped face up on his bunk. McPherson was taking no chances of a repeat performance of the free flight he had taken.

He looked at his friend lying on his back, his hands cupped beneath his head. J.C.'s eyes were open and his thoughts were in Los Angeles.

"It didn't do any good, J.C." Liverlip had lighted a cigarette, his upper lip wetting a quarter of its length, "She's a shrewd kid! I pitched the line," he paused looking for reaction from the reclining Malton. Seeing none he continued, "the whole line, but she wasn't having any! That gal's playing it by the books. Christ! The way she throws that damned engagement ring around."

"What's wrong with that?" J.C. said, his eyes closed. The image of the girl before his eyes, "She loves the guy. It figures - at least it does to me."

McPherson drew deeply on his cigarette, the thought provoking conversation calling on seldom used mental concentration. "I'm not so sure. She acts like she does. She says she does. She has a ring to show she does, but the whole set-up doesn't sit right with me."

Malton opened his eyes and turned his head to his buddy. McPherson had put into words the thoughts that had lurked in his own head that Saturday night. Lurked, true, but which had never fought their way to cognizance. He saw the small Marine in a different light.

"The guy's parents were there," Liverlip continued. "It was a nice scene. Two happy families, and a gyrene they were entertaining as part of the war effort." He crushed the cigarette beneath his heel, "a real nice day - outdoor cooking, talking of the war and smiling significantly at Jodie when they spoke of peace finally coming." Again he stopped, "Don't get me wrong, it was nothing they said or did, but somehow it all seemed too pat - too much of a family affair."

Malton listened silently, re-enacting the scene of the barbecue as Liverlip spoke. Somehow he couldn't put Jodie into the picture.

"Kind of gave me a funny feeling," McPherson was saying, then he added thoughtfully. "Jodie didn't seem to be a part of it. She didn't say much, just prettied up the joint, her and that sister of hers." He smiled. "That babe goes for me." He lowered himself on the bunk, the smile became lecherous on his lips.

Silence prevailed once again in the immediate area of the two bunks. J.C. had listened to the words of his friend, analyzing them. He didn't understand the feeling he felt. Attracted to the girl, thus, any man would be, but it seemed to end there. Yet he thought of her frequently, his dreams even finding her creeping in. Perhaps it was the age old code of the sexes. Perhaps it was the urge of conquest which he felt now.

"J.C." Liverlip's head was on his right hand as he looked at the closed eyes of his friend. Malton's head nodded slightly. "She sure wanted to know a lot about you!" he hesitated. "When I went into the house to help her carry some drinks-out, she really pumped me. Kept looking at the phone." He stopped then added quietly as he put his head back on the bunk. "Think you could score there, buddy?"

The words carried over to Malton. His eyes still closed, the words slowly sunk into his consciousness. Finding no resistance, they traveled to his heart.

Beneath the cupped hands under his head he felt the blue letter - the fragrance wiping out the smell of the barracks around him. Evening chow call sounded!

Liverlip sat in the slop chute with a disturbed Lasher. No letter from Judy had arrived in the mail call that day. Malton approached through the crowded room. Smoke hung heavily in the air, his own pipe clenched between his teeth adding to the heavy odor filled man made fog. He sat down opposite Lasher. Turning to Liverlip he asked.

"Got any change?"

Liverlip and Lasher reached into their pockets, pulling forth the silver therein. Dropping the coins on the table, they looked questioningly at J.C.

Malton smiled. "Got to make a call." Scooping up the money, he rose from the chair, its wooden legs scraping the tough floor.

"Where to?" McPherson asked nosily.

Malton was already walking toward the door. Over his shoulder he said "L.A."

Lasher watched him go, then turned to McPherson, the questioning look still on his face. The little Marine too was gone, running to catch up with J.C. Lasher watched them disappear, then shrugging his shoulders, sadly stared into the flat beer before him.

"You calling Jodie?" Liverlip ran to keep up with Malton, stumbling on the uneven ground in the darkness of the night. J.C. walked toward the lights of their barracks, unanswering.

The pay phone booth of the barracks stood on the outside, along the upper end of the oblong building. Some thoughtful telephone people must have realized there was no privacy inside the building.

J.C. entered the booth, the light going on as he closed the glass folding door in McPherson's face. He inspected the phone books hanging on their chains, selecting the Los Angeles directory. He slowly thumbed through the pages to the F's. Running down the lists of Franklin, he frowned. Hell, there must be a thousand Franklin's in the Los Angeles directory. He didn't even know the street or her father's first name. He became aware of McPherson's attempts to push open the door of the booth. Malton took his foot away from the door and permitted it to crack open.

"The number is Inglewood 7-1544" Liverlip said, his lips pushed back in a huge grin. Malton permitted the door to open even further, careful that the light didn't go out.

Grinning, Malton put a nickel in the slot and gave the operator the Los Angeles number. As the operator rang the number he deposited the requested change into the slots above the mouthpiece. The phone rang four times before a feminine voice answered.

"Inglewood 7-1544?" the operator asked. When the voice confirmed the number she added, "I have a long distance call for this number from Camp Pendleton, California. Go ahead, please."

Malton fought back an urge to replace the receiver. "Hello, may I speak to Jodie, please?"

"Just a minute." the voice was metallic over the miles of wire. Malton heard the phone come into contact with wood, then quickly it was picked up again and the youthful voice asked excitedly "Is this Doug?"

"No." Malton smiled at the disappointed voice as an "Oh" came through the receiver. In the distance the voice called for Jodie. After a moment which passed slowly for Malton, the phone at the other end was again picked up.

"Hello!" the musical voice was slightly breathless.

"Hello, my lady." J.C. twitched at the corny sound of his voice.

"J.C.!" the voice was loud in the receiver. "Where are you? You sound so far away."

Malton smiled, "Camp Pendleton is a long way off," he paused. "Got your letter today! I'm giving you the call I owe you." Malton cursed himself. He was infuriated at his lack of finesse.

"But long distance. I thought servicemen were always broke," laughter juggled in Malton's ear.

"I am, but I'm a man of my word." He paused, rousing courage as he approached the real purpose of his call. "Jodie. I've got a pass for this weekend. OK if I see you?"

The silence at the other end of the line made J.C. regret again the call. He was a fool, a damned fool.

Jodie sat quietly, the anticipation which the question brought welling in her breast. Impulsively, she switched the phone to her left hand, where the engagement ring was hidden from her eyes. "All right." She was surprised at the decisiveness in her own voice. "J.C. I'll meet you in Long Beach. It'll be easier then you coming all the way here. Think you can find the Pike? I'll meet you at the entrance."

Malton thought for a moment orienting his knowledge of Long Beach. "Good," he said planting the information in his mind. "I'll be there at 4:30 Saturday. O.K.?"

The voice was far away "4:30 at the Pike." Scarcely audible Jodie continued, "Goodbye, J.C."

The click of the receiver at the other end of the line had sounded a minute before Malton replaced the phone on the hook.

"What the hell you up to, J.C." McPherson's voice was distraught as Malton came out of the booth. "You've had two weeks liberty in a row. You have the duty next weekend." He stopped flustered, then again he shouted, "You don't have liberty this weekend."

Malton smiled as they climbed the barracks steps. At the door he turned to Liverlip, "But you do!" The smile broadened. "I told the orderly we were trading weekends." Quickly he entered the barracks leaving an open mouthed McPherson on the porch.

Lying on his bunk, Malton stared sightlessly at the darkened ceiling. Taps had sounded and the occupants of the barracks tossed in their fruitless search of the bunks for a comfortable sleeping position.

Meet her in Long Beach because it would be easier, J.C. thought. The reason was logical, but how much truth was in her request. He remembered McPherson's account of the Franklin home and her parents attitude of their daughter's love life.

True it would be easier, but Long Beach was a long way from questioning faces in Inglewood. Sighing, he turned on his side, the vision of the beautiful blonde, and disturbing girl already intruding his dreams. Liverlip sat dejectedly on the Post Exchange steps as laughing, happy Marines clambered aboard the three gray dilapidated buses which were already filled. It was Saturday noon and liberty call had sounded in the clear, warm Southern California air. Throughout the vast military base similar scenes were being repeated many times as all training activities ceased for the weekend. Only the raiders in tent camp were still on duty. No rest or liberty for those hardened cruel killers. Most were cutthroats, good only for the deadly lot for which the Corps had assigned them.

J.C. had entered the second bus early and settled in a window seat facing the P.X. He smiled at McPherson sitting with his head between his hands, his lip protruding far out of line with his other features. The duty N.C.O. boarded the bus and checked passes, abrupt with the liberty bound Marines. Lucky bastards, he thought as he looked over the passes carefully. The bus driver started the motor, and then swore as it gasped several times and stopped. The passengers groaned and then watched the drivers second attempt to get the old motor running. Most of them had experienced the necessity of getting out of similar busses on the road to L.A. when the transports had broken down. A loud cheer sounded as the motor caught and muttered its discontent at the ordeal to which it was being put to. With a clashing of gear the bus began to roll. Through the dust swirl the action caused, Malton waved to Liverlip. The small Marine dramatically raised his right hand and offered an obscene sign in return. Malton laughed as the bus turned the corner of the P.X. and moved onto the paved main road which led to the main gate some fifteen miles away.

The lumbering bus clung to the side of the highway as cars sped by on the outside lane. The seaward 101 route was packed with cars, almost all filled with sailors and Marines bound for Los Angeles. Malton sat contentedly puffing on his pipe as the scenery whisked by. He was sitting on the inland side and the flat land with its misty mountains in the background spelled a release from the military aspect of Camp Pendleton. Occasionally a farmer with his team of horses broke the monotony of green as a plow turned over the rich brown man irrigated soil. What a country! Someday, he thought after this war was over he would come back. Not to L.A. but to one of the small communities which lined the coast between Los Angeles and San Diego. Pensively he turned the towns over in his mind - Carlsbad, San Clemente, Corona, Del Mar, Laguna Beach - Laguna Beach - the name of the small town sounded good on his lips as he thought of the famed resort town through which they had just passed. An artist colony, the strange glass fronted homes clung to the side of the coastal range, looking over the Pacific toward the island of Catalina. Less than 5,000 people lived in the informal community, where shorts were the daytime garb for male and female alike. This is where he would settle after the war - this is where he would write his great works of art. He smiled as he thought. Gradually his eyes closed and joined the majority of training tired Marines in dozing.

The clock at the Long Beach traffic circle information bureau said 4 P.M. as he got off the bus. Only a few other Marines debarked from the bus with J.C. The bus roared back into the heavy line of traffic as Malton stood getting his bearings. The ocean was two miles to his left and he was too tired to walk even though he had time, he noted. Running across the street between cars he took a position in the proper fork leading from the circle. Thanks to the war, uniforms were a badge of honor and only a dozen cars passed before one stopped and he was again a part of the whirring traffic. The ride took him to Ocean Boulevard. Thanking the middle-aged male civilian driver, he stepped from the car and glanced at his watch. It was 4:10. Gazing down at his travel weary greens he entered a fast press shop which cluttered liberty towns. 10 minutes later he was again on the street heading to the Pike, a mile long amusement area famous throughout the western part of the country. The streets were crowded with the ever present servicemen, 95 percent of whom were sailors from the fleet visibly anchored in the great harbor.

His long stride carried him toward the meeting which had been foremost in his mind since Wednesday. He still had not answered convincingly to himself his feelings toward Jodie Franklin, yet his pulse quickened at the impending meeting. He crossed the wide boulevard and moved down the small side street toward the arch which was the entrance to the Pike. His eyes scanned the crowd of pleasure seekers who were entering the amusement park. A tightening of his throat greeted his spying her standing at the ocean side end of the arch.

Jodie Franklin was uneasy waiting for J.C. She was well aware of the eyes which went over her body in the minutes she had stood there. Every one of the sailors who passed the arch looked at her, some whistling, others just peering longingly in her direction. Even the three sailors who stood at the opposite end of the arch weren't responsible for the nervousness she felt. They were making remarks about her, laughing. Some of the words even reached her ears. She was used to being stared at undressed even in the eyes of men. She realized that she was beautiful, even more so today. She had picked her clothing carefully today, had taken more pains than usual making up her face and combing her long golden hair.

Her hands now patted her sky blue dress at the hips. A conservative dress by all the standards of seductive garb, high necked and plain, but on her it was loveliness. Her taut hard breasts were molded against the plainness of the material and her legs were enhanced by the spiked shoes she wore. In her hair a band of the material of her dress formed a tiara that set off its blondness.

She had spent so long, getting ready that Sally, her sister, had besieged her with questions as to her destination. She had merely smiled, unanswering. Her mother had posed a problem, however.

"My, you're really dressed to kill." her mother had said. "Where to today that calls for such an outfit?"

She hadn't been able to look her mother in the eye as she gave her the answer which she had planned for days. "Oh! We're getting our portraits made for the yearbook today," she had lied. "Then some of us are going downtown for dinner."

Mrs. Franklin studied her daughter carefully, noticing her uneasiness. Something was wrong, she had noticed it for a week. She daren't interfere with her high strung daughter. She'd learn when her elder daughter was ready to tell her.

Jodie watched each approaching Marine. She wasn't even sure she remembered what he looked like, but why did her heart pound so? She saw his walk long before she made out his face in the crowd. She wouldn't recognize him, she laughed inwardly, yet she knew his walk.

Their eyes met and held through the crowded street. She watched his dark eyes brighten with recognition, then leave her face and travel down her body. She did not mind his examination, did not object to the desire which mounted as they passed on her breasts. Unconsciously she arched her back slightly, aware that the outline of her firm breasts tortured him. When his eyes again met hers they were not in the least embarrassed at being detected in their exploration. A wave of passion swept over her, her lips dry beneath the soft pink lipstick she wore.

He stopped a pace from her, smiling, "You'll get raped in that outfit one day, my lady."

Her face burned, and her full lips fell open astonished by the greeting. Quickly she regained her composure and laughed lightly and musically. J.C. took her hand gently but possessively in his. Turning he walked slowly through the archway of the Pike, not unaware of the envious looks cast in his direction by the three sailors who now moved out into the stream of pedestrians. The girl walked hand in hand with the Marine, her blonde head reaching his shoulder. The touch of his hand had not lessened the emotion she felt. He tightened his grip as he moved her toward a bench which sat uninhabited near a huge fountain spraying water from the image of a sea lion. Malton waited till she had seated herself facing the ocean, her back to the fountain. Then he lowered himself on the bench far enough away so he could sit sideways and look at her, his arm on the back of the green bench.

"I have until Monday morning," he said matter-of-factly looking at the side of her lovely bronzed face. "What have you planned for us?"

The question was more of a demand. She turned and faced him, unsure of herself with a man for the first time in her young life.

"I've got to be home by midnight," she said quietly as she looked deep into his amused eyes.

"I'm going with you," he said, then added before she could speak. "Your folks don't know you're here, do they?"

She lowered her eyes and fidgeted with the clasp of her small gold handbag. She said so low that her voice was almost lost in the cascading water behind them "No!" Then she looked up and stared straight into his eyes. "And I don't know why I'm here either."

Gently he took his hand from the hard bench and placed it on her soft shoulder. "Frankly, I don't know why you are either." He wasn't smiling. "What is it with you, Jodie? You've done your best to let me know that you're happy! And that damned ring! Is it a symbol - a God that protects you from the world? Look at me - " He ordered as she looked down at the ring. He drew his lips into a hard line. "You don't love that damned sailor, do you?"

Tears formed in her eyes. She wanted to run from this place, from this Marine who could read her inner, private thoughts as if they lay bare for all the world to see. Run far away from this cruel, heartless man who played with her emotions, hurt her deeply and then openly laughed at her discomfort. She hated him - hated him with the strongest desire she had ever felt.

"Yes, I do!" she literally screamed at him. "I always have and I always will!"

Through her tears she saw he was laughing, his straight white teeth startling his contrast to his sun leathered brown skin. He stooped and gently took her hand.

"Good! That's what I wanted to hear," he said astonishingly. "Then let's not treat me as if I were a home breaker." His eyes were soft. again and he continued in an encouraging gentle voice. "You're an attractive girl, my lady, a damn desirable woman. I'm a gyrene who is man enough and vain enough to have your company." Again his eyes became serious, "But I'm not going to rape you, though God knows I want you. Can't we be friends for just a few hours and let the rest go. You're the boss, but remember, don't unlock the door, or by God, I'll lock it behind me."

His words soothed then disturbed her. Damn his black heart, she thought. Gradually, as they sat there not speaking, her self-confidence returned. He was no different from any other man, once again she felt she could control him as she had the others. A frightening thought tightened around her heart. But could she control herself.

"What's the verdict, my lady?" Malton waited, dreading the answer she might give him.

She smiled, "Let's ride the Ferris wheel." Her decision had been made the Wednesday before when he had called. She feared the Marine, but she also felt the magnetism with which he attracted her. They rode the Ferris wheel, and the roller coaster, and the whip, and the flying swing seats. They laughed and held each other tight through the breath-taking rides. The hours passed quickly and soon the dark California night had descended upon them.

"Hungry?" he asked as they turned from the milk bottle throwing concession stand, a huge rag bed doll in her hands.

"Famished," she answered. "It's late! We'd better start home."

The plural pronoun slipped easily from her tongue. Both were aware of it, but neither so much as blinked an eye. The fact had been established long before on the park bench. He glanced at his watch, the short hand resting on seven. "We still have time to eat. Have any suggestions?"

She hesitated. She knew of many places in the area, but the possibility of meeting someone she knew disturbed her. She looked up at the Marine walking straight backed beside. Suddenly she knew. She didn't care who saw them!

"There's a good restaurant on the highway to L.A. All the college crowd goes there. They serve the best spaghetti on the coast." She looked up at his face bright in the lights of the midway.

He looked down at her smilingly. He had caught the full meaning of her words. "You're the boss." he said.

The taxi stopped in front of a neon lighted ramble down building on the Ocean Highway. Traffic whizzed by as J.C. paid the fare and long strided after Jodie.

"It's better inside," she answered his unasked question.

The smell of hot peppers and tomato sauce met the opening of the door of Jospe's. The room they entered was dark but inviting. On the red and white checkered table-cloths, candles burned in wine bottles affording the only light. As they walked unescorted to a vacant table J.C.'s eyes roamed the walls. Typical Italian scenes, hand painted by an experienced hand, covered their entirety. Vainly he searched for the hidden lights which illuminated the scenes. It was a comfortable room he thought as he held the chair for Jodie. There was a peacefulness here that was in sharp contrast to the blaring calliope of the midway they had just left. From somewhere the soothing music of an Italian folk song softly but unobtrusively completed the scene.

"Like?" Jodie's voice was quiet in keeping with the atmosphere created by the dining room.

Malton nodded his head, content to relax in the crude but comfortable chair. He looked about the room, amazed to find it was almost full of talking people. He marveled at the acoustics of the place. Unspeakingly he congratulated the mind who had conceived this oasis in the mad rushing world of 1943.

"Goot evenin, bambinos." Malton was jerked back to reality by the voice.

He turned and looked at the white aproned, heavy set, mustached waiter who stood at the table.

"And what will the Marine and his lady have?" Without waiting for a reply the wild eyed Italian continued, his mouth full of teeth reflecting brilliantly in the candlelight. "The lasagna it is - " he raised two fingers to his lips, blowing a kiss to the ceiling.

J.C. and Jodie laughed at this character from a Neapolitan movie. Looking inquiringly at Jodie who nodded, Malton said, "I don't know what that is, but bring us two orders, Please."

"Gracias," the waiter smiled, "and a little red Italian wine, not?" he winked knowingly. "It makes the heart beat a little faster, makes the food -" again he threw the kiss to the ceiling.

"Yes, that will do fine!" J. C. said laughingly. The fat waiter rolled off to the kitchen and was back immediately with the bottle of wine. Pouring two glasses of the rich, flowing liquid, he again "gracis'd" and disappeared into the back room.

Malton raised his glass, held it to Jodie in a silent salute and they both sipped the strong wine. It flowed warmly through their body, causing Jodie to shudder a little. J.C.. put his hand on hers across the small table. The room, the wine and the loveliness of the girl across from him, reflected in the wavering light of the candle, affected him as he had forgotten it was to be affected.

"This place should be carted up and sent near every service base in the world," he said, his eyes roaming about the room. "The war, loneliness, the damned insanity of it all seems so far away from in here." He was talking aloud but it was as if he were a witness to the scene, he had forgotten such places existed. "The people in here are protected from the insanity of the whole damned mess," he repeated. "Look at them, look at me: Basking in this peacefulness. Content with good food and strong wine, oblivious to the world outside clamoring to move on. This is the way life should be. Slow and enjoyable. A life that could be relished and reveled in with no fear of what tomorrow will bring." He looked at the door, seemingly unaware of the girl's eyes on him. "Out there, not more than two miles away, lie battleships, aircraft carriers! All the implements of destruction - the tools with which men will kill themselves as well as each other."

He held his training hard hands open before his face, "And these! They hold a rifle, a machine gun. They aim, they squeeze a trigger, and off somewhere a scream testifies that the weapon was well made, the hands well trained. But there, lying on the cold dark jungle floor, or on the bottom of the ocean will lie a corpse - lifeless:" He paused his eyes staring into the flaming candle, "when he could have all this just for the asking! Peace, quiet, relaxation and life."

Jodie watched the Marine bare his soul. For the first time in their short acquaintance she saw beneath the hard shell he put forth to protect himself. The dark, cruel, laughing eyes were now sensitive to the pain and revulsion he felt deep within. Slowly she put her hand atop his, and waited for him to again lift his head.

"Why are you in it, J.C. if you feel so strongly about it?" she asked him quietly, sympathetically, wanting desperately to know what drove this Marine and all others like him on.

Malton continued to stare into the flame. The question had not shattered his concentration, rather, it had merely put into words what he had unspokenly asked himself many times before and which now lay in his mind. Brusquely he broke some wax from where it had gathered on the wine bottle.

"I don't know." He stopped, not believing his words. Softly he continued. "I thought I knew when I put my name on the enlistment paper. I was going to fight because that's what was expected of me. The disgusted looks thrown my way as I went about the business of getting an education while others were off fighting finally began to affect me. I didn't want to go, to war - knew then that it was senseless, useless. I laugh at the belief that this is the war to end all wars. Hell, my father fought in the original war to end all wars in 1914. This won't be the last war. In twenty years - or less the world will be at each other's throats again - and twenty years after that, the world - if there is a world left, will resume this - periodical struggle to equalize the human population. NO! It wasn't that I wanted to fight! The senselessness of it all infuriates me! Perhaps I'm trying to prove to myself that I'm no coward! Not afraid to kill or be killed."

His voice had raised to a high pitch as he spoke. The loudness of it, now shocked him back into his shell. He glanced across the table at the pity in Jodie's eyes.

Suddenly he laughed. "Perhaps I know why I joined - especially the Marines. You know they say that the German fights for the Fatherland, and the British fight for the Motherland, but that Marines fight for the Hell of It - and souvenirs!"

They both laughed, the tension broken as the fat waiter approached with the steaming plates of lasagna. Malton glanced at his watch as they alighted from the bus. It was 11:45. The bus left a quietness in the Inglewood night as the beautiful girl and the hardened Marine strolled hand in hand down the street. Homes along the suburban street were alive with lights and people. Pre-war cars were scattered along the narrow street, most of them idle as the result of war-time rationing.

Jodie was inwardly trembling, her hand clasping Malton's tightly. She had steeled herself to the scene they were about to face, but the sudden proximity of home had its effect. J.C. was not unaware of the tension disturbing the girl. He felt sorry for her uncomfortableness. His hand poured strength from it but he knew the battle for control the girl was fighting. At the head of the walk of the Franklin home he could see the head of a woman sitting in a chair facing the fire, and a pajama clad young girl sitting on the sofa, her legs doubled under her, reading a magazine. He stopped and turned to Jodie.

"I can leave you here!" The words were full of meaning. The touch of deep affection had crept into him during the enjoyable hours of the evening. He felt a deep concern towards her happiness. What had started out hours before as a war-time flirtation had all but consumed him.

Jodie looked up at his face reflected in the street light. She could leave him here now, she knew and the episode would be ended. It was the expected thing to do. A night out with a serviceman - her small contribution to the war effort. Unseeingly in the darkness his eyes were burning into her very being.

She tightened the grip on his hand and walked to the door.

Sally Franklin answered the door, her pin curls clinging flatly to her head.

"Where you been, sis, we've - " she stopped speaking, her eyes finding the Marine in the semi-darkness "Oh" she whispered and held the door open wide.

Malton felt his hand being released and followed Jodie into the foyer, uncomfortableness and uncertainty walking with him. What the hell am I doing here? Jodie unhesitatingly strode into the living room and smiled at her mother who had turned in her chair.

"Mother, this is J.C. Malton." she said, false gaiety in her voice. "I met him at the party last week."

Malton stood to one side of the fireplace his overseas cap in his hands, uncomfortable at the scrutiny he was undergoing at the hands of Mrs. Franklin and Sally. Mrs. Franklin smiled and extended her hand.

"Welcome to the Franklin manse, J.C." her voice rang true, not false J.C. realized. Immediately he liked the woman. "How was the show, Jodie?"

She was laughing, and J.C. joined her. He looked at Jodie, her face red with embarrassment. "Oh, Mother!" Jodie exclaimed. She sat on the sofa, indicating J.C. was to sit beside her.

"Wow! What a hunk of man." Sally sat on the arm of her mother's chair and dodged the slap aimed at her.

"Time for you to go to bed, Sally," her mother said decisively. "And me, too." She rose from the chair and moved to the sofa where J.C. fidgeted with his cap.

"I'm very happy to have met you, J.C." she said and then continued her words not emphasizing the look of concern she wore. "I hope you'll visit us again, soon."

He thanked her and watched her gracefully walk from the room. Jodie sighed an audible sigh of relief.

"I like her!" J.C. said, emphatically voicing his thoughts. "And I can see where my lady gets her beauty."

Jodie smiled and rose. Walking to the window, she slowly drew the drapes. "Time for me to leave!" J.C. said as he rose. This was getting too hot - it was too ripe for trouble.

Jodie turned from the drapes, her fair beauty outlined in the multi-colored material. She walked toward him, a smile on her face, barring his path to the door.

"Where are you going?" she said softly her lips motionless, "Wait here, I'll be right back." Malton sat in the chair. Mrs. Franklin had occupied and drew his pipe. Filling it, he drew a light from the fireplace with a taper from the mantel. He leaned back comfortably. Muffled voices came from somewhere in the house. He closed his eyes, content once again in a real-honest-to-goodness home. He dozed off immediately, his pipe slipping from between his teeth awakening him.

"The picture of contentment." Jodie's voice came from the wall wide arch which separated the living room from the foyer. "The only thing out of place," she said as she walked toward him, "is the uniform." She sat on the edge of the chair, her right hand resting lightly on his shoulder. Quietly she said, "Mother says you're to stay here tonight if the couch won't be so uncomfortable."

J.C. was surprised at the invitation. Somehow he had thought that the older woman would be happy to see him go. "Thanks." He smiled matter-of-factly accepting. "I've slept in far more uncomfortable places in the past months."

Softly, she laughed and braced herself on his shoulder as she lost her balance. J.C. moved and pulled her down in his arms, her body cradled in the chair. She gasped and started to pull herself up, then stopped, completely happy in his arms.

He looked down at her, his left hand gently rubbing her ear beneath the blonde hair highlighted by the fire. "Jodie, you're in trouble" his voice was almost soundless. "It sounds crazy, I know, but this has stopped being a game."

Gently she placed her small white fore finger on his lips. "You said I was the boss, remember," her eyes were bright, tears welling deep within them.

Tightly she closed them as she continued. "I don't know what it is. It doesn't seem possible that I've just been with you one day - a day that the image of Ed," she spoke the word inaudibly, "has been blotted out - all I can see is you and those eyes - those damn eyes," her finger traced his eyebrows and down his face.

Gently J.C. lowered his lips and closed them on hers. Hunger inflamed by the touch exploded and the kiss became hard, demanding. His hands caressed her slim body and found their way to her breasts, cupping them gently but firmly, first one then the other. She quivered at the touch and her lips parted. Instinctively his tongue shot in and out of her mouth, an insane urgency upon him. Her body moved slowly, undulating under his touch. Time and place were forgotten. His fingers found their way to her legs bent over the arm of the chair, slowly moving up the silkiness of her stockings until they came in contact with her warm soft skin of her inner thigh.

Gasping she pulled away and almost jumped to her feet, her face tortured with the desire that she felt. J.C. sat there, his throat dry and his lips still smarting from the kiss. Slowly the passion passed from his eyes and he smiled up at her. "I told you, you'd get raped in that dress," he said softly, the grin broadening.

The tension in the girl broke, her body still tingling from his touch. She laughed quietly, a note of hysteria. tingling the sound.

Cautiously she bent over him, her hands pinning his arms to the chair. "Goodnight, J.C." she said, gently necking him on the lips. She turned and was gone from the room.

"Goodnight, my lady," he said more to himself than to the girl. He stood from the chair, his body still pulsating from the nearness of the preceding scene. Again he filled his pipe and lit it, standing with one hand on the fireplace gazing into the fire.

He heard a rustle in the hallway and turned, his breath drawn quickly by the sight.

Jodie stood framed in the archway, the fire playing on her body. The thin full length nightie was sheer and he could see the bronze of her legs through the flimsy blue negligee she wore. In her arms before her she held a blanket and a pillow. Inwardly he cursed at the obstruction. She smiled at him and standing sideways she placed the bed clothing on the chair by the archway. Quickly she turned and was gone, but not before her semi-hidden body had been scanned by the Marine.

"Christ!" Malton bit furiously into the pipe stem!

Completing his toilet J.C. stretched out as well as he could on the narrow couch. Sleep came easily in the silence, interrupted only by the crackling sound of the dying fire. His night was filled with dreams - dreams of Jodie clad in the blue negligee. He tossed and, turned, fighting to conquer her. Finally peaceful sleep came, the dream turned to just the image of the girl standing over him. Quietly the ghostly figure stood over him, looking at him, then the form bent over him and gently kissed him on the lips.

Malton awoke at six a.m. Habit of rising at that hour at camp carried over to liberty weekends. Stretching he pushed the blanket from him and donned his green trousers and silently, so as not to awake the sleeping house, went to the lavatory at the end of the hall.

He stood before the mirror rubbing his hands through his disheveled hair. Suddenly he stopped, moved closer to the mirror and brushed the sleep from his eyes. His eyes studied the image in the mirror. His hand went to his lips and gently removed the trace of lipstick which remained. Slowly he smiled. He had not been dreaming.

Breakfast went pleasantly enough, the Franklin's doing their utmost to make him feel comfortable and a member of the family group. The fresh country eggs and sausages were well prepared and hot, unlike the dehydrated eggs and Vienna sausages served in the mess at camp. As the three almost were finished with breakfast, Sally monopolizing most of the conversation, Mr. Franklin entered the kitchen. Immediately a strained, unaccountable tension replaced the carefree happiness - which had existed moments before. Mrs. Franklin introduced the short, unkempt man who was Jodie's father. A pulpy, bulging body sitting uncomfortably beneath a flabby, paunchy face. The eyes, sunken deeply into sockets beside a bulbous nose were bloodshot and sad. As J.C. took the man's soft, strength less hand, he saw that the eyes were sad, sad with what, Malton knew not.

Gradually the strained air departed from the room and once more Sally, who no longer wore the curlers of the night before, rambled on about her high school cronies, the U.C.L.A. football team, how much she liked the Marine Corps, and every other item she thought would impress Malton. The Marine smiled through the barrage, occasionally offering an opinion which fell unheard on the youthful ears. The girl was young, but in her features and quickly developing body she showed promise of becoming a real beauty. God pity the men then, he thought as he watched her antics. As he observed the scene he could see Jodie's disapproval of the scene being played by the young girl. Once, when J.C. and Jodie's eyes met he was surprised to see that the disapproval was also aimed in his direction.

"What are you two planning for today?" Mrs. Franklin's voice was a godsend as she interrupted Sally. Jodie and J.C. looked at each other, the Marine having no idea what course the day would take, and frankly content to remain here in this family inner circle.

"The car's available! I won't need it and there's some ration coupons in the glove compartment." George Franklin spoke for the first time, his voice thick and husky, unnatural sounding in contrast with his soft body.

"There you are," said Mrs. Franklin in a stage voice, "a beautiful warm California day, and a car full of gas. What does that suggest."

"The beach!" Sally was wide-eyed with excitement, but the youthful exuberance dissolved at the look on her mother's face.

"For two, it's a nice day for a beach party." Grace Franklin said, emphasizing the number. "Ever been on a beach party, California style, J.C.?"

Malton was beginning to feel the tempo of the words, although he still couldn't comprehend the action of Grace Franklin.

He could not understand the intention of her throwing her daughter and the Marine together under the circumstances. "Never have," J.C. said turning to Jodie who also was staring at her mother not quite believing the words which had been spoken. "How about it, Jodie?"

The girl turned to him, and without another moments hesitation said, "It will be fun!"

Moments later, the kitchen was a place of clanging dishes as all pitched in to clean up, one mess before starting another. Suddenly Malton found himself alone in the kitchen with Grace Franklin, Jodie having gone to the other extremities of the house to get her beach apparel. Sally had slammed the rear screen door as she was off to the neighbors to borrow a swim suit of a man who was "just the same build, wow:" of Malton. While Grace was preparing a basket lunch, George had gone to gas the car.

The silence fell heavily in the Franklin kitchen as Grace went about the task of cutting huge slabs from a ham, and expertly placing the makings of a picnic in a wicker basket. J.C. sat on a stool, smoking his pipe, his thoughts busy.

Grace turned from the table, she looked at him and saw him studying her. She waited. Malton shifted the pipe from his mouth to his right hand, bluish smoke curling from his lips. "Why, Mrs. Franklin?"

Grace didn't need any more of a question to know what J.C. was talking about. She turned from him, again fiddling with the picnic basket. "You don't know Jodie very well, yet" the voice was steady, almost inaudible. "You know she's engaged?" Not waiting for an answer she went on. "It's a match that his folks and I always wanted, but somehow they weren't drawn to each other - not really - until the war started and Ed joined the Navy." She turned towards the Marine and sat in a chair.

"Somehow, I think you already have sensed something unreal about the engagement. She's too sure, too willing to isolate herself from everyone and everything. True," she looked straight into the Marines eyes, "I want her to marry Ed, I always have, but I want more than that to be sure it's the right thing for both of them - I don't want a divorce on my hands."

She spoke the final vehemence that Malton wondered if she was speaking only of her daughter alone or if she was also referring to her marriage with the alcoholic.

Malton slowly drew on his pipe, his teeth clenching tightly on the stem.

When he spoke, it too was quietly with the pipe still in his mouth, "Where do I fit into the picture? There's the possibility that I might fall in love with Jodie," and he hesitated, then determinedly continued, "she might fall in love with me."

His words brought a smile into Grace Franklin's eyes. "Perhaps. I realize that! I noticed - realized is more like it - last night! You're a guinea pig, Marine." She laughed lightly. "If Jodie is going to be faced with a third party - you're the perfect party. As Sally said, you're some hunk of man. I'm not going to push Jodie into marriage with Ed, and you're going to be the villain. If she comes away from you unwavered in her plans, then she'll be all right with Ed, if she doesn't," she shrugged, "I made a mistake."

J.C. had listened, not surprised by the trend of the conversation. He sincerely liked this woman and admired and respected her honesty for what she had done. J.C. climbed down from the chair as he heard footsteps in the hallway. He smiled as he said, "I'm going to enjoy my part in this play, really enjoy it."

They were both laughing as Jodie came into the kitchen, "What are you two up too?" She was not smiling.

"A private joke, my lady." J.C. said as his eyes canvassed the girl. Uncontrollably he sucked in his breath, making the final words almost inaudible. Jodie wore blue shorts, light both in color and material. Her full golden legs were visible up to a line of loveliness just below the fork where her full hips majestically extended the fiber of the shorts. Her breasts thrust themselves out majestically from a pullover terrycloth jersey.

Again J.C. laughed as he turned to Mrs. Franklin. "Really enjoy it," he said. This time Grace Franklin didn't laugh with him.

J. C. sat in the disreputable 1939 model four door car. Long ago it's green paint had become foggy from the results of the California sea air. It had long since seen better days, but it was transportation and its droning motor was much quieter and more efficient than the gray bus which had brought him to Long Beach the day before. He sat beside Jodie as she expertly weaved in and out of the Sunday traffic.

Leaning against the car door he occasionally - bravely took his eyes from the traffic and watched the girl. He marveled at her ability to handle the car - marveled at her beauty and marveled at his control which stopped him from placing his hands on the breasts which were so provocatively thrust forward. Once she turned and saw his eyes on her. She smiled and turned her eyes to the highway again.

"I thought you said we'd put on our suits at the house," he said, unembarrassed at her having caught him coveting her. "You can't have a suit on beneath that outfit."

She laughed and gingerly took her right hand from the wheel. Slowly she reached for the bottom of the jersey and raised it with the grace of a dancer, the kind he had seen at the burlesque house in Dago. A flash of bronze skin showed for a moment as she pulled it above her flat stomach, then quickly tatted it back in place. "Two piece," she laughed at his discomfort.

Malton felt his hands grow clammy and perspiration dampen his brow. He wanted her so badly he could take her at this moment. He thought of the expression on Grace Franklin's face as they had left the house. You have need to worry, he thought.

"I'll say it again!" he said as he filled his pipe. "I like your mother. She's a pretty wonderful person and damn smart." He hesitated, then continued not sure of his next words. "You're father seems the right sort too."

Quickly the expression of Jodie's face changed and her body stiffened. The contentment she had felt was changed to one of uneasiness. Hate hardened her face and her lips were drawn and white through her lipstick: Malton watched her carefully. Not once, he realized now had she spoken a word to neither her father, nor he to her. Something was terrifyingly wrong between father and daughter. He waited for her to say something but only quietness filled the car.

Malton sighed and turned to the window. The country was strange to him. They had long since left the city and had passed through Santa Monica and its beach homes of the movie stars. The road marker showed they were on Route 101 heading north. Almost two hours had passed since they had left Inglewood, but he knew that most of the time had been consumed in city traffic. His watch said that it was almost noon.

"Where are you taking me, my lady," he laughed, "to San Francisco and your swabby?"

Her manner remained frigged and he realized that his attempt to change her thoughts of her father had opened the way to another troubling trend.

"Hey, my lady," he said as she didn't answer, "there's someone else in this car between you and me."

She smiled and turned her head momentarily and flashed him a lovely, everything's all right smile "Won't be long now. Wait till you see this beach. It belongs to a friend of mine from school," she stopped at his frown. "I called her before we left. They're having guests in town, but said we're welcome to the beach and the house!"

The music on the car radio had broke the silence. Neither spoke, Malton leaving the girl to her driving as he watched the mountains becoming more steep on the highway. Traffic had thinned out and the car rolled along feeling the strain as Jodie accelerated to 70 miles an hour. As she suddenly slowed up Malton turned his eyes from the right surprised that the ocean was no longer visible on the driver's side of the car.

Jodie cautiously turned the car off on the dirt lane that left the highway on her left. As they passed two stone towers which breached the lane, he caught the name "Sinclair's" on a rural type mail box.

The car bounced down the rough road, a trail of dust curling behind them. Two miles of dirt road through ragged trees and vegetation brought them to the Sinclair's private beach. Buried in a cove the white sand shone brilliantly in the sun beneath a flat roofed cottage of some size. It was constructed of California redwood and faced the sea. Jodie stopped the car and they got out, the girl walking to the side of the house, Malton followed, not unduly impressed by the magnitude of the scene. The sea was blue and endless before him with the beach sheltered from prying eyes by massive bluffs on either side. It truly was a private retreat – lovely with its long white sandy beach and peaceful with nothing but the call of sea gulls to disturb the quietness.

"I found the key," Jodie proudly held up a silver key. "Kathy told me where the extra one was hidden."

They walked to the front of the cottage which was glass paned along its entire length. Drapes protected the interior from the fading qualities of the sun. Jodie placed the key in the door and pushed it open. They stepped into a large living area, finished inside with native pine. The floor was rough and covered with white fluffy rugs. Furniture, seemingly placed idly but actually with a decorator's eyes, had as its focal point a huge stone fireplace whose darkened interior showed it was not just a show piece. Off the large room through open doors, J.C. could see bedrooms, five of them, each merely cubby holes, and a small kitchen with gleaming cooking utensils hanging from a ceiling bracket. One door was closed and Malton smiled as his mind surmised its purpose.

"Some beach house," J.C. whistled. "It's some beach house." He turned just as Jodie pulled open the drapes the sun, dancing through the glass. Again he whistled as the sea was picture framed through the opening. War seemed far away from this setting.

Jodie turned from the window, her lovely body silhouetted against the blue green ocean in the background, a smile on her face. "This is heavenly!" she said as she moved to the center of the floor, her fingers caressing her thighs, Malton watching every move, his eyes glued to the trim figure of the girl.

"You remember Kathy Sinclair, don't you? She was the other blonde at the party. Her father is an executive producer at Warner Brothers. They built this several years ago for a movie and he bought it after they stopped shooting."

J.C. remembered the girl vividly, as well as the soldier who had pawed her most of the evening. He nodded, a smile on his lips.

"Ready for a swim?" Jodie asked as she sat in a plush green chair already removing her white sneakers and blue socks. J.C. grunted agreement and began to remove his blouse, his mind and eyes never moving from the girl.

Deliberately aware of her audience Jodie crossed her arms in front of her body and delicately grasped the bottom of the jersey. Slowly she drew it up over her body and pulled it over her head. J.C.'s eyes were glued to her thrusting breasts outlined in the white bra of her bathing suit as her raised arms lifted their beauty. Her body was a beautiful bronze, soft sensuous shoulders and flat hard stomach, golden against the small bra which covered her breasts. She smiled at him and he realized he had stopped unbuttoning his shirt in his attentiveness. Self-consciously he fumbled with the remaining button of the tan shirt and pulled it from his hard, training torso.

J.C. Malton's dog tags flapped on his hairy chest, it too brown from the California sun. The muscles of his arms bulged and rippled gracefully - this time he was being surveyed closely.

"Let's go!" Jodie shouted as she rose, quickly unzipping her blue shorts and stepping from them as she ran to the door and raced across the sand. Malton unbuttoned his trousers and removed them as he watched the slim body through the huge window. Her body moved gracefully across the sand, her lovely figure straining at the confines of the brief white suit. He hitched up the yellow trunks he wore and ran from the cottage to the ocean's edge, Jodie already deep in the water, swimming strongly to a raft which floated several hundred feet from the beach.

Diving into the water, he marveled at its warmth. He cringed at the saltiness of the ocean as he long stroked his way to the raft. Jodie was sitting on the edge of the tilting raft, her feet dangling in the water. He pulled himself up beside her breathing heavily from the exertion of the swim.

"Pretty slow, Marine." Jodie laughed as she playfully punched his heaving stomach.

Malton lay on his back on the raft shading his eyes from the blinding sun. "Haven't used those muscles for a long time," he wheezed. Gradually he felt the wind returning to his lungs and propping himself on one elbow looked toward the beach.

The sun reflected glaringly on the full windows of the cottage. From the vantage point he could see the solitude and privacy of the setting. The glass house was completely surrounded by semi-tropical vegetation and in the distance he could see the cut in the trees which indicated the dirt road winding toward the highway not even visible from the raft. His eyes caught the impressing bluffs which hung close, it seemed to the raft. He marveled at their craggy, unscaleable height, his eyes playing to their extremities where they were lost in the sea. No ship was visible on the horizon, They were truly in a retreat - far from inquisitive eyes.

"Why did you bring me here?" he quietly asked of the lovely back.

Jodie swung her legs from the water, dripping onto the smooth surface of the raft. She drew her legs before her and rested her face on her knees. She looked into his eyes, her face open and frank. She laughed quietly, the sound tinkling against the small waves which rocked the raft gently.

"Mother wanted me to test myself, didn't she?" Malton startled at perception with which she had detected her mother's plan. "Could you think of a better place?" Her right hand gently indicated the setting.

J.C. looked at her, his eyes taking in the beauty of her slim, rounded legs and thighs, the cleft which her position emphasized where the bronzeness disappeared into the white bra.

"You might be sorry," he said as his free fingers traced a pattern on the lower part of her legs beneath her knee. She violently shook her head, the wet blonde hair fluffing itself out.

"I don't think so!" She watched the fingers reach the softness of her thigh, entranced by its caressing softness. "I think I know what I want, but," she frowned, "I've got to prove it to myself also." She reached down and stopped the wandering fingers as they touched the material of the white trunks. Quickly she rose and gracefully broke the surface of the water with a dive. Malton watched as the head emerged from the water, her body undulating as she tread water.

"Come on, sissy, catch me!" she shouted as she turned on her back and floated in the tide.

Malton awkwardly dove into the water and took out after her. As he approached the girl turned, she let out strongly for the beach. His strong stroke took him closer to her, but as he neared, she slipped beneath the surface of the water. J.C. followed, his smarting eyes making out her white suit in the shimmering depths of the sea. He came up behind her and reaching out he spun her around, his strong arms encircling her body. Struggling they came to the surface, laughing. His lips found hers and slowly they sank beneath the water. He pressed her body to his feeling the points of her breasts against his chest. Suddenly she struggled, and breaking from his grasp gasped for the life giving air above. Chokingly she exclaimed.

"You'll drown us both!" Splashing salty water into his eyes she swam the few yards to the beach and stood there waiting for him. J.C. treaded water, unable to reach the beach in his telling condition. Gradually he swam ashore and pulling his shorts into place walked through the surf toward her. Again she ran to the house this time, Malton slowly following.

Entering the house, Malton found one of the bedroom doors closed. Crossing to the bathroom, he grabbed a towel and dried himself removing the bathing trunks and putting on his green trousers. When he emerged from the bathroom, vigorously drying his hair with a towel, he found Jodie in the kitchen, a floor length terry cloth beach robe tightly wrapped about her. He watched from the doorway as the girl took the food from the basket, placing it on the table. She hadn't heard him enter and startled when she caught sight of him in the doorway watching her.

"Don't stand there," she laughed. "How about a drink, something cold and icy," she added when he nodded. "There's the makings at the bar in there."

J.C. turned and went to a bar which was partially obscured by a dividing wall in the large living room. Experimentally opening the cabinets beneath the bar's counter, he found a small refrigerating unit, glasses, and a wide selection of whiskeys, rum, and gin. Calling on his memory, he concocted two large icy planters punches. He had just finished shaking the ice when Jodie entered carrying a heaping tray of sandwiches and potato salad. Placing the food on a large round short table before the fireplace she sat on the floor, her bronze legs visible above her knees. J.C. brought the drinks and sat across from her. She sipped the potent drink.

"Umm, that's good!" she said throwing back her head. "What is it?"

"Planter's Punch," he laughed, "and it punches too."

They talked as they ate, of school and home. "Are you going back to college?" Jodie said as she put down a sandwich and leaned against the rust colored couch behind her. She closed further the gaping robe which clung to her figure.

"Yes!" Malton said thoughtfully, lighted his pipe. "When, I don't know! It looks like a long war! But I can wait! I always wanted a college education - so did my father but he had to quit high school to go to work." He bit on his pipe. "We sure have it over his generation. I want to write - don't laugh! I always dreamed of writing the great American novel! Maybe the war has its good side. I certainly am seeing all phases of life - all types and temperaments of people - motives, drives, desires - I'll know what I'm talking about, even here in the states - and when I get over there," he nodded toward the horizon of the sea through the glass windows.

Jodie gasped inwardly. Somehow the thought of his going overseas had seemed far away in the peaceful setting. "When? Soon?" Her voice held a sense of urgency.

Malton rose and tapped the ashes from his pipe into the empty fireplace. He laughed loudly, "Now, this would be the time to say yes, and take you in my arms and empty my desire! Isn't that the traditional scene - a man about to go to the wars - maybe never to return - how could a woman deny a man about to die for his country?" He looked out as a red glow foretold the sinking of the sun into the sea and then turned to her his eyes sweeping her face, her bright green eyes and her full sensual mouth. "No, it'll be a while yet, well after Christmas. We're not yet halfway through the training period at Camp Pendleton."

She sighed with relief and gracefully struggled to her feet, the top of her robe opening slightly, the fullness of her breast exposed momentarily. Malton gasped as he realized she wore no brassiere. She moved beside him, her back braced against the stone fireplace. Quietly they stood for a few minutes watching the blueness of the ocean turning gray in the enveloping darkness.

"I'll miss you!" Jodie said almost beneath her breath.

Malton turned to her, watching her lips quivering in the semi-darkness. His emotions were heated. He wanted the girl more than he had ever wanted anyone before. He fought down the caution which plagued him - she knew what would happen here! Damn her - damn her mother. Jodie turned slowly toward him, want showing in her eyes. Quietly she said, "Mother was right."

He took her in his arms gently, his lips finding hers. He pressed her to him, her arms tight about his neck, her breast buried into his bare chest. Slowly his hand reached the knot of her robe and slowly he untied it. Gently he pushed her from him and slipped the cloth from her shoulders, it falling in a fluffy pile at her feet. He looked down at her body, the white breasts and torso vividly in contrast with the bronze skin. He again took her in his arms and cupped his hand about her full and ripe breast, the nipple hard against his hand. She moaned quietly and he slowly picked her up in his arms and carried her into a bedroom, as the sun sank completely beyond the horizon. Twilight had come, but the two bodies on the bed merged as one were unaware of all save the tingling passion they fought with heaving bodies to quench.

The night air blew cool through the open window as the young couple drove down 101. In the distance the lights of Santa Ana shown dimly, twinkling in the clear night. Malton would catch a ride there and would be back at Pendleton by 1:00 A.M.

Jodie's head rested on J.C.'s shoulder, her eyes closed as the Marine slowly kept the car in the right lane of traffic. They had not spoken much since they left the cottage earlier, nothing needed to be said after they had lain in each other's arms. Finally they had slept only to awaken to the fact that he must leave and head back to the base. They had dressed silently and stood for a moment before the cottage watching the moon rise over the ocean. She had slipped her hand in his as they walked to the car and drove away from the retreat. Only then did he realize that she no longer wore the engagement ring.

"J.C." the voice was quiet on his shoulder. "What's going to happen now?" There was trace of feeling in her tone, as if to suggest that she had offered herself to him of her own accord - the future lay in his hands.

Gently, he took his right hand from the wheel and laced the coarseness of it over her smooth hand on his knee. "This is only the beginning of my life," he said evenly, the voice unreal coming from the hard features of his face. He continued slowly, the words coming unnatural and before from lips. "I always thought I had my life pretty well planned. College, a career of writing - somehow a woman never seemed to enter those plans." He smiled, his eyes still on the road. "Not that I haven't sampled feminine company before - I did, often at college, but no one ever meant any more than an evening of enjoyment, companionship - until now."

She felt his reluctance to go on. She raised her head gazing intently at his profile. "And now?" The question was demanding.

He tightened his hand on hers. "Now I want to share that life." He hesitated and then said emphatically, "with you!"

Raising her face to his she quickly but tenderly kissed his cheek, then sighing she returned her head to his shoulder.

"What about your mother?" the thought kept returning to his brain and finally he put it into words.

She squeezed his arm. "I think she knew all along!"

In the darkness he thought for several moments and then slowly nodded his head in agreement.

The weeks passed quickly - every weekend that he had liberty found Malton at the Franklin home. He had worried about the scene which would take place when he again faced Mrs. Franklin. But his fears were groundless, he had been almost overwhelmed by the reception he received. Sally had soundly kissed him and Mrs. Franklin had taken his extended hand and squeezed it tightly, a smile proclaiming her acceptance on her face, Only Mr. Franklin was cool and offered neither congratulations nor objections.

Malton and Jodie spent long hours together in the months that followed learning little things about each other. She had a sudden temper, and when it flashed J.C. could hardly believe it was the same girl who was so beautiful and gentle. They argued over trivial things and quickly made up in soft lingering kisses. She wrote to him daily, the blue envelopes ever present at mail call. Sometime she wrote in the boring class, but more often just before she went to bed, pouring out her feelings for him.

One such letter brought a frown to his face and he read it several times in the few minutes of solitude he had during the day. The slop chute crowd had gone from the barracks and all was quiet save for the scratching of pens and pencils as men wrote home. J.C. climbed into Liverlip's top bunk and lying on his stomach took the letter from its envelope for the fourth time.

"My darling, It's perfectly still in the house tonight - all are asleep save me and I'm writing this before the fireplace. In the semi-darkness I can almost believe you are here on the sofa as you were that first night. This is going to be a difficult letter to write, but I've thought about it all day and I think I've made the proper decision. Darling, don't come up this weekend. I do want to see you, it pains me to think I won't have you in my arms, your lips on mine, but I think it best if you don't distract me in what I have to do.

Ed's coming down from San Francisco this weekend, and he called wanting to talk to me. I told him in a letter what had happened at the cottage, all of it, and you and I are truly in love! I returned his ring the next day. But he wants to talk to me and I feel I owe him that! Do you agree? So, I'm going to see him and talk to him.

Remember I love you! I love you and I'm yours as I've never been to any other,

All my love, Jodie.

Malton placed the letter before him. He didn't understand the feeling he felt. He was actually glad that she was going to see the sailor, but he didn't know why. He filled his pipe and lighted it, thinking. He cursed his lack of confidence in the girl. Somehow the whole thing had been so easy - winning her! Was she really in love with him or was she looking for an out with the sailor all the time. Furiously he became disgusted with himself. He loved the girl and she loved him - he was certain - almost certain.

He tapped his pipe vigorously on the steel tubing of the bed, the ashes dropping down on Liverlip who had entered the barracks.

"For Christ's sake! Watch it Mac." Liverlip brushed the ashes from him, some still on his face. He hoisted himself upon the bunk sitting on the edge. "Another letter from Jodie. Hell, she'll want to marry you next."

Malton turned over on his back. He gazed at the ceiling. "She does," he said almost nonchalantly.

"Well, I'll be a turd-bird." Liverlip's mouth hung open, a look of disbelief on his flushed face. "You're not serious! What about you! You feel the same way?"

Malton lay motionless for a moment, the question sinking deeply into his brain. Then slowly he nodded his head.

"Well, I am a turd-bird." Liverlip stared at his buddy, still not grasping the full meaning of the conversation. The week had dragged for Malton. Even the letters were hollow comfort. He sensed, or was it his imagination, that conflict raged in the writer. He had traded back the liberty he had owed McPherson and spent the weekend in camp.

He now lay in the almost deserted barracks. Most of the troops were on liberty this Sunday night. The luminous dial on his combat watch indicated that it was almost 2400. He couldn't sleep, having lounged on the bunk all day, dozing off occasionally. Somewhere in the night he dimly heard a phone ringing. He had just dropped off to sleep when a hand gently shook him. He opened his eyes. Lasher was standing over him, a smile on his face. "Telephone call J.C."

Malton grabbed for his trousers, thoughts on an emergency at home racing through his mind. He ran down the barracks steps, his untied laces flapping. He reached the booth and breathlessly took the receiver to his face "Hello."

"Hello, darling," the voice was full of affection at the other end.

"Jodie!" he breathed more evenly, relief in his voice. "What's the matter?"

The metallic voice laughed across the miles of wire. "Nothing's the matter. Everything's perfect." She stopped then continued evenly. "Ed just left. I love you darling and I wanted to tell you." Silence fell across the wire, "Hello, are you still there, J. C.?"

He gathered up his voice. "Uh-huh. Thanks Jodie now I can go to sleep. I'll see you next weekend - no - wait. Christmas is Thursday! I've got a three day pass. I'll be up early   Wednesday evening.." He stopped then, lowering his voice he continued "I love you, my lady!" He took the phone from his ear and hung up. He didn't remember re-entering the barracks and climbing into his bunk. Sleep came quickly and in the darkness a smile played across his lips.

Christmas week was indeed strange for J.C. Malton and all other Midwesterners and Easterners who spent Christmas of 1943 in Southern California. The climate was not inductive to thoughts of the Yule season. The hot, dry western sun beat heavily upon perspiring troops as they continued their stepped up combat training. The sound of Christmas carols did not ring true to the ears of the easterners as the grass remained green and free from snow. Only the brilliant poinsettias, in bloom everywhere, seemed Christmas.

J.C. managed to pick up presents for the folks back home at the post exchanged. They weren't much but each was picked out carefully. He smiled as he wrapped them and mailed them Monday - he doubted very much if they would arrive at their destination before Easter. He drew heavily on his back pay to purchase the gifts, the largest amount for a small diamond ring he took a longtime selecting at the P.X.

Wednesday, December 24 was a day of bedlam at Camp Pendleton. No field problem had been scheduled for the troops in anticipation of the half day holiday which preceded Christmas. The morning was filled with idle drill and blackboard sessions, the instructors too chomping at the bit waiting liberty call.

Half the training group had Christmas Liberty - the other were scheduled for a similar extended absence from duty over New Years. J.C. had put in for

Christmas without a moment's hesitation. This was the one holiday which meant the most to him of all those during the year. Inwardly the pain of being away from home gnawed at him, but since he had been accepted into the inner circle of the Franklins, the day had been looked forward to with added anticipation. J.C. bent over his shoes, applying the Kiwi polish which brought a high luster to their surface. It was nearly one o'clock and already bus loads of happy Marines had wheeled off to the liberty towns of the west coast. He wasn't in a hurry – there would be no scramble in search of holiday activity for him – his three day pass was already filled with the plans of his second home.

Bill Lasher sat on the lower bunk across from Malton watching him. Lasher had decided to stay in camp over Christmas. J.C. looked up at the heavier Marine now, his eyes spelling their sympathy for the fellow West Virginian. He admired him tremendously, feeling a closeness with him which he felt with no other buddy. It was not just that they were from the same section of the sprawling nation, but the oneness of thought which existed between them. Both felt the need for their being in the service, but each was not sure if the entire situation made sense. Often their thoughts dwelt on the same subject as they did now.

"Going to call Judy tomorrow?" the question was unnecessary but Malton felt good as he asked it.

Lasher smiled and flipped ashes from his cigarette to the deck of the barracks room. "You know I am," he frowned, "if I can get through." He drew slowly on the cigarette and casually looked about the room to see if there was anyone within earshot. "J.C.! How about being my best man?"

J.C. slapped the shoe with the shine cloth, then looked up at his friend questioningly. "Judy coming out? When?" He was happy that the pair had made the decision for he knew that neither he nor his friend would get back across the Ohio River before they were shipped overseas.

"Sometime after the first." Lasher flushed with the thought. "I've talked to the Chaplain. He said we could hold the ceremony at the chapel in the ranch house at San Margarita."

J.C. put the shoe carefully on the deck so no speck of dust would dull its brilliance, then rose and went to his friend, clasping him on the shoulder. "Great!" He tightened his hand on the muscular shoulder, "I'll be damn proud to be best man."

"Thanks." Lasher said and again a silence fell between the pair, their thoughts preoccupied with the forthcoming marriage. To himself J.C. thought, "I hope she makes it in time."

"Ready, J.C." Liverlip stood at the foot of the aisle spotlessly decked out in his liberty uniform. On his head he wore a new piss-cutter, jauntily tipped to one side. In his arm he held his great coat, a necessary precaution against the coldness of the California nights.

"In a minute!" J.C. pulled on his blouse, carefully smoothing the folds on the breast pocket over his wallet in his shirt. His green uniform had been brushed free of knap with hours and hours of labor. How it shone saltily in the sunlight. Over his hair, cut short again the day before, he placed on an overseas cap. Reaching into his foot locker he pulled out his buster brown belt, its blitz clothed buckle shining brilliantly. He pulled the belt tightly into place, put his pipe, tobacco, and lighter in the pocket of his great coat and saluted mockingly toward Lasher.

"See you Sunday morning, Bill," he said, and followed McPherson down between the bunks to the stairs which led to the ground floor and the Los Angeles busses.

Lasher stood and walked to a window. He watched the pair cross the green grass to the Post Exchange and board a bus. He put a cigarette in his mouth, a worried crease on his forehead. He knew all about Jodie - J. C. had confided in only him - but something bothered him about the situation. He had a deep respect for his friend's intelligence but he knew what tricks a lonely man's heart played on him. As Lasher turned from the window, his mouth silently. formed the words, "Be careful, J.C."

"Hand me some tinsel," Jodie stood on. a small ladder, her curvaceous body deliciously outlined in a bright red sweater and green slacks as she gingerly and systematically placed tinsel on the tall pine tree before the large picture window.

"Here you are," J.C. stretched as he handed up to the girl a wad of tinsel. He was in his shirt sleeves, his tie removed. He patted the girl on the leg which reached out as Jodie leaned forward to place tinsel on a bare branch.

"Hey! Gyrene!" she screamed. "Be careful of the merchandise."

"What are you two up to?" Mrs. Franklin's voice came from beneath the tree as she arranged the tiny reindeer and their present, weighted sleigh in the folds of the sheet which had already been sprinkled with artificial snow.

Mrs. Franklin was contented - well almost contented. The house was full of warmth and the spirit of Christmas. The signal for the decorating activity had come with the arrival of J.C. an hour earlier. He had burst into the house, his arms laden with crudely wrapped presents. She had watched the love jump into Jodie's eyes as she took the gifts from his arms and had herself replaced them as she kissed him lightly. The hard looking young man had lifted Sally from her knees and kissed her and had even pecked her cheek as he called Merry Christmas. The house, especially the living room had been heavy with the Yule Season and she had smiled comfortably to herself as she saw the happiness and contentment which the activity had brought to the tired features of the Marine.

"How's that?" Jodie had climbed from the ladder and stood beside the Marine, her arm linked in his. The four inhabitants of the room stood silently listening to the heavenly strains of Silent Night as they looked at the brilliantly lighted tree. Mrs. Franklin snapped off the room lights and the cheerful glow of the tree lights sparkled peacefully in the gloom.

"Just like home," Malton's voice was low as he looked from the crackling fireplace to the green tree sparkling with gay decorations. "Sure makes one feel a part of living again." He hadn't realized he had spoken aloud nor was he aware that three sympathetic pairs of eyes were fixed on him.

"How about some eggnog?" Mrs. Franklin asked as she started for the kitchen.

"With or without?" Sally scampered after her mother.

The older woman slapped the younger girl on the rear and answered , "For us, with - for you - without."

"Oh, mother! I'm not a child." The voices were lost in the swinging door. J. C. laughed and took his tired body to the couch and dropped down upon it.

Jodie gracefully crossed the floor, her golden hair changing color in the reflection of the various colored Christmas tree lights. She pulled her legs beneath her as she sat beside J.C. on the sofa. Gently she rubbed her index finger across the forehead and closed eyes of Malton.

"Tired?" she asked and continued the caressing as he slowly nodded. His body had taken on the aches which always traveled the muscles and tightened the nerves which bound them after the training had stopped for several hours. "J.C." Jodie said softly, "Will you go to midnight services with me tonight? I think you'll enjoy them."

Malton opened his eyes and looked up at the vision which sat over him. The eyes were bright and shining with love and the happiness of the evening. He was tired, but he couldn't refuse her tonight. "Sure! I'd like to," he lied.

"I'll be back in a few minutes," she said as she rose and rushed from the room saying over her shoulder as she left. "We'll have to hurry!"

J.C. settled back in the softness of the sofa and looked at his watch. It was nearing 11:00 pm. He closed his eyes and reveled in the warmness of the fire. He didn't hear Mrs. Franklin come in and startled as she put the glass on the end table near him.

"Asleep?" Mrs. Franklin asked and continued seeing his eyes open. "Here's to happiness for us all and Merry Christmas." She raised her glass and waited until he had done the same and they both drank easily of the white yellow eggnog. Mrs. Franklin sat on the arm of the sofa before the fireplace and looked at Malton.

"Done any thinking of the future, J.C.?" she asked. "How much longer do you have before you are shipped out?"

Malton slowly filled his pipe, his thought formulating his mind. "As near as I can calculate, we should be leaving around the end of January." He paused, "Of course I can't be sure."

Mrs. Franklin looked into the fire, its embers snapping as they burst from the log. "I haven't asked Jodie about it," the statement was strange and disturbing to Malton. "Do you two plan to marry before then?"

Malton studied the woman, her tone had indicated her feelings on the subject and the words had brought to the surface the decision he had buried in his sub-conscious mind. "I don't know," he honestly replied. "What do you think we should do?"

The woman turned to the Marine, the mother instinct forcing itself to the fore, "How old are you, J.C. - 20?" She continued as he nodded. "Jodie's 17! I think you're both too young to marry, especially in war time. You've known each other such a short time - and you're going overseas - what if you should" - she stopped ashamed at the frightening statement she had been about to make. She raised her right hand to her face, then straightened her shoulders and looked at the Marine who had not moved during her words "I'm sorry - I shouldn't have - ! I won't stop you if you decide to marry."

Malton rose and went to the woman. He gently placed his hand on a trembling shoulder. "Everything will be all right. We'll decide carefully, I promise you."

Mrs. Franklin put her hand over his. She felt deeply about this Marine, had faith in his judgment. She smiled as she heard Jodie's footsteps in the hall - it was her daughter whom she was not sure of.

J.C. Malton sat in the vastness of the crowded church, every seat filled by intent worshipers. Sprinkled among the civilian clad congregation were the servicemen, some with parents, others alone, or like him with a young girl beside him. The smell of incense and burning candles twitched his nostrils as he sat in the pew watching the impressive services on the altar before him. He had never before been witness to the pageantry and ceremony of the Catholic Church and he was awed by the pomp and solemnity of the midnight service. He remained sitting as the congregation rose, knelt and sat during the proceedings. Behind and above him the rich, young voices of the choir lifted the traditional and beautiful carols of the Christmas season.

A sweet, relaxing feeling settled into the muscular form of the Marine. For the first time in months he was completely relaxed and contented. He looked at the back of the lovely blonde head of Jodie kneeling before him. An unexpected thought came swiftly but gently across his mind - the service that he had not been eager to let interfere with his life had brought him happiness, contentment, and love. He looked toward the altar - the God represented there was not of his faith but he nodded almost imperceptibly and silently whispered thanks.

The young couple fought their way through the crowd before the Church who stood wishing season's greeting. Several times Jodie stopped and talked to friends whose eyes always sized up the Marine with her. J. C. smiled as he realized that the story of the broken engagement had of course traveled the rounds and the smile broadened as he realized that he always came out second best in the unspoken comparison with his predecessor.

Finally they found themselves clear of the congregation having refused the last offer of a ride home. The night was dark and crisp, clouds blackening. out the bright glow of the moon. Jodie put her arm through J.C.'s, drawing warmth from the nearness.

Jodie snuggled closer to J. C. She looked up at the Marine. "Did you enjoy the service?"

J. C. put his hand over the gloved tiny one on his right arm. He spoke softly "It was peaceful." He hesitated groping for the proper words. "Amongst those hundreds of people, all with different problems, difficult cares, there in that church for two hours, there was a unity of purpose, to pay homage to the Christ Child. Forgotten were the individual problems, the personal desires and ambitions - even I felt it. It was peaceful and - beautiful." The last word was said with some embarrassment but it was the only suitable word J. C. could muster.

"I love midnight mass." Jodie sighed "The services are more elaborate and joyful, then those of the regular Sundays." She tightened her grip on the Marines arm. "I'm glad you were there with me."

They walked in silence down the street; houses were ablaze despite the hour. Gaily lighted decorations framed the windows of the homes and inside, the Christmas trees were ablaze and J.C. smiled, so were obviously, some of the people. Occasionally they passed people staggering under the weight of highly decorated parcels and happily offered Christmas greetings. It was a night of rejoicing and good cheer.

J. C. turned down the street on which Jodie's home sat. They could see it glittering in the distance. Suddenly the moon forced its way through the clouds and daylight seemed to burst over the city. The couple stopped in the deserted street shocked by the brightness of the night.

J. C. slowly reached into his breast pocket inside his great coat and pulled a small case. He looked into the questioning eyes of the girl. "Merry Christmas, my lady." Gently his lips covered hers, his fingers meanwhile opening the leather case. As their lips parted he held the box before him. The small diamond glistened in the moonlight.

"J.C.!" The words came in a sob as Jodie took the ring from its velvet seat. "It's beautiful." She took her glove from her hand and J.C. gently slipped the ring on her finger. Slowly they were drawn together, their arms about each other as their lips met in a firm kiss.

"Merry Christmas." The greeting was followed by laughter. Standing in the middle of the street was a police car, its two occupants grinning broadly at the couple on the sidewalk. Self-consciously Jodie and J.C. drew apart, embarrassed smiles on their faces as they saw the police car. "Merry Christmas." they said in unison as they resumed their steps up the street.

The Franklin house was dark save for the Christmas decorating the front and the tree burning in the picture window. Jodie took her key and handed it to J.C. who fumbled with the lock only to find the door unlocked. They quietly entered the house, not wanting to awake its sleeping occupants.

A movement in the living room drew their attention. Mrs. Franklin was sitting in the large chair before the fire, napping. A frown crossed Jodie's face as she went to the side of the chair and gently shook her mother. The older woman startled, then looked past Jodie to Malton and then beyond, disappointment in her face.

"What's the matter, mother?" Jodie spoke the words as if they didn't need answered. Mrs. Franklin started to speak, but only a sob emerged

"The no good --- " Jodie shouted and then turned to J.C. tears welling in her eyes - grabbing her coat she rushed from the room, the sound of violent crying following in her wake.

Malton stood embarrassed, unable to determine what action was called for. Slowly he moved to the couch and sat down drawing his pipe from his pocket - then he had been right about Mr. Franklin, the thick voice, the bleary eyes! He was an alcoholic. What a hell of a time to go off the wagon. Mrs. Franklin sat sobbing in the chair, the flames from the fireplace dancing on the small rumpled handkerchief she held to her eyes. J. C. drew slowly on the pipe, watching her, trying to determine what he should do, if anything. He couldn't explain to himself how a seemingly happy family could suddenly crumble within its own home, yet he had the feeling, it had happened before, often. The strained atmosphere which prevailed when Mr. Franklin was a member of the group had been plainly evident before, and now it had finally exerted itself into the open. He almost smiled at the thought that the family skeleton had emerged from the closet, Mrs. Franklin took the handkerchief from her face, and turned to the Marine, her eyes red from the tears. Again she tried to speak but the words could not come through her emotional upset. J. C. drew the pipe from his lips, and leaned forward.

"Something I can do?" his voice was quiet, soothing.

Mrs. Franklin shook her head vigorously, her right hand to her face. She spoke in a halting tear filled voice. "It's none of your concern, J.C." She wiped a tear from her cheek before she continued. "My husband is an alcoholic. He's been off the stuff for six months, but tonight"- she couldn't continue, her voice cracking with the tears that choked her.

Malton rose and went to the chair, sitting lightly on the arm, he gently placed his hand on the woman's shoulder, "Where is he?"

Mrs. Franklin gained control of her voice once again. "He called from a bar on France Street." Malton recognized the main artery into L.A. "He was so drunk he could hardly talk." Again she wept furiously.

J.C. slowly got to his feet and put his great coat on. He moved silently to the hallway as he pulled on his barracks hat. "What's the name of the bar?"

Mrs. Franklin looked up and some self-confidence forced its way through her depression. "Floyd's. But J.C. you don't have - "

"Get some rest." J.C.'s voice was calm but carried with it a command. He opened the door and walked into the night, Most of the houses were now dark as he walked quickly down the street toward the broad thoroughfare, most families having exchanged gifts and retired for the night. Once again, homesickness, spurred on by the sad situation in the Franklin home, returned to him. He visualized the tall Christmas tree, his father always bought one too tall for the room, on its platform and the three trains racing through the country-side scene his brother had constructed, covering a good fourth of the living room. At the bottom of the platform were gifts, literally dozens of them for every member of the family, and toys for his young sister. Toys too young for her, but his parents didn't want to shut out the joy of a child's Christmas - they prolonged childhood - he smiled as he thought of more for their own sense of Christmas than for any other reason. He saw the dining room table, set with the Christmas candles and the Yule cakes and candies that were so much a part of the Malton's Christmas celebration. And activity - lots of activity as the members of the Malton family and their relatives busily opened up the gifts and loudly enthused over the too large clothing and the too loud ties and sweaters, thanking and gratefully kissing the giver. It was a common ritual and scene throughout the United States he realized, but it was his own dream - one he wished with all his heart to be a part of tonight.

He pulled his coat closer about him as the dry, cold California night pierced the wide spaced threads of the green greatcoat, he sunk his hands deeper into his pocket as he reflected that the hot days turned into cold, crisp nights in this climate.

The increasing numbers of cars racing through the intersection ahead brought him back to his present situation and he inwardly cursed as his thoughts turned from the cheerful and happy Malton home to the turmoil and depression of the house he had just left.

His eyes pierced the night to the right and left as he reached the thoroughfare trying to recall to his mind just where he had seen the neon lighted sign before which marked the Floyd Bistro. To his left he saw a twinkling blue light several blocks down and he turned his steps in that direction. Several minutes later he found himself in front a dirty clapboard fronted bar. The sign above flickered on and off, the "l" in the name dead. He turned to the door and opened it with some difficulty. He grimaced at the decrepitness of the place and he entered the small, dimly lighted, smoke-filled room.

Again he cursed, as his eyes traveled from the bar where two or three sops bent over their beer to several occupied booths. What kind of people go into making up this world he thought. Christmas Eve and some bastards have no way of celebrating the happiest and brightest of holidays than to hole up in a stinking dirty bar.

A door marked with a badly carved head of a man opened and George Franklin, staggered out, his shirt and tie askew and his fly opened beneath his wide open suit coat. He didn't seem to recognize Malton as he wobbled his way to the bar where a double shot glass stood filled waiting for him. He clumsily climbed onto a bar stool, successful only after a second attempt. With one motion he raised the glass and slowly sipped the liquid continuing until the glass was empty, then replaced it on the bar with a motion to the bartender to refill it.

Malton shuddered as if the whiskey was going down his throat as he walked up to the unkempt drunkard. He placed his hand firmly on Franklin's shoulder and swung him around on the bar stool, his eyes digging hardly into the limped sightless ones of the drunk.

"Come on, Mr. Franklin! You're going home!" the words were softly spoken but broke from the thin line of Malton's lips like a whip. As he spoke he pulled and held up the man.

"Don't wanna go home!" the voice flowed and the words all ran together, then a faint recognition came into the eyes. "Oh! It's Marine. Have a drink!" he laughed without humor. "Or maybe Jodie wouldn't like that," he spoke the word Jodie as if it were strange to his lips.

"Where's your coat?" J.C. asked as he searched the room. His eyes met those of the two drunks at the bar.

"Let 'em alone," one hissed. "Let the poor bastard have some fun!"

Malton looked hard at the drunk who spoke, then said through pitched lips. "Shove off, mac!"

"Why, you sea-going bell-hop," the civilian stumbled from the stool, too drunk to stand up still. He was about 25, Four F, Malton decided as he gently leaned Franklin back on the bar and met the staggering charge of the drunk with a crushing right hand to the nose. Blood flowed from the man as he crumbled to the floor. J.C. quickly turned just in time to duck a beer glass that the other bar sop was throwing. One of the whores at a booth screamed as Malton stepped over the inert form on the floor and pulled the second drunk from the bar. A stab of pain raced through his right fist as he squashed another nose. The man slumped slowly to the floor as Malton released him. J.C. slowly surveyed the semi-dark room, relaxing as he saw that no further opposition was forthcoming.

"Where's his coat?" he asked the bar-keep who had not moved from his post behind the bar with his hands under the counter on a black-jack he saw now he would not have to use. He nodded to a lone coat on a rack at the end of the bar and watched Malton pull the passed-out Franklin's arms through the sleeves. J.C. pulled the drunken man to his feet and slid his head under the limp arm.

"What's he owe you?" Malton paused in front of the bartender.

"Nothing - he's square with me," the bartender lied.

Malton went to the door and nodded to a young teenager, who had risen from a booth to open it. As they passed through, the Marine and the drunk, they half-turned and Malton said wryly "Merry Christmas."

The night air revived Franklin and he mumbled inaudibly to Malton's inquiry as to the location of the car. The Marine checked the automobiles at the curb and spotted the dilapidated Franklin transportation. He opened the door and gently helped the older man into the passenger's seat. He closed the door and went around to the driver's side, pausing to light his pipe to settle his tossing stomach. His right hand ached as he did so and he smiled as he saw the slit knuckles beneath the street light.

Behind the wheel, he fumbled through Franklin's pockets until he found the keys and turned the car toward the man's home.

"Best time I've had in months," the voice startled J.C. as he awkwardly handled the old car. He glanced at the man slouched beside him, his eyes closed, but his voice strangely clear. "I don't regret it a bit," Franklin chuckled. "No one to ignore me, no one to frown at me - no one to hate me – just that little ole bottle and me - good old friendly bottle," the words drifted off and snores took their place.

Malton looked down at the man, the heavy words remaining in his thoughts. Somehow he understood their meaning, the man was drunk, true, but he knew what he was saying. Malton suddenly realized the loneliness that was the man's life, he had seen the way the three women of the Franklin clan had treated husband and father - with contempt - hatred - Jodie never even acknowledged his existence, his very presence. Whatever the man was - whatever he had done he deserved more help in his battle with the bottle than he was getting.

Malton stopped before the house, now dark save for the glow of the fireplace in the living room. He half-dragged, half-carried the drunken man to the door which opened when they reached it. Mrs. Franklin wordlessly closed the door behind them and then led the way down the hall to the master bedroom. Malton carefully placed the man on the bed and removed his shoes, the stench of alcohol almost unbearable in the room. He straightened up and looked at Grace Franklin who, now that the man on the bed was not cognizant of it, was tenderly and endearingly brushing the dark, smelly hair from his forehead.

Silently J.C. left the room and turned into the bathroom. Switching on the light he surveyed his right hand. Blood had crusted on the split knuckles, gingerly he felt for the broken hones which were not there. Placing the hand below the faucet he winced as the hot water crept into the broken skin, then he opened the medicine cabinet and taking iodine from it poured it over the wound. Gasping from the effect of the medicine, he covered the knuckles with several band-aids. Crude but it would serve the purpose.

Making his way down the darkened hall he found the bedding already prepared on the sofa. He drew the picture window drapes and undressed, slipping between the crisp sheets favoring his aching hand. He lay on his back, his eyes watching the dancing shadows from the flames on the ceiling.

The rustle of silky lingerie caused him to turn his head toward the archway. In the dimness of the glowing embers of the dying fire in the fireplace, Jodie padded soundlessly over the carpeting, only the crinkling of the flowing folds of the golden nightgown and wrapper. She sat on the floor beside the sofa, her right hand finding his where it rested atop the blanket.

J. C. cringed at the pain which raced through his body at the touch. Instinctively he jerked the hand from her.

"You're hurt" her voice, soft in the quietness was emotional. "What happened?"

J.C. laughed, slowly putting the aching hand above hers, bracing himself against the pain. "Several of your father's cronies objected to his leaving their company." Quickly he continued, noting her stiffening. "No one got hurt, your father's ok."

"Is he?" The word were spoken with bitterness. In the soft light of the fire, her face was hard and her eyes shone with a hate that was intense and lingering.

J.C. shouldered his body on the couch until his head rested raised on the arm of the sofa. He looked at the girl - the hate and distaste in her eyes were unnatural and likewise distasteful to him.

"What is it, Jodie?" his voice was steady and forceful. "You've never spoken to your father when I've been around - not only that, but you've ignored him completely. What's the reason?"

Jodie's head was resting sideways on the sofa seat, tears glistening in her eyes. J. C. could see her struggling with herself debating inwardly if she should disclose her secret. Slowly she moved her head close to his, her eyes averted and her cheek on his chest.

"My father," the word was strange coming from her lips - J.C. had never heard it spoken in that manner before, "is an alcoholic - has been as long as I can remember. It was pretty miserable for mother to put up with - he'd come home drunk and beat her - he doesn't even remember doing it. You've seen him sober - quiet and a damn good engineer - that's how we've got this," she indicated the beautiful home, "but when he's on one of his binges he's mean, disgustingly so."

She stopped and J. C. waited. So far she hadn't told him anything that he had not guessed. He waited watching the girl who once again had shifted her position until her back, white beneath the silky wrap rested against the couch. She stared into the fire, now almost dead. Slowly her voice came and filled with emotion."Some nights it was worse than others. He was mean and - and insane," a sob broke the word. "He'd beat mother - I could hear her moan, and then when she was almost unconscious he'd - "she stopped unable to go on the tears rolling down her face.

J.C. took her in his arms and turned her face to his chest, his jaw was knotted - he visualized the girl in her room holding her eyes to shut out the sadist scene in the next room.

"One night," J. C. was surprised as the room was again filled with the emotional voice, "he came home worse than usual. I heard him come in knocking thinks about as he staggered through the darkness. He was almost falling as he felt his way through the hall. I was terrified and had pulled the pillow over my head to close out the sounds when he burst through the door of my room. He was groaning and grunting mother's name. I couldn't move I was so stupefied. It wasn't until he had pulled me from the bed and torn my gown off that I could scream. The sound made him more insane. He hit me and grabbed at me." She shuddered at the thought, "If mother hadn't come in and somehow pulled him off I would have died."

The tears flowed uncontrollably now and J.C. smothered them against his chest. He swore beneath his breath. Damn him! Now he understood the atmosphere that existed in the house. His lips were dry as he gently soothed the girl with his hands, his own pain forgotten. Gradually the tears stopped and the girls breathing became more natural. Gently he slid the head to the couch and gingerly freeing himself lifted the slim body to the couch. Silently he covered the girl and stood above her, his lips dry. Slowly he pulled on his trousers and sat in the huge chair placing his greatcoat over him. The fire was almost out as he looked into it.

What a mess this was. Somehow he couldn't bring himself to hate the father, he knew that the man's actions when drunk were brought on by his life - or lack of it when sober. His thoughts turned to the mother - the efficient, friendly but cold Mrs. Franklin. He closed his eyes - and made up his mind - his plans called for marriage to Jodie. He was taking her out of this morbid situation.

The pre-war Dodge sloshed down rain swept Route 101 toward San Diego, Camp Pendleton its destination. J. C. Malton strained his eyes through the small arc made by the hesitant windshield wipers picking his way through late afternoon traffic, all headed toward the military bases set on the lower tip of California. Jodie sat close beside him, drawing warmth from his body.

Occasionally, as she did now, she spoke. "Are you going to call home?" She smiled, her whole being happy as she remembered the announcement of their coming marriage, and the effect it had on her mother, surprisingly enough she had smiled and had seemed earnestly happy at the news. The smile slowly turned to a frown as she recalled that her mother's happiness had quickly turned eagerly from sadness over her father's exhibition of the evening before.

"I'll call tonight." J. C. took his right hand from the wheel and placed his arm around the girl. He smiled down at her, "They will be surprised - and happy," he added though he didn't actually believe it. "Jodie," his voice was questioning, "what about these instructions I'm to take. Do I have to?"

The girl laughed musically and squeezed his arm tightly. "Don't worry, honey, they're nothing. Only we Catholics have to make sure when we marry those of another faith, that the victim knows what they're getting in for. You know it's for keeps in the eyes of our church."

J.C. nodded in the gathering gloom. The rain still fell heavily and he fumbled for the headlight switch and muttered his thanks when Jodie pulled the switch. He knew a little about Catholicism at least about the rule that forbade divorce - he agreed with that, but the rest of the dogma of the Roman Catholic faith was a mystery to him.

"There's a Catholic Chaplain at the base. I'll see him first chance I get," J.C. said.

"Make it tomorrow." Jodie again squeezed his arm. "I love you, J.C." her face crashed against his sleeve.

J.C. smiled and felt his deep love for the girl and his want for her gnawing deeply at his insides. The rain seemed to be letting up and the setting sun high above the storm clouds turned the horizon on the sea beside the halfway to a fiery red.

A line of cars waited at the Oceanside entrance to Camp Pendleton, their headlights slowly creeping toward the sentry who was checking passes at the main gate. J.C. stopped before the poncho clad Marine, the latter flashed a flash light into the interior.

"Just driving into thirteen area." J.C. said, "she'll be right back."

"Better be," the Marine laughed as he stuck a temporary stamp on the windshield and waved them on.

J.C. slowly accelerated and shifted gears. The winding road climbed the hill past numerous areas, each one laid out in the same manner with barracks buildings sitting at angles about a central area where a long building holding the area library, P.X., and slop chute squatted beside a large assembly and theatre building. All the buildings save the P.X. were ablaze with lights and in the early evening darkness, figures huddled against the piercing rain, shuttled between the buildings.

The marine and girl rode slowly, their impending separation leaving them quiet and thoughtful. The lights continued to flash past with the miles and area 13 soon loomed before them, it too, bright with lights. J.C. turned into the motor transport area and backed the car back on the camp highway. He drove several hundred feet back from 13 Area, and pulled onto the berm of the road and turned off the motor and lights.

"Thanks, my lady," he put his arms around her body and pulled her face close to his. "I'll see you week after next." Her face was softly lighted from the area's lights behind them. Softly he placed his lips on hers and the kiss turned from a gentle one to one of want and desire. She clung to him and responded with the want she felt.

Brusquely he pulled away and reached for the door handle. "I love you," he whispered as he opened the door and stepped into the rain, and slammed the door. Jodie rolled down the window the rain hitting her on the face.

"J.C. See the chaplain tomorrow." she called.

Malton laughed and walked into the rain toward 13 area. He stopped and turned as Jodie started the motor and he watched the red glow of the tail-light disappear into the night.

The two Marines plodded through the early January rain. The mud slashed through the tongues of their combat boots and oozed down their already damp socks. Malton pulled his helmet liner covered head deeper into his poncho.

"I don't know, Lasher," J.C. said through the rain. "There's more to this religion than I had imagined - it's got me pretty well snowed."

Lasher laughed, his teeth chattering from a chill as he did, "That's just the way I felt at first – seems - to take a lot of faith to be a Catholic, and it's difficult to accept so much of the dogma in such a short time. But," he smiled as he thought of Judy, getting ready to leave tomorrow for Camp Pendleton. "It's worth all the doubts."

J. C. turned to his friend and silently agreed with him. They had just left the Catholic Chaplain's quarters, Lasher completing his instructions and J. C. still mired down in his fifth lesson. Slowly he shook his head, the rain sliding off like a dog drying himself. The chaplain had made it clear from the beginning that he did not have to turn Catholic for the Church to recognize the marriage, but the Marine would be required to agree to many conditions, most important to him, and one that cost him the most doubts was the requirement that any offspring must be reared as Catholics. He didn't object to Catholics, many of his friends both at home, in school, and now in the Corps were Catholics. Frankly, he admitted to himself now, he had always admired their determination and conscientiousness in maintaining and keeping the rules and requirements of their faith. But still he didn't feel, at least at present, the drive that would compel him to become a Catholic, and he wondered how the relationship in the Malton household would be with he being the only "non-believer" in the home. Inwardly he smiled, there would be plenty of time to resolve the question. It was still raining the next day at Camp Pendleton, but the gloom that hovered over Lasher and Malton's sacks was not as a result of the rain pelting down outside. Their orders had been changed, their training had been cut short, embarkation day was set for early next week. The news had been broken at roll call that morning.

"Damn it!" Lasher sat on the lower bunk, his right fist slamming into the rolled up mattress at his side. Again he cursed, the words strange from his lips. "Damn it!"

Malton lay on his back, his eyes searching the ceiling. All about him the Marines were squaring their gear, most elated at the word that they were shipping out. It was apparent to anyone caring to notice who were the married men by the efficient but sullen way they went about the task. It was a depressing Saturday.

Lasher suddenly rose from his bunk. "Where you going?"

J.C. swung into a sitting position, his eyes peering intently at the squat Marine.

Lasher stopped and turned to his friend. Slowly his lips began to move." I'm calling Judy," his eyes were misty. "She'd better not come." He swiftly fought his way down the crowded aisle.

J. C. jumped down the top bunk, his thoughts on Jodie – he had better contact her. He was scheduled for liberty that weekend but he imagined it had been called off since the orders had been cut for their departure.

He followed the path Lasher had made through the equipment and went to the head. The sound of running showers surprised him. He saw Liverlip at the far sink and fought his way through towel clad bodies. McPherson was lathering his face to shave some highly imagined whiskers. He turned as he felt Malton's presence.

"Aren't you going on liberty?" His eyes were wide with amazement.

Malton felt a knot forming in his stomach. "Hasn't liberties been cancelled?"

"Hell no! Hurry up if you're going to make that 10 o'clock bus."

J.C. gazed at his own face over McPherson's in the mirror. He couldn't read what his expression said. Gingerly he felt his face. He could pass up a shower and shave until he reached L.A. Quickly he turned and made his way to his bunk and began changing into his liberty clothes. He was almost finished when he spotted Lasher slowly walking down the aisle between the bunks, his hands thrust deep into his pockets and his head hanging.

J.C. went about finishing dressing. He turned and held out his tie to Lasher who leaned heavily against the row of cots. Lasher took the ends of the tie and began knotting it. His eyes clung to the khaki material, a tear slowly descending down his cheek.

"She left at 9:00 this morning," Lasher said softly as he gave the knot a final tug and slipped it between the points of the collar.

J.C. rode with his eyes closed, his body bouncing with every bump of the bus. Liverlip sat beside him, his mouth continually spouting words that Malton was oblivious to. He was deep in thought, his present and future laid out before his closed lids. He fought for the decision that would not come. In a matter of hours he must face Jodie and tell her of the change in orders, but what of their plans for an elaborate wedding. The invitations had already been sent out he knew, dated three weeks hence. Would she agree to a hasty marriage tonight or would she want to wait? But the question in his mind at the moment was what he wanted to do.

The decision would not come easily. His thoughts formed one solution and then threw it out. The bus rolled on and so did McPherson's one-sided conversation.

It was getting dark as J.C. stepped down from the bus and turned down the narrow side street. Slowly he walked in the gathering gloom, his hands thrust, unmilitary deep in his trouser pockets. His eyes seemed to be looking at the houses and the children playing before them for the first time although he had seen them dozens of times before. The white stucco of the homes with their pale tile roofs shone eerily in the semi-darkness.

Inside the homes, lights were already chasing out the night and the pleasant odor of cooking food drifted to his nostrils. Sadness accompanied his slow steps - these people were going about every day chores, not realizing what they really meant. He knew - at least he was now beginning to realize the importance of a cluttered sidewalk with the toys - bicycles, baby carriages, and wagons - the sweet smell of close cropped grass in the gathering dew - the shiny brass knobs on the doors, the hot water that awaited only the manual command to rush steaming and clear - the light that came on at the flick of a switch - the music that floated from the handsome cases but most important of all - the security, satisfaction and sense of well being that came from four walls about you - a home.

He smiled to himself - all this had seemed so commonplace to him before, so common, in fact, that never before had his thoughts dwelled upon them. Now they lingered, encouraged by the realization that soon - too soon he felt - they would no longer be a part of his every day world – they would only be a memory - a memory to hold fast to and savor with longing and anticipation. All this, his eyes quickly took in the entire block before him with its pangs of home, would be replaced by what. The smile broadened as he recalled stories of cramped quarters in the stinking holds of ships and the feeling that aloneness even with one's thought was impossible. And there were the stories of the jungle, its heat, its foulness and its lack of everything civilized - and the inhabitants of the jungle, malaria carrying mosquitoes, lecherous ants, and terrifying land crabs and death dealing Japanese.

He hadn't realized that he had stopped before the walk leading to the Franklin's. He didn't know how long he had stood there staring at the home. Startled by the opening of the front door he made his way slowly up the walk, taking his hands from his pockets and unconsciously adjusting his blouse.

"J.C. Is that you?" the voice came from behind the screened door, its owner hidden in the darkness, but its tone disclosing it to be Jodie. Recognizing him she added, "We've waited dinner for you. You're late."

He was being scolded he knew and the smile which was still on his face softened even more. He was late, all right. He had purposely taken his time with the shave and shower at the downtown Y.M.C.A. The biting spray of the water and the splattering of the water had given him his first moments of solitude, and time for thought.

He entered the darkened foyer as Jodie held the door open for him. Once inside his eyes tried to penetrate the darkened room. Finding no one there he took the girl in his arms and kissed her hard upon the lips. His mouth silencing the beginning of an exclamation - her lips responded and she clung to him tightly . Drawing his lips from hers, he continued to hold her close, the fresh clean scent of her hair tingling his nostrils as they lay against it.

"Wow!" Jodie whispered, a laugh in her voice. "It was worth the wait!" She pulled herself from him and taking his hand led the way into the dining room where J .C. was relieved to find only Sally and Mrs. Franklin seated there.

"Hi, Gyrene!" Sally called, her mouth full as she shoveled another forkful of roast beef toward her mouth.

"Sit down, J.C." Mrs. Franklin smiled, her eyes testifying that she was really pleased to see him. In the weeks since that first announcement, she had more than accepted the Marine as her future son-in-law and had more than gone out of her way to let him know it.

J.C. sat at the table and the meal resumed. Sally talked of her latest boyfriend, evidently a big wheel on the high school campus, and J.C. smiled at the occasional scolding her remarks brought from her mother and a sister. Several times he felt Jodie's eyes on him and he smiled, but her eyes were prying and it was clear to all save Sally that all was not well.

"Mother, if you and Sally want to catch the early show, J.C. and I will do the dishes." Jodie finished drinking her coffee, her eyes looking straight at her mother. J.C. finished the last spoonful of dessert, pretending not to see the play between the girl and her mother. As he brought his napkin to his mouth he casually glanced at Sally, her face red and her mouth just twitching to speak.

"Fine!" Mrs. Franklin had made up her mind. "Any objections, J.C.?" She spoke his name but her eyes were fixed sternly on Sally, he realized.

"I haven't had mess duty for a month," Malton laughed. "I guess the dishwater won't curl my fingers."

"Let's go Sally," Mrs. Franklin rose from her chair and left the room, Sally dutifully, if slowly, following her.

The sound of the front door closing brought but another noise to mingle with the sound of dishes in the kitchen. J.C. stood by the drain table, his clumsy, roughened hands adroitly trying to rub the pattern from the dish he held. Jodie stood at the sink, her small hands submerged in the dishwater. The dainty apron she wore added to the picture she made in a soft, fluffy white sweater and blue skirt. Malton continued to rub furiously, trying to plan his strategy. Soon he would have to tell her, and then what? He watched the graceful arms gracefully move the soapy hands - her breasts outlined even more in the white sweater, heaving heavily.

"When do you leave, J. C.?" the words were spoken softly, but they cracked like a whip across the room. They were alive with feeling, but spoken as if they had been rehearsed silently. She turned slowly to him, the soap suds dripping unnoticed to the floor. Tears suddenly welled in her eyes and flowed down her cheeks. Again she spoke, but this time her voice heavy with emotion. "When?"

J.C. dropped the wash cloth to the counter and took a step toward her, his right hand brushing a tear from her cheek. Impulsively his shoulders jerked, "Monday, Tuesday, I don't know for sure."

Suddenly she was crying hysterically, jerking herself from his reaching hands and running into the hallway. Malton stood there a moment, he could hear her muffled sobs coming from the living room. Slowly he turned to the sink, his forehead creased with a frown. Deliberately he put his hands into the soapy water, feeling for any stray piece of silverware. Finding none, he pulled the stopper and watched the suds swirl down the drain. Flushing the sink he dried his hands carefully and hung the dish towel on the rack. During these minutes his thoughts tried to form in his head, but utter confusion held sway. He had been surprised by the outburst, stunned would have been more accurate. Jodie was high strung, she had proven that before, but this outburst had merely confused him more. He thought he had made his decision there in the shower of the Y.M.C.A. but now he wasn't sure. Wasn't sure, the two words hung there in his thoughts, and slowly what had been bothering him for the past several weeks, since he had seen the Chaplain, exerted itself upon his conscious being.

Malton stood leaning with his back against the sink, his mind disturbed and his heart revolting. The Chaplain had made it perfectly clear there in the office back at camp.

"Son," Chaplain Frank P. O'Brien was a large, dark, hairy man with a voice that carried a heavy touch of the old Sod in it. "Forever is a long time, and your lifetime is but a small part of it. When you marry this girl it's for your lifetime, but for her, because of her religion it's forever. There'll be no dissolving of the vows once you both have taken them." He paused seeing the concern in the Marine's face. "Now don't misunderstand, my boy. I'm sure you are positive that this is the wife for you, just as I'm certain the young woman has decided, but I must point out the danger involved. The acquaintance has been about two months you said." The Chaplain had made his point well!

Now Malton pushed away from the sink, his hands trembling slightly. Wasn't sure! His heart cried out that it was sure, his senses cried out that they wanted, needed her, they were sure, but his mind wasn't sure. He loved the girl now, he was sure, but what would happen in the year, two years, three years or more that he was overseas. How deeply can a memory be planted in 90 days, how long will love last under these circumstances? And what if he was killed - the possibility had come into his mind for the first time.

Brusquely he cast the thought from his head and forced himself to walk into the dark hallway that let into the darker living room. No fire burned in the fireplace. He felt for the lamp that stood inside the archway. Across the room he heard the heavy breathing of the girl on the couch, catching occasionally in a sob. Finding the light he switched on the dim floor night light on the base. His eyes became accustomed to the soft warmness which now shrouded the room.

Gently he went to the couch where Jodie lay on her stomach, her left leg still dangling in the position where she had first dropped. Her face was turned toward the wall, her head buried in the pillow. J.C. sank to the floor beside the sofa and gently stroked the golden hair. "You knew it had to come," he said softly, his voice little more than a whisper. "We got word this morning. The orders weren't very definite about the exact date." The body on the couch didn't move. Brusquely he turned the head toward him. "Snap out of it! Hell, I'm not the only one who ever went overseas."

The girl seemed to gain her composure. Quickly she pulled him beside her on the couch, her lips clinging to his. Gently he began to caress her back, his fingers dispatching comfort to the trembling girl.

Suddenly she sat up on the couch, her skirt creeping over her knees as she did so. She sat with her back against the corner of the couch. She pulled his head against her firm breasts. He rested there, the beat of her heart clear against his heavy head.

She brushed a tear from her eye. "I'm all right now," her voice belied the fact. "When do you have to be back?"

J.C. drew his hand against the rough material of her skirt where it covered her outer thigh. "Tomorrow at 6:00 p.m." Again he felt her breath come in a gasp.

She turned his face upward and crashed her lips fiercely on his. He felt control of his emotions quickly leaving and he fought them knowing there was a more trying scene coming.

"What about us?" the words were almost whispered in his ear as she bent over him once more.

J.C. felt his heart beat faster. His tongue was thick in his mouth. "What about us?" The question served as a trigger on the girl. She almost thrust him from her and pulled herself away from the support of the couch back.

"We can get married tomorrow!" The words were spoken in a tone he had not heard since they had first met. "Isn't that's what you want?" The last word was almost a scream.

J.C. rose and walked to the fireplace. He drew his pipe from his pocket and slowly began to fill it. He fought for the right words. "Yes, I want to marry you, but," he was stopped by her cry.

"But, what!" She stood up and placed herself beside him. "What are you trying to say?" she screamed.

Malton looked at the girl's face. It was a face he had never seen before. On it was ugliness, fear, anger, and hatred. He was shocked, but he heard himself saying, "I think we should wait until I get back. I don't know enough about your relig - "

"Shut up! Shut up!" she screamed her hands to her ears. "Religion - that's a poor excuse! You don't love me!" Her face twisted with rage. "Want me, yes! But love me - NO!" She raced to the closet by the door, grabbed his coat and hat and flung it at him. Calmly she said, "Get out! You've had your piece of ass! That's what you wanted. Get out!"

Slowly Malton walked toward the door watching the girl. Stunned by her sudden fury and her more sudden change of form, he was speechless. As he reached her he stopped, groping for words.

"Get out!" she hissed, her eyes wild.

Malton opened the door and walked out into the night. As he reached the middle of the walk he heard the screen open. Jodie stood in the light of the streetlight. "You forgot something!" She raised her right hand and flung a shiny object that sailed past Malton's head. Slowly he turned, not looking back on to the ground where the engagement ring lay somewhere in the grass. The bus stop was a block away.

"Malton!" the voice called loudly through the nearly deserted barracks. "You're wanted on the phone."

J.C. swung his legs over the side of the bunk. Tiredly he rubbed his eyes with the backs of his hands. Glancing at his watch he gingerly forced himself to his feet. It was almost 10:00 a.m. Walking briskly he pushed his shirttail into his trousers, he hadn't bothered to undress when he came into the barracks at 4:00 A.M. The trip to the base had been a slow and lonely one. Not many servicemen returned to the base on Saturday night, but then not many went through the ordeal which he had the night before.

Finally, fully awake he went into the orderly room where the phone sat on a table off the hook. The duty N.C.O. slouched in a chair, his feet resting on the table and his overseas cap draped over his eyes. He looked up as Malton came in and nodded toward the phone. Malton picked up the receiver, only then the reality and importance of a long distance call hitting him full force.

"Hello!" His mouth was dry and his lips cracked as he spoke.

"J.C.?" The voice at the other end was unnatural, trembling with emotion. It was Mrs. Franklin. "J.C. I've been trying to get you since early this morning. Is Jodie there?"

The words smacked his senses with an echoing crash. "Jodie?" he managed in a low voice, his head spinning. "No, she isn't. I haven't seen her since last night."

He could hear the woman crying at the other end of the line and he felt helpless to comfort her. The duty non-com had pushed his hat back and straightened up his ears. He was missing nothing! Finally J.C. spoke again. "Mrs. Franklin! What happened?"

The sound of a handkerchief being used was audible at the other end of the line, then sniffles, "I don't know. Sally and I came back from the movies and the house was dark. Did she leave with you?"

J.C. began to vibrate with fury - fury at himself and fury at Jodie. Desperately leveling his voice he said, "No." He wanted to tell the woman what had happened but material was classified about their leaving and he didn't want to mention his impending departure and the consequences over the phone, especially with this over-bearing non-com listening to every word. "We had a disagreement, and," he could punch the leering, smiling face of the corporal sitting before him. "I left. She was upset, but I'm sure she's all right. Don't worry Mrs. Franklin."

"Where could she have gone?" the voice hinged on panic and Malton broke in an effort to squelch the possibility.

"Have you called all her friends?" He knew she hadn't. She wouldn't have wanted to spread the story of her daughter's absence amongst the gossipy college girls. He was sure that she had thought Jodie and he had merely eloped. He imagined her fright had begun when she had found him at camp.

"No." the voice was calmer, resigned to the task before her. "I'll start now J.C. I'm sorry." The voice stopped and there was a second of hesitation before he heard the phone being replaced on the hook.

Slowly he replaced the dead phone he held in the cradle and turned toward the door.

"Woman troubles, mac?" the corporal was chewing noisily on an apple, his lecherous eyes displaying his immense enjoyment he was receiving from the episode. J.C. turned in the doorway and stared momentarily at the pimply corporal, his eyes hard and cruel. The duty N.C.O. stopped chewing and stood with his mouth open. His slow brain wasted no time in figuring he had better end the staring bout. Dropping his feet to the floor he began shuffling some papers on the table. Malton turned and made his way up the steps to the upper deck where his bunk lay. He passed almost noiselessly down the row between the double tiered bunks, most now deserted. Next to his own sack, Bill Lasher slept deeply, his night having been one of tossing and turning, his thoughts on the train carrying Judy which was slowly making its way westward. Momentarily he forgot his own troubles as he felt a pain of compassion for his friend.

As noiselessly as possible he swept to the top bunk and lay upon his back, his hands behind his head and his eyes closed. The damn fool - the little damn fool. He had recreated the scene at the Franklin living room many times enroute back to the base and lying in his bunk before sleep had come. He had strained to wipe out the vision of the girl, the ugliness of her face in the soft light, the coldness and contempt with which she had ordered him out, the refusal to listen to anything he had tried to say, but the memory would not leave, had rather persisted in his thoughts.

Gradually, the early sharp pangs of hurt and regret had left and it was replaced with a feeling of well-being - well-being in that he had made the right decision. He really hadn't known her, the magnitude of her temper, the full scope of her possessiveness, the limits of her understanding. And so he had finally gone to sleep but not entirely unhindered with the feeling of love, of wanting, which he felt for her. He knew he still loved her as much as he had ever had, but now he realized that it would take a long period of companionship, of becoming really familiar with each other, a period of understanding and resolution. Then, and only then, could their life together be happy, if they still desired to marry as Father O'Brien had said "for the rest of their lives."

Somewhere a bugle sounded, calling the men to chow. J.C. didn't move, the need for food was not demanding and he thought he had better stay close to the barracks phone. It was a long day, one filled with conversation with the awake Lasher. Both men spoke freely of their troubles, finding comfort in the understanding they both offered.

The phone didn't ring for J.C. that day, nor did it ring for him for two years thereafter.

Monday was filled with packing of the small amount of gear each man was to take with him. His rifle was carefully checked and his issue of warm weather clothing. The clothing list which was posted in the barracks brought some raised eyebrows as it included topcoats. Locker boxes were emptied and all a man's possessions were jammed into one sea bag. At noon another order was posted on the bulletin board. The replacement outfit would leave at 0800 the next day by truck for the ships at San Diego.

Malton stood next to Lasher as they read the bulletin. J.C. looked at Lasher, whose expression changed not a fraction. His jaw was set, the ordeal had left its toll and resignation had deepened the lines in the forehead. The ringing of the phone downstairs caused J.C. to think of his own concern for Jodie. With pulse rising he heard the orderly jogging up the steps of the barracks. "Parker! Telephone!" Malton's face relaxed but his heart still pounded furiously.

"Hells Bells!" The words shot youthfully from Liverlip's mouth. He sat on a bare mattress on the lower bunk beside Lasher. All about the barracks men sat in small groups talking quietly. The room was bare, all sea bags had long been loaded in trucks, now nothing remained but bare mattresses on the bunks and the men. The clock over the barracks door read 11:00 A.M. The marines had been waiting since before dawn but the trucks that were to take them to San Diego were still grouped outside. Officers and non-coms bustled about outside, checking and re-checking.

"Stand at ease, Liverlip." Malton sat on a top bunk, his legs dangling, from over the side. "Hurry and wait! It's the story of the service."

A commotion started at the and of the barracks. An orderly staggered in, two mail sacks slung over his shoulders. "Mail call! Last one! Come and get it!" The Marine climbed on an empty foot locker as the troops crowded about him. Names were sung out, followed by "Ya's" and "Here", as the men collected the valuable missives from home. At last every letter had been dispatched and the men sauntered slowly back to bare bunks opening the letters.

"Here's your collection!" Liverlip flipped up two letters from the floor level to J.C. Malton's breath caught as he noticed that one was the familiar blue of Jodie's. But it was not the small square, rather large and a different shade of blue.

J.C. turned over on his back and tore the letter open, his heart beating fiercely. The writing was Jodie's familiar fine hand.

"Dear J.C.,

I don't know where this will reach you, but I felt I had to write! You'll never know how you broke my heart Saturday! Has it only been two days? It was cruel and heartless the way you tore apart everything that was between us! I married Ed yesterday here in San Francisco. He loves me and wouldn't hurt me for the world. I hope you're satisfied!

"Love, Jodie"

Malton lay still for a minute, his face ashen, his pulse pounding. Slowly his muscles relaxed and a grin crossed his face. How lucky can a man be? He had been spared a life with this madwoman. Suddenly he began to laugh, the sound of it reaching the far corners of the barracks room. Faces turned in the direction of the laughter and watched. Lasher and McPherson trying to quiet down Malton, but their efforts were in vain.

The laughter became more hysterical and mad.

A Lieutenant appeared at the barracks door. "O.K. Men! Fall in!" Slowly the ship pulled from the slip in San Diego, another load of Marines heading for the combat zone. At about the same moment, a westward train was pulling into Oceanside, California. A trim, attractive girl of 25 stepped from the train, her eyes wide with excitement as she looked about for her fiancé.

Judy Francy looked the length of the station, her excitement turning to anxiety. Impatiently she waited. It would be a long wait.

The firing on Peleliu was blazing the gathering gloom. Movement of men digging their foxholes deeper at the thought of approaching night and the inevitable infiltration by the Japs brought the filthy Marine back from his reverie. Slowly he took the blue letters and reached into his pack. His grimy hand withdrew over 20 such missives. Every mail call had brought them, each forwarded from his Camp Pendleton address, each carrying the same memory provoking scent. Each one unopened. Carefully he untied the cruddy string that held the letters. Meticulously he placed the new one on the bottom, chronologically according to the post-mark, and then he placed the packet back into the pack.

Malton turned to read the letters from his mother, thoughts still on the blue letters in the pack. Someday - he thought - he might read them! Their contents were loaded with dynamite, he instinctively knew. Someday - maybe, he added in his thoughts - he might read them.

Chapter 8

The entire southern tip of Peleliu had been secured by the 7th Marines and equipment and supplies were quickly obscuring the island. Near the east coast a battalion of 155 mm Long Toms had been set up in a bombed out Japanese Coastal gun area. The huge circular pits which once served the Jap guns were being used as a C.P. post and a sick bay.

Malton sat on the edge of the Command Post pit talking with a friend he had known back at Guadalcanal. The Fifth was moving into the lines soon and J.C. as well as all the rest of the Marines were taking advantage of every moment of relaxation.

It was D Day plus 5 and the island which was to be secured in 72 hours fought with the tenacity of demons - demons who refused to be driven from their man made caves. The southern tip of the island - only one fourth of the actual land area had fallen, but the ridge - Bloody Nose Ridge and the valleys and ridges that lay in her bloody shadow had defied all attempts to take it - the Japs were holding - and killing the Marines in great numbers as each attack formed and tried to scale the sharp coral edges.

It had been three days since Fagan had been shipped from the island - J. C. had waved as the landing craft carrying the wounded Marine and many more like him to the comfort and security of the Solace. A deep void had formed in those three days - a void which left Malton actually lonely for the first time since he had joined the 1st Division. True, McPherson had tried to step in and take Cold Steel's place, but the little Marine was obnoxious as hell. As he was now as he approached Malton at a run.

"J.C. - I got some news." He panted as he drew alongside the sitting Malton and dropped down on the concrete also, his legs dangling over the edge of the pit. "Hey, Malton!" he said as he realized he was being ignored.

J. C. slowly turned and glanced at Liverlip. Christ - he was a pain in the ass. But as he looked his soaring temper settled. The poor bastard was just a kid and he did try to do the right thing - but Christ - he sure could be a pain in the neck. "What is it, Liverlip?" He was sorry he had used the hated nickname as soon as the words had slipped out, but he wanted to hurt the little bastard for some reason.

McPherson drew in the lower lip which had earned him the title. Self-consciously he tried to bring his two fat, cracked lips together, which was a physical impossibility. "I've got news," he said half-heartedly, his pride hurt. He admired Malton - had taken him for the one man in the company to look up to.

"So you said." Malton said as he slowly drew on the pipe now loaded with some tobacco which he had managed to bum from a buddy in the artillery outfit. That friend now slowly walked away from the two, realizing some sort of two-sided combat was going on - a combat he knew nothing about and wanted to know no more. "Well, you going to tell me, or have you forgotten Doug?" He used the man's given name with a grin on his face and pronounced the word clearly.

Liverlip also smiled - the grin growing bigger as he recalled the news. "Cold Steel's back!" he exclaimed.

J. C. almost let the pipe slip from his lip. His jaw dropped but he quickly clamped the pipe tightly between his teeth. "What the hell did you say?" Not waiting for an answer he landed on his feet running, heading in the direction where the third platoon was bivouacked. The area was a good hundred yards distance but Malton made it in brief seconds, his brain still trying to rationalize the words which Liverlip had said.

The third platoon, all six of them were huddled together with Fagan as the center of attraction. Konkright obviously pleased, and his right hand was on the New Englander's back, slapping it unconsciously. Fagan stood calm, his composure returned. He stood motionless, seemingly unaware of the questions being hurled by the Marines. His eyes were looking urtively about, searching the area. Suddenly a brightness appeared in his eyes as he caught sight of the rapidly approaching Malton. Gracefully he shouldered his way through the crowd and walked out, straight as a ramrod, to greet his friend.

J.C. stopped running, his face flushed and perspiring from the effort. The two men came together, Malton's right hand firmly clutching Cold Steel's left arm.

"So you're back?" he said quietly, a grin beginning to form on his face. "I thought you'd be back on the canal by now. What happened?"

Fagan dropped his eyes from those of J.C. unconsciously not wanting to show with his eyes the feeling which was so obvious there. "Couldn't talk the docs into it", he said quietly, "tried my damndest - told them that I was no good out here with my friggin' finger gone, but you know what those pill rollers told me?" A fake frown obscured his features.

Malton shook his head, not believing that the lanky Marine had pleaded to be sent back to the states - he was dubious! "The bastards told me to use this friggin finger!" he exclaimed as he held up the middle finger of his right hand.

The men of the third platoon, who had once again formed around him burst out laughing at the sight of the long middle finger stark against the bandaged stump of the forefinger. Malton stared hard at Cold Steel, his jaw set. "You lying bastard!" He said through his teeth, "I bet you jumped ship - you're a lying bastard."

Fagan looked at his friend, an innocent expression belied by the smug look which shone from the hard eyes.

Fagan had been back to the third platoon now for five days - five days in which the rebounding power of America had taken another laurel. Troops which had been standing in reserve off shore in ships had been thrown into the bloody battle. Even the depleted 5th Marines had received some replacements - men who had not had much time to adjust to the workings of a combat team because of their recent arrival at Pavuvu, but who had been placed in replacement battalions and carried along as possible replacements for the combat regiments - but, according to the commanding echelon, they were just along for the ride - since they would not be needed.

These men, fresh from the states and given no opportunity to mold into the regular squads, platoons, and companies as a part of a combat ready team - had now been committed to battle to fill the alarmingly depleted ranks. They had begun to pay for that ride! The third platoon had received seven of the replacements - starry eyed men whose stares as they were introduced to the battle begrimed men, registered the disbelief they felt. There had been a consolidation also in those days of rear area duty - the third and a similarly depleted platoon had been joined, and a lieutenant from the replacement battalion had been placed in command.

Lt. Gary Marshall was green - greener than the clean dungarees he wore with the shiny gold bars on his collar. His clean shaven face was youthful, his blue eyes shiny and clear, devoid of the "look of death" combat brings. Malton had stared incredulously at the baby face, blonde youth when he called the platoon together the day before.

"Stand at ease, men!" he had said to the already fully relaxed men. He bounced jauntily before the uneven ranks, his slim figure lithely moving in the loose fitting ranks. "I've been asked to lead this platoon in the coming action. As you probably know, it will be my first experience in actual combat - and I'll look to you men to cooperate. Do I make myself clear?"

The older men, Blue, McPherson and the rest smiled with their mouths. Fagan just slowly shook his head.

"Now, the word is that we'll be moving up in a few days. In the meantime, let's see if we can work out some mutual procedure. That's all, Sergeant!" he indicated Konkright. "Any questions, men?"

Malton stood speechless – this sad case was a prime candidate for one of those shallow graves down on the beach. Fagan shifted his feet - his hand fondling the handle of the jungle knife.

"Marshall -" he spoke through his thin lips. The lieutenant who had begun to turn slowly faced the slim Marine - his eyes questioning the omission of his title. A retort to the effort was coming to his tongue when Fagan continued, his knife now unsheathed and his left thumb and forefinger testing the blade's sharpness. He looked at the blade as he spoke. "You'd better take those bars from your collar." Again the lieutenant's mouth opened as though to speak, but Fagan's timing was perfect. He spoke softly as to the knife. "They reflect real nice in this sun - the Japs try to pick off the officers first too!"

A crown of disturbance had begun to form on Marshall's face - then the logic of the private's words sank in and the youthful smile blossomed once again across his face.

"Thanks, private." He said and awkwardly worked on the bars with strikingly clean hands.

"That's O.K." Fagan seemed determined to have the last word. "The rate of mortality among second Lou's is the highest in the corps they tell me," he spat. "We want you among us as long as possible."

Lt. Marshall's fingers stopped. His face clouded - a look of uncertainty and a trace of fear entered his eyes. Then he turned and slowly walked away. The smiles broadened among the combat veterans and the looks of amazement on the boot's faces showed that Fagan had added more followers. A smiling Sergeant Konkright shouted, "Fall out!"

Fagan and Malton sat with their backs against a communications jeep in total darkness listening to the operator whirling the dials trying to pick up San Francisco. Earlier two linesmen had scaled the shattered trees of the rest area and strung an aerial - the radio operator had been sure he could pick up the states and Malton and Fagan had joined others around the jeep several hours before. Darkness had fallen quickly and the operator was still fumbling with the dials, an occasional curse spiking his actions. Many of the Marines had wandered away but the two buddies had merely said they had nothing better to do and tomorrow they would be moving into the lines - a word from home would be welcome.

"What do you think of the replacements?" The words were the first spoken in more than 30 minutes. Malton spoke between his teeth which were clutched on the bit of his pipe. "How do you think they'll react?"

Several minutes passed before Fagan answered. "They'll be scared - damn scared. Some will panic - but they'll learn fast," he smiled in the darkness, "just like you and I did."

Malton drew deeply on his pipe, "What about Marshall?"

Fagan reflected, "He'll probably get killed tomorrow or live to be a hundred." He paused, but Malton knew he wasn't finished and waited. Fagan continued, "Why the hell do they send guys like that out here. He's too damn young - he'll always be too damn young. He thinks this is all a game, something he can tell the kids when he gets back to Notre Dame."

"He's from Notre Dame?" Malton asked, once again surprised at Fagan's ability to gather all the facts silently and unknown.

"Yeh! I heard him telling Konk last night." Fagan softly said, "He's a real college cut-up that guy is. Was a junior and decided to join up. Sounds familiar, doesn't it?" He poked his elbow into Malton's side gently, bringing a gasp and then a curt laugh from the squat Marine. "Got tired of campus capers, he told Sarge, and decided to see what war was like - Christ, is he going to find out!" the voice was bitter. "You know the bastard is really a cut-up! He told Kong that he was a member of the Notre Dame glee club and tore an audience apart one night. Seems the guys were on tour and they wore tuxes. Well, one of the guys who was in the first row never changed to black socks, but wore loud argyles beneath his black pants. So what does Marshall do - he's standing in the second row right behind this guy and during one number he reaches forward and slowly pulls this guys trousers up during the singing of the Lord's prayer. The audience died with convulsions, Marshall said, at the sight. He also added he was no longer a member of the glee club."

Malton was laughing hard - he tried to speak but couldn't, his mind visualizing the sight of the socks against the blackness of the trousers.

"We'll have to keep an eye on him." Fagan said softly, his mind working, "or he'll get us all killed."

The laughter stopped as the words sank in. Malton blew out a smoke ring. "He's not a bad guy - a character - but not a bad guy. Let's hang close tomorrow."

Fagan's grunt was lost in the sudden voice which broke through the whistling and static. "I got Frisco!" The radio operator exclaimed proudly. A dance band, Tommy Dorsey, was playing music from the Top of the

Mark hotel, the announcer disclosed. The soft, harmonious music attracted occupants of the surrounding area, who sat quietly listening to the music from home. Thoughts of loved ones welled in the lonely hearts at the unfamiliar but sentimental music.

"And now, ladies and gentlemen," the voice of Tommy Dorsey came through the night air, "the Pied Pipers will sing a song which is sweeping the country."

The music started and the vocal group came in on the chorus "Dream - Dream when you're feeling blue - Dream, that's the thing to do" - the words struck deep. Among the homesick men - they listened, heads bowed to the grounds. The song came to a climax "Dream - and they might come true - so Dream, dream, dream."

The band started another song immediately but the words to the previous song lingered. Malton drew harshly on his pipe - for the first time in months an old ache forming in his heart, Jodie - the vision of the small beautiful girl, the blonde hair reaching her soft shoulders, the curved breasts which were firm and perfectly formed. He thought of the loveliness and softness of her - the pride and happiness at knowing she loved him - and the magic of possessing her completely. The day at the beach was relived, his body aching at the remembrance.

"Why don't you read the letters?" Fagan's words were soft, meant only for his ears. Malton startled - unaware of his friends knowledge of the letters. Of course Fagan had been told of the girl in Los Angeles but how did he know of the letters.

Malton laughed, "You're a mind reader, too?" Then he became serious again and became silent, his mind busy with the thoughts of Jodie.

"I had your pack when they evacuated you." Fagan spoke matter of factly, not embarrassed. "Why didn't you open them?" he said.

Malton was silent for a moment then he answered haltingly. "She's married to someone else."

"That tough titty." Fagan was blunt. "So you're a puritan - but she's got something to say to you - she's writing, isn't she? Wise up, Malty - mail's mail

- no matter whose wife it is - besides I'd like to hear what she says."

Malton had listened half-heartedly. But what Fagan had said began to strike home. For perhaps the first time he realized that he had wanted to know what was in the letters. Suddenly he made up his mind. "O.K. I'll read them tomorrow."

Fagan spoke louder and sterner, "Tomorrow may be too late." The music softly came to a close. A bright voiced, resonant announcer took over the microphone.

"Time for the latest news, brought to you today by the Friar's Home Loan Company," the voice droned on with the commercial, the words bringing snickers from the congregated men. "And now the news - the report from the war front today is good. Peleliu - the tiny atoll in the Palau group has fallen to the troops of the United States. A bloody battle, described by correspondents as the grimmest of the war, has been waged for the past nine days, with the seasoned veterans of the famed First Marine Division forced to dig the enemy from the caves of the ridge which has come to be known as Bloody Nose. Casualties have been heavy, the government has censored our correspondents from disclosing the exact amount, but they have been the highest of any campaign thus far. But today, the battle is at an end - the island has been secured - Bloody Peleliu has fallen! In the European campaign - "

The voice happily continued on - the words lost on the ears of the men of the Fifth Marines! All they had to do was to lift their eyes and see that the battle of Peleliu was not concluded; indeed the island had not been secured. Bloody Nose Ridge had not fallen - tracers from machine guns shot at each other through the skies, the boom of the Long Toms coughed their lethal death over the Ridge to the north - the island was not yet still - or would it be for weeks to come. Death had not been shed as the constant companion of every man on the coral atoll. And these men of the Fifth were only too aware of the fact - tomorrow they were going back into the lines!

The metallic voice stopped finally and once again music filled the night, the thundering sound of the big guns adding unrealistic sound effects.

"Let's shove!" Fagan said as he scrambled easily to his feet. "It's going to be a long war! Maybe not here, the man said the war's over on Peleliu! Better get some sleep though, the walk up on the ridge for souvenirs is liable to be pretty strenuous."

J.C. smiled as he awkwardly got to his feet using but one hand, his left cradled over the bowl of the pipe, hiding the glow of ashes. Wordlessly they walked side by side the short distance to their foxholes. About them the sounds of men field stripping their pieces were audible - fingers did not fumble with the parts in the total darkness - they had been trained long ago. Malton reached his foxhole first, and dropping into it, began arranging his gear, already prepared for the next day in order it would not cramp him during the night. He became aware that Fagan had not gone on to his own foxhole, but stood over him.

"J.C." Fagan pronounced the name quietly, his words did not contain their usual harshness.

Malton stopped arranging his pack which he used for a pillow, "Yeah?"

"Listen, Malty! I'm not an expert on these things, but you're not doing the right thing about those letters," he paused waiting for a rebuttal, but Malton lay on his back listening. "That gal meant a lot to you - I can tell. I've see you look through your mail for the blue envelopes - so she married another Joe - so what! You yourself said it was out of spite." In the darkness he shook his head. What a crazy mixed up kid! "But you were partly responsible - the gal must have nearly been crazy with uncertainty. It's the damn swabby to blame - the bastard is a friggin fool to have married her just like that. Read the letters buddy - it won't hurt anything - might do you good." He was gone, Malton hadn't heard him leave.

J. C. stared at the stars overhead, the Southern Cross magnificent in its brightness. Beneath his head he was conscious of the letters in the pack - her perfume penetrating the dirty canvass. Slowly he rolled over and pressed his face into the pack - he would read the letters - tomorrow!

"Fall in." Sergeant Konkright assembled the Third Platoon with the first light of the day. It was September 25 - D plus 9 on Peleliu. Around the southern tip of the island troops of the 5th Marines were forming - forming to return to the lines. The replacements' faces were drawn - reflecting their feelings of what lay ahead. No such reflections were visible on the sunburned faces of the old hands - but they merely wore masks - the fear was there!

Lt. Marshall stood before the platoon, his face bright and scrubbed in contrast to the bearded faces of the veterans. The damn fool is gonna get killed sure, Fagan thought.

"Here's the word." The lieutenant began, "The Fifth Marines are going to go down the east shore and attack the ridge from that side - the 7th Marines will go in from the west. The 3rd battalion is staying behind. They're going to cross over to Ngesebus later. Any questions?" he waited.

"Lieutenant," Fagan once again spoke up at the inquiry. Marshall stared at the private. "You'd better get rid of that bar painted on your helmet cover."

Marshall took off his helmet and stared at the black perpendicular bar he had painted so carefully on the camouflaged cover.

Fagan gracefully took off his pack and opened it. His hand fumbled for a minute and then withdrew a cover from the pack. "Use this - it's a spare I picked up from a guy."

The words sank into Marshall's mind. Absently he took the helmet cover and discarding the carefully painted old one, slipped Fagan's "spare" on. His mind envisioned the dead man who had been the previous owner.

Troops about them began to move and Marshall led the 3rd platoon into its proper position. The men spread out in skirmish position - the seasoned hands wordlessly directing the newcomers wordlessly like mother hens.

The Fifth Marines were going to battle once more. All told they were but a little over battalion strength. Replacements had not nearly been able to fill the ranks. The troops reached the fringe of the airstrip and Bloody Nose stood stark and naked before them. An air signal guided the men around the strip. It was hot - damn hot and already the exertion of walking had turned the green uniforms black.

Malton turned once checking the position of Fagan. The lanky Marine, through the strange perception which existed between the two, took that moment to glance in Malton's direction. Their eyes met and though the lines of his face didn't change, a smile was in his eyes.

J. C. smiled back and then turned back to his own line of march. He recognized the meaning of the smile, for he knew that Fagan had been watching him when he had read the letter in a blue envelope that morning. His thoughts strayed back to that moment, shortly before first light. His night had not been a comfortable one - he had tossed and turned. Long before dawn he had fully awakened and lay in the coral hole - waiting for the light to come.

He had carefully taken the water-proof pouch from the pack and in the half light strained to find the first one he had received. Lying in the foxhole waiting for the dawn, he had decided that he would start at the beginning. He had argued the point with himself - one segment of his being demanding he read the last one - the other, the first.

Finding the earliest post marked one, he carefully put the others down. His fingers were trembling as he tore open the blue envelope. Carefully he withdrew the single sheet. He turned it over - only half the back side was filled with writing. His eyes caught the words – "Love, Jodie". He stared for a moment at the neat feminine writing. The odor of her perfume, dim now with age, reached his nostrils, and left him a little heady. Holding the letter with his fingers along the edge, he turned it carefully in order not to run the writing ink with his perspiring hands. He sank down in the hole and slowly read - his eyes hungry for the words.

She had taken some time to decide to write, he smiled to himself.

March 23, 1944

"Dear J.C., Perhaps you'll be surprised to receive this letter - I'm surprised to be writing it - believe me I've started many times only to tear it up and throw it away. It's been two months since you've left - ship's sailings are not as well guarded as the authorities like to believe, you see - it seems much longer than that.

I'm back at mother's house as you can see by the return address." Malton
frowned - it was still *"mother"* only, not *"mother's and dad's."*

*"Ed has shipped out - he's on an aircraft carrier now, but he's supposed to
be stationed at Ulithi, wherever that is. J.C. I'm sorry; That's all I can say - I'm
sorry. I don't expect you to answer but I just can't go on not writing to you. Try
to remember me - remember me as I was before that day - Please!*

"Love, Jodie."

Malton walked through the sand on the beach - his mind on the words
- he remembered the letter almost word for word, though he had only read
it once. He was remembering her - remembering her before he had stormed
down the street that night. His arms swinging at his side could feel her in his
arms - her golden hair next to his face. The letter had been short, the words
clear. She was sorry, she said - a single word which could mean so little - but
could mean so much. Absently he kicked at the sand with his striding right
foot. It seemed a long time ago also to him, the old wound that had turned
numb with the passing months again throbbing in his heart. The weight on
his mind had been lifted by reading the letter but now another problem took
its place. Suddenly the frown left his face, a smile replacing it. Why worry
now - he was six thousand miles away and he would be away a long time.

"Hit the deck!" Konkright's words preceded momentarily the explosion
of a 150 MM heavy mortar shell. The 3rd platoon buried themselves in the
sand. Their approach had not been unnoticed by the Japs and the positions
on the damnable ridge had responded to the sudden heavy troop movements.

"Let's go!" Konkright shouted - giving the orders which should have
come from the platoon leader. But that Marine was dazed by his introduction
to enemy fire. He followed the directions of the Platoon Sergeant feeling his
way in the battle for men's lives. The going was now perceptively slower. The
Fifth Marines spreading out even further, corpsmen busy answering the calls
for aid which each shell brought forth.

At last they had reached a sheltering border of trees which had stood up against the devastating ship fire. Through the shattered trunks, the men of the Fifth got their first close look at Bloody Nose Ridge. It stood stark white against the blue sky, a strewn mass of coral, littered with the remains of trees. Ridges, ravines, and crags were now visible - belying the distant view of a solid rise of rock.

Cautiously the Fifth moved down the coastal road which ran at the base of the Ridge. The movement stopped and the troops turned to the west and dug in as best they could. The Ridge boomed ominously before them. The Fifth Marines had arrived at the jumping off spot.

"Keep your eyes open and your asses down." Konkright drifted from position to position, making sure the men were all set. He paused a moment longer with the newer men, giving reaffirming pats on the back and making sure a veteran had the new man in tow. "Who you guys goin' to wet nurse?" he asked after lighting up a cigarette behind the fallen tree where Fagan and Malton had dug in while awaiting the assault.

"Rah! Rah! Boy." Fagan jerked his thumb indicating the lieutenant who even now was exposing himself by sitting on - the wrong side of a tree. Fagan spat, "The bastard is goin' to die today for sure. Hey, Marshall!" he called and when the green louie turned in his direction he with his hands covering his head to take shelter behind the tree, "you're going to get that guy pissed off at you."

Konkright said with a broad smile on his face, "Or maybe you'd rather wear those bars he has in his pocket."

"Hell, no!" Fagan shouted, "that's why I'm trying to keep him alive. You guys all get yourself knocked off and they're sure to make me take over this friggin' platoon or what's left of it." He shifted his pack on his shoulders. Malton recognized the truth in what Fagan had said under the guise of a joke.

A new man, Rollins, serving as a runner, ducked through the brush and stepped behind Lt. Marshall, now safely behind the tree. The two talked for a few minutes, then Marshall nodded. Scanning the area he signaled the Sgt. Fagan and Malton tail along.

"Sit down!" Marshall indicated a rotten tree trunk. "Regimen's says we're to push ahead at 0930." They all checked their watches, 10 minutes to go, "we're to scale that crag to the left. Make it to the top and hold tight. Got it?"

Malton looked at the crag - it stood outlined against the higher ridge in the background. It was completely devoid of all vegetation, the white coral glistening in the sun. Quickly he estimated the distance - 300 yards all uphill. His experienced eyes searched for protective coverings, they found little, just clumps of coral which had been thrown away by blasts of shells tossed shoreward by the cruisers and battleships. Squinting his eyes against the reflection, he made out a shadow - approximately 150 yards away, a ravine - there the trouble would be. The ground rose slowly until it hit the ravine and then sank - how far it was difficult to say - and then it climbed straight upward to the peak.

"How long will it take us to get there Sergeant?" the lieutenant glanced at the peak - it looked so near.

Konkright studied the problem - then looked at Malton and Fagan. "That ravine's going to be tough. It's exposed almost all the way - open at the left and right, and nothing behind it but the ridge."

"We gonna get support?" Fagan was cleaning his fingernails with the tip of his knife. The question carried no overtones, but both Malton and Konkright knew they were there.

"It's a concentrated push. Command figures there are dozens of crags and ravines between here and the Ridge. All units will push up and onward. Check your positions, keep the line straight. We've got 24 men. Break them up into 4 squads, make sure seasoned men are put with the new ones. Malton you take one, Fagan another." A look of astonishment swept Fagan's face. Before he could speak Marshall continued, "Sergeant, get those two corporals from the other platoon to take over squads. Keep as many old groups together as you can. Any questions?" He looked at Fagan expectantly.

"I ain't no squad leader?" the voice was sullen, the eyes diverted to the point of the knife - Fagan's jaw muscles twitching as he flexed them.

"You are now!" .Marshall snapped, authority in his voice, "and it carries corporal stripes in this outfit. Any questions Corporal Fagan?"

Fagan merely grunted and busied himself with his knife, too frustrated to speak.

"Good!" Marshall's voice carried a twinge of victory - finally he had outlasted the salty private. He checked his watch. "We've got five minutes. Shove off and get set up. Malton you take the point, Fagan the left, Smith the right and Brownell the rear. Good Luck."

The three enlisted men shoved themselves away from the tree. Fagan crouched beside Malton as he ran. "The son-of-a bitchin' boot!"

Malton laughed, "I take Blue and Peterson, and three of the new guys. You take Richardson, Young and three new men. Keep your eye on me buddy." He slapped Fagan on the rump and scampered in the direction of where he knew Peterson was dug in. He called his new squad together and briefed them as best he could. Peterson and Blue listened attentively to every word, quickly sizing up every word. The new men, a young hillbilly from Kentucky with a huge chew trying to hide the smooth unshaven face; a city slicker from Chicago who wore his dungarees as if they were a zoot suit; and a drawling, tall, muscular Texan who Malton picked for strength, listened but did not hear. Lighten, the Kentuckian, looked unblinkingly at Malton, the words lost in the cloudiness of an undeveloped brain. The Chicagoan, Rinter, smoothed his helmet liner thoughtfully, and McKean, the Texan, stared at the ridge, seemingly comparing it to the hills of Texas around Medina.

"We're to deploy as skirmishes. Be sure to keep your distance and interval. Remember McKean?" He indicated the only man with an automatic rifle. "You keep behind me. O.K. When we move out, odd number men to the left, even to the right. Sound off," he called. The men counted off, each man remembering mentally the position he was to take. Malton glanced at his watch - almost time to move! He turned to his left and indicated all set to Marshall. The second hand pointed straight up and the day came alive with the whistling of shells passed overhead as the Navy pounded shells into the east side of Bloody Nose. J.C. fastened his helmet strap, grabbed his rifle in his left hand firmly and caressed the trigger plate with his right.

"Let's go!" he signaled with his right hand and the point took its position. Cautiously maneuvering his men into positions, five paces apart, he crouched forward and slipped from the protective brush. He braced himself for the small arm fire which he expected and could feel the surprising elation at the lack of it. He quickened his pace and wove between the blasted coral, his eyes peeled for any sign of movement before him - for spider traps, for caves beneath the ledges which had become discernible as they moved forward. The going was tough as he led the men upward, the sun beating down unmercifully on the Marines. The torn coral offered no foot holes for men, they slid backward, stumbled as loose coral moved beneath them. Shoes and clothing were torn by the sharp rocks as they fell to the ground occasionally to mark their advance.

Malton lay beneath a ledge, curling under it to escape the heat. Braced against it, he pulled out his canteen and took a sip of the warm rust tasting liquid. He smiled as the new men, themselves under cover, followed his example. He strained his eyes, squinting in the sun and mentally placed the other elements of the platoon. He saw the dark figures moving and shuddered as he picked out the form of Marshall walking erect, some 30 yards to his right.

"Down you bastard," the voice of Fagan cut through the din of the shells. The lanky Marine tossed a small piece of coral at the lieutenant. Startled, Marshall threw himself to the ground. Fagan smiled.

"Let's move!" Malton called and climbed over the ledge. Machine gun fire greeted his exposure and he clung to the ground, painfully cutting his body as he scampered for a protective crag. His ears and eyes picked out the enemy position. It sat 40 yards up the hill, the muzzle of the machine gun poking its nose through an ingeniously constructed dugout behind a fallen tree. Larger pieces of coral had been wedged along the side and offered protection from the flanks. Smoke hovered as the muzzle swung to the left, sending chunks of coral flying as it plowed into the area just occupied by Fagan's platoon.

Malton sensed rather than heard someone crawling near him. He cautiously turned on his side to see Marshall crawling toward him.

"Wait for another burst," Malton called, "and then move fast." As if in answer, the mambu spat again, this time to the right as Smith moved up. Malton heard a cry of pain as a bullet hit one of the men. The lieutenant crawled quickly beside Malton, ducking his head close to the deck as the machine turned its attention to him.

"We've got to get that gun," he yelled into Malton's ear. The squat Marine almost laughed at the obvious maneuver. "McKean!" the lieutenant called. "Keep those guys low." Swinging on his right side he indicated Smith to move up and then quickly rolling over he motioned Fagan to attack. "Let's go!" he yelled to Malton.

The three squads broke from their positions, crouching as they ran. The machine gun was swung in all directions, the gunner undecided where to shoot first. The maneuver took three seconds, and the lieutenant signaled to hit the deck. Now the machine gunner started firing - fruitlessly. The platoon had advanced 10 yards - they were now deployed 30 yards from the machine gun position. The machine gun was firing frantically, swinging from right to left.

Marshall unclasped a hand grenade from his bandolier and held it up for the left and right squads to see. Quickly hand grenades appeared in the hands of Fagan and Smith. Marshall pulled the pin and released. His lips moved as he counted and then he drew his arm along his side and with a smooth motion spiraled the grenade toward the machine gun nest. Two other grenades joined it in flight. The seconds seemed endless, then three loud detonations sounded and the Marines burrowed themselves deeper into the coral. Fragments of coral chipped by the exploding grenades kicked up dust around the prone Marines. As the sound echoed into the ravine, Malton cautiously raised his back.

The machine gun lay outside the nest, the tree roiled away. Two bodies pierced with fragments hung head down on the coral sides, blood rolling from the limp bodies.

"Let's go!" the lieutenant called and crouching low he raced to the pit. Malton followed more cautiously, as he reached Marshall's side, the lieutenant snapped the safety on his carbine and emptied the clip into the five motionless bodies in the hole.

J.C. pulled at the lieutenant's arm and dragged him down beside the tree. "They're dead. Don't waste ammunition."

Marshall looked at Malton, sweat pouring from his pores, his face smudged with dirt. His eyes shone brightly with exhilaration. Cockily he said, "You're right."

Fagan was staring at the pair. A new respect had come into his eyes. The lieutenant had made the right move. Maybe he would live through the day.

The men of the Fifth were spent. They had been in the lines since September 25, and someone's pocket calendar indicated it was October 11 - they had been under the constant strain of battle. Casualties had been heavy as slowly, ravine by ravine, crag by crag, they had pierced the "china wall", a cliff that brought exposure for the few seconds it took for a Jap to draw a bead and hurl a deadly bullet from his long 31 caliber rifle. Ridges dubbed "Waddie" and groups of hills named "Five Brothers and Five Sisters" all fell beneath the constant attack of the driving Marines. At last the final objective loomed around "Dead Man's Curve" and nicknamed "Baldy." The Japs constantly harassed the men of the Fifth - not banzai charges but concerted, well-planned sneak assaults. Many nights during the two week sortee on the Ridge were constant hand grenade battles - often climaxed in hand-to-hand combat.

And now "Baldy," was to be taken - the peak which had taken such a heavy toll of the Seventh Marines.

Fagan had joined Malton in a shallow shell hole. J. C. munched on a moldy candy bar - he offered some to Cold Steel but the lanky Marine shook his head in refusal.

The two men were walking nightmares, their clothes were torn and tattered - no longer green but a dust color. Their skins were the same color except the faces which were covered by a fortnight's growth of beard and by the accumulated dirt of the campaign. But it was their eyes that were strange - they seemed phantom-like, hollow, and unseeing. Combat men had come to call it the look of death. Fast on the heels of the stare would come combat fatigue - the battle would have to be concluded soon.

"I lost Lighten last night," Malton said. "Found him this morning in his foxhole - throat was slashed," the voice was emotion free.

"Lost two myself - same way." Fagan spat. "Hell, I was only 30 feet away; I didn't hear anything. Those bastards are sly all right! How do you figure Baldy," he indicated the bleak knobby ridge.

"Loaded with caves! Check those crevices - everyone holds an opening. Christ, I'm tired." He dropped on his back, relaxing for the first time in days - he counted on the alert eyes of Fagan.

"Read another letter?" Fagan asked without taking his eyes from scrutinizing the ridge.

"No - Haven't had time!" Malton sighed.

"Read one now! I'll wait." The words were an order rather than a suggestion. He turned his back to his friend. Malton smiled at the action and silently slipped the pack from his shoulder and shaking, not from any emotion, he was too tired for that, but from weakness.

"Saddle up in 10 minutes.," Marshall's runner scooted from dug-out to dug-out. "How's your old lady?" Fagan called as the runner went by quickly. A smile creased the young private's lips.

"Still alive - still alive." The words held an inflection of disbelief and Fagan shook his head also. Not only still alive but with a hell of a lot more energy than any of the rest of the beat up platoon members had.

Malton sorted through the blue envelopes. He hadn't read any since the first one. Now he searched for one - found it and tore the envelope open. A smile crossed Fagan's eyes as he heard the paper tearing. "Save the envelopes, buddy. Air mail paper makes the best ass wipe." J. C. had not heard him for already his eyes were hungrily pouring over the contents of the letter.

July 18, 1943

Dearest J.C.:
Sorry, I haven't written for a week, but I've been pretty ill lately. Mom says it's to be expected during pregnancy."

(J.C. read the opening paragraph over again - his eyes disbelieving what he had read the first time. Finally the truth sank in. Embarrassed he mentally counted. A frown crossed his face. Quickly he read on.)

"The doctor gave me some pills and they seem to help. You should see me - don't look slim like the girl you remember.

"J.C. I've thought a lot about what I wrote you before. It wasn't fair for me to tell you the things I did - I realize that now! I understand that you've enough to worry about. I shouldn't have complicated things by that letter. I can imagine how you felt opening it so far across the ocean - I'm pretty outspoken - but I'm sorry. It seems I'm always saying that word to you. Funny too - you're actually the only person I can remember saying that to in all my life.

I keep wondering where you are. The newspapers are full of stories about the Marines on Saipan, but that's the 2nd Marine Division and I know you're with the first. I keep wondering if you are all right, if you're hurt - I know you're not dead, because I haven't had any of my letters returned. Well, time for bed. Goodnight, my darling.

All my Love, Jodie

Malton put the letter down, his confused mind racing with a million thoughts. He sifted through the blue envelopes. One of them contained the letter to which Jodie had referred. He glanced at his watch - three minutes to go - he didn't have time to look through them all. Fagan turned at the sound.

"What's the good word, Malty?" Fagan had a rare grin on his face as he spoke.

Malton dropped the letters back into their waterproof pouch and carefully placed it into the crusty stiff pack. "She's going to have a baby." The words didn't come easily.

Fagan stared perceptibly. He peered steadily at J.C. watching every move. "Yours?"

J.C. raised his head from the hidden letters in the pack and returned Fagan's frank look. "I don't know," he shook his head in confusion. "She didn't say when it's due." His words were barely audible.

Fagan shifted his pack and tossed away his cigarette and rose to his knees getting ready to rejoin his small squad. "Forget it for now. Check that hill over there - that's enough to think about. It's not going to be easy." He scampered across the coral, his words hanging in the air behind him.

J. C. watched him go and then slowly turned to Baldy. The image of Jodie gradually left and the caves in the peak took its place. Fagan was right. This was no time to be worrying about anything.

"Move out, skirmishes!" Lt. Marshall shouted as he moved forward. Almost as soon as the men had left their places of concealment, the enemy opened up with small weapons a little more than a hundred yards away.

The Third platoon raced down and through a ravine which had ridges on both sides. They reached the end and immediately began trying to scale Baldy - the gradual slope was exposed to Japanese fire that seemed to come from above. As a reporter later said, "The Marines seemed unmoved by the withering fire - they scaled the ridge that led to baldy, they clasped roots, fell over rock faults and crevices. How they made it, God only knows."

Every turn produced cave openings! It seemed every time they blinked their eyes another cave appeared. Malton shook his head at the numerous caves - and from every opening came scathing fire, deadly fire. The cry for "Corpsman" came often and more painfully. "Take cover - for Christ's sake - take cover." Marshall's voice called. The order made men dive for what seemed like protecting cover only to find that their cover faced another cave. Men suddenly were hit as they lay, "Runner, go back down, and call for a smoke cover."

Before the runner could move, the rear squad were already firing from their rifles, grenade launchers, smoke shell. The entire ridge soon became obliterated by smoke.

"Move up - use grenades in every cave you find." Marshall called. The platoon instinctively groped upward, tossing hand grenades into the bowels of the caves. More grenades were brought up by negro supply troops.

Malton breathlessly moved up. McKean at his side, a bear on attack. He carried the heavy automatic weapon on his hip firing into every opening.

An hour passed, then two, three. Finally Marshall reached the summit and as he was joined by the other members of the toon, held his hand holding the carbine over his head. A whining 31 caliber bullet took the carbine right out of his hand as it passed perilously close to his head.

Malton clutched the ground, conscious of Fagan at his side. He turned to his buddy and smiled. Now Peleliu had been secured, every inch of the island covered, but he knew that beneath him in the bowels of the caves, hundreds of Japs still lived – would still kill and would until bulldozers closed up every opening. That operation would take months - but the men of the First Division would not do it - that job wasn't for combat troops.

Chapter 9

All hell broke loose! The two by five mile long sand spit was suddenly awakened from its Pacific blackness by the flash of tracer bullets across Bloody Nose Ridge. This was Peleliu, aftermath of Guadalcanal and prelude to Okinawa.

The receding light of a far off flare picked out the cautiously creeping form of Shep Masters, Corporal, United States Marine Corps, as he skirted Beach Red - the same Beach Red which several days before had fulfilled the promise of its name with the blood of landing Marines.

Unconsciously contracting his body against the sudden brightness, Masters carefully continued his treacherous route back to his outfit. Damn the luck! He had taken too much time down at the beach. The sudden tropical darkness had caught him unaware.

Stopping briefly to get his bearings, Masters chanced standing upright. He wasn't a tall man, in fact, nineteen could hardly be considered a man. Stockily built, his face belied his youth. The week's growth of beard that had been left unattended since the landing scarcely seemed more than a stubble. Not a killer by trade, Masters had chosen the Marines when war broke out because of a movie he had once seen. The "Glory of the Corps" as depicted had decided his fate.

It hadn't taken Shep long to find out the difference between movies and reality. The Corps with its flashy blue uniform was a thing of the past. The fighting Marine was in for a living hell - check his outfit.

The 1st Battalion, Seventh Marines, had been relieved from its positions on Bloody Nose Ridge just before sunset the previous night. Only sixty percent of the battalion had been relieved - the rest had already found their relief on hospital ships and in the division cemetery. Peleliu had proven to be the bloodiest, hottest damn hunk of coral in the pacific.

After the relief battalion had taken over the lst's positions, Masters and the rest of the battered First had moved south two thousand yards and bivouacked near a destroyed Japanese coastal gun emplacement.

Sleep that night came easily. Even the 155 outfit, behind blasting away at the enemy, couldn't disturb their sleep of exhaustion.

These thoughts rushed through Master's head as he picked his way around the destroyed barb wire barriers that had failed to halt the onrushing landing force. Shep had been to the Sea-Bee camp on the east coast. The Sea-Bees, work horses of the Navy, had been assigned the task of making the reef lined harbor accessible to cargo ships.

The older men of the Sea-Bees had a deep feeling for the younger Marines and were known to share everything they had with them. So after last night's sleep, Shep had decided to hustle some of his souvenirs to the navy - besides, it was well known throughout the Pacific that wherever the Sea-Bees went they were sure to bring plenty of good chow. Shep figured he could use a cooked meal - these damn K rations did nothing more than constipate a guy.

The glare of white crosses against the light of the tracers told Masters he was heading in the right direction. The coral of the island defied the digging of graves - the dead were buried on the beach where scooped sand made a fitting grave for brave men who had died to obtain it.

A few hundred yards more and the bivouac area would be at hand. By the eerie light of battle, Master's face showed the scars of battle. He looked older than his nineteen years, his features were hard - written across them was the history of the Pacific war. Death and brutality had been witnessed by the cold gray eyes. The same arms in which buddies died had wrought revenge while cradling a flaming M-1. He had aged decades since joining the corps as soon as he had reached seventeen. The Marine Corps wasn't for weaklings.

Twenty-three months had passed since he left the states - twenty-three months and three major campaigns. This was the last - one way or the other.

The chips were down and he knew it only too well! He had laughed when he talked about it with his buddies. It was a laugh without humor.

Just how much could a guy take? Guadalcanal, Cape Gloucester and now Peleliu. The First Marine Division really got around but it wasn't a very pleasant itinerary for a South Pacific cruise.

Masters couldn't see his watch - it must be close to nine o'clock. Another night! The days were bad enough but the nights seemed never to end. Back stateside, nights were something to be enjoyed with a gal or the gang. Then later, sleep, restful sleep! On these damn rocks, night meant endless hours of darkness with unfriendly sounds spanning the distance between you and where the enemy had last been seen.

Shep's fingers tightened on his M-1. He had left camp early that morning and was anxious to get back to his sack and some more sleep. He must be nearly to the area now. The distance hadn't seemed so far this morning.

"Halt!" The voice cracked across the night like a Jap 31 caliber bullet!

Masters froze! Then he slowly relaxed, realizing it was the sentry of the bivouac area. He had made it o.k. He started forward again.

"Halt! Give the password!" This time the voice was colder.

Holy hell! The password - he didn't know it! He'd left the camp before it had been posted and after reaching the Sea-Bee camp he'd been so busy eating and snowing his friends that he hadn't given it another thought.

He stood motionless, his finger still tight on the trigger of his rifle. Instinctively, he knew that the sentry's finger was tightening too - on the trigger of a rising gun!

What a joke! Or was it so funny? He knew he couldn't call out that it was Shep Masters. Even if the sentry was someone he knew, and with all the replacements lately, it probably wasn't, the orders before landing on this rock had been explicit! The enemy was the best the Japanese had, the Imperial Japanese Marines, and ninety percent of them could speak English fluently! The password was to be enforced.

"The password! Quick!" The voice was higher, pitched with the growing tension of impending danger.

Masters realized the sentry was going to shoot, and wouldn't miss! He was less than twenty feet from the guy and silhouetted against the tracers on the ridge.

So this was it. After all he had been through, he was going to bow out at the hands of one of his own kind. Fate! He had known that this was going to be his last campaign, but damn if he had expected to end it this way.

In his thoughts he could see the telegram in his mother's hands:

"The President regrets to inform you that your son, Corporal Shep Masters was killed on Peleliu by a United States Marine security sentry for failing to volunteer the password of the day."

Fire! Shoot and get it over with. The fool was taking long about it. Or had it been only a second!

The fire from the ridge was diminishing. The lines were settling for a night of infiltration by the past masters of the art. He knew, the Japs had taught him well on the Canal! Dawn would bring a Banzai charge. He wouldn't be here to withstand it - he was getting his now.

"The Password!" The click of the safety concluded that the last warning had been given.

A wave of hysteria overwhelmed Masters. His tongue grew thick in his mouth, his eyes blurred, but with typical Marine bravado, he slobbered?

"Beats Me!"

Masters braced for the bullets, his own voice echoing in his ears "------beats me ---- - beats me------beats me!"

"Pass!" The sentry said in a voice deeper with relaxation.

What the hell! Masters was dumbfounded. Nevertheless, he made his legs carry him forward before the guy changed his mind.

"Better be quicker on the password if you want to stay alive, Mac!" The sentry whispered as Masters walked past him.

A bewildered Masters groped his way among the protective foxholes until he found his own. He slid into its damp depths and reached for his poncho. He located it covering the frame of his buddy Ray Thomas. Thomas groaned and turned over.

"Where the hell you been for so long?" Without waiting for an answer he added, "if you gotta go to the head don't forget the password," he leaned closer.

"It's Peach Tree! Get it, Peach Tree!"

Amid the screaming and the whirring of 155's, a strange sound awoke the sleeping bivouac area. Heads broke through restraining mosquito nets, fingers tightened on rifle triggers. All eyes focused on a small group of struggling humanity.

Corporal Shep Masters, U.S. Marines, was putting up a terrific fight, but it was a hopeless one. The husky corpsmen, it took four of them, were gently but forcefully dragging the hysterical Marine to the Battalion Aid Station.

The look in Shep's eyes was not a pretty thing to see. Rationality had disappeared from the grayness, replacing it was the insanity watching Marines had seen in the fanatical faces of Banzaing Japs.

Back at Master's foxhole other Marines were gathered around Ray Thomas who was thoughtfully lighting a cigarette. "What the hell happened to Shep?" one asked.

Thomas looked up at the speaker and at the other inquiring and puzzled faces. Taking a long drag on his cigarette he unseeingly looked toward the front lines. Letting the smoke pour through his lips, he said –

"Beats me!"

"SOUVENIRS"

CHAPTER 10

"Let's go, Fagan, Malton." Lt. Marshall approached where Malton sat on an upended 50 gallon gasoline drum, Ben Badger, one of the replacements, unnaturally wielding a pair of scissors and clippers. Fagan sat crossed-legged against a tree, his old campaign hat pulled over his eyes.

Malton looked quickly from Fagan to the Lieutenant, who stood grinning, his face clean shaven, and his carbine held lightly in his right hand. Malton blew some hair clippings from his nose and said, "Lieutenant, don't you think you've got enough! Christ, we're going to get into plenty of trouble going back up there", he indicated Bloody Nose Ridge.

"Don't dope off on me Malton!" Marshall laughed heartily. "Who's going to give us trouble?"

"Colonel Ferkal!" Fagan spat, speaking for the first time. He pushed the brim of his hat with his right thumb. His eyes squinted in the sharp sun.

Marshall continued laughing. "We're not going to meet up with him! We'll steer clear of the C.P. area, drift around to Old Baldy. Should be plenty swords left in those caves."

Fagan slowly got to his feet, felt to make sure his knife was secure and then grabbed his rifle, slamming his hand smartly against the wooden stock. He quickly flicked his eyes at J.C. A look of "What the hell you going to do?" passed between the two.

"Hey, I'm not finished." Badger shouted as Malton scooted from the barrel from beneath the shears left snipping in the air.

"You've ruined that crop enough already," Marshall laughed. "Come on with us Badger, we'll cut you in on the profits."

"Thanks, Lieutenant," the Southerner drawled, his thin face already burned bronze in the sun, "but make my money here. It's safer."

Marshall left a trail of laughter behind as he started across the airstrip toward Bloody Nose. Fagan and Malton followed at a respectable distance, although not all their hesitancy coming from respect. They didn't want to get too close to the madmen who constantly seemed to be heading for trouble.

"And I was looking forward to a day of rest and relaxation." Malton moaned.

"You should know the Corps better than that," Fagan said looking at the Marine Corsairs which were taxing down the almost perfect airstrip that had quickly been patched by the Seabees. "If you're not kept busy with some unnecessary duties, then some crazy lieutenant got to take you souvenir hunting." He dropped his words as the fast pacing Marshall slowed and let them catch up.

"What you guys beating your gums for?" he asked. Malton tried once more, "Lieutenant, you've got enough samurai swords. Hell, we've taken at least a dozen from these caves." J.C. referred to the two previous trips the lieutenant had made, accompanied by whom he considered to be his best two men. Acting against strict orders from each battalion commander and put into strict written form by Colonel Ferkal, Regimental Commander, they had scampered around the caves pulling away enough of the concussion loosened coral to achieve entrance to the closed caves. In several hours each time, they had come across enough dead Jap officers among the enlisted men killed by accurate fire from the Long Toms and Naval shells, to well supply themselves with the valuable samurai swords.

"Yeh, but there are still enough suckers among those pilots to peddle them, and the men sure enjoy that whiskey." Marshall increased his pace as he passed a group of air personnel who looked at the dirty combat troops with deep suspicion.

Malton laughed silently. Marshall was sure an operator. True, he shared all the liquid proceeds of his dealings with the non-combatants with his men, but, damn it, he sure took chance.

"Better not pass that Seabee outfit's area. They might be looking for you.," Fagan said from a non-committal face as they approached the living area of the Seabee construction battalion who were working on the landing strip. "They don't stay fooled long," he added.

Marshall grunted and stayed clear of the well furnished living area. The Seabees were the wonders of the service, able, because of their highly skilled members in all mechanical areas, to make the most of any situation and make nature work for them. But they were always so busy in their chores, that they seldom had time to search for the souvenirs prized so by those back home. Marshall had taken a leaf from the "make-do" manual of the Seabees themselves to trap them into buying worthless "souvenirs."

Japanese battle flags were in great demand throughout the island. The small white flags had the symbolic red "meat ball" in the center. Fagan surprised and befuddled his men as he asked each if they had white handkerchiefs. The white handkerchief itself was a luxury and because it was, most men had had some sent from home. It was not happy men who surrendered the handkerchiefs to the lieutenant. Then Marshall, under the wondering eyes of the men had fashioned an oval from a piece of aluminum he had salvaged from a Jap plane destroyed on the strip. Carefully and painstakingly he kneaded and formed the aluminum until it made a perfect round circle about eight inches in circumference. Sending McKean to the mobile hospital area with a requisition for a case of iodine and merthiolate, he waited. The men sat and watched, confusion on their faces while Marshall just sat and waited grinning. When McKean returned, telling of the argument he had got at the hospital area and producing only a dozen bottles of the medication, the smile broadened, indicating it was more than he needed.

Unrolling his blanket from his pack he placed it on the top of oil drum. Grinning as he thoroughly enjoyed his wide-eyed audience's admiration, Marshall flattened out a well laundered but worn white handkerchief on top of the blanket. With a flourish, he placed the shiny aluminum cylinder carefully in the center, then, holding the aluminum down firmly he poured the mixture of the iodine and merthiolate into the home made die. He watched the reaction as the fluid spread on the porous material. Then with a flourish he withdrew the aluminum. Already drying in the hot sun, the mixture of iodine and merthiolate turned from a dark maroon to a shimmering red. The astounded men of the 3rd platoon saw before them the birth of a Japanese flag, complete with meatball. True, the iod-metha mixture ran a little beneath the aluminum but with practice came perfection and soon a gross of Jap flags, thoroughly aged by rubbing in the coral dirt, were on their way to the Seabee Battalion where the demand far surpassed the supply. But Marshall was not inferior to the situation, and the Jap "flag" factory turned out the desired quantity of flags.

Malton smiled as he thought of it now as they passed along the coastal road.

"Check that sign!" Lt. Marshall called as a huge crudely painted sign jutted at the side of the road.

Fagan read, "Run - Don't walk! Sniper in hills! Has open shot with machine gun." Fagan spit derisively to the ground and started forward.

"That sign ain't kiddin, mac!" A marine followed the voice from behind a thicket. Malton recognized a shore patrol, S.P., on his sleeve. "This Nip has picked off seven men in the past week! He ain't got the word that the islands secured."

"Why the hell don't they send a patrol up there after him?" Marshall said amiably.

The S.P. shifted his chew to the other side of his mouth and stared at the thinnish Marine. "They have, mac! Only they can't find him. Patrol's been up there diggin' around. Lot of caves up there! Can't find him. Patrol just sittin' up there someplace now, waitin' for him to show those pearly teeth.'"

"Let's be some bait," Marshall said and began walking rapidly down the narrow road toward another sign some 300 yards away which evidently had been erected out of the Japs line of fire to protect approaches from the opposite direction. Malton and Fagan exchanged shrugs and started off at a dog trot behind the lieutenant who had opened up a gap. The S.P.'s voice trailed after them.

"Forgot to tell you. He's using a machine gun." The words quickened the pace and Fagan and Malton zigzagged as they ran. Marshall had lengthened his stride and was looking furtively toward the ridge on his right. All three seemed to be expecting to hear the metallic rattle of the Nambu momentarily.

As they reached about half-way across the danger alley, they weren't disappointed. Like a cheap typewriter gone mad, the Nambu sent hot lead flying down from the ridge. Its voice followed the whine of bullets as they clattered the coral. The three Marines had swept the terrain as they had moved for places of protection and now dove for a ditch that ran on the left side of the dirt trail road. Bullets followed them into the hole, one kicking dirt into the face of Marshall as he followed the example of Fagan and Malton and elongated himself in the deepest part of the ditch. It didn't offer too much shelter - only a narrow ledge of coral rock thrown from the tires and treads of trucks and tanks and forming a rise protecting them at all.

"Don't move!" Malton said, "He's got us dead in his sights." As if in answer, a round burst cut the coral ledge above them. It was lowered noticeably.

"That patrol better get busy!" Marshall said. "We can't play clay pigeon too long."

The Jap played a coy game. Not firing for several minutes, he waited until the Marines below him could not stand the rigid position and then moved a muscle - then the Nip let fly another burst, each one lowering the level of the ridge another inch or two. 10 minutes passed then fifteen, then 20 and the sweat and blood of the three trapped men ran together as the slivers of coral began to prick through their clothing as the ledge before them became negligible.

"We've got to move to another part of the ditch," said Marshall. "I'll go first - scoot backward. You two wait until the firing starts then scrounge forward as fast as you can. The ledge looks higher and 15 feet before you." Before the two enlisted men could object to his moving first, thereby endangering even more his own life, the lieutenant scooted backwards rapidly. The Jap was caught by surprise and the moment of reprieve saved the lives of the three men. Marshall had covered 10 feet in the interval and ducked just behind a fresh ledge of tire cast coral above by the time the Jap opened up, aimed far enough away so Malton and Fagan could take their dry skin searing, swim. The angered sniper sent his emotion by squeezing twenty rounds, mostly toward Malton and Fagan who had moved last. The bullets scattered the coral above them, but for the moment their position had been secured.

Fagan blinked his eyes to clear them of coral dust. "You know," he shouted. "I think that bastard is shooting at us." The words hung in the air, then their full meaning struck Malton and Marshall and their laughter filled the air. A loud explosion on the ridge drowned out the laughter. The patrol had found their prey.

The trio remained motionless for a moment, listening to the deafening roar echo through the crags and ravines of the ridge. As the sound of the hand grenade subsided the angry hoarse grumble of a light machine gun renewed man's answer to natures quiet. Finally all was silent - cautiously Malton rose from the ditch, his body searching the unprotected air for any further Jap bullets. None was forthcoming. Fagan and Marshall followed, shaking from their clothing the coral dust. Voices sounded upon the ridge.

"Looks like they got him," Fagan said and started up the hill toward the human sounds.

"Forget it," Marshall said, as he lighted a welcome cigarette and blew a deep lung full of smoke into the clear tropical air. "Let's go on! It's getting late." The lieutenant started up the road once more.

Malton heard Fagan mutter under his voice referring in his manner his opinion of the officers the Marine Corps deemed fit for command. The road narrowed sharply and soon the well beaten terrain seemed to engulf the tire tracks. Heavy equipment, most made inactive by Japanese fire weeks earlier, cluttered up the countryside.

Although the trio encountered few Marines, occasional work parties were salvaging good equipment from the equipment lying still.

The formal battle for Peleliu had been over for a week now - as Fagan had said, "Now the historians will be the sole beneficiaries of the battle of Peleliu. They'll sift through the monumental piles of orders, counter orders, directives, battalion histories and finally come up with a decision as to the relative merits of the campaign - but one question will remain after they have decided whether Peleliu should have been bypassed - and. that question will have to be answered by each of us in turn - whether alive or buried in the coral. "What the hell was I doing on Peleliu?" He had shaken his head and sighed, "I hope enough of them come up with the right answer to have made it all worthwhile."

The elements of the First Marine Division - the First, Fifth, Seventh and Eleventh Marines were standing by to be returned to their rest camp at Pavuvu while members of the Army's 86 Combat team tried to wedge the Japanese still alive from their cave positions, many of which had been blasted shut, but many which had never been located in the mass of coral deception known as Bloody Nose Ridge. The island was officially secured on this late October, 1944 day but hundreds of Japs in the interior of Bloody Nose Ridge did not get the word. Fortified with plenty of water, food and ammunition, they waited until the Americans became careless - then struck.

It was into the area of old Baldy that Marshall led them, seemingly unaware of the dangers which lurked behind each shadow on the crags about them. Fagan and Malton both had their weapons at the ready, scanning the ridges to the right and left.

Marshall stopped and putting his hands to his head, shielded them from the glaring sun. "We'll go up there - I remember some caves behind that crag." He pointed to the portion of Old Baldy which had almost spelled the end of the 3rd Platoon.

"You bet he remembers," Malton said through pursed lips to Fagan, "this guy's strictly nuts. Keep your eyes open."

"Why the hell didn't he get killed that first day?" Fagan said aloud as his gray eyes poked into the ridge's surface. "It could have saved us a lot of suffering. Hey, lieutenants better stay low," he yelled at the upright form of Marshall which was picking its way up the face of the ridge.

"Don't call me that," Marshall whirled around frowning. "You tryin' to git me killed?"

"Wouldn't be such a bad idea," Fagan answered harshly. "Before you get us killed."

Marshall's frown disappeared and his face broke into a wide grin, "Let's go, boots!"

The smell of dead and decaying bodies was overbearing in the area and the three Marines constantly tried to rid the arid taste by spitting, the saliva drying almost as soon as it touched the hot coral.

"Here's a good one," Marshall called as he stopped before a cave opening recess which was not too tightly sealed with blistered coral. "Fagan, you stand watch," he added as he put down the carbine he carried.

Bending his back to the task, Malton joined the lieutenant in scooping and throwing aside the coral in what appeared to be the thinnest part of the cave opening. After half an hour the smell of decaying flesh wafed forth sickening from the opening. "Ripe ones in there!" Marshall said wiping the perspiration from his face with the already saturated sleeve of his dungaree shirt, "Nobody's been into this one yet."

Fagan handed Malton his weapon and a blank stare as he took the stocky Marine's place at the mouth of the cave. The fresh pair of hands soon had an opening large enough for a man to crawl into.

"Stand clear," Marshall cried with his blue eyes bright with excitement. "I'll go in." Taking his rifle in his hands he wedged his way into the dark cave - Malton and Fagan waited, their eyes on the opening, "Get the hell away from that opening. I can't see a thing," Marshall's ringing voice sallied forth.

Malton moved but Fagan was too occupied to do likewise. He was watching an approaching group of five Marines, led by a barrel chested figure with a side arm. "We've got company," Fagan said quietly.

Silently the two Marines watched the men approach. The barrel chested individual seemed to breath fire with every step, his hard body and firm step belying the age written on his face. No insignia or rank was on the dirty dungarees.

"What are you men doing here?" the barreled one's voice bull frogged as he stood before the two Marines, who instinctively seemed to be standing at attention. "Damn it!" the man said angrily. "I asked you what you were doing here."

A disturbance at the cave opening overrode the need for an answer. A slim shiny sword shaft slowly began to show itself. One of the new arrivals quickly swung his rifle to the target and snapped off the safety. Malton grabbed the man's arm before he could pull the trigger. The barrel chested man motioned with his hand and the other Marines put up their weapons.

"Got me a beauty!" Marshall's dirty, sweat streaked face appeared at the opening of the cave followed by his foul smelling body, fresh from the unsealed grave. He took in the men about him and smiled. "Hi, ya," he said, his teeth white in the sun.

"What the hell are you doing in there?" the barreled chested man said angrily.

Marshall's face clouded at the tone, and his face reddened. "I'm checking on casualties."

The barrel chested seemed about to explode. "Don't you know there's orders to the effect that no one is to go into the caves for any reason - to get souvenirs least of all."

Marshall drew himself to his full height and with command in his voice shouted "Who the hell do you think you are talking to me like that! By God, I'll have you court-martialed for that. I gave those orders! I'm Colonel Ferkal."

Cold Steel Fagan and J. C. Malton, seasoned veterans of the 5th Marines, turned white at the words - slowly they turned to the barrel-chested man - his face now red with anger.

His lips trembled as he opened his mouth and let forth the voice that had started in his chest. "Like hell you are - I'M COLONEL FERKAL!"

The bivouac area of the Fifth Marines had been added to. A shelter, three sided with Jap corrugated tin and roofed with the same material had been erected. It was fronted by a poncho and completely surrounded with barbed wire. A sentry stood before the compound. Lt. Gary Marshall was the lone occupant of the 5th Marines brig.

Malton stood a short distance off leaning against a truck. "What do you think they're going to do with him?" Malton asked as he drew on his pipe.

"Going back to the states - General court-martial." Fagan was sharpening his knife - he spat on his whetstone. "Gonna miss the guy."

Malton sighed, "Me too. He sure took us off the hook by saying he ordered us with him."

"Well, he did, didn't he?" Fagan said spitting again on his whetstone as Malton nodded in agreement. "At least there's one good thing about it!" Malton looked up questioningly.

Fagan spat on the stone. "At least he won't get killed like he was sure headin' for."

J. C. sadly shook his head in agreement.

"JAP-A-DAY"

Chapter 11

For the first time since leaving Pavuvu months before, J. C. Malton was clean - the cleanliness which comes with relaxation. His body had finally been rid of most of the grime it had borne through weeks of fighting by a fresh water shower, wonders of wonders, at the Sea-Bee Camp the day before. And the shave, he now rubbed his hand over his smooth face, smooth in its one day's stubble, in comparison with the growth it had carried before.

Even the hot humid death filled air of Peleliu had been cleared by the deluge of rain which had swept over the Palau's earlier in the day, had brought some life to the devastated terrain and had settled the coral dust which blinded the eyes and throttled the throats of the Marines. Elements of the 1st Division had already departed Peleliu by this 25th day of October, and the 5th Marines had already gathered the salvageable gear and were standing by for the order to move aboard one of the ships which even now were unloading supplies down on the beaches.

The rain had passed on and the cleaned evening air was fresh. J. C. sat on the edge of a coral rock ledge which rimmed a coral cove on the southern edge of the island where the 5th Marines had bivouacked awaiting their evacuation back to the "rest" camp at Pavuvu. The blue water stretched endlessly before him, the setting rays of the distant sun shimmering upon the calm waters. The surf, a scant 25 yards from him beyond the crystal white sandy beach, gently lapped the shore. The setting was peaceful - far removed it seemed from the terrors of war. But Malton knew, without turning, that whereas the scene before him was one of peaceful serenity, behind him was total devastation, the fury of man's hatred expounding the earth.

"Want company?" the voice was that of Cold Steel Fagan. Malton startled - his nerves belying his outward calm. He never would become used to the stealth of his buddy.

"Sit down and light up," Malton said without turning. His own hand reached for his breast pocket and pulled out his pipe and tobacco - carrying the blue envelope which also was in the pocket. Glancing quickly at Fagan, he replaced the letter for which he had sought solitude for reading, and succeeded, in the pocket. Unhurriedly he lighted his pipe, drawing deep upon the tobacco, another prize he had acquired on the previous day's sortie to the Construction Battalion's camp. He leaned back against the hard surface of the ledge and looked up into the darkening sky at the stars which already were asserting themselves.

"What did she have to say in that one?" Fagan said quietly. He hadn't moved his eyes once since he had sat down, Malton was sure. Malton closed his eyes and drew deeply on the pipe, the smoke filtering through his teeth. He removed the pipe from his mouth with his left hand, a dull pain from his wound testifying to the rain which had fallen earlier. Slowly he pulled the letter from his pocket, "Read it."

Fagan turned for the first time and looked from the proffered letter to Malton. He shook his head, "Tell me what's in it, if you want, but I'm not going to start now reading other people's mail."

Malton smiled at the incongruity of his friends statement. Then his mouth straightened, "I just picked this one out. It was written on September 8 - the day we left Pavuvu for Peleliu." The last words were said with some nostalgic. "She said that for some reason she felt close to me, as if something were about to happen. Said she was frightened - afraid that something had happened to me." He stopped, unable to say the words which were clear in his mind - the words were tremulous on the perfumed blue stationery.

"J.C. darling! I'm so afraid for you! I love you so! I'd die if something happened to you!"

Malton opened his eyes to find Fagan staring at him through unblinking cold gray eyes.

"What about the baby?" Fagan's words shattered Malton's thoughts - brought a blush to his face. For the first time the words in the letter struck an unharmonious note. The baby – she had spoken words of love while carrying another man's child.

His words were hard, "It won't be born until November." He gave a curt laugh, "You don't have to count. It's not mine. She told me that."

"What's her husband's name?" Fagan asked innocently, his eyes searching the calm sea.

"Hell, I don't know!" He glanced at the return address - there the clear hand had written Jodie Farlin. "Farlin - I guess." He began to ask why he had asked, but Fagan's movement stopped him.

Fagan took some letters from his side pocket. "We had mail call today - while you were down here," he explained as he thumbed through the pack. Selecting one he said, "This one's from Seaman Ed Farlin!"

Fagan held out the air mail letter. J. C. stared at it for a minute and then took it awkwardly in his hand staring at the heavy male handwriting.

"Want me to leave?" Fagan started to get up.

"Sit still," J. C. answered absently as he tore open the envelope. He pulled the one page letter before the envelope and forgetting the presence of Fagan, began to read silently. Fagan watched his buddy's face as he read. As the eyes penetrated deeper down the page, the expression on the sunburned face of Malton changed from surprise to anger and then to a total blankness.

Finishing the letter he held it down to his side, staring at the sea. From his mouth came heatedly, "The son-of-a-bitch". Fagan waited, his eyes intent on Malton.

Malton became aware of his buddy's presence, "You read it!" then added forcibly as he thrust the letter to Fagan. "You read it!" Fagan strained his eyes in the rapidly closing darkness and read half-aloud.

"Dear Malton,

This is the damndest letter I've ever had to write, but it's the only thing to do. My wife (that's a laugh) is in love with you, not me! I know it now and

*should have known it when she came to San Francisco. But I wanted her so
much I could taste it, so I closed my eyes to everything and married her. I had
her - her body anyway, but looking back on it now, I know her tears were not
of love - at any rate - love for me. We've made a total mess of the whole damn
thing. She's miserable, she tells me. I'm miserable - and I don't know how you
feel! Frankly I don't give a damn.*

*Anyway! I'm sick of it! She's all yours. The only thing I'm thankful for is that
there won't be a kid to complicate matters. Good luck, Marine! You'll need it!*

Farlin"

Fagan put the letter down and joined Malton in his scanning of the sea.
He didn't speak while the stocky Marine refilled his pipe and lighted it, then
offered softly, "Who were you calling a son-of-a-bitch?"

Malton stopped midway in a puff on the pipe stem and turned to his
friend. His face was still drawn with anger. Slowly he said, "Both of them -
me! Hell I don't know."

"What you going to do now! Write her or him or both?" Some levity had
crept in Cold Steel's voice.

Malton recognized the humor and futility of the situation and a smile
crept over him. "Neither!" He said. "I was going to write Jodie. Matter of fact
I was plotting the letter when you came up. But now, now! Christ, How could
she not tell him she was going to have a baby?" Furiously he tapped the ashes
from his pipe against a large chunk of coral, knock both a chip from it and
the bowl of his pipe. He caressed the chip in the pipe repentantly.

Fagan stood up and tossed a piece of coral into the ocean now shimmering
in the moonlight. "Take-it easy, Malty," he said thoughtfully. "That girl's
really mixed up. She's got the yearns for you as bad as Farlin had for her.
Sure, she didn't tell him he was going to become a father, but," and he paused
to emphasize the words, "she didn't let you believe it was yours! That would
have made it easy - do you follow me?"

Malton didn't answer. the words registering in his mind - accepting the truth of them.

"Besides," Fagan continued, "we got work to do tomorrow - You and I are on patrol over on Jap a Day." With that he left Malton to his thoughts.

October 26 dawned with a misty, low hanging carpet of fog. Again during the night that specialty of the Pacific, a rain squall, cast a torrent of water over the sleeping Marines - Marines who immediately forgot that during the days of overbearing heat and sunshine they had prayed for rain. But now as the sun tried to burn its way through the overhang, the rain had stopped and the warmness of the new day brought a steamy mist from the rapidly drying clothing.

Cold Steel Fagan and J. C. Malton stood on the east coast of the southernmost tip of Peleliu straining their eyes to make out the island; islet was a better description, which had come to be known as Jap-A-Day Island. Dimly through the mist and ascending daylight, the island drifted in and out of view. It sat squat on the sea, no more than a hundred yards long and 50 yards wide. It was thickly covered with tropical vegetation, save for five tall coconut trees which tops were not now visible in the mist.

"Tide's almost out," Fagan commented as his eyes traced the water line on the beach. When the tide was out, a man of average height could easily walk across the smooth coral bottom of the ocean the five hundred yards from Peleliu proper to the small islet without wetting the buckle of the belt around his middle. But at night and during the daylight high tides, it was necessary to swim the distance.

It was this easy accessibility which had earned Jap-a-Day its name. During the night, Japs, mostly alone, swam or walked from Peleliu to the island in the safety of the darkness. Where they holed up during the day, God only knew. But at night, they burrowed out of their holes like rats and some, usually on a night, made his way to Jap-A-Day, and the following morning, armed two men patrols searched the bushes of the island for the Japs - and usually found their quarry and exterminated them - thus the name Jap-a-Day.

"I'll take the lead," Malton said as he tested his leggings to make sure they were tight. "Stay clear of me," he instructed.

Fagan nodded and followed the squat Marine into the calm sea. The sun had succeeded in burning away the haze and the pair furtively scanned the beach for any movement, their fingers lightly fondling the trigger guard. The pace was by necessity slow and they felt as if a pair of eyes was peering down the sights of a Jap 31 rifle at them. The partial protective cover of waist deep water was reached and even after their feet were moving upward toward the small atoll, they chose to remain low in the water.

Malton reached Jap-A-Day first and dashed into the thick vegetation, gulping deeply of the air after the exertion of the crossing. Fagan followed and crouched beside J.C., his breath causing his thin frame to expand unevenly.

"Someone's here," Cold Steel said through his teeth. "About 40 yards down the beach," he indicated the area to his left. "Saw the leaves move." His words came haltingly with each gulp.

J. C. hadn't seen anything. "You sure? Could just have been a rat or a monkey," he said. Fagan shook his head in disagreement. "It's a rat alright, but I can smell him way over here. Let's go."

Fagan cautiously moved through the brush away from the beach on which they had landed. He was like a cat as he stealthily pushed back the vegetation and wiggled his lithe body through the jungle in a half circle. Malton followed the slight trail left by Fagan, the tenseness of the chase bringing saliva to his mouth.

Five minutes later Fagan had completed his semi-circle. Slight break in the dense foliage offered the first opportunity for any visual observation. Fagan stopped and pointed to a clump of bushes immediately before them. Straining his eyes, J. C. could dimly make out the back of a man crouched beneath a shrub which blended well with the tan-green uniform. Malton smiled as he realized that the Jap was watching the beach for their approach. Fagan waited until J.C. looked once again in his direction and then whispered soundless for the other Marine to stand to the side of the bush.

A sudden blast of dynamite, sealing another cave on Peleliu echoed across the water. Seizing the opportunity J.C. lunged into the position indicated by Fagan, lying quietly once there to see if the movement had been heard by the Jap. Evidently it hadn't for the Jap seemed to stand up a little to try to see the source of the explosion.

Fagan signaled to J.C. to be ready then cupping his hands over his mouth shouted, "Hey! Stinkin' Jap." The words peered the stillness. The Japanese soldier whirled, terror in his eyes. Moving instinctively he dashed from his shelter, a knife in his hands. In the next moment the click of Fagan's rifle misfiring was quickly followed by the thud of Malton's rifle barrel as it crushed the skull of the Jap.

J. C. stood over the Jap, looking at the barrel of his carbine which he swore now sported a curve - which the designer had not inserted in his plans.

"Thanks," Fagan said quietly. Clearing his piece, he rammed another cartridge into the chamber and pointed it at the Jap's head.

Malton held out a restraining hand. "Hold it, Cold Steel. We have been ordered to take prisoners for interrogation. He's harmless now. Let's take him back."

A look of disgust crossed Fagan's face. "Shit." he spat. "Prisoners. What the hell is this corps coming too." He turned away in disgust.

Malton's face creased in a smile, quickly wiped out as he heard the Jap stir beneath him. The nip gingerly felt his head, moaning slightly as he sat up. Slowly his eyes focused on Malton's feet and up his body to his face. Graciously he spread his hands and bowed, mumbling incoherent words.

"He's all right now," Malton called to Fagan who had lighted a cigarette and was contemptuously glaring at the Jap who tried a smile which was lost in the effort. "Keep an eye on him," J. C. said. "I'll check the rest of the island." Before Fagan could object he added, "There aren't any more, if there were, they would have bunched up."

As quietly as possible Malton took a turn around the islet, confidence building with every step. There weren't any more Japs on Jap-A-Day - it had filled its daily quota.

A burst of fire caused him to drop to one knee. It was an M 1. Quickly Malton raced to the clearing where he had left the Jap and Fagan. Cold Steel stood with a grin on his face - his M 1 pointed down, its clip expended into the head of the Jan - it was no longer a head.

"What the hell did you do?" Malton shouted, staring incredulously at the morbid picture.

Fagan casually took another clip from his cartridge belt and thumbed it into the breech of the M-1. "The guy asked me to shoot him," he explained. "Pointed to his head and begged. You know how those guys feel about being captured." His eyes were expressionless.

"Yeh," Malton said as he started back across the beach to the water's edge. A curious question racing through his brain. Was the Jap telling Cold Steel to shoot him as was fitting for a Japanese soldier? That seemed logical. He looked at the grinning Fagan behind him - the Jap hater - the cold, merciless Marine - or had the Jap merely been trying to tell Fagan that his head hurt from Malton's lusty clout with the rifle?

The cold water of the ocean turned Malton's thoughts back to the unopened letters in his pack in the regiment's bivouac area. The answer to the question could be answered by but one man, and he lay dead with his brains spread all over Jap-A-Day Island!

The battle was done,
The victory was won,
But fear lived on.

"6 P.M. DEADLINE"

Chapter 12

"Greetings to my young Marine friends on Peleliu. This is your Oriental girl friend, Tokyo Rose, bringing you the latest music from the states and the latest news from the war front." The voice, coming from the jeep short wave radio, was sensually husky.

"Turn that bitch off!" one of the older marines surrounding the jeep shouted. The night was dark and unaccustomedly free from the tracer bullet trails that had lighted the Peleliu skies for the past month and a half.

"It's a beautiful night here in Tokyo and I know it's the same there on Peleliu. A night just made for romancing. How do you think it is back home in the States? And what about your girlfriends and wives? Are they sitting at home? -- or are they taking advantage of this moon with someone luckier than you? You know your women better than I do - What do you think?"

"I said shut that bitch off!" the older Marine cursingly climbed off the hood of the jeep and disappeared into the darkness. Mail from home had been scarce and the tone of his wife's letters when he did get them had started his battle weary home-sick mind thinking. What was Gloria doing that kept her from writing more often? The bitch! Bitch! "Have you boys heard the latest Glenn Miller record "Sentimental Journey"?   It was just released last week. As you listen to it remember that the U. S. Government estimates that one out of every five G.I.'s will receive a "Dear John" letter. Here's Glenn!"

The strains of the lilting song pierced the silence of Peleliu. The music drifted over the bivouac area and hundreds of Marines lay in their sacks or sat in small groups listening and longing for homes far away. Doubts crossed many a mind. Unfounded fears blossomed from the seed planted so skillfully by the sugary voice of the American traitor, Tokyo Rose!

"Where the hell does she get those records?" Cold Steel Fagan sat cross-legged among his band of cut-throats whet-stoning his ever sharp jungle knife.

"It's simple!" Ross Miller, chomped on his chew slowly, spit with the wind and called on his great mass of unconfirmed scuttlebutt. "We ship them to her! Guy told me that the government sends her a copy of every record cut. They figure that's one way to keep us up on the latest songs."

"Sure, that's right," Cold Steel never looked up as he spoke, "the state department sends a special courier in the president's plane! He drops in at Tojo's Palace, has tea, talks of the horrible conditions in the world, and then takes off again for home."

The laughter spread throughout the area. Miller mumbled something and then spat again. "What's your explanation, then, hot shot?"

The laughter stopped. Everyone strained to hear the words of the calculating Fagan, who was more often right than wrong.

Cold Steel tested the edge of the razor sharp knife, "The way I figure it, they get the record from one of those South American countries who's palsy with both sides in this fracas. We trade with them to keep the bastards on our side and they trade with Tojo and the paper hangers for the dough involved." He looked up at Miller, imitated a wad of tobacco in his jaw and spit into the wind.

The music faded away, "A special announcement now to the brave Marines oh Peleliu - the young and doomed men of the First Marine Division!"

"Hey, that's us!" The troops crowded the jeep once more.

"I have a sad duty to perform. I've been informed that the 1st, my favorite division, soon will be completely wiped out. The Peleliu you so gallantly fought for and which now holds in its bowels 1,241 of your dead, also holds enough charges of explosives to blast the island into the depths of the sea. Yes, it's true! The Empire took precautions in case the strategic island ever fell. The entire island has been embedded with a circuit of explosives and is controlled by a switch at Babelthuap, up north! Impossible, you say! Look about you at the caves hewn from the solid coral rock by the ingenuity of our troops! The date of destruction is near. Tomorrow, October 28, at 1800, the switch will be thrown and Peleliu and the First Marine Division will be no more. It saddens me, my young loves, but in the words of your own dead General Sheridan, "War is hell." And now, I'm too distraught to go on. I'll close with a recent release of the Pied Pipers. It's called "Dream!"

The melancholy music was scarcely heard by the stone-faced men huddled in the darkness. The entire island was still for a moment and then the quietness was broken.

"Well, I'll be damned." Cold Steel had stopped stoning his knife. Suddenly the entire island became alive with activity as the word was spread by mouth to its far extremities. Within an hour the sixteen thousand Marines remaining on the island had heard of Tokyo Rose's message. The first reaction was of disbelief, but as time went on the thought of the hand carved intricate system of caves became more and more the measuring stick of the truthfulness of the story. Reports, scuttlebutt or truth, began to be distributed. Large caches of explosives had been deep in the coral during the actual battle for the island. Scuttlebutt racked the island. Fear began to creep into the faces of battle tired men. They faced a known enemy without fear but this was something else again.

"A hell of a way to die!" Chick Young sat on the edge of an overturned, burned out Jap tank. About him in the brightening sun were Fagan, Miller, Wagner, Badger and Malton, each with his own thoughts turned toward the 1800 deadline that evening.

"I still can't believe it!" Wagner, opening and closing his fist on a grip developer, said. "Tons of explosive planted on this rock. It will sure make a huge boom."

"Check those guys moving closer to the beach," Fagan spat toward Beach Red where operations in the past several weeks had slowed down, but where, now, a mass of humanity was already beginning to form.

"Around seventeen thirty, you'll find me down there, too," Miller shamelessly said. "Don't know where I'll swim to, but swim I will." The laughter was hollow. The attempts at bravado were weak and scarcely hid the lines of fear which roamed the faces of brave men.

"What's the latest word Richardson?" The tall thin, muscular Marine who joined the group wore the same expression as his colleagues.

"Division has men combing the island. They don't hold much faith in Rose, but they're not taking any chances." He propped his back against the tank and fixed his gaze on the beach area.

Malton, the West Virginian, watched him and imagined the turmoil that was going on in that keen brain. A favorite of the squad, Richardson was respected and admired by the men who knew him best.

Richardson sat immobile, his eyes on the beach, but his thoughts thousands of miles stateside in California, on Mary. Mary, how he longed to hold her, reassure her that all was well. He recalled the night before he left Comstock.

The path along Farrell's Lake had been bright with moonlight. Hand in hand they walked, silently and thoughtfully. Theirs was a love that needed no words. They had been inseparable since their sophomore year in high school, three years before Jim, at the University studying law, had managed to resist the shock of Pearl Harbor and remained in college, but with the coming of spring 1942, he spent the entire spring vacation convincing his parents that he had to join the service. Mary took no persuasion. She knew his burning desire to get into the fight.

They came to Flat Iron Rock and Mary sank to the grass, her back braced against the rock. Jim knelt beside her, skipping stones on the smooth surface of the lake.

"It had to be the Marines, didn't it, Jim?" Mary's eyes were on the lake.

Jim stopped throwing and looked long at her before he spoke. "The Marines? Yes, I thought about it of often! All volunteers, mostly young guys like me, strict but responsible discipline! Yes, it had to be the Marines!"

"And the first to fight! And the most difficult battles! You must get into actual combat! Don't mind me! I understand!. It's just that I love and need you so!" Her eyes clouded. "Please come back, Jim, Please!"

He lowered himself beside her and held her close. "I'll be back - I'll be back!" He leaned his head back and gazed deeply into her eyes, "I'll be back!"

The tank's treads dug into his side and as he shifted his position he saw Malton's eyes on him, and he flushed.

"Well, check the civilians!" The rasping voice of Platoon Sgt. Konkright broke into their thoughts. "Off your asses! We've got to get our gear together. Ships pull in day after tomorrow!"

"Think you'll be here, Serge?" Cold Steel was back to honing his knife!

The serge's face clouded, "Forget the scuttlebutt. Now move!"

The group pulled themselves to their feet and began to rearrange the gear for the tenth time. No idleness in the Marine Corps. The more active you were kept, the less time for thoughts.

The battle for Peleliu had been over for a week, organized resistance had come to an end, and mopping up operations were going on at the northern tip of Ngesebus, a small island north of Peleliu which was joined by a causeway. The ships were due to take the division back to Pavuvu in the Russell's. The day was filled with frantic action as commanders tried to keep the men's thoughts from Tokyo Rose's announcement of doom.

Scuttlebutt had the division's anti-mine team finding the central control point of the demolition. Scuttlebutt had it that the charge had not been found. By 1700 the island was a mass of activity. All attempts to find evidence of explosives had failed. The island command had issued precautionary measures. Regimental and battalion commanders were on a stand-by measure. Troops were ordered to dig fox holes. At seventeen-thirty troops began to filter toward the beach. Ships anchored off shore pulled back into the sea.

"I'm going to the beach!" Chick Young stopped digging. Everyone stopped his feverish shoveling. "If this island's going up, I'm going to get ready to jump in the ocean." He started walking toward the beach.

The squad looked at each other and then one by one made their way behind Young. The beach area was jammed with other Marines who had the same idea. Fear was distinguishable on all faces save Cold Steel who sat near the water line whittling at a piece of deadwood.

Eyes every moment glanced at watches. The minute hand crept toward 1800. More and more men crowded the beach area. Enlisted men and officers quietly took places in easy access to the water. 1750! Anxiety mounted with the passing minutes. Suddenly one Marine jumped into the water. Willing hands drew him back to the sand. Where was there to go? Cold Steel watched the action, then slowly pulled his long frame to his feet, gingerly placed his knife into its sheath strapped to his leg and turned to his buddies.

"If I going to die, I'm going to die like a man!" He began walking inland toward the battalion bivouac area. All eyes in the area watched guiltily and then one by one, Richardson and the rest, with Chick Young bringing up the rear, followed sheepishly.

Fagan reached the area, sat beside the nearly finished foxhole he had been digging, pulled his cigarette makings from his breast pocket, rolled and lighted a cigarette. The others joined him.

Silently he passed the cigarette from one to the other, all with heads bowed. Richardson looked at his watch. "30 seconds to go." The heads raised slowly! The eyes still had the look of fear, but pushing the fear aside was the glint of pride. Each gazed at the others.

Suddenly shouting rose above the silence that had prevailed over the island the past five minutes. The small group turned toward the beach. Marines were slapping each other on the back. 1800 o'clock had come and gone. The farce was over and boisterousness tried to hide the shame that each felt.

"Wonder what new record Rose will have tonight?" Cold Steel was again stoning his knife. Smiles spread over the squad's faces.

Richardson pulled out his wallet and took out Mary's picture. His lips moved silently, "I'll be back."

"MAN OVERBOARD"

Chapter 13

"Don't that ship look good?" It was more of a statement than a question which Cold Steel Fagan spoke. The crowded landing craft pitched and tossed as it headed ungracefully toward a large APA which stood anchored off Peleliu.

No answer came from the standing Marine, so unlike the crouching troops who had made the inland trip on September 15, almost seven weeks before. No answer was necessary to the quiet, spent, filthy Marines whose eyes looked upon the squat converted merchant ship as truly a King's Castle after the misery each had seen on the coral hell behind them.

So we're really leaving, thought J.C. Malton to himself, leaving that damn scorching rock. His head turned from the APA - 604 was the number, and looked over the faces of the men of the 3rd Platoon who were getting out. Some he knew well, they had shared combat before - Cold Steel, Liverlip, Blue, Richardson, Peterson, Young. Others he knew only slightly, personally that is, for though they had fought well beside the old timers when they came in as replacements, there had been little time to exchange backgrounds, ideologies, and philosophies.

There were Badger, McKean, Wagner among others. Men whose fighting ability he had come to respect. And the others, they lay dead beneath the hard coral back on the island or wishing they were dead back in a base hospital.

"Sure was the longest 72 hours I've ever spent anywhere," Chick Young spoke - his naturally thin frame now emaciated, his thin face hollow beneath the high cheekbones.

A snicker arose from the boatload. Seven weeks they had suffered, fought, suffered and died on the tiny island which the head brass had said would be secured in 72 hours. But the bitterness which had been existent so strongly before had tempered with the passing days and now, as the landing barge banged against the side of the ship, almost forgotten in the joy of leaving.

The Marines scrambled expertly up the net, carrying much less than they went in with. Fagan and Malton had but half of their packs on their backs, and they were loosely packed with personal belongings - no rations of food or ammunition, no gas mask to tangle with. The rifle which still was the only essential item of equipment. Even the heavy steel helmet had been discarded, but not the camouflage cover, the symbol of a Marine. It proudly was worn over the fiber of the helmet liner.

The Marines made a sorry looking sight as they dragged themselves single file down the uncovered passageway on the starboard side of the ship to an open hatch which led to troop quarters below. Sailors watched them incredulously, marveling at their filthiness, their thinness, the look of death so prevalent in their eyes. The Marines knew they were the object of the stares and tried, not quite successfully, to hold themselves erect as they moved down the passageway. The contrast between the two groups was startling to anyone caring to make the comparison. The ship's company fresh from the states still had the bloom of civilization about them - they were clean from fresh water showers, clean with their machine laundered blue coveralls, clean with their hot water shaved faces. The sailors, at least most of them, were getting their first look at what combat does to a human being.

Malton followed Fagan down the passageway, forcing his uneasy legs forward. His healing arm ached from the unaccustomed climbing. He was perspiring and uncomfortable, but happy.

He barely noticed the sailor who was sitting on the rail as he approached, but the almost forgotten odor of after-shave lotion caused him to glance at him. A smile formed, here was a poster sailor - immaculately dressed with even his shoes shined. He wore his white cap perched cockily on the back of a well-groomed head, a lock of black, toniced hair bumbling from under the front, falling across a sun-tanned forehead. The eyes beneath were blue - a startling effect against the sunburned face which was handsome and beautifully unlined. A waxed mustache arched over the full lips from which dangled a cigarette - but the crowning effect was a silver ring which hung from his left ear. He was talking to another sailor half hidden beyond him.

His lips moved contemptuously as he watched the Marines pass before him, "I'll sure be glad when we leave this two bit island and move up where real fighting is."

The words struck J.C. a blow in the face, the crotch and the stomach. He felt sick! Suddenly anger flared and he automatically stuck out his wounded arm and pushed the sailor hard. A startled cry left the lips of the hurtling man just before they were submerged in the ocean.

J. C. grinned at the surprised look on the face. "Man overboard!" he called. But the alarm was not necessary. Sailors and Marines alike had turned to the rail and a line was tossed to the gulping sailor!

"Grab that man! Toss him in the brig!" the voice bellowed from above. The officer of the deck, his face flushed, pointed at Malton from the bridge. Several sailors moved in, but Fagan and Konkright headed a corps of Marines who were prepared to disillusion the arresting detail.

"Easy you guys!" Malton said softly, a smile on his face. "Did you see his face when he hit?" The grin broadened into a laugh. "It was worth it. Take it easy - the brig has privacy I won't have with you guys."

Smiles appeared on the Marines faces. The tension had broken and laughter arose, sailors and Marines joining voices. Below them, the sailor had started up a Jacob's ladder, his mustache drooping and his earring absent.

"What the hell's the commotion, Lieutenant?" Captain Jonathan Hearkit, his pouch bobbing, joined his officers on the bridge. His face was round, his lips almost lost in the chubbiness of his cheeks.

The Lieutenant smartly saluted, and the Captain carelessly returned it seeming only to be waving away a fly which could be buzzing near the peak of his baseball cap. "Marine tossed one of the ship's company overboard. I've ordered him to the brig." The last was said with pride of accomplishment of being equal to the situation - according to the book.

A frown fought its way beneath the layer of perspiration which covered the face and found its way into the deep sunk eyes which were shaded both by the cap and a bulbous nose. Damn it! He had known there would be trouble with the Marines - he had shuddered when the ship had been ordered from transient duty between New Caledonia and Guadalcanal to the combat area. The barbarous sons-of-bitches were always causing trouble. Espirit-de-corps shit! They were uncivilized savages. The globe-circling woman from Washington had been right when she recommended that the Marines should be put on an island off the coast of the U.S. and civilized before being permitted to re-enter the country. Well - he'll show them! He'd fix it so that there wouldn't be any further trouble - he'd make an example of this Marine that the others would not soon forget.

"Set up a court martial for the bastard. Make it in the ship company officer's mess!" He checked his watch - it was 1000, "at 1100."

The Lieutenant gulped, "A general, sir?"

"For Christ's sake, no - the court martial fits the crime - don't you know your manual - it calls for a deck!" He turned and disappeared in the chart house - his big behind waddling as he walked.

The red faced Lieutenant, his victory of a few moments before turned into defeat felt the grins which appeared on the duty enlisted men on the bridge. "Stand by your posts - look alive now." He fled from the bridge, his humiliation biting deeper.

Malton stretched out full length on the iron cot in A.P.A. 604's brig, a peaceful smile on his face. He moved his body luxuriously on the soft mattress, the first he had seen since leaving Pavuvu. He had tested the wash basin and commode which were also part of the brig's fittings. He was in heaven - not even the impending court-martial seemed to deter the comfort and privacy which he had not enjoyed for what seemed years - indeed!

Propping the pillow up against the bulkhead, he lighted his pipe and drew deeply of the smoke. Outside the thick, but resonant, steel sides of the ship, final preparations for embarkation could be heard - all the troops must be on board. A gentle rocking motion, and the increased vibrations always present with a moving ship testified to the fact that indeed the trip back to Pavuvu had begun.

Pavuvu - what a beautiful sounding name for such a lousy hole. It had been the Marines "rest" camp - the 1st Marine Division's rest camp after Cape Gloucester. The island lay in the Russell Island group, some sixty miles from Guadalcanal. It was completely unsuited for a "rest" area as it was for the training necessary for the next invasion which was always mandatory after each operation - necessary because of the number of replacements necessary to replenish the division. Pavuvu was too small, too wet, and infested with the largest rats in the world. The exhausted Marines "rest" after Cape Gloucester began with building a camp - Pavuvu was uninhibited by anything but rats - and this job was made impossible by the ankle deep mud which the torrential rains fed every day. Fagan had commented, "More guys went Asiatic on Pavuvu than on Cape Gloucester."

And now the First Marine Division was heading back to Pavuvu, island whore of the Pacific. Smiling faintly Malton thought that even Pavuvu would look good after red hot bloody Peleliu.

"O.K. Mac," the young sailor peered through the barred small window of the door. "Guess they've got the party ready for you." The key clicked in the door and creaking lustily, the steel door opened wide. The sailor stood there, a rifle in his hand - he looked unhappy and slightly frightened at the unkempt Marine.

J. C. smiled, "Relax, I'm not going to try to take that rifle away from you. I've enjoyed your hospitality." Still clenching the pipe between his teeth, he moved past the sailor, automatically contracting his nose against the always present body odor. He was surprised that there wasn't any - then his grin broadened as he realized this was a clean living swabby and not a stink hole crawling Marine. He blinked his eyes and squinted against the glare of the bright sunlight as he reached topside, unused to its brilliance after the darkness of the "private" chamber he had just vacated.

"Head aft - to the first ladder," the sailor ordered, uneasy under the angry stares of the Marines who stood and sat on the deck. Acclimating his eyes to the sunlight, J.C. smiled unconcernedly at the dirty faces, inwardly feeling proud that they had not rushed to the fresh water showers but had stationed themselves near the brig hatch waiting. He spotted Fagan who was sharpening his knife on the whetstone - an awesome maneuver which the sailor did not fail to see.

"How you guys making out?" Malton called. "I've got it made. Steel cot, mattress, my own private crapper and sink, I'm traveling first class." Then he added mean fully, "You guys keep your noses clean. There isn't room down there for any more - and the privacy is great - great."

An irregular wave of laughter passed from the group - but the eyes were still hard, mean and itching for trouble. Fagan viciously passed the blade on the stone, his eyes on Malton. "You tell that son-of-a-bitchin' fat captain we're getting restless." A murmur of agreement rose from the Marines.

"Break it up," a Junior grade Marine officer from battalion headquarters company had seen the gathering from the transient officers country deck which was far removed from the ship's company's area and came down to investigate. "What's the bull session for? Speak up Sergeant!" he indicated Konkright.

Malton had reached the top of the ladder and the voices were indistinguishable to him as he made his way through a bulkhead and down a passageway. Immediately the difference from the troop's area was distinguishable. He had thought the brig area was heaven, but now he realized it was only his faulty memory of what real living was like which had formed the conclusion. Here, everything was immaculate - the door to one of the officer's staterooms was open and in his hurried glimpse he recognized the touches – a bookcase, desk, wide bed, wooden armchairs , and framed large pictures on bedside tables - that only a semi-permanent duty could offer.

He followed the short, but now more relaxed, orders of the guard as he made his way down passages. Finally he was halted before a door over which "Officers Mess" was lettered. The guard pounded sharply once on the door and thrust the bulkhead sharply open at an answer from within.

The sailor indicated Malton in - and the Marine stepped into a rectangular room about 40 feet long and 25 feet wide. The mess tables had been pushed together at the far corner and a long oaken table stood directly across the deck from the door. Behind the table sat the Captain, perspiring in full summer uniform complete with field scarf. Flanking him were two junior officers, uncomfortable in like dress. An enlisted man sat at the end of the table, a pad before him ready to take down the proceedings.

"Bring the prisoner before the bench," the Captain said, seemingly unaware of the perspiration which had already soaked his collar and was working its way through the blouse of the uniform. His face was red, his eyes were hard - he was in his glory.

Malton stepped before the desk standing at stiff attention trying to hide the humor he felt at the ridiculous sight. He was amazed at his lack of emotion - complete lack of concern toward the court martial.

The Captain nodded toward the Lieutenant on his right who hurriedly consulted the manual before him, obviously unfamiliar with the proceedings.

"Name, rank, and serial number?" the officer said, glancing uncertainly at the Marine.

Malton almost burst out laughing. He composed himself and offered "J.C. Malton, Corporal, U.S. Marine Corps 35 42 67," he emphasized U. S. Marine Corps.

The Lieutenant hadn't heard, again checking the manual. He held it before the Captain who read and then nodded. Clearing his throat Captain Jonathan Hearkit spoke in his high pitched voice, "Corporal: You are charged with an offense which dictates a deck court martial. You are entitled to defense counsel."

"Waive counsel!" Malton snapped from his stiff attention. His harsh voice whipped through the room, causing the lieutenant to drop the manual with a thud. Captain Hearkit's face became more red, he banged his hand on the table.

"Call Seaman John Korthan," the Captain almost yelled, his face bursting forth another flow of perspiration.

Malton heard movement behind him - he had been unaware that the aggrieved sailor was in the room. He sensed that the Seaman was standing to his left, well away from the "mad" Marine.

"Seaman Korthan," the Captain tried to bellow but failed miserably. "Tell your story."

The sailor cleared his throat and his voice when at last he found it, bore evidence that he had not as yet, overcome his ordeal. "Well, sir -" he started, then cleared his throat again, still tasting the salt water. "I was sitting on the rail, minding my own business -" Sounds like he's rattling in school Malton thought wryly, "talking to Seaman Walters, when this Marine pushed me over the side." Tears seemed to well in his eyes. "That's all there was to it sir - I don't know why."

Captain Hearkit humph'd several times then confidence in his voice said, "Anything to add to that Corporal?"

Malton grinned watching its effect happily on the Captain. "That's about it, sir. Nothing to add."

Captain Hearkit's mouth drew in a straight line. He'd teach this wise Marine and the rest of them too. They wouldn't forget Captain Hearkit and APA 604 for a long time.

Hearkit drew himself erect in his Captain's chair. "Corporal! You've endangered the life of a seaman in the United States Navy. It was a serious act and I'm going to throw the book at ---"

Captain Hearkit didn't complete his sentence, for at that moment the bulkhead banged open and disclosed Regimental Commander C. W. (Barrel) Ferkal. Behind the chesty Colonel stood two of his officers including the headquarters company lieutenant who had appeared amongst the troops earlier. Barrel thundered across the deck, his swagger stick pounding into his hand – his granite jaw set and his black eyes throwing fire. He stopped beside Malton, looked him up and down and then gave the Captain the benefit of the mad eyes.

"What the hell is goin' on here?" The words were furious and held no respect for Captain, a full Captain, who outranked him.

Captain Hearkit seemed to wither before the assault of the Colonel, but he managed to assume an authoritative air. "We're holding a court martial."

"With one of my men?" he thundered. Not waiting for an answer he added, "Why the hell wasn't I informed?"

The captain's anger smoldered, the perspiration flowing freely. He looked at Barrel's rank, "Lieutenant Colonel!" He emphasized. "This is a Navy matter and we're entirely capable of handling the situation without the Marine Corps help."

"Since when!" The Colonel's retort drew a smile on his officer's faces and that of Malton. "When it involves one of my men, I'm involved! What's the charge?"

Captain Hearkit was beginning to regret the matter. These damned Marines - the officers were as bad as the men - lunatics, savages. He indicated to the Seaman, "Tell your story, Sailor."

Seaman Korthan shared the Captain's uneasiness, but valiantly repeated the story as he had told it before. As he concluded the Captain was relaxing in his chair once again, once more confident of his position.

"Is that right, Malton?" the Colonel had been surprised to see the same Marine who had been involved with the fool Marshall in the souvenir escapade, when he had stormed the room. Didn't he ever stay out of trouble?

"Yes Sir!" Malton said and the Captain relaxed even more. The Colonel frowned staring at J.C. with anger. Then he swung to the sailor.

"What were you talking about when this man pushed you over the side?" The words were less harsh but still carried a sting.

Seaman Korthan shuffled his feet and slouched somewhat under the strain. "We were just talking about the war, nothing in particular, sir." His voice was tinged with fright, his eyes wavering.

Colonel Ferkal sensed his opening. He shouted, "What were you saying, sailor!"

Korthan looked pleadingly at the Captain only to find bewilderment there. He began to talk. "I don't remember exactly, but it was something to do with the island, I think. Something about being glad to get out of here and moving up where the real fighting was."

As he concluded, a stillness fell over the cabin. Stunned expressions on the Marine officers faces turned to drawn lines of anger. Suddenly Ferkal's face reddened, and he beat the swagger stick savagely in his fist. He turned and stood before the sailor, his face a mask of hatred – the swagger stick beating a tattoo in his palm.

Suddenly he swung back to the desk and placing his hands upon it leaned over it and stared into the gasping face of the Captain. His voice hissed almost through clenched teeth, "You court martial Malton and you'll have to do the same with every Marine on this tub - including me!" He stood there, knuckles white on the table.

Captain Hearkit shifted himself uncomfortably in his chair. He looked at his aides, whose faces were focused incredulously on Seaman Korthan and then at the angry faces of the Marine officers and finally to the only composed man in the cab. Malton was smiling.

"Humph!" The Captain tried again, "Under the circumstances, we had better secure this court."

Ferkal continued to stare at the Captain a minute, then swung on his heel and started from the room waving Malton behind him.

Malton, still smiling fell in between the Colonel and the junior officers, and the quartet strode smartly through the bulkhead leaving a flushed and disconsolate Captain Hearkit behind.

The Colonel moved out of earshot and then stopped, whirled and faced Malton, a stern expression on his face. "Can't you keep your ass clean, Corporal?" Then his face softened and turning he let drift over his shoulder. "You'll make a good Marine someday."

Malton couldn't see his face, but he knew Colonel Ferkal was smiling.

"THE DITCHING"

Chapter 14

November 10, 1944, dawned with its usual brilliance wherever on the scattered face of the earth U. S. Marines happened to be. Guadalcanal during the third year of World War II proved no exception. Elements of the 1st Marine Division, fresh from the hell island which was Peleliu, were already training for their next assault, but November 10 was a special day, one to be looked forward - for this was the anniversary of the founding of the Corps. Training schedules were forgotten - it was a day of celebration!

Marines hurried through morning chow and then quickly but carefully prepared for the review which would signal the beginning of a full day of celebration and liquid nourishment. Expectancy replaced the tired boredom which always followed a battle.

The review quickly materialized and the battalion soon found themselves formed for the traditional greetings from the Commandant. Lt. Colonel Ranna stood straight as only a career Marine can before his troops. Many of the faces before him were unfamiliar to him - replacements who had taken the places of those left behind - beneath the coral of Peleliu. In one hand the colonel held the ever present swagger stick; in the other the birthday greetings of the Commandant. His thin mustache twitched as he cleared his throat.

"Men, the Commandant sends his greetings. I quote --" He read rapidly, his deep voice rich with a Southern accent. The old timers smiled. The greetings were stereotyped, they had heard them before. "That's it! All training procedure will be discontinued until 0800 hours tomorrow. Each man will be given a beer ration of 6 bottles. Enjoy yourselves, but don't overdo it. I don't expect to see anyone fall out when sick call sounds tomorrow. Platoon leaders, dismiss the troops."

Staccato voices ordered, "Toon ten-shun, Fall out." The parade area rang with a strange sound - laughter, carefree, wild, laughter!

"Carter," yelled the quartermaster sergeant as another six cans of beer were lined up!

"Yo!" Carter grabbed his six cans and quickly headed back to the tent area.

Domenico, Egan, Faccinto - all took their ration and joined the parade to the privacy of their own tent!

"Fagan!" The name brought catcalls, whistles, profanity and Cold Steel himself forward.

"I'll take my six and Brabern's too, Sergeant." The blue eyes pierced their way past the hawk nose. He wasn't smiling.

"Like hell you will!" The fat quartermaster sergeant's face turned red with anger! His head jerked down the list. Frank Brabern's name had a line through it, followed by the letters K.I.A.

Fagan stood there a second longer, his long fingers clamping the six cans of beer in a vise. His battered face showed no emotion, then his slim bony shoulders shrugged, and he turned and walked off, oblivious to the quietness that had joined the ration line. The afternoon shower didn't hinder the celebration which was by now in full swing. The beer ration had been supplemented by all the types of rot-gut that could be bought, borrowed or stolen. Stills along the banks of the Tenaru poured forth raisin juice that had not yet been aged. The entire battalion area rang with drunken laughter.

Suddenly the laughter dissolved into roaring cursing. Down a company street came a parade of drunken Marines. Squirming in the grasp of four shouting, staggering, huskies was Cold Steel Fagan. The procession proceeded past the neat rows of coconut trees, picking up inquisitive followers. The mob trudged through ankle deep sand to the water line. Waiting for a wave to come in, the quartet began the chant, "one, two, three --!"

The lanky form of Cold Steel soared helplessly through the air plunging spread eagled into the surf!

Drunken laughter greeted Cold Steel as he pulled his grime saturated clothes, which clung to his bayonet thin body, ashore. The laughter subsided as the troops caught the look in Cold Steels eyes. Sand flew in all directions as Cold Steel took after the next victim.

In a matter of minutes there was a constant procession of bodies hurtling through the Pacific sky as other Marines joined the select corps of drunken dunkees. Soon there was not a dry member of the crowd surrounding the "port of debarkation." Those from the tent area who came to the beach to find out what was causing the excitement soon found out. Suddenly Cold Steel stopped his darting from one heaving crew to another. He had spotted the next victim.

Lt. Harrington had just returned from the communication tent where he had ascertained that all equipment was secure. His thinning hair and punching bag shaped stomach disclosed his years. A telephone company district manager from Pennsylvania, he didn't quite fill the pictures of the Marine poster. Quiet and efficient, he was appreciated if not fully respected by the communications crew.

He had stopped along the first row of palm trees and was watching the by-play on the beach. The one beer he had gulped had reacted quickly, and its effects were still apparent in his eyes. He did not seem aware of Cold Steel, Miller, and Ross encircling him. His first reaction to the grasp of Fagan was of surprise, then quickly recognizing their intent he relaxed and chuckled. Let the boys have their fun, they had earned it - God only knew.

The warm, salty sea snapped him to reality. He wondered how his fellow officers would react to this indignity. As he waded ashore his fears were allayed as he saw his contemporaries in the process of being given the same treatment. He laughed and joined in the search for incriminating dry clothing.

The recreation went on for an hour until not one dry Marine remained in camp. The novelty was wearing off when Sergeant Carston, soaked by the ocean and a quart of jungle juice he had been saving for an occasion, staggered down the main company street and fell into a mud hole that was perpetually full as a result of the daily rain that fell on the canal. About 15 feet long and five feet wide, the "pond" was deep enough to hide a body stretched flat. Fortunately a group was prowling the street for dry gyrenes and saw Carston fall in. Whooping with delight they dragged the drugged Sergeant from his bed of mud and took his limp body to the ocean's edge and gave him the dousing his spattered condition called for.

Interest was again aroused in the sport and everyone received another heaving, but this time the dunking was prefaced by an invigorating mud bath.

Captains Thomas Griffen and Fred Barker, U.S.A.F., unfortunately picked this day to visit the Marine Post Exchange down the road from Henderson Field. The unfortunate aspect was the fact the P.X. was situated in the middle of the tent area which was the scene of the sporting exhibition. The two air force officers visited the P.X. frequently. The Marine P.X. had a better selection of cigarettes and shaving gear, it being common knowledge on the Canal that the supply dump where luxuries were stored after arriving on the island was always visited in the still of the night by "Marine Work Crews." This visitation was never proved by the port authorities but by the same token was never doubted.

As the pair neared the P.X., Cold Steel and his crew turned a tent corner and spotted them. Cold Steel smiled without smiling and ordered, "Charge."

The Air Force men were dumbfounded as they were seized and dragged through the dust. Finally Captain Barker found his voice. "What the hell! Hands off, you bastards." He tried to free himself but his arms were pinioned by Cold Steel.

"What's going on? Let go, I'll have you men court-martialed! Are you rock happy?" Incredibly dumbfounded by the action he saw before him. The mud puddle surrounded by wide-eyed laughing Marines.

Finally Captain Griffin, a straight D-I football player from the University of California at Los Angeles, realized that this was not according to the book and joined in the vocal protestation. The two were ceremoniously lifted at the brink of the mud hole.

Griffin tried to free himself from the obviously demented Marines. Failing he cried out, "Stop it, damn it! You'll be court-martialed! Where the hell is your commanding officer?"

A face merged from the depths of the mud hole, dripping with the red deposit of the canal. The face softened into a grin, "Someone looking for me?" he said moving over for the company that splashingly joined him.

Chapter 15

"It looks like the Southeastern hills of Ohio!" Malton leaned against the crude shelter he and Fagan had constructed against the uncertainty of the Okinawan spring.

"Ohio can't be much then." Fagan spat a slivery, muddish trail of tobacco juice into a small puddle left by the spinning wheel of a jeep in the soft ground. "It's gonna start raining soon - and then this picnic will be over." Fagan added, looking discerningly along the horizon, beneath which sat the largest floating armada ever assembled in the Pacific.

Cold Steel looked from the sky around the side of the hill on which they sat, nothing but thin groves of trees between them and the China Sea. Nothing, that is, save what had once been the carefully cultivated fields of the Okinawans, fields which had been trampled by the thousands of feet of the invading Marine and army troops. The scene about him was reminiscent of a staging area rather than a combat zone. Marines of the First Marine Division stretched out over the terrain almost as far as the eye could see, some sitting, some lying, beside hastily and crudely dug foxholes. It was D + 11 of what had turned out to be the strangest and weirdest of all the First's landings.

The battle plan had called for the First and Sixth Marine Divisions, the latter a newly formed outfit, but staffed with veterans of Guadalcanal who had been rotated to the states and were now back for the second time around. The plan called for the two Marine Divisions to land at Yantan point, turn north through the mountainous terrain where the enemy was expected to put on his stand. In the meantime, the 77th and 96th Army divisions were to turn south from the airstrip and liberate the Okinawans in the heavily populated Shuri and Naha areas. The 77th, most respected by the Marines and affectionately dubbed the "Dog-faced Marines", invaded little Ie Shima Island, which held a strategic air strip.

But the Japs had exasperated the intelligence by almost completely deserting the Northern part of the island, save for a few snipers, and throwing the bulk of their troops and heavy equipment - south, right in the path of the Army Divisions.

And so April 12, D + 11, found the Marines of the First Marine Division once again entrenched on the slight rising terrain which ran from Yantan Field down to the beaches on which they had landed but a short time before.

"When we going into the lines?" Alex Blue sat leaning against the dirt which he had thrown from his foxhole. The question was aimed at any of the four who sat at the immediate area, none doing any act of warfare more useful than Miss Blue who cradled one dirty-dungareed leg over the other as he rubbed the sole of his shoeless foot - the pain got worse each day.

"Why the hell don't you turn into sickbay with those Goddam feet?" Liverlip said over his protruding lip, his hands pulling at the one lone hair which had forced its blond way through the baby skin on his chin.

Miss Blue dropped his eyes from Malton who had also noticed the anguish which had come over the older Marine's face as he took over his clod hoppers. Alex said apologetically, "They don't hurt too much - just get cramped in these shoes - don't bother me too much," he sniffed in his habitual manner.

"Well, they sure as hell bother me - they stink like hell - Man, they're already dead and waiting for the rest of you to catch up," McPherson held his nose and rose to the laughter which was led by Miss Blue.

He watched McPherson waddle down the hill to where another group of men lounged and smiled as the little Marine reacted the prescribed way by bumming a cigarette. He sighed as he pulled on a clean pair of socks, his last, "I'm still wondering when we're going to move in down there." He jerked his head south where the sound of gunfire was almost lost in the noise made by the heavy port equipment on the beach,

"Heard any scuttlebutt, Fagan?"

Cold Steel put his hand to his mouth and closing his fist, threw the large wad of tobacco behind him and then spat several times. "Don't know how those guys stand that stuff! Thanks," he muttered to Blue who offered him a cigarette. Slowly he lighted it, then inhaled deeply of the smoke, sighing as the pungent smoke filtered away the harshness of the chew. Titling his head to the south he said, "Nothing for sure been said, but the word I get - "

Malton and Blue both leaned forward for they knew that when Fagan did offer information, which was seldom, it was usually next to being official, "the Sixth is going to be assigned to the west coast - Naha lies in that sector, and the First will move inland of them - through Shuri."

Malton sifted the information. "What about the 2nd - are they coming in?" He referred to the 2nd Marine Division which were still sitting off shore waiting for the word they were needed. They had been held in reserve of the combined Marine and Army troops - which had been labeled the 10th Army!

"No word on them," Fagan said as he blew a smoke ring in the still warm air. "It looks like they won't be needed."

Blue laboriously struggled to his feet, "Well, guess I'll sack out - it's going to be dark soon."

"Guess he'll sack out -" Fagan muttered almost to himself scanning the sky and watching the darkness which appeared far off to the west more unerringly over the setting sun and enveloping the remaining light as it did so. "Poor Miss Blue - that guy is really aching - wish the hell he would turn in to sick bay - I've never seen feet so swollen." He eyed Malton who was filling his pipe and who now looked over the edge of a bluff where he could see activity near the Battalion Command Post. His eyes squinted as they tried to pierce the gathering gloom to the C.P. which now had attracted more than its usual share of junior officers.

"Miss Blue will never turn in to sick-bay - you know damn well he won't, those feet of his will fall off first - looks like some action at the C.P." he concluded, rising in order to better see over the bluff which rose half-way across the 400 yards which separated the battalion C.P. and Fagan's and Malton's foxholes.

Fagan spun around at J.C.'s words and rose to his knees. Silently he studied the somewhat quickened movement of the figures barely visible in the deepening shadows. Then, he slowly sat down again and almost automatically drew the jungle knife from its leather scabbard and began to test the inevitably razor sharp blade. He spoke without looking up from where his thumb slid along the 6 inch blade. "Better get set - we're moving out."

Cold Steel Fagan had been right, as usual. Malton reflected two hours later as he rested his shoulder against the carriage of the 50 caliber water cooled heavy caliber machine gun, its nose poking through the hastily filled sandbags which had been rigged around the likewise hastily dug foxholes toward the blackness of the night, pointing Malton knew toward the water lapping silently on the beach 300 yards before them. He sensed through the darkness, similar foxholes, or more correctly, machine gun pits on both sides of him - he had heard, indeed had seen some, that there were over 200 such emplacements strung along the beach, each fortified with machine guns and crew of two Marines.

"What time is it?" Fagan yawningly asked from the depths of the pit, his back resting against the comparatively soft sandbags. He mouthed his lips, yearning for a cigarette which he couldn't have smoked if he had since the smoking lamp was out.

Malton placed his hand beneath the left sleeve of his dungaree top and cupping the dial of his luminous watch drew it out on his wrist. "2300, man, we really set up in a hurry - where the hell are we anyway? Those trucks sure seemed to go a hell of a long way," he added as he winced at the memory of the torturous rear-end shattering ride.

"Off Kadena Point," Fagan softly said. Then he jerked his head ineffectively in the darkness. "There's a short fighter strip up there somewhere," he paused contemplatively. "The front lines must be a mile south – it's sure quiet down there."

"You think the Japs will really try a landing here tonight?" Malton said softly.

"If they don't, there is going to be a lot of red faces in intelligence." Fagan snickered. "J.C. felt a sick feeling in his stomach."It will be like shooting in a shooting gallery. You think they know we're wise to the landing."

Fagan slid down to the bottom of the emplacement. "We'll know by morning, Salty. Call me when you get sleepy," he said quietly and Malton knew that he was already half asleep.

In the unnatural quiet, J.C. looked about him. All along the line he knew that the thoughts of the men in the pits were the same as his. They hadn't been told where they were going or even that they were pulling out. The first indication came when the 6 x 6 trucks of the battalion motor transport pulled up to the command post. When the word was passed to board, the men, still ignorant of the mission, already had their packs on and rifles slung. The convoy had raced down the dirt roads of the island moving quickly, always within sight of the China Sea. They had been joined by other trucks, seeming to come from all parts of the occupied section of the island. Some with troops - others with only loads of ammunition and machine guns.

Both troops and machine guns had been unloaded at Kadena point and after a hurried reconnaissance by the officers, in the almost total darkness the men had been paired off and spotted along the beach. Work crews appeared from nowhere and within a half hour emplacements had been dug and sandbags filled.

And then the word had been passed. 10th Army intelligence had found out that the Japs - in regiment strength would attempt a surprise counter - landing behind the lines. The best of the Imperial Navy's troops in the Ryukyus would strike quickly and with an offensive launched against the Southern flank, would pinch and destroy the troops in the center, thereby destroying the majority of the allied forces on Okinawa.

So the 1st Battalion had been called from their standby positions to pull a surprise of their own. Armed with machine guns borrowed from rear area troops, the Battalion had been instructed to wait until the troops were on the beaches and then, at a given signal to throw lead as fast as the machine guns could at the Japs, who could then go no place but to their honorable ancestors.

"It's going to be a slaughter," Malton said half aloud and then startled as he heard a body crawling behind the emplacement.

The click was clearly audible as two safeties snapped of rifles. Fagan leaned forward, his body tensed and waiting for a command to move into action. Malton stilled his finger which encircled the trigger of the M.1. Lightly he encroached on the curved finger rest, his eyes piercing the night tried to catch sight of the intruder.

"Lillian – Lillian." A voice called as the password of the night was given. The muzzles of the rifles rose ever so slightly in an almost imperceptible motion of lessening of tension. The body came tumbling into the trench, heavy boots slapping the withdrawn legs of Fagan.

"Sorry." Carple, the new battalion runner gasped, both as a result of his exertion and of conscious fright at his new found existence in the combat area.

"What's the word?" Fagan grunted, unconsciously falling back into the gun pit, his shoulder blades against the hastily placed sand bags.

"President Roosevelt is dead," the words were almost whispered. "Report was just picked up on the shortwave." Without another word Carple was gone, a vacuum quickly came over the emplacement. Neither Fagan or Malton moved, their eyes, indistinguishable in the darkness were disbelieving, the mouths slightly agape,

"God damn it!" the sound waifed across the emplacement toward where Malton leaned over the machine gun, his unseeing eyes clasped where the incoming waters of the ocean met the yielding sands of the shoreline. The words were not spoken irrevently, but carried a tone of despair, anguish, and sorrow. "God damn it".

Malton half turned to Fagan, his right elbow hitting the ammunition tin and clanking loudly. He strained his eyes trying to focus them on his buddy - it was impossible. "It's hard to believe -" he sighed.

"He's dead." Fagan said with authority, the same authority he had expressed when disallowing the scuttlebutt which always accompanied the landing on an island. "He's dead - all right."

Cupping his hands around his mouth, he pulled his shoulders up around his cheeks and his knees hard against his elbows. In the human cave thus created, he lighted a cigarette, the glow from the match hidden by his sheltering form. In the darkness Malton could hear him suck in the smoke, then exhaling, blow the smoke away from his eyes. "You can bet your ass on this - this war killed him!" he paused, taking another drag on his cigarette - "killed him just as if he had been shot between the eyes on the front line. What a hell of a time he must have had - endless days of decision making - and then nights of sleeplessness - how the hell could he sleep knowing that by his orders - indirect though they may be, men were being maimed and killed thousands of miles from their native shores. The problems which must have been tossed into his lap from top level decision. Should the Normandy front be opened? Should the troops land on Iwo and Okinawa - Should the thousands of lives be lost on landings which would garner a few acres of soil? How do you imagine he faced the dark of his room at night? Don't you think he saw the faces of those men lying dead on the beaches, the faces of mothers and wives as they looked down on the yellow sheet of telegraph paper, the faces of young children as they tried to grasp the meaning of their fathers never coming back to them, never again entering the front gate with a toy he "just happened" to see as he was leaving work - and all those faces peering down from the darkness - all asking the same question - "Why?" How do you think he answered? What could he say? That they had died for the rights of man - that democracy might live - that aggression might be halted. Perhaps he could answer that way, but how shallow and empty the words would seem - how devoid of reason to those who cared not to face the thought of democracy prevailing, of aggression halted, of the restoration of the rights of man - could not, did not want or care about all those pretty words without the loved one who would make all these things what they were meant to be, and whose death had made them meaningless." Fagan halted his tirade, realizing he had raised his voice until it was clearly audible several foxholes away. He smothered the limp cigarette beneath the heel of his boot and whispered almost to himself, "God rest his soul."

Malton leaned against the barrel of the machine gun - knowing that an answer was neither expected nor needed. Half to himself he said, "The glory of victory is for the living." He had read the sentiment somewhere but he couldn't recall where, but for the first time he realized the truth it unfolded.

"You're right, Salty," Fagan softly said and Malton startled, not realizing the words had carried to the reclining Marine. "Everything belongs to the living, most of all the glory of victory!"

"Here and on a dozen other islands stretching between the Ryukyus and the States there are over 10,000 guys who went down for the last time. Each one's death, senseless though it may seem, was needed to gain the victory, that specific victory. And as the death count rose so did the land area increase - you might say that the dead bodies were used as stepping stones to the eventual victory and without them victory was not possible." He sighed, "We've been lucky, buddy - you and I - we've been using those stepping stones and have basked in the glory of the victorious living, but how long can it go on - when is it our turn to be stepping stones?"

Malton had listened to Fagan speak, speak as he had never heard him speak before - it left him stunned - and the last words ran through his body in a cold shudder. The fatalist Fagan had never contemplated death at least not verbally - and now he referred to it in the same breath as he did his own being.

"Knock it off Cold Steel," Malton tried to hide the uncertainty and uneasiness he felt. "What the hell's the matter with you - Christ, I've never heard you talk like that before," he paused trying to bring to his lips the right words to snap the prostrate Fagan from his sudden association with death. "You're the guy who said there was meaning to the whole damn thing, a meaning which made all the suffering and anguish worthwhile - What the hell!" He slammed his helmet to the deck of the foxhole, in the process skinning the knuckles on his left hand.

Cold Steel Fagan smiled in the darkness. He spoke softly, "I haven't changed my philosophy, if that is what it is, I still believe that there must be an aggressor and guardians of the freedoms - must be, that is, until we finally destroy each other, and then the world will resort once again to peace - peace, because civilization as we know it, will no longer be a part of the scheme of things - yes, I still believe in our "cause'," and in the darkness Malton could sense Fagan smiling, "but I don't think in those first hours and days after those back home get the word, that there's much thought of the "cause" we're fighting for - instead the grief and pain is almost unbearable. At least there won't be too much of that for me." he shifted his weight and rose to his knees, cutting off any answer which Malton may have given. "Sack out - I'll take over the watch."

J.C. slid from the sandbags which lined the front of the emplacement and pulling himself along the damp night soil propped himself against the warm packs which Fagan had just left. The moon fought against overwhelming odds to poke its nose through the dense overhead of clouds which dotted the horizon and a soft light emerged over the sea, silhouetting Fagan against it, as it would the landing crafts of the Japs as they tried to surprise the Americans. Malton through drooping half slits of eyes watched the closest friend he had ever had. The lanky Marine sat leaning against the machine gun, one hand draped affectionately across the barrel. He didn't stir a muscle as Malton watched - he was deep in thought. Slowly J.C.'s eyes closed and he fell into a fitful sleep, his dreams pierced with the sight of Fagan, rock-like, looking with unblinking eyes at the horizon.

A land crab crawled stealthily across the foxhole in search of food, his tentacle came in touch with Malton's relaxed hand, the tentacle tightened ever so gently and then relaxed as the hand tensed and threw the land crab across the sand, the voice of the hand's owner cursing softly as he pried for a cut. Finding none, Malton looked at Fagan, who had moved - at least so it seemed, since he had dozed off. Looking at his watch, J.C. realized it was less than an hour until full daylight would be upon the Ryukyus. He crawled to a position along Fagan, and squinting his eyes, looked to sea, "See anything?" he asked Fagan.

"They're there -" Cold Steel said calmly and continued his scrutiny of the water. To himself the words were repeated - they're there - he could feel and sense the presence of the Jap landing force, just as he had sensed them in those early days back on Guadalcanal. "Got your bayonet on your rifle?" he asked.

Malton nodded and felt the rifle just to make sure the deadly steel was firmly in place. He turned again to the sea and watched all along the line, there was an unnatural silence and he knew that some 500 other Marines were looking out to sea, each waiting - waiting for the order to fire - three quick bursts of a 45 caliber pistol. Pick your targets carefully they had been instructed, keep pointed straight ahead, don't cover too wide a field of fire or the path of machine gun bullets would over-lap. No sense in wasting ammo, the orderly had laughed without humor.

There! He had seen movement away from shore. He closed his eyes for a brief moment and then opened them again. There, he could see the outline of small boats about 400 yards from shore. He strained his ears, listening for the sound of motors above the breaking of the waves. None were forthcoming. He nudged Fagan and slowly pointed his finger. Fagan nodded and then slowly traced his own finger from left to right. Malton almost gasped as he followed the arc of the finger. His eyes could make out small landing craft from as far to the left and right as he could see.

Again he listened for motors and still he heard none - then his ears picked up a sound heretofore foreign to the stillness, the lapping of oars. Silently he pulled his head down and watched from the cracks between the piled sandbags. Now, with the passing minutes he could better make out the approaching landing craft. Navy Higgins boat - each could carry but little more than a squad - but God, there seemed to be hundreds of the small dark blurs upon the sea - hundred thick for as far as the eyes could penetrate out to sea, and to the left and right.

"It's gonna be a real nice morning." Fagan said softly, his eyes sighting along the cross-line of the view finder of the machine gun. J.C. moved closer to the machine gun, his shoulder brushing the tri-pod. Almost unconsciously his hands moved along the belt of 30 caliber bullets, loosening the coil from the can so that when the gun started speaking, there would be no jamming. "Christ - how many are there - the water's full of boats."

Fagan chuckled deeply in his throat. "Better than 5,000, D-2 says: Watch them! They have no suspicion at all that they are being suckered."

Malton hadn't taken his eyes from the beach and thus it was that he saw the landing - three hundred pairs of feet hitting the sand almost in unison, quickly followed by an endless of others. Cautiously they spread out on the deck, their officers jabbering out orders.

The first wave moved up the beach, and another wave took its place on the beach front. Malton tensed - when the hell were they to get the word to fire? The Japs were scarcely a little over 100 yards away. He almost pulled his face from the crack in the sandbags, certain that he could be seen as easily as he seeing the enemy. The invaders moved closer, each line spaced 20 yards apart. Malton strained to see through the ranks to the beach. He was able finally to make out the last wave of boats pulling into the beach. The other boats had already backed off the surf. Malton gritted his teeth - the front line was but 35 yards from his position, he could almost make out the features of the Japanese who led the group in front of J.C.'s and Fagan's line of fire. What the hell were they waiting for?

"Psingg: Psingg: Psingg:" The shots broke the deadly silence and the breaking dawn of a new day was filled with the deep-throated staccato voice of the 30 caliber machine guns. Fagan pressed the trigger of his water cooled machine and sweeping the muscle slowly from left to right and then right to left, cut a deadly swath through the ranks of the attacking Japs. J.C. fed the machine guns belt expertly through the breach of the heavy caliber gun. His eyes, wide and stunned by the sight of falling bodies. In each face he saw the same expression which the platoon leader had worn when he had heard the pistol shots and felt the hot burning lead dig into his body. J.C. waited for the panic to set in, but none came. The Japs kept moving onward, walking, crawling, over the bodies of their comrades. The lines never faltered and the fire took life after life. As soon as one man fell before Fagan's sights another seemed to measure himself in his place.

"Won't they ever stop?" Fagan jerkily said as he continued to pour death into the advance hordes. His teeth chattered as the back-lash of the machine gun shook his body. The end of the belt jumped from the ammo box and J.C. quickly opened another one and pushed it into the breach as soon as the slim brass bullets disappeared through. He would not look back at the Japs, he told himself as he heard the first bullet on the new clip slam into the chamber, but as soon as the machine gun spoke again he could not keep his eyes from the scene of utter humiliation and death. He raised his eves just in time to see a Japanese Lieutenant, decked out in full ceremony uniform, ribbons and all, clutch his stomach and fall, but a dozen yards from the front of the emplacement.

Suddenly there were no more men racing up the beach. A heavy pallor of gun smoke hung over the beach in the graying dawn. Firing still was going on - and strain his eyes as he would, he could not see the object of the firing.

"Cease Fire: Hold your fire!" The word was passed down the beach. "Reload and stand by! Everyone hold your position until further word."

Dawn rushed upon the scene, and with each brighter ray, the eerie scene on the beach took more stature. The bodies, and Fagan had been right, there must be 5,000, were piled deep on the beach, the light green-gray-tan of the Jap uniforms almost hid the sand on the beach. Death, in all its ugliness, was unavoidable. The bullets of the 30 caliber machine guns had done their job well - some of the bodies were torn apart, faces were blown away, legs and arms were amputated and flung about the other dead. Slowly Malton's eyes traversed the scene. A soft sun was forcing its way through the rain clouds which promised rain.

Up and down the line there was not a sound. Man after man, position after position, stood unmoving, looking almost unbelievingly at the death he had helped create. And then the silence was broken as men turned from the havoc and became sick, retching sick. It was the only sound which could be heard over the area.

"Check that pistol, J.C." Fagan said softly and Malton followed his line of sight and he saw the Lieutenant he had seen earlier as he fell before the onslaught of the machine gun. His helmet had fallen over, revealing a crop of coarse black hair, cut short. From the hair and dripping to the ground was a fine trickle of blood which flowed from a wound behind the ear. He was lying on his stomach, his head buried in the sand, both hands were extended as if he had tried to brace himself as he fell. It was in his right hand that held the pistol that Fagan had referred to. It was a German Luger and it was polished to a high glean. The fingers of the Jap seemed barely entwined within it.

"It's a German Luger, isn't it?" J.C. asked unnecessarily, his eyes clinging to the glistening barrel. Did it move, or was he imagining it?

"Yeh! The bastards know a good piece of equipment when they see it." Fagan lighted a cigarette freely now that daylight had cast its light over the island and the smoking lamp was again lighted. "Heard that they had a corps of secret intelligence before the war which visited foreign companies testing various objects which would help them in the war. What they couldn't buy, they copied." He gazed squinting at the Luger. "That's no copy - it's the real thing." He moved his legs in preparation of leaving the foxhole. "I'm gonna have it."

Malton firmly placed his hand on Cold Steel's right shoulder, preventing him from leaving the foxhole. "Ease up, Cold Steel," he said authoritatively, his mouth set in a firm line. "The word is to stay put, no souvenir hunting until they secure the beach."

Fagan didn't answer, but he did not move to throw off the restraining hand. Instead he casually began to check the machine gun, industriously brushing off the sand which had accumulated on it. Malton watched him fondly handling the weapon and relaxed.

And so daylight came to Okinawa Shimo, pearl of the Ryukyus, the first rays of the sun as they peeked their soft rays though the bulky clouds. The rain which Fagan had predicted was not far away over the horizon. The northern part of Okinawa was in peace, the Okinawans already back toiling in the fields which had suffered a minimum at the hands of the conquering Marines, the crop still intact, especially had the troops disregarded the vegetables after their briefing that the land had been fertilized by human feces. But the southern Okinawan land was not so lucky. Even now a heavy gray, white cloud of powder smoke hung lazily over the battlefield. Naha, the proud city of the east, lay devastated, its paper houses flattened by the heavy fire of the Americans. Only the skeletons of the few concrete buildings bearing testimony of what a fine city it had once been.

And in between these two opposite, one of seemingly untouched peacefulness, the other of utter destruction lay the quiet beach below Kadena Point, not quite in the battle area, not quite in the rear area. It was quiet this morning, quiet save for the rumblings of heavy artillery shells whizzing overhead occasionally on their journey into the enemy positions not so many south. Small arms fire was not a part of the morning scene. The Japs beyond the lines of the Marines were waiting for a signal that the beachhead had been secured and that the pieces movement was beginning. But the signal was not forthcoming - would never be forthcoming from the beach below Kadena Point, for the landing attempt had not been successful. A Piper Cub Artillery plane flying lowly overhead held two opened mouthed Marines. The sight below was fantastic - their eyes could clearly see the machine gun emplacements stretched out for a mile along the beach and could almost make out the dark shadowed sleepless eyes of the two Marines who watched them fly over from their positions in the sand bagged pits. There was no sign of recognition, no sign of any activity at all, just the casual glance as the shadow fell over them.

But it was the beach which stunned the fliers. The sand which had been white when they had passed over yesterday had changed colors. Now it was a tan-green-grey, only occasionally did the whiteness of the sand break through the wholly foreign covering.

"Jesus Christ!" One of the spotters swore softly. He added louder over the hum of the single engine to his fellow airman. "There must be 4 or 5 thousand of them on that beach."

The other spotter spat out the window of the Cub - it didn't remove the feeling of sickness that strangely had begun to run through his stomach. "That's what all the shooting was about at dawn. Let's get the hell out of here. It makes me sick."

The pilot nodded and banked inland, his eyes catching a group of men making their way through the mass of bodies as he did so.

Malton watched the same group from below. It was a platoon moving up the beach - the security platoon. Their movement was spiced occasionally by one of the men stopping and poking at one of the bodies with the tip of a bayonet, and even less occasionally motioning to a trio of corpsmen who followed behind, in turn followed by a dozen sets of stretcher bearers. Then the bearers raised a limp form and cautiously made their way inland through the line of emplacements toward the temporary sick bay which had been set up.

"Humane, isn't it?" Fagan's voice startled Malton who had been so intent on the beach scene that he had forgotten Fagan. Now he looked at his buddy whose eyes were black with hate and whose lips were drained free of blood. "Wonder what kind of treatment we'd get if we were in their place -" He spat "not much, you can bet your ass." He spat again, this time toward the lieutenant before him, his eyes resting invariably on the pistol. Quickly his eyes switched from the body to the advancing security platoon which was still several hundred feet down the beach. "Those bastards ain't going to get that pistol!" he said slowly but affirmatively. "J.C. keep me covered, I'm going out."

J.C. once again grabbed Cold Steel's arm. "Stay here - you're going to get your ass run up," he spoke harshly.

Fagan laughed and shook the hand from his arm. "Nobody in that details going to see me - they're too busy with what's in front of them - they're not about to step on any guts. Cover me, Salty, I'll be right back."

J.C. once again tried to restrain Fagan, but the determined Marine merely writhed from the grasp and slipped over the protective sandbags. Cursing to himself, Malton dropped behind the machine gun and grasped the trigger bars with his hands. Where the hell was the crazy bastard, he cried to himself as he lost sight of Fagan who had dropped on the other side of the sandbags.

Raising his head from the sight, he rose to the fullest angle permitted by the kneeling position in which he was. He caught sight of the camouflage helmet cover of Fagan's bobbing before him. He sighed a breath of relief and again sighted in on the machine gun. Move over, he muttered to himself. Move over Cold Steel. The lanky Marine though hunched over as he crawled forward was blotting out J.C.'s view of the Japanese lieutenant. "Circle - Fagan!" J.C. cried out - his head jerking, trying unsuccessfully to pick up the prostrate Jap in the cross-lines of the machine gun sights. But Cold Steel had disregarded the one principle that had played such an important factor in the Marines victories over gun emplacements and block-houses - covering fire could only be effective if the men furnishing the firepower had at all times an unobstructed view of the target - but Fagan was not giving J.C. an unobstructed view of the target - rather he was hiding the target, hiding it so effectively that it was impossible for Malton to train his weapon to provide the covering fire. "Cold Steel! Circle!" Malton yelled louder, the blood vessel in his right temple twitching.

Fagan, standing now almost fully erect over the Jap for the first time realized what Malton was yelling about. He took his eyes for a moment from the head of the Jap and scanned the sand for - a place to step. In that instant, the report of a German luger broke the silence of the beach.

Fagan felt the heat of the blast of the Japs pistol and his eyes caught the sight of the big round hole in the barrel of the Luger. Then his head seemed to explode - funny no pain came with the explosion, but just a huge display of prothenics, he hardly felt the jar as his body hit the deck, and his ears did not hear the wild firing of the machine gun as Malton expended round after round into the now dead Jap. In the brief instant between life and death Fagan smiled - at least no one would mourn for him - he had done what had been asked of him, had paid the supreme sacrifice and now he was one of the long list of casualties. As the darkness fled from his eyes, and the brightness of eternity swept over the slim, lanky, hell for leather Fagan, his features relaxed in complete acquaintance to death - he would not be mourned.

But the stilled Fagan was being mourned, mourned by a wet-eyed Malton who held the lifeless body's head free from the sand. About him, the security platoon probed more viscously with the pointed bayonets, digging furiously into the vitals of the corpses which littered the sand. There was no need to check to see if the Jap lieutenant was dead. - not enough being left after the fuselage of Malton's bullets to tell that it had once been human.

Miss Blue, Chick Young, and Liverlip all knelt in the sand beside Fagan. Each stared grimly at the serene expression on the relaxed face of the Marine from New England. In the middle of his forehead, a neat round hole, dark with congealing blood, gave the only indication that Cold Steel had not taken the opportunity to catch a fast nap.

"He's dead!" J.C. Malton said absently, conclusively. It was an unneeded statement but the others nodded. Somehow it seemed that it had to be spoken in its finality.

"Better break it up, boys," a tall Captain, his carbine dangling from his right hand, said. He shook his head as none of the men around the corpse made a move. An old-timer, he thought. You could always tell, the way the buddies just stared unmovingly, unbelievingly at the corpse. Well, that's the way this fucking war goes. It spares a man until everyone begins to think he's immune to death, and then he catches one, "The burial detail will take care of him." Damn it to hell, he thought as he moved once more among his platoon, booting a corpse of a Jap with the heavy toe of his boondockers right in the face.

One by one the quartet of friends pulled away from Fagan, each saying good-bye silently to the old friend, each swearing vengeance in his behalf. It was not until two stretcher bearers came and stood a few feet away that Malton finally stirred. He rose slowly to his feet and looked about him. Quickly he stooped and picked up the Luger, its handle smashed by one of the machine gun bullets. He stared at it, hate turning his eyes black, then bending he slipped it into the dungaree jacket pocket of the dead Marine. He looked at the two stretcher bearers, and as if they had understood his meaning in unison, both nodded. Malton looked once more at the face, a face that had become so familiar. J.C.'s lips moved soundlessly. "So long, buddy." Then he turned and walked to the gun emplacement, his face now lined with sadness and anger.

Men are known to crave
The pride of being brave
But when death seems near
All men know fear.

Chapter 16

The sound of small arm and machine gun fire in the distance came muffled through the battalion C.P. tent, bright with the light of a dozen Coleman lanterns.

"I remember a night on Cape Gloucester," the major was saying as he sat on a camp stool, a black cigar smoldering from the side of a chiseled face - one that looked as if it had been carved from a piece of granite. The jaw was jutted to a small cleft that was predominate in the unlined features. His cheekbones were high, and the small steel blue eyes were set deep beneath bushy dark eyebrows which were a shade lighter than the black short cropped hair. Flourishing the cigar, Major Joe Meldrum continued, "The battalion was sitting about a thousand yards from the beach, two batteries of 105 pointing toward the hills. We were firing support for a push which was scheduled for 0700."

The five other occupants of the Command Post sat quiet, resolute in the knowledge that they were in for a snow job. Pfc. Jim Craven sat at a field telephone switchboard which hadn't buzzed for an hour, a fact which disturbed him. He impatiently had wished he could send out a call to a field telephone, but the Major had nixed the suggestion. Staff Sergeant Pill Patten, the communications chief bent over a brewing pot of java, his thought also concerned with the line of communication that had been, in his opinion, been dormant much too long. Two enlisted runners likewise gathered around the cooking coffee, thankful they had not been called upon to penetrate the dark Okinawan night. Only 2nd Lieutenant Howard Thompson, battalion intelligence officer, listened intently in his camp stool, his eyes glued respectfully on the handsome face of the Major. "The campaign had been a rough one for all of us, the ordeal of flushing out the damn Japs had been complicated by the rain which fell continuously. All the heavy equipment had been bogged down by the mire, even our guns were tied down near the beach, able to fire only at maximum range."

For which you were undoubtedly grateful, Sgt. Patten thought with a smile. He had heard the Major sound off before.

A big talker, a newcomer to the infantry battalion, he had just returned from rotation to the states and been assigned as executive officer after the landing and initial objectives had been secured.

"I was tired, I remember," the major continued, "no sleep, constantly wet." He arose and proceeded to drink the coffee which a private offered. "Suddenly about 0300 we began to get rifle fire from our right flank. I dispatched Headquarters for a company in support of the sentries. The battle, and it did develop quickly into that, was a vicious fire fight, indicated that a large group of the Japs had circled the front lines and converged along the beach." The black-out curtain parted and a runner entered. His face was drawn from lack of sleep and his eyes had an emptiness which characterized front line troops. His rifle was slung over the right shoulder of a begrimed set of dungarees

Major Meldrum looked up, disturbed by the interruption. As the runner approached, he waved him off and continued. "Well, we deployed all available men to the right flank when gunfire could be heard from Jap 31's, could be heard on the left flank." He took another gulp of coffee and looked at the runner who appeared ready to speak. "It was a hell of a situation, let me tell you. The men were near panic and I could tell that morale was sinking fast. I thought carefully and then assigned the third battery man, the guns had not been set up for lack of space, to the left flank. Christ it was rough. We were pinned in. Japs to the left and Japs to the right, the sea in front of us and no place to go except inland and that was out too. Our troops could not move the guns and damned if I was going to let the Japs have those artillery pieces."

Holy hell, Patten thought, was this a snow job. He looked at the runner, who again had inched forward, his mouth ready to speak. Patten wanted to warn him to be quiet until the oration had been completed but he was damn if he was going to draw the wrath of the hero.

"Sir, I've got an urgent report and -" the runner had spoken. Patten drew into his shell awaiting the wrath of the Major. He didn't have to wait long.

"Shut up!" Major Meldrum was on his feet, his face turning crimson and his body shaking with rage. "Stand at attention there when before an officer. You god-damned turd bird. Don't you know better than to interrupt an officer when he's talking?" He stumbled over the words, his finger gesticulating at the ram-rod-stiff runner. Slowly the Major sank into the camp still, his face returning to its normal atabrine pallor. Methodically he re-lighted the cigar which had gone out in the barrage of words.

Puffing contentedly he resumed his talk of heroics. "It certainly looked bad. I radioed to regimental headquarters and the orders were explicit. 'Hold at all costs'. Let me tell you I was up to here in Japs. Then it came to me and I reacted immediately!"

Here it comes, Patten thought as he looked again at the distraught runner wondering what message he had carried through the Jap infested countryside.

"I ordered Battery A to swing its guns to the right Flank and Battery B to face the left flank. There they were, eight 105's back to back. Then I personally supervised the setting of the short fuses and ordered the falling back of lines of troops." He chuckled. "I imagine they were surprised at the orders. When they had all drew between the guns, I ordered the gunners to sight along the muzzles. Suddenly the firing stopped - the Japs realizing they were not receiving any answering fires. We stood there waiting in the silence. An hour must have gone by, it seemed like four, then the night came alive with the screams of the charging Japs. Screams of "Banzai" filled the air. I ordered the men to hold their fire and signaled for a flare to be sent up. As it burst open ahead, its light showed approximately a 1000 Japs, half attacking from each direction. The flare startled them, and they seemingly paused. It was then I ordered fire and the 8 guns spoke as one." He laughed loudly. "The shells fell a scant 200 yards from our positions and the screams of the dying Japs must have been heard all the way back to Tokyo. We fired three volleys in rapid succession and when the smoke cleared, the remaining live Japs could be seen scurrying back into the underbrush. When dawn broke we counted, over 800 dead Japs. I say it was a job well done."

The Major relaxed in the stool, his face flushed with the emotion of the telling of the story. Outside, strangely the firing seemed closer. Shutting his eyes Meldrum reveled in the awed respect of the second lieutennt. Slowly the Major became aware of the scuffling of the runner. He opened his cruel eyes and stared at the slovenly man with contempt.

"Well relay your message, private!" he ordered between his teeth.

The runner relaxed and Patten noticed a trace of humor in the sunken eyes. "Sir, the company commanders have been trying to reach you for two hours. The lines must be cut."

Meldrum paled noticeably. Craven pushed a button and whirred the hand ringing crank. He waited a minute and then turned from the switchboard and nodded his agreement.

"Go on man, what's the message." Meldrum was out of his chair.

Now the runner's eyes were dancing. "Sir, the Japs have infiltrated the lines and are attacking on the front. The companies have fallen back. They want help from your division."

For the first time Meldrum actually became aware of the closeness of the firing. His face was ashen and he again was trembling but this time not from anger. Patten was at the field TBX radio, one of the runners cranking the power apparatus. He raised Division Command and relayed the message. Turning he caught a glimpse of Meldrum's end leaving the tent. His eyes fell on the runner who now was laughing openly.

The night was a hectic one, small arms fire drew within a thousand yards of the Command Post where the battalion commander, awakened, took over efficiently and quickly. The division troops soon were on hand and after a steady and ferocious fire fight the Japs were driven back and the line was established farther inland than it had been before.

"Where's Major Meldrum?" Colonel Trod Hampton, battalion commander, spoke over the lip of a steaming cup of coffee. The firing was far away now and the tent flap had been thrown open with the coming of daylight.

Receiving no answer from the men within the tent, the colonel sat in the camp stool, a look of contempt on his face.

A commotion outside brought the colonel to the tent opening. His eyes bulged with the sight.

The hero of Cape Gloucester was walking toward him, his hand furiously scratching through his clothing. His face was no longer carved from stone but was puffed with the bites of a million fleas. Snickers were audible from the men around the tent. In only one place could a man be bitten by that many fleas - in the tombs the Okinawans had hewn from the sides of the hills!

The "hero" was transferred the next day back stateside, but his night of bravery was the main source of conversation for months thereafter.

Chapter 17

Peace had quickly laid its heavy hand of impatience over the island of Okinawa. Throughout the indeterminable number of roads which crisscrossed their narrow, dusty roads, the troops of the Marine corps and Army who had, but a few short weeks before, been preparing for the all out assault on the fortress of Japan, were now impatiently performing invented duties while awaiting orders to return home. The "beating of gums" was a constant pastime among the troops and each newly posted list of orders attracted triple its usual number of scanners.

Such was the life of the 1st Battalion, as they spent their hours policing the area, building semi-permanent mess halls and generally securing their tents where they clung in neat, company street fashion across the dusty road from the white sandy beach which met the cool, blue waters of the China Sea.

The days were doubly long for these fighting men, those that were left. J. C. Malton sat on the edge of his bunk, his eyes staring sightlessly across the 10 foot creek which ran beyond the end of the company street and into the browning leaves of the trees which covered the hills in the background. The tent was silent, save for the occasional rustle of a turned page as Ben Badger perused War and Peace in the quickly gathering darkness. Like the other occupants of the tent, the men in the area were mostly silent - silent which prevailed naturally at this time every day as the men, tired from the "cooked-up" chores of the day, lay or sat thinking of their chances of making the list "sure" to be published the next day. Others were trying to recall memories which they had cast from them during the many months they had spent in the Godforsaken islands - cast from them because of the heartache and misery the thoughts of home and loved ones brought to the days and nights stuck far from their comfort and love.

J. C. felt the presence of the letter beside him. He had taken it from the hand of the mail orderly earlier with unfeeling hands. Now he felt it beside him, unopened and unread. But he felt also another presence, an unseen one, of an unsmiling face - whose piercing gray eyes spoke for the unmoving lips. Malton shifted his glance to destroy the image of Cold Steel, but it returned as it always did - a Cold Steel who was lean, tall, and hard, not the Cold Steel who now lay buried beneath the cold, damp, autumn Okinawan earth.

Malton shuddered and silently as he did continuously since that day on the beach, said a prayer for his friend - the only real friend he had ever had in his life.

"Who's the officer of the day?" The voice came from a pudgy face which stuck its head beneath the rolled up flaps of the side of the tent. Loren Iverson wore his cartridge belt and carried his helmet. "You're luck, Lorrie," McPherson smiled through his mosquito netting.

"The duty roster had Ferguson, but the scuttlebutt has it that "Jumps" traded with him."

"I'll be a Japanese whore's bastard," Iverson shouted, pulling his head from the tent amid the laughter of Miss Blue who was in the process of dropping a boondocker to the deck of the tent.

J. C. smothered a grin and watched Iverson go down the company street, toward the duty shack. He had reason to be unhappy about the unfortunate choice of Officer of the Day. "Jumps" was the bone of the outfit. The most cursed, hated and feared second louie who had ever been member of the battalion.

J. Frederick Whelan had earned his nickname the first night on Okinawa. Fresh from the states and the short Officer Training School at Quantico, which turned civilians into Gentlemen and Officers in six months' time, he had been attached to the First Marine Division shortly before they had departed Pavuvu for the Okinawan campaign. An eager beaver, he had been ignored by the wizened and respected officers of the command who attributed his obnoxious use of the manual as God's word for every situation as the judgment of one who had never been in combat.

But J. Frederick had cast his fate soon after dark on that first wonderful day on Okinawa. The Marines of the First Division had stormed the beach with the memory of Guadalcanal, Cape Gloucester, and Peleliu still fresh in their minds, and were unprepared for the total lack of enemy opposition which greeted their unopposed landing on the beach. For some reason, his highnesses imperial forces chose not to defend the beaches and indeed, not much of the northern end of the island at all. Dusk had found the battalion at their objective for the second day, beneath Yantan Airfield. The happy and pleasantly relieved troops dug in without undue haste for the night, the release of the pent-up tension evidentin the loud voices and carefree bantering.

It was indeed unprecedented night for the men of the First Division. The first night on a newly assaulted island and sleep was possible. And sleep was not long in coming the troops. Within ten minutes after darkness had fallen, within the depths of the foxholes, the peaceful breathing of the men attested to the fact that their sleep was untroubled.

It was in the hours around midnight that "Jumps" had earned his nickname, for he crawled from fox-hole to fox-hole awakening the troops warning them of an impending Japanese parachute attack. Thereafter sleep was impossible as the men lay on their backs gazing at the stars as they twinkled in the clear sky overhead, each star during the course of the night being mistaken for a parachuter at least once during the hours of darkness. The men never forgave the lieutenant for the loss of sleep as not one parachuter ever appeared, and easily turned their feelings to hate when it was learned by the Colonel's orderly the next day, that no warning had been given by division, and indeed the Colonel had known nothing about it. So "Jumps" had been tagged upon the louie, and "Jumps" it remained long afterwards.

J. C's smile faded as his gaze fell upon the blue letter beside him. Again he knew that the vision of Cold Steel Fagan was looking down upon him, watching, waiting and helping to plot his decision. Sighing resignedly, he picked up the blue envelope in his hands and drew deeply of the scent which waffed from the paper. Slowly he tore open the flap, glancing needlessly at the return address embedded on the paper with the neat feminine hand.

He unfolded the letter aware that an even deeper silence had come over the other occupants of the tent. Their eyes were averted, and each seemed occupied with some other task, but in actuality each was aware of the stress and indecision the letter was causing J.C.

Malton read the words which he knew the letter had contained. The tone had been established with the conclusion of the actual fighting.

"Dearest J.C.;

I received your letter (am I kidding, it was just a note) and it brought a twofold disappointment - first its arrival discounted the theory I had that you were on your way back to the states and secondly I can read your letters and sense that you are not too sure of the sanity of all this. I can feel your hesitation in every word. It's there and I can read it between and in your words.

Darling! I love you! It's as simple as that. Perhaps it is wrong! Perhaps no good can come out of it, but there it is. I love you and want you - want you so much that I can hardly bear it. I'll be awaiting your call when you hit San Diego - you said perhaps it would be best if you didn't call - but somehow I feel that you want to see me - almost as much as I do you - You'll call - I know you will.

All my love, Jodie"

Malton carefully folded the letter, his mind retaining the words. I'll call - yes, I'll call. Damn it. He cursed silently to himself. He'd call - you're damn right he'd call. He wanted her so badly that the pain in the pit of his stomach cut off the air. But was it all physical emotion. The love he felt, and he knew he felt it - was it solely for sexual release or was it the everlasting longing of perpetual sharing which he felt.

He glanced up from the envelope so quickly that he caught Miss Blue staring at him. Alex quickly made a great show of cleaning the barrel of his M 1, but his already bronzed face darkened even more with embarrassment. J.C. smiled and rose to go over to his buddy's bunk.

"Halt! who goes there?" Iverson's voice carried across the creek from the darkness beyond.

J.C. stopped in the tent, instantly conscious of the complete immobility which had developed over the darkened battalion area. Iverson, from the sound of the voice was at the east outpost and surprisingly not asleep as had become his custom since the war had come to an end. That war or no war, the sentries were issued live ammunition in case any fanatical concentration of Japs decided to try a banzai attack. Now every man in the battalion area quickly noted the accessibility of his weapon.

"Halt! Give the password!" Iverson's voice carried its natural tone. The words were issued calmly and without malice. Some of the tension left the men of the battalion in their tents. The consensus if one had been taken, would have been that some boot had strayed beyond the perimeter of the camp while taking a natural call of relief and had stumbled into Iverson's zone of patrol.

"I told you, mate, to give the password or I'm going to blow your ass off!" Iverson's voice had lost some of its calmness, and anger had crept into the tone. Every man in the tent area was listening - waiting - and when the safety clicked off the rising gun, every breath was held.

"You asked for it - you bastard!" The words were scarcely out of Iverson's mouth when the deep throated cough of the rising gun sounded across the darkness. Complete silence followed the last clap of the gun. Not one among the battalion members moved, save those who, having already grabbed their rifles, tightened their fingers around the trigger guard.

"Corpsman!" The voice was Iverson's, but panic had replaced the calmness. "Corpsman, I've shot Lt. Whelan." The words closed in and sank into the minds of the men. Miss Blue was the first to move in J.C.'s tent. Dropping his stock of the rifle which was totally useless in its disassembled state he started through the tent flap.

"The stupid bastard was sure to get it someday. The stupid bastard!" He trailed behind him.

The movement of Sgt. Blue seemed to snap the rest out of their semi-stupored inactivity. Malton, grabbing his dungaree jacket followed the heavy set Marine as he joined the tide which - poured from the tents along the company streets. Miss Blue was right. It was inevitable that the chicken-shit "Jumps" would get it.

The bastard was lucky to have come through the Okinawan campaign alive, Malton thought. He had constantly needled the men until it was but a matter of time before he caught a slug from one of them.

Malton thought of the time on the forward observer post above Naha as he merged with the hastening troops. He had the watch during a dark night at the outpost and the Nips were all around the post. His finger had been taut on the trigger during his two hours watch and when "Jumps" had relieved him, he had sneaked up to him and touched him on the shoulder. Whirling, he had jammed the Browning into the lieutenant's stomach, not knowing to this day why he did not pull the trigger.

That's what had happened now - he thought. The dumb bastard had pulled that trick before - skirting around the outposts to see if the sentries were doping off on duty. The chicken-hearted stupid bastard.

"Holy Hell" Miss Blue exclaimed through pursed lips as J.C. joined him as he knelt beside the grotesquely doubled up and prostrated figure of Lt. Whelan. Blood almost entirely covered the khakis from numerous bullet holes exposed in quivering light of a Coleman lantern which someone had had the foresight to bring.

"Coming through!" Corpsman Jay Culver yelled as he shouldered his way through the crowd, his first aid medical kit slung over his shoulder. "Get the hell out of the way Liverlips," he pushed McPherson from his position hanging over the wounded man. Culver quickly began probing, taking a quick diagnosis with eyes and hands. With effortless sureness he began stopping the flow of blood which continued to escape in dangerous proportions from "Jumps". Without lifting his head from ministrations, he said, "Get the hospital jeep!" Three of the troops jumped in answer.

Iverson stood at the rear of the loose circle of Marines who watched Culver trying to preserve the ebbing flow of life as it escaped the inert form of Whelan. Hanging, muzzle down was the sentry's gun, held loosely in the stunned man's grasp. His face in the soft illumination was ashen, his eyes cloudy and unfocused. The reason which is the vital and distinguishing characteristic of the human race was not apparent in the expression of Iverson's face. He was numb, his consciousness telling him that he was responsible for the scene before him - he could have averted it - could have exerted more patience - after all - he did know - his conscious told him - who the figure silhouetted in the darkness was - he had meant to scare the son-of-a-bitch - teach him once and for all that this shit of being gung-ho was for the birds - but what had happened when he had started to fire a burst over the intruder's head - what had caused the barrel of the gun to zero in on the gut of the shadow figure - what had caused his finger to continue depressing the trigger, until the entire clip had been expended? Iverson shuddered and a cold sweat broke from his sickened body. His finger loosened on the stock of the gun and it dropped noiselessly into the soft turf.

The headlights of two quickly approaching jeeps flashed across him on their way to a halt, accompanied by screeching brakes on the large knot of men.

From the first jeep leaped out Colonel Mackenzie, his right hand pounding his swagger stick into his left. He rapidly strode through the path which automatically opened through the circle. He stopped before the actively hunched back of the corpsman, his eyes taking in the entire situation. When the corpsman looked up, the Colonel softly but coarsely said "Is there any hope, Corpsman?"

Culver stared into the deep eyes of the Colonel. He saw that the answer was already there. "Not much, sir" he said, then seeing the stretcher being brought from the second jeep, he ordered "Bear a hand men! Gently."

Willing hands carefully raised the suffering body a few inches which others slid the stretcher into position. As he was lowered onto the stretcher the eyelids of the lieutenant opened with - a great deal of effort. Colonel Mackenzie and Corpsman Culver quickly bent over the stretcher as they saw the lips quivering as if to speak.

The death mask which the face of "Jumps" had turned into was ashen with the eyes narrowly slitted - the twin nostrils contracted as the lungs fought for every breath of air which could be forced into the body. The dry lips, drained of all blood parted and in a whisper barely audible to the ears of the bent over men said, "He hit me with the first bullet and kept the rest of them right in there." The last words trailed into the darkness, to be joined by mattering of the circle of troops.

Culver rose and indicated for the stretcher to be placed in the jeep. Once again a path opened up in the crowd and the body was rushed to the jeep and with horn blowing the jeep raced toward the Naval Mobile Hospital some 18 miles down the highway.

Colonel Mackenzie walked back towards his jeep, then paused, his eyes catching Iverson standing stiffly and still away from the others. Turning he walked up to the sentry and stood close to the unnerved man. Softly, in almost an undertone, he said "Iverson! Are you on guard duty?" Iverson didn't move, but continued to stare unseeingly at the spot where his bullet had dropped Lt. Whelan. "Pick up your gun, son!" Colonel said, then with a snapping voice, "Pick up that gun and mount your post, Private."

The words penetrated through Iverson's semi-consciousness. He startled and then quickly picked up the gun and snapped to attention.

Colonel Mackenzie turned on his heels and walked away. The troops followed and soon the stillness was broken only by the subdued whispers in the tents as the men recounted the chain of events as their minds remembered or fabricated them.

"Yeh! The poor bastard died just as we rounded Pourdi Point," Corporal Frank Hatfield of the Battalion's Motor Transport Platoon said. He was almost hidden in the midst of a crowd of Marines. At their fringe, J.C. Malton, Alex Blue, and Ike Garber leaned up against the ambulance jeep, its motor still warm from its frantic, but futile dash down the earthen roads of Okinawa. In the deep darkness of the moonless September night, their faces were dimly silhouetted against the Coleman lantern which lighted the command post in front of which the jeep stood. "I tell you it was weird." Hatfield continued, "There we were, flying over that friggin' road, my horn blasting like hell, and Doc yelling for me to hurry and there Jumps was, a sort of a smile on his bloody face - mumbling -" He shrugged at a question, "nah, I don't know what he was sayin'!"

A voice imperceptible to the group around Hatfield slowly spoke from the heavy darkness behind Malton and his crew. The words were unmeant for other ears. "He hit me with the first one and kept the rest of them right in there," Loren Iverson mumbled from the deep recesses of the night.

The Board of Inquiry which was held according to the manual as the result of the death of Lt. J. Frederick Whelan had perhaps the shortest term of existence ever recorded in the annals of the Marine Corps.

When it was time to summon witnesses, every man and officer of the battalion was willing to testify, and honestly, that they had heard Private Loren Iverson carry out the Red Book's instructions in challenging an unknown person in a combat zone. The thing that could be seen preying on the minds of the division officers who were on the Inquiry Board, was how each man knew and remembered the exact words of the sentry. But when Colonel Mackenzie, himself, took the stand - a mere camp chair set up near the Board of Inquiry's table in the mess hall of the Battalion, he corroborated the men's testimony exactly - adding that in the stillness which descended upon the area following the first command to give the password, every word and movement made was clearly audible to the entire complement of the battalion.

The decision was not long in forthcoming. After a deliberate but rapid conference - it was necessary to confer to uphold the respect for weighty decisions the august body was compelled to render. The Chairman of the Inquiry Board, a full colonel who gained his chair of authority on the grounds that he he had a distinguished law firm in Frehennan, Louisiana, population 127 - cleared his throat, adjusted his overseas cap which had slipped over the glassy hairless scalp it theoretically rested upon, and pompously drew his rotund 235 pounds from the not too steady camp chair. He surveyed the mess hall - half filled with battalion officers, and curious others of the President pronounced gentlemen, and with the witnesses who had been permitted to remain after giving their version of the incident - their number had been cut down after the board quickly realized, after 15 men and officers had testified, that the story would be always the same. As a result there were a godly number of disappointed marines, dressed in their mattress pressed and spring marked khakis, who had offered to give their recounting of the accident in order to later tell their grandchildren with pride of their part in the gory mess.

A bead of sweat rolled down from atop the bald part of the Colonel, sneaked from beneath the edge of the overseas cap and splashed with salty pain into the malaria contracted pupil of his eyes. He brushed the eye irritably with the back of a sweaty, salty hand and merely succeeded in irritating the tender organ all the more. Once more he cleared his throat to get the attention of his captive audience. But the effort was not needed for every pair of eyes, save one had watched the civilian Marine struggle to his feet and awaited the decision of the Board quietly, but nevertheless anxiously.

Colonel Chairman fixed his gaze, at least focused his lone remaining clear eye on the person who sat erect on the accused bench, but with his head staring into the coral dust floor. Finally Private Loren Iverson, whether from the Colonel's not too withering eye, or from the silence which had fallen over the mess hall, raised his head and seemingly sightless eyes met the Colonel's.

"It is the decision of this Board of Inquiry, created according to the rules and regulations as set up in the Standard Operating Procedure, of the United States Marine Corps, that the death of Lt. J. Frederick Whelan, U.S.M.C.R. 88 42 67, at the hands of Private Loren Iverson, U.S.M.C.R. 65 53 47, was accidental. It is the further finding of this board that Pvt. Iverson was performing his duty as a sentry as required to do under the General Orders, regarding the standing of a watch in a combat zone - and that he was completely justified in firing upon and taking the life of the deceased Lt. J. Frederick Whelan, who according to all the witnesses at this proceeding failed to offer the correct password." He looked about the mess hall again until his eyes rested once more upon Pvt. Iverson. "It is only a higher being and the defendant who knows whether the Lieutenant was recognizable in the darkness." He paused then continued quickly, "This Board of Inquiry is dissolved." For a moment the men in the room remained seated and then, one by one, they filed out. Some stopping to rest a hand on the drooping shoulder of Iverson who sat staring into the sand.

"Iverson's leaving - being shipped home on the next roster," Miss Blue offered a few days after the Board of Inquiry met, as he entered the tent where J.C. sat on his cot, aimlessly running a swath through the bore of his rifle. Malton looked up at the words and slowly nodded.

"Guess it's for the best," he said, once again resuming the needless cleaning of the rifle. "He's in bad shape. Konkright says he hasn't eaten in days - he's taking it pretty hard."Miss Blue flopped on his green blanketed cot, easing his throbbing feet. He lighted a cigarette and inhaled the smoke, filtering the smoke through his teeth as he spoke. "The boy is really gone. The medic's say he really flipped - won't say anything but "He hit me with the first one - and kept the rest right in there." He puffed again on the cigarette, then continued softly, "I think he'll not snap out of it either - he'll have the memory of "Jumps" with him the rest of his lore. It's like when we were kids -I remember one time, lying in ambush once for a guy - must have been around 12 at the time -I just wanted to scare him a little, but when I jumped out of the bushes he was so startled he tripped and fell and hit his head on a boulder. I remember standing over him - he was out cold. I was scared, damn scared that I had killed him. I was the happiest guy in the world when he snapped out of it."

Malton put his reassembled rifle on the sling he had attached beneath his cot. "You think he knew it was Jumps?"

Blue flipped the cigarette into the creek beside the tent and shrugged, then added as if to himself. "I kept asking myself - What would have I done?" Then he yawned, rolled over and closed his eyes.

Chapter 18

J. C. Malton had made up his mind - and now he sat on the edge of his bunk with a writing pad on his knee braced upon a shelf of a homemade locker box he had fashioned from an ammunition case. Between his fingers was a stub of a pen - his initials now faintly embossed on its black shell casing. His tanned thumb and forefinger of his right hand rolled the lusterless pen between them as J.C.'s eyes looked unseeingly through the deserted tent into the heavily descending darkness beyond. At the center of the tent a Coleman lantern, its steady bright flare of light, non-flickering inside the shelter of its glass case.

Slowly J.C. looked at the paper, its lines of royal blue ink sharp in contrast against the harsh whiteness. The words were stilled, the tone of uncertainty visible and readable in every word. He looked past the paper, down into the shelf where his foot rested, at the pile of blue envelopes which held within them no uncertainty, but determination. He sighed - he had made up his mind - had weighed the circumstances which he must face - the resentment and perhaps unacceptance of his decision by his staid middle western family - but he was going back to California, was going back to the house in Los Angeles, was going back to Jodie, and to hell with the consequences. He had tried to analyze his decision, but it did not fall into the commonplace - at least he thought it didn't - but, he smiled, the burning desire for her did play a major role in his decision - the long months which had dragged into years had taken their toll - and the memory of Jodie, her beauty, her softness - was associated with home. He had argued it was only because she had been such a vital part of his last days in the states - perhaps, but no person, no thing returned to his thoughts as she did - Yes, he was going back, but how in the hell could he put it in words in a letter.

Malton crumbled the paper from the pad, and balling it, threw it across the tent. It almost hit Jim Richardson who was just ducking his head to enter the tent flap.

He laughed as Malton began to stammer an apology, "That's a heck of a welcome for a guy!" Richardson never cursed.

"Wasn't expecting company, I thought everyone was sitting in on the movie?" J.C. said through his laughter. It was true that he wasn't expecting company - least of all Jim Richardson. Not that the Californian wasn't liked and respected by the crowd - he was and had been a vital part of the company since before the Peleliu invasion. But something had happened to Richardson in the past year - something which had caused the muscular youth to draw within himself - to keep closed mouthed and more and more to himself. Fagan had offered that it was woman trouble - the old salt had warned the others to lay off the lad and let him work out the problem himself and that's the way it had been played - by ear.

Richardson dropped on Miss Blue's unoccupied cot and said sheepishly, "Couldn't stand it. It was one of those boy meets girl, boy loses girl, boy gets girl soap operas." He noticed the writing pad on J.C.,s knees. "Hey, I'm not interrupting you, am I?"

J. C. put the pad inside the case shelf next to the neat pile of blue envelopes. "No," his face reddened. "I'm trying to write a letter but the right words just won't get on paper the way I want them to."

"I know what you mean - I had the same trouble myself," Richardson said, a far-away look coming into his eyes.

Malton took note of the Marine's use of the past tense. He instinctively knew that Richardson was referring to his own deep personal problem. He decided to elaborate on his own. "I've got this letter to write - to a girl - and - well, the girl's married - ," he stammered and stopped, confusion and embarrassment creeping into his tone.

Richardson nodded slowly, his head causing a shadow on the wall of the tent. "It's tough, I know -" he halted his eager flow of words with an effort. The words were fighting to be spoken but he stifled them.

Malton had hardly heard - he was deep in his own thoughts. "She's married - but it's not the right marriage. She - loves - me." The words were embarrassing when they were spoken aloud, but now that they had been uttered he flung out the rest of it, "and I think I love her - well - I do love her - and I'm trying to tell her that I'd be coming back to - her."

Richardson was listening, sensing the agony and indecision which were in this man - suddenly he felt compassion for him and he began to speak, slowly at first, then with the eagerness of one who has held a secret for a long, long time. "I know - I know. I've had the same problem - guess all you guys knew that I was having trouble - I was grateful that you didn't try to interfere." He sighed and drooped on his back on the cot, his hands cupped beneath his head, staring sightlessly at the dusky top of the interior of the tent. Malton was listening to his words, knowing the words were being spoken aloud for the first time and were merely expression of an inner struggle which had long raged. "You remember my speaking of Mary?" Malton nodded needlessly, also remembering that the name had not been uttered by Richardson for almost a year.

"Well - we were engaged and we'd planned to be married as soon as I got back to the states." He drew a deep breath and his jaw set tighter, "When we got back to Pavuvu from Peleliu there was a letter waiting for me - a dear John letter, I guess they call them - she said the usual things that she had met someone and that she had married him. It sort of threw me - I didn't know what to do - I tried to write, but I was so darn mad, the letter sounded like a kid who had just had a petty love affair broken up - but I wasn't a kid," he smiled shyly. "At least not any longer, and this wasn't just a puppy-love affair with me – it was the real thing - and I thought it was the same with Mary - I was really thrown - I couldn't understand it. For over two months I kept asking myself why? - why did she suddenly throw me over for someone else, and then I got another jolt in the form of another letter from her -" he stopped, the face filled with emotion. "I never thought it strange that no one else wrote to me about the whole darn mess - and this one, she begged me to forget her - said she knew I was brooding when I didn't write - said that I wasn't to think about her anymore, to forget her - that was for the best. And then she clinched it - said she was going to have a baby - that she was very happy and that I'd never hear from her again - that we both had a new life to plan for and it would be better if we didn't write." He stopped and lay staring at the darkness at the top of the tent. Then he rose up on one elbow and looked to where Malton sat looking at him, respectful attention evident in his face.

Richardson waited a few minutes more, anticipating rather than expecting a question. When none was forthcoming he continued. "I was going through a living hell - at first I wanted to keep it all to myself and then, later, I felt I must confide in someone, but by that time I had withdrawn so far within myself that there was no one with whom I was close enough to talk to. And so I kept it to myself - the hurt was terrible enough but it was more than that - my pride I could quell, but I really loved Mary, had projected my whole life on the promise that we would be together always, and now there was no future - at least no future with Mary - and without Mary I felt there was no future - Damn it, it almost tore my heart out."

J.C. had assumed all that he had heard - you didn't live with men all these months in such close proximity, without sensing what was going on within the hard shell they attempted to throw around them. And Richardson's story was not novel - it was but one that went on with the course of the war happening to men of every class and station. It was tough but so what - his thoughts were interrupted by Richardson's resumption of his story.

"And then about five months ago I received a letter from my father, which indeed was a rare occasion, it too carried a jolt - that's why Mom had him write it instead of her. He said in the letter, that he didn't know whether I had heard it or not, but Mary "was expecting" - I swear those were the words he used "was expecting". He went on to explain to me all the things he should have five years ago about the birds and the bees. I almost had to laugh when I read the fumbling explanation of the drive and urgency which exists between the male and female, but suddenly as I read, something began to reach me as to what he was trying to say - Mary wasn't married! Mary wasn't married and was going to have a baby."

Malton leaned forward straining to hear as Richardson had lowered his voice to a steady drone. "Somehow, I didn't believe it, and there was a brief spell there when I actually hated my father, calling him a liar - Mary wasn't like that- didn't have any of the characteristics which would let a guy make her - I should know - I dated her for almost - it seems all my life. She wasn't free with her affection - I should know." The words were strained and Malton saw how much this Marine had wanted the girl called Mary -it was evident in every phrase, every expression on his face in the light of the steady Coleman lantern light.

Richardson continued, "It was then that I really was confused, but with the hurt and pain which I felt at the knowledge, the bare knowledge of the existing conditions that I felt a strange elation - Mary wasn't married and wasn't going to be from the further information in my father's letter. And then the real agonizing inward struggle really began. I hated the sordid mess - hated her and the coming baby and the father - he being the only other in the picture. Who was he? How did he come into our lives and with undoubtedly unconcern plant the seed that had thrown the planned pattern of life of two people so far out of kilter." And what about Mary? It was not difficult to interpret her action of writing to him. She didn't want to ruin his life - had thought it better that he think she was married and that they were no longer the destined pair they had always assumed.

"What did you do?" for the first time Malton had spoken, his voice soft.

Richardson gently nestled the back of his head in his hands before he answered. "I suffered - suffered like hell! Raging a battle within me! Forgive her, one part of me ordered! Who was I to judge? I loved her didn't I? The arguments were strong, but the other voice was just as tenacious. Forget her! She's a slut! What she does once, she'll do again!" He stopped and sighed, "then after several months I had convinced myself." The assurance of his voice attested to the fact, "I loved her! Would always love her - and without question accepted the fact that she loved me. Who knows what happened! Perhaps she'll tell me - at any rate, I won't ask her. It's been rough but finally I made up my mind and decided to write to her, telling her all! It was tough," he chuckled, "just like the trouble you're having, but finally I got the words down and sent out the letter."

"Did she answer?" Malton asked, his head bent forward in anticipation.

Richardson nodded, "I received the letter at mail call today." He pulled a small white envelope from his breast pocket with gentle care. He didn't ask if Malton wanted to hear it, but took the single sheet from within, unfolded and began to read.

"Dear Jim, You'll never know how wonderful it was to hear from you again. You'll never know what it meant to me. I frankly thought that my life had outgrown its usefulness. I couldn't begin to tell you what these past months have been to me. How can I ever explain it to you. Oh, I know I could give all kinds of reasons for that one mistake I made, loneliness, longing for you - but they all sound so hollow. I made the one mistake - and you can believe this - one time I went out to a party - one time I was ever near a man - one time tried to stay my longing for you - and it happened - how? I've asked myself the same question thousands of times - and no logical answer presents itself! And so I found myself pregnant! I almost lost my mind - I even thought of killing myself, but I went to the little Church on Maple Street - and sat there for hours - and in my own way thought the thing through. That's when I wrote to you - It's been difficult! I'm pretty much an outcast amongst the good people of the town. And so I've been pretty much on my own - Thank God my parents have stuck with me and comforted me - the father? I've never seen him since - to be frank, I don't even know his name - a serviceman, long since disappeared amongst the multitude. He'll never know he cast a son! But my darling, how your letter put new life into this mixed up world for me. I'll always cherish the letter. You are the most considerate, deserving man in the world. I don't deserve you. I'll be waiting for you and then we'll start our lives together. It will be difficult - especially for you - I don't think your parents will be too pleased about it. I love you, and always have - only you.

All my everlasting love,
Mary"

Richardson folded the letter and smiling put it gently into his breast pocket. Malton watched him, realizing he was completely happy and content. But there was a question which kept forcing its way into his consciousness.

He spoke slowly, "What did you tell her in that letter you finally wrote?"

Richardson rose slowly, thrusting his hands into his dungaree pants. He continued smiling, "It came hard as I said, but I had thought it out, completely. I simply told her that no matter what she had done that there was no purpose in my life without her." He moved slowly toward the tent flap, his back towards Malton, and the words drifting softly over his shoulder. "I said that I wanted her to marry me - and together we'd raise the boy as if he were my own." He looked over his shoulder and the smile deepened. "And you know what J.C. I'm kinda looking forward to start the job."

With that he was gone - gone into the darkness of the Okinawan night.

J.C. stared into the inky blackness after him - a sense of wellbeing spreading through him. Unconsciously a smile broke the astonished look on his face. He knew Richardson would be good to his word and he would wager his entire pay resting idly on the Marine Corps books that the two would live out their lives together happily and would soon forget that the boy was not their own.

Malton took up his pad again, and with a look of confidence began his letter to Jodie. He was coming back. Maybe it wasn't the right thing to do, but yes, he was coming back to Jodie!

Chapter 19

The war was over! The war which seemed to have no end in sight, at least to the men stuck on the hell-hole islands of the Pacific, had come to an end with such rapidity that it was difficult to comprehend the magnitude of it.

One day the troops, none too happy about not being returned to New Zealand as they had been assured they would be after the Okinawan campaign, were going through the training grind for the next assault, and the next. The troops were busily engrossed in the chicken-shit drilling and policing which characterized peace time corps life. The details sifted through on the wings of scuttlebutt. The Air Force had dropped a huge bomb, atomic, whatever-the-hell that meant on two Japanese cities and the Nips were calling uncle.

"What a bomb that must be," Badger said quietly as he rubbed the dust from his dress shoes, shoes he hadn't worn in well over two years.

"TV's a lot of bull-shit, if you ask me." Liverlip offered, trying to plaster his hair down as he sought to line up his reflection in the fragment of mirror which Alex Blue had nailed to the center pole of the tent.

That tired Marine, his face belying the litheness of his youthful looking body, stopped in the act of adjusting an uncomfortable field scarf, glanced irritably at the back of the small man. "The scuttlebutt said that those bombs," he paused and continued reflectively, "and they dropped only one on each city, killed almost everyone in the city."

"Bull-shit!" Liverlip repeated scornfully.

"One bomb that can kill over 100,000 people and burn the whole damn city," mattered Badger, continuing absently to shine his shoes which now glistened brighter than the mirror which hung precariously on the pole.

"Bull-shit!" Liverlip unoriginally said again as he turned nonchalantly from the mirror. His face dropped to J.C. who was carefully inspecting his rifle for any evidence of dirt - he found none. Liverlip stood over him, "Do you believe it, J.C.?" His mouth turned up in a half grin waiting for the college man's confirmation of the impossibility of the story. He watched while Malton carefully placed the weapon on the green blanket on the bed. J.C. looked about the tent where the others, though seemingly intent on their own preparations, were listening for his answer.

"Yes, I believe it." The heads all turned toward him as if on a swivel as he continued, "Just why don't you believe it, Liverlip? I know why!" His voice contained a hint of the anger which filled his body - anger at the Japs, at Liverlip - all stemming from Fagan's death. "You can't imagine the Japs surrendering - can you? None of us can - we've seen them die rather than live - you've seen them kill themselves rather than surrender: Miss Blue and I saw them come on, thousands of them, when they were being cut down like wheat with a scythe. We all saw hundreds jump off the cliff at the southern end of this island to their deaths on the rocks below, and I've seen a no-good-son-of-a-bitch, instead of surrendering and living, kill Fagan. That's why you can't believe, why none of us can believe, of the slant-eyed bastards surrendering." He paused, groping for control of his voice while he filled his pipe. "But they've surrendered, all right - surrendered because they finally came up against something they can't understand." He looked at the questioning eyes about him, questioning all except Badgers who knew what he meant "Yeh! Can't understand! They could fight us when they were on the same ballistic level with us, even though most of their equipment was inferior. Let's face it, they made up for their limitations in material with fanatical fervor. And all the time we kept them on the defensive they were hoping and dreaming for a miracle. The miracle came, all right, but we came up with it. One bomb which can destroy a city and kill hundreds of thousands. How long do you think the island of Japan would last if we planted those bombs daily for a month?" He lighted the pipe. "I believe it, all right. The odds got too high and Papa Tojo saw that the end of the glorious empire, literally and figuratively was about to fly overhead." He drew placidly on his pipe. "The official war in the Pacific is over, but I wonder if the Nips still in the caves and hills on some of those islands will ever believe it. There will be a lot of men dying in the next few years from the rifles of "defeated" Japanese."

The end of the softly spoken decision was met with silence, only the sound of Ben Badger's brush against the leather cracking the wordless air. Then suddenly the tent came to life as from dawn the company strut came the words. "Fall out! Fall out!"

From the gaping mouths of the tents came the Marines, walking carefully on the coral which had been placed as streets between the rows of tents. The sight as they fell into ranks was unusual - unusual that is from any such formation they had fallen into recently because of the garb of the men - ay, their overall appearance.

The khakis they wore were salty-made that way by constant washings of bleach saturated water - These were not the set of khakis which had been broken out on various occasions of relaxation back at the rest camp on Pavuvu. Rather they were the one complete set, salty set which was kept for just two special events - liberty and general's inspection. And the Marines were now lining up for a general's inspection.

The well whitened tan khaki trousers were joined by cut-down khaki shirts, not hand cut down, but professional tailored back in the states. The shirts clung lightly to the well-hardened trunks of the men, outlining the bulging chest lines and narrowing at the waist. The clothing was surprisingly well pressed, allowing for the absence of irons. The secret lay in the folding, which every Marine knew, had been taught so well. And since the end of the war and the issuance of cots and mattress pads, the time honored corps method of pressing had been put into use. The shirts had been folded to crease them down the breast pocket lines on both front and rear, and the trousers had been folded to crease in a straight line. Then the two were placed between the canvass cot and the mattress pad and nature took its course in the sight of the Marine on the mattress pad.

It was a proud platoon which faced Pl. Sgt. Konkright this the 15th day of September, 1945. True there were not too many old faces among the many, but each man in the ranks had earned his position there by facing the enemy on Okinawa and not giving way. Sgt. Konkright looked down the ranks, passing occasionally to meet the eyes of the old hands Malton, Blue, Young,

Garber, Badger, Richardson, Peterson, McPherson, Wagner. In that halting, but fleeting glance there was a comradeship which did not take even the form of a smile but which each felt. Missing were other faces, faces which had been gone since the beginning - Brabern, Carter, many, many more, but most noticeable was the absence of Cold Steel Fagan. Konkright straightened his shoulders, which had begun to slump a little during the past campaigns.

"O.K.! Shitheads!" he said affectionately. "Let's dress up the ranks again. McPherson, straighten up that field scarf," he continued to criticize - it was his job though they all looked pretty damn good to him - pretty darn good.

Satisfying himself that he had wounded their pride and that the men would struggle even more to outdo themselves, he right-faced the platoon and marched them smartly down the company street to the area which had been cleared as a drill field. He expertly maneuvered them through the other forming platoons and turned them into their proper positions.

And there they stood - waiting.

The late summer sun was hot as it beat down on the heads and shoulders of the Marines standing at stiff attention awaiting the appearance of the inspecting party. Small beads of perspiration grew into large drops as they rolled down the faces of the men probing their stinging ways into their eyes and mouth. But the men moved not a muscle beneath the clean, but darkening with sweat khaki. There they stood, the 1st Battalion, Fifth Marine Regiment, First Marine Division - the best damn fighting outfit in the world they liked to believe and damn willing to take on anyone who disagreed.

A whirl of dust announced the arrival of the inspecting party. Each man fought back the impulse to swish his eyes to the two jeeps which had pulled up before the ranks, but discipline was stronger than curiosity and the eyes bored straight ahead.

Led by Master Sergeant Curt Fraley, a 25 year veteran of Nicaragua and World War I, the brass bore down on the first rank of troops. In the party were Major Phelan, Colonel Mackenzie and the inspecting general, Lieutenant General Franz Culpet. Bringing up the rear, writing pad in hand was Lt. Capet ready to jot down any violation which might pass from the lips of the General. Slowly General Culpet moved down the ranks, swagger stick tapping gently into the palm of his left hand, a pride he drew from the lean, strong Marines. Infrequently he would pause at an unusual specimen of Marine and thrusting the swagger stick beneath his left arm, would take the piece from the hands of the Marine. Then easily swinging the piece into position without dislodging the swagger stick, he would peer down the barrel. Grunting satisfaction he would thrust the rifle back at the Marine whose hands would come up invisibly from his sides to catch the piece and replace the bolt.

"Smart looking outfit you have here Colonel," General Culpet said softly as they moved around the first rank to the second.

"Best damn battalion in the best damn regiment in the Corps!" the Colonel growled from deep in his barrel chest. Major Phelan smiled outwardly at the words, and his chest expanded even more from the words of his regimental commander than from the general. He was so taken up with his own thoughts that he was unaware of the General's next words.

"You have a Wagner in your battalion, do you not, Major?" The words were warm and friendly as he gracefully moved down the ranks.

Major Phelan was taken aback at the mention of Wagner - truly one of the men in his outfit, a Marine whose name did not altogether fit well into the mouth of a general of the Marines. "Yes, sir, Wagner is one of my men. He's in A Company."

"Good, Good!" the general muttered. "Point him out to me when we get to his outfit, please."

Private Cordyn Wagner III stood stiffly at attention in the fourth and last row of the platoon, perspiration falling freely from the strikingly blood eyebrows which matched the close cropped hair now wet beneath his overseas cap. His face was handsome, too handsome, in fact, to belong to the masculine sex. Bronzed by the hot sun which had beaten unmercifully upon it for the past two years, the face was unlike those of his fellow veterans. It did not show the scars of war, indeed were not marred even by the yellow atabrine tinge the others wore so conspicuously. The straight nose and square chin was that of a male model, and the blue eyes were soft and harmless. But if his face was too feminine, his body was not. Cordyn Wagner III owned the most masculine body in the entire battalion. Beneath the smooth lines of his khaki shirt lay relaxed bulging muscles, filling the cut-down tan shirt to its capacity. The chest, huge though now immobile, tapered to a thin waist, clinched tight by a salty web belt. His legs were hard, hard not only by the conditioning of the Corps, but hardened even more by the physical development program he had set up for himself.

For Cordyn Wagner III was a muscle man - not by nature - but by the use of weights and exercises. He had found time during his sojourn overseas to exercise his body according to the physical culture program he had bought prior to leaving the states. Every move to a rest area had found him pestering the engineering battalion for lengths of pipe and concrete. Finding large food cans at mess dumps he concocted barbells, securing the pipe into the cans with the concrete. Crude but effective, the homemade weights had helped develop him into a mass of muscles - muscles which were picturesque but not helpful in his duties of a BAR man.

He stood now in formation, his muscles beginning to cramp. Private Cordyn Wagner III, a private because that was the way he wanted it. He did what he was ordered to do, but nothing more, for his one thought in life was body development and nothing else. Private Cordyn Wagner, the pride of Talisman Lake, Washington. His father, the other men in his outfit had found out, but not from "Bar-bells", was one of the most influential men in the state of Washington - a lumber baron. It had been reported, and not too exaggeratingly, that Cordyn Wagner II, was owner of more than a third of the virgin lumber in the Northwest State. But one would not know it from associating with "Bar-bells", his manner was not of the socially prominent, rather that of one from the wrong side of the tracks. He lived slovenly, spoke as a street urchin and discarded any of the luxuries which were so vital to the others. All Cordyn Wagner III wanted, desired, and lived for it seemed was the crumpled physical culture manual he kept beneath his straw mattress and the barbells propped beneath his cot.

And now he stood, stiffly erect, the Marine's Marine waiting in the infernal heat for the inspection to be concluded. It was a child's game he thought. Grown men standing like tin soldiers in formation. Well, as Sherman had so nobly said, war is hell. A smile turned the corners of his mouth up slightly. It wasn't the war that was hell, it was the damn regard to the Marine Corps Manual. In combat, the book was at its best, but the petty regulations it demanded for rear area and peace habitation was assinine. He'd take combat any time if it hadn't been for the lack of time and facilities for his rigid muscular schedule.

It was just this moment, as Cordyn Wagner III's body had relaxed as the governing mind had shifted from reality to daydreams that the inspecting party swung sharply around the rear of the third rank and down the fourth. Lt. Capet cast an unhappy look at Wagner who hadn't realized he was next to being the object of the inspecting general's attention.

"Straighten up, Wagner!" Lt. Capet's lips didn't move as he silently threw the words at the inattentive Marine. The words jolted Wagner back to reality and almost imperceptibly he drew his roaming muscles to firmness and drew to his full 5'11".

"This is Private Wagner, sir!" Lt. Capet had swung around after alerting Wagner and now faced the general, who looked at Wagner with some disbelief in his eyes. Those gray eyes traveled first from the collar of the Marine to the sleeves of the shirt, looking for some rank or at least rate. Hesitantly he turned a wary eye on Major Hanna, not sure that some sort of trick was not being played on him. He found no reaffirmation there - so he again focused his eye on Wagner.

Softly he spoke, "Glad to see you, Wagner. I told your father that I'd check in on you. How's everything going?" The words seemed to contain the embarrassment ever present when a command officer tries to speak with an enlisted man on a social level.

Wagner blinked several times fiercely. Who the hell is this guy, he thought? What did they say the inspecting general's name? The face did look familiar. Crisply he spoke. "Just fine, sir. Everything's just fine."

The held breath of Major Ranna and Lt. Capet started a slight breeze as they released it. The perspiration was a little heavy on Major Ranna's forehead. He shuffled his feet, trying to start a chain reaction and duplication on the part of the generals, but that august gentleman merely looked with added scrutiny to the young Marine in front of him.

"You've certainly developed into a fine physical specimen - since I last saw you - How long has it been since you accompanied your father to Washington - two years?" The general's eyes continued to be attracted to the lack of rank or rate adornment on Wagner.

Barbells screwed his face into an attitude of concentration. Hell, I don't remember the pompous bastard, he thought, but aloud he said, "Yes, Sir, Two years, Sir."

The general umpth'd several times and with a condescending smile moved down the, ranks, leaving Wagner to his interrupted day dreams.

Thirty minutes later the inspecting general was rocking gently in the officer's mess, a glass of iced bourbon and ginger ale in his hand. Sitting uneasily about him were the Command Officers of the regiments headquarters. The only relaxed officer other than the general was Colonel "Barrel" -- who had a constantly drained triple header in his hand.

The General drew deeply on a cigar, let the smoke escape from his exaggerated oval shaped mouth opening into a ring, and watched it drift toward the ceiling. All ears waited for the pearls which were certainly going to drop from his lips.

"Tell me, Major," he said, still watching the smoke as it disintegrated against the wooden rafters of the ceiling. "Why is that Wagner boy still a private?" Without awaiting a reply he continued, "I understand he's been overseas 24 months now."

Not a word of reply was forthcoming. In the silence which followed - words had no place - the general looked into his drink, the colonel looked over his cigar to the Major, the Major glared at the Captain, the Captain's face became red and he glowered at the lieutenant, and the lieutenant finding no one else to pass on the rebuke, hastily made a notation in his little black book.

"I'll be a no good son-of-a-bitch!" Cordyn Wagner III spoke vehemently as he sat down heavily on a log in the battalion's makeshift outdoor movie area beside Malton.

"What's the word, Barbells?" J.C. asked innocently drawing contentedly on his pipe.

"I've been given the shaft - the royal shaft," Wagner composed his muscles and sank into a semi-comfortable position.

Malton held the pipe away from his face and watched the smoke, blue and seemingly transparent, curl from the burnt bowl and drift meanderingly in the draft toward the center of the tent. Troubles - everyone had troubles, but they never amounted to anything. He smiled - what the hell kind of trouble could Cordyn Wagner III have? But he didn't have to ask for that worthy Marine was already pounding the ears of the occupants of the tent. J.C. focused his ears and listened and came in of the proper frequency just as Wagner was saying, "and I get this call from the company command post." Cordyn was leaning against the tent post flexing his muscles and watching them as he talked, "and that fat Major Cundrum sat there. The sweat running down the barrel of his stomach and turning the front of the shirt wet. "Wagner," he says pompous as all hell. "Wagner, you've been down in the ranks for over 2 years now and your permanent record card says that you're due for a promotion." Why, the lying son-of-a-bitch, I don't rate anything but a court martial. Well, anyway he holds up a pair of sergeant's stripes and gurgling in that fat gut of his, he says, "Take these back to your tent son, and have your buddies pound them on." Can you foster that - a friggin' sergeant from buck ass private - what's this friggin' corps comin' to."

The men in the tent sat immobile for a minute and then burst out laughing followed by the others as they figured out the sudden promotion. The story of the General's dialogue in the officer's mess had been passed on by the mess man.

"Brown nosin'!" Liverlip snickered. "Brown nosin' the brass!" He held his thumb and forefinger to his nose. He sank down on his bunk feinting fear as Wagner advanced on him.

"Knock off that shit!" Wagner thrust at the small McPherson who cringed exaggeratedly on the green clad bunk. "I never brown nosed anyone in my whole friggin' life and I haven't started now. It sure burns my ass!" He moved back to the center pole. "What the hell am I going to do?"

For the first time Alex Blue joined in the conversation. He raised his eyes until they met Wagner's. "Don't be a fool, Wag!" he said loudly. "Don't do anything. Take the promotion. No one gives a holy damn how you got it. Rates don't come easily in this outfit." He looked down on the two stripes on his khaki sleeve, caressing them with his eyes.

"Bull shit!" Wagner spat over Liverlip to the exterior of the tent beyond. The spittle curved gracefully over the bunk, but nevertheless spattering some of the wet fringe area on the cowering Marine. "I don't need any stripes - I'm doin' fine - have been for a long time. Those friggin stripes'll just mean trouble." He chortled, "Sgt. Wagner - shit, I ain't no more sergeant material than hard-assed Liverlip there." He sneered at the insulted McPherson.

"Forget it," Malton said. "The guys know you didn't have anything to do with getting the stripes. It won't make any difference."

"I just don't want to be a sergeant!" Wagner's voice rose and carried with it conviction. "I want to be a buck-assed private from now until they survey me from the Corps. What the hell can I do?"

Malton laughed and said jokingly, "Go punch the adjutant in the mouth - he had to put the papers through." The tent filled with laughter at the words and everyone, including Wagner, roared at the story of the three stripes. Some rot-gut was produced from somewhere, in the manner in which only Miss Blue could produce it, and drinks were passed around as the men pounded the stripes onto Wager's arm. It was indeed a jovial and carefree group in the company tent area that night. All holds had been lifted and the men for the first time in years completely relaxed, the realization at last making its way into the inner beings that the war and its danger of impeding death had passed. With lights out, men in a happy and somewhat drunken mood, slipped off into sleep.

The dawn broke slowly over the fall colored land and with the dawn, the early morning mist hung heavily from the windblown and shell racked trees of Okinawa. Activity still awaited the call of the bugler. The company street was quiet and motionless save for the occasional dust of coral which blew as the warm ocean air passed through the row of tents, across the five foot wide creek which ran parallel to the ocean, and bent the knee high grass in its race to the foothills of the Kobe mountains which rose majestically a mile from the battalion area.

J.C. Malton was following the path of the breeze as he sucked on his pipe in his tent which rested at the company street along the creek bank. He had awakened at the first light of dawn and had tossed and turned, trying to go back to sleep, but he had been unsuccessful, perhaps because of the overt amount of rotgut he had drunk the previous night, or because of the recurrent nightmares on that night on the beach - the night whose dawn had brought death to Cold Steel Fagan. Finally he had resigned himself to awakefulness and had quietly propped his head against his extra blanket, rolled firmly to take the place of the pillow he hadn't felt for over two years. He did this silently so not to wake his slumbering tent mates, whose snores were as diversified as the forms from which they were emitted.

Peacefully he watched the trickling water of the stream, becoming keenly aware of the necessity for relieving himself - but nutting off the effort so as not to disturb these few minutes of solitude which were so rare in the process of war and the resultant formations of troops. His eyes lingered on the clear water momentarily and then they rose to the friend of brownish green beyond. The land was virgin - save for a few invisible spots, to him at least, where shells had felt for hidden troops. His eyes half-focused on the hills, seeing more than the open ridges whose faces were scarcely discernable at this distance.

A patch of white stood out amongst the black of the hills. Almost unconsciously his eyes lingered on the patch of white which moved slightly in the otherwise stillness of the montage. Suddenly his vision focused on the white, and the pipe was drawn slowly from his mouth as J.C. leaned forward it held his eyes, as if the few inches would help. The white was moving. Malton drew his bare frame from the cot and stood erect outside the rolled up tent flaps. He shielded his eyes from the sun which was just coming over the distant ridge.

"I'll be a corps happy qyrene!" Malton said in a whisper as he stood motionless watching. The white patch was surely moving from side to side forming a half circle. Attached to the white cloth was the arm of a brown clad man who was moving toward the stream - some 500 yards away. There were three other men walking beside the flag waving Japanese, all in the uniform of the Niponese army. They seemed to be floating toward Malton, their feet and legs hidden to the hip in the tall grass.

J.C. jumped over his cot, tipping it over in the process. Unconscious of his nakedness he grabbed his M 1 from the rack, Miss Blue had constructed around the center pole of the tent. As he opened the breach and jammed home a clip he found his voice and ailed in a loud voice, "Japs!"

The Marines who had been dead asleep a moment before as they, as one, rolled from their cots to the safety of the deck and instinctively crawled to their weapons. They had heard the one word before in their sleep. Alex Blue was the first to voice the question which all had in mind as he pulled his rifle to his bare body.

"Where?" his voice was thick with sleep. The others too looked to Malton from their crouching positions, an odd sight as five bare assed men prepared to meet the enemy.

"Out there - coming this way!" Malton said as he moved out of the tent opening. Cautiously Blue, Liverlip, Peterson and Badger followed, each in a crouching quick moving step. They spread out automatically in the company street, each watching the white cloth swing in its arch.

"Japs coming!" Miss Blue yelled. "Corporal of the Guard! Japs coming." It took but seconds for every tent in the battalion to be emptied as over 600 men, most completely naked, spread out over the area in combat readiness, rifles at the ready. The sound of clips being jammed into breaches and bolts slamming home clattered and broke the morning stillness.

"Hold your fire!" The commanding voice belonged to Colonel Ranna who had taken the time to pull on a pair of cut off khaki's - after all, it was difficult to strap a cartridge belt and pistol over bare skin. "Sgt, get five men and follow me!" he added as he moved over the plank footbridge which spanned the creek. Konkright signaled to Malton and four others who were in the proximity. J.C. for the first time realized he was naked and self-consciously moved forward with the others.

"Looks like Minskys," an anonymous voice called in the security of the troops. The words brought laughter as each man suddenly realized that this was the most bare-assed army ever assembled. But along with the laughter there was a seriousness which the laughter did not succeed in covering.

Malton saw, as his bare feet crossed the bridge that the Japs had stopped some one hundred yards from the creek, but the flag still waved. The other Japs had their hands high over their heads.

They were a sorry looking lot – these, his Imperial Majesty's finest. Gone was the arrogant self-assuredness which the Orientals had possessed in the early days of 1942. The war was over - though J.C. doubted if they knew that their unconquerable land had indeed been defeated - conquered without a foot being placed on the land by the hated Americans. But one thing these men did know as they bowed from the knees as the Marines approached. At least their war - the last war was over. Their clothes - uniforms they had once been, were in tatters and the skin which was exposed through the rips in the material was blotched by the bites of mosquitos and flees. Their tiny bones jutted against the taught skin, and the veins on their faces stood out in the thinness of the starving faces. They had had enough! Their war was over.

"Jesus Christ, they stink," Malton said aloud as he looked over the scaly remnants of humanity which had now fallen to their knees, and with arms stretched far before their palms on the dew damp deck held their heads face down. "What the hell they sayin'?"

Indeed, there emitted a strange sound from the diverted faces of the men. It was a shrill, chattering sound which pierced the ears and brought to memory the voices which filled the darkness on Peleliu.

"Shut up, you bastards." Malton almost thought it was someone else talking before he realized the words had come from his mouth. Bitterly, he kicked dirt over the Japs whose bodies tensed as the rich loam struck them.

"Easy, J.C." Konkright spoke softly - then turned his head to see if the men in camp were covering the surrounding terrain. Grunting his satisfaction, he moved toward the Jap who had lead the group into the area. Gently he jabbed the muzzle of the rifle he was carrying into the pit of the back of the man who had remained motionless with his companion. Had it not had been for the sounds coming from beneath the bowed heads, the objects might just as well been stones.

The touch of the steel brought the head of the Jap up instantly. Konkright stared down into the face of the nip. The eyes were steady - the hard look - the steadiness of determination - of one not knowing fear. But behind the hard eyes lay the shadow of despair, of uselessness. The jaw was set - the mouth firm, but the fire had gone from the eyes - yes! It had been there, once, but all which remained now were the physical signs - the heart had long since deserted. Konkright motioned the man to his feet with his rifle, and without an apparent shifting of a muscle, the man was on his feet. He stood a head shorter than Mike Konkright's 6'2". Starvation had long since drained from the Jap soldier any muscle. But even in the tattered uniform, his body emancipated by malnutrition, the bearing of a man of the sword was evident. Evident in the straight military manner in which he stood - strongly evident in the chiseled face, from whose deep sockets burned the black eyes.

"Do you speak English?" Konkright asked quickly, watching for the reaction which would more surely answer his question than any words which would come later. The man's facial muscles did not quiver, the eyes did not contract, did not blink - nothing about the man had changed in the slightest.

"I speak English, sergeant," the man's lips scarcely seemed to have moved, but the words were firm and strong. "My men do not speak or understand English."

His words surprised the capturers. Malton swallowed his spittle. The words had been enunciated perfectly. As perfect as a speech teacher, the thought formed in J.C.'s mind. J C. looked at the little man more closely now. He was an officer, strange how his words had identified him where his uniform had not. Konkright had been surprised at the words of the Jap, but had managed to hide it save in his eyes, which became more alert - he was sure the Jap officer had caught the change, just as sure as he was that he was smiling at him, inwardly now. He cleared his throat. "Name and rank -" then added, "what outfit?"

The Jap seemed to become even more rigid and brought his heels together, the frayed and torn rubber sandals making no sound. "Captain Osake Hywisku, 02341," he spoke firmly, his eyes looking straight past Konkright, then his lips tightened as he continued, "My regiment is not required information according to the rules of the Gene -"

"The war's over Captain," Konkright interrupted, his voice strong and deep had obliterated that of the Jap's.

Captain Hywisku sucked in his breath and for the first time showed an emotion, the emotion of uncertainty. He focused his eyes incredulously on Konkright.

"The war is over?" The perfection of his English had slipped, his shoulders seemed to sag and the hard jaw line had now become limp. His eyes were disbelieving.

"That's right - the surrender papers have been signed and it's over," his feeling was evident as Konkright continued. "All over."

Captain Hywisku dropped his head amid the jabbering of his companions who had sensed that something had stunned their leader and they were wishing to be apprised of it. Hywisku spoke but briefly, his face averted. The jabbering stopped as the words sunk in. One by one the men fell back on their hunches, shock on their faces. Malton stood watching them. These men were his enemies - one just like them had felled Fagan, but now it all seemed different. These men were just like he was, not the deformed maniacs he had forced himself into seeing in battle, and now look at them - they were completely defeated, both physically and mentally - wait until they hear about the bomb, he thought mirthlessly.

"What the hell did he say to the crummy bastards?" a rifleman from A Company snarled, scratching his crotch unselfconsciously. He spat trying to clear his nostrils of the unwashed odor which waifed about the Japs. The Japanese Captain regained some of the composure he had lost at Sgt. Konkright's words. He drew his body erect and saluted the Marine Sgt. "Sgt, we surrender to you! We have no arms as you can see," he shrugged. "No food - nothing to surrender save our poor miserable bodies." He looked to the east where but a few hundred miles lay his beloved Oashu. "All our countrymen have laid down their arms?"

Sgt. Konkright nodded, "All but a few like you who were cut off and didn't get the word." He tossed his head in the direction of the hills which were now visible as the rising sun burned off the haze. "Any more of your troops up there?"

Captain Hywisku smiled, "Many - all starving - all unwilling to surrender." The smile faded "They are awaiting the resurgence of His Imperial Majesty's forces. They will not like to hear that the dynasty is no longer."

Malton was studying the Captain. He didn't look the part of one who would so easily surrender. The eyes, the jaw, were both significant of the type who committed hari-kari rather than surrender, turn over their arms and themselves to the hateful enemy.

"Why did you surrender Captain?" The Jap turned to Malton as he heard the words. Steadily the fierce black eyes studied the speaker. He seemed to be about to answer them, he slowly raised his shoulders and let them fall.

"Let's go," Konkright motioned the prisoners to their feet. "Take the point, J.C. You other men, flank them. I'll bring up the rear. Shove off, J.C."

The strange procession moved rapidly toward the battalion area. Four small Japanese soldiers, clothes hanging limply from their bodies walked erectly, all but hidden amongst the heavier and taller naked Marines who bounced along, their rifles held at the ready. It was a strange sight indeed which entered the camp area.

"Corporal of the guard!" Colonel Ranna yelled and as the running corporal arrived, his duty belt white against the tan of the khakis, added, "Detail your guard to supervise the prisoners. Feed them and then take them to the C.P."

"Aye, aye, Sir!" Corporal of the Guard Sanders sharply saluted and quickly assembled his men and took the prisoners down to the beach where the odors of breakfast preparation waged and won the battle joined by the smells of the sea.

"Captain!" Colonel Ranna was speaking, sitting in his commandeered bamboo chair in the officer's mess. He leaned comfortably back in the chair - a cool scotch and water sitting on the round table before him. He blew a trail of smoke skyward as he again spoke to the Japanese officer who was politely eating American rations. "Captain, you mean to say that you didn't know the war was over?" He seemed to find the fact difficult to comprehend.

Captain Hywisku smiled, the accomplishment no easy maneuver since his closed mouth was already occupied chewing the first hot food the connoisseur of delicacies, as he had fancied himself before the war, had digested in over two months. "When you're not on the offensive, Colonel, the lines of communication often fail. And my men and I," he stopped as he thought of the remnants of his once fine company, "well, we've heard no news at all since we were wiped out during the early days of the fighting." Gingerly he touched his right shoulder, whose skin pulled even now, over the wound which had taken him out of the battle.

His oriental face, handsome and unlike the artist sketches of the Japanese, as chow mein is from the Chinese regular fare of rice and fish, darkened. He had lived through a period of frustration and uselessness during those days when his wound had managed to heal itself - he had offered no assistance - in fact had wished for the shadow of death to cross his face once more - conclusively this time. He had not wanted to live after the cursed Marines had overrun his position on Kuki Mountain. The position was impregnable;

no one could take it away from the emperor's men. No one - but the position had fallen before the phosphorus shells, the flame throwers, and the bayonet of the Marines - and he had fallen with the position, a bullet piercing his yellowed skin. Darkness had followed the initial shock of the bullet and he had not been aware of the Marines as they overran the position. Unaware of the dead comrade who had fallen over his body and who had taken the job of the advancing Marine's probing bayonet in his lifeless body. When finally he had regained consciousness, an earth less silence had descended upon the hill. His limbs were cramped from the dead weight of the Japanese soldier who had fulfilled every man's dream of destiny by dying for his Imperial Majesty. The smell of spent gun powder mingled with the sweet heavy odor of blood, but the gunfire and rifle fire had stopped. Exploringly Captain Hywisku had lifted his head in the late afternoon light, first to the left and then to the right - each way the scene was the same – devastation. Devastation for the Japanese, his people. They lay about him - dead, all dead. He tried to move to help these, his own, and then for the first time became aware of the pain in his shoulder.

He prodded with his finger, both front and back. The bullet, it had been a bullet and not a piece of shrapnel which had pierced him, had passed on through, and even now the blood was beginning to clot. Carefully he slid his weight from under his human cover. He rose to his knees and scanned the woody terrain. No human being moved, his own were dead and the victorious Marines had moved on with the momentum of their drive. Even now he could visualize the green clad, bearded monsters descending on the opposite side of Kaki Mountain. Cautiously he explored the area, taking from the corpses the meager rations which were stuffed in the cartridge holders which long since had last been filled. He had found a sheltered cave and awaited darkness. Secure that the men returning from the ridge would not take the trouble to check out every likely hideout on their descent - and that the supply troops would not have the courage to explore for the enemy, but if the enemy appeared, would fight, fight hard until the infantry took over and then would revert to their unnatural fear.

There he waited for the Okinawan night to descend. Several times he heard the voices of the Americans as they passed close by. Once he had chanced to look from his hiding place. How easily he could have placed a bullet in the head of one of the Marines. Unaware of his presence they had, after being sure that none of their superiors were watching, gone through the pockets of his slain comrades, taking what they wanted and wanted only, discarding the useless. He had grimaced as one flung piece had fallen close to his position - a picture of the gallant warrior and his wife. He had brought blood to his mouth as he dug his teeth into his lips to prevent his anger from causing him to fire at the pimple faced youth who had so callously desecrated the dead soldier.

But no Marine came close to his shelter. No telling what he would have done if that had occurred. But darkness had finally come and with it shielding cover, he had vacated the dark, dark confines of the crevice and moved silently and stealthily into the hills. His shoulder pained him and he could not remember much of the ordeal of that night. How long had it taken him to reach the unseen line that separated the enemy from his own kind? He did not remember, time had not been important! Ah, he didn't even know when he had passed through the American lines. In his foggy memory of that night months before, he recalled shying away from the knots of enemy troops who had pocketed his path, but he had not had a single encounter. How easy it had been to slide by without being discovered - how true were the tales of the patrols who had recounted their infiltration of the enemy lines.

Colonel Ranna had patiently waited, experience telling him that patience with the Japanese was essential. He had lighted a cigar and now it was half smoked. Watching the Niponese Captain, whose eyes were cloudy with reminiscing, he knew that the time for talking was not at hand. Still he had to find out. He could see the general now, wanting information about the groups of enemy troops who were in the hills. "Do you think they'll surrender, Captain?" He watched Hywisku carefully.

Captain Hywisku turned his eyes back to those of the American Colonel. He shrugged almost imperceptibly. "My people are not given to surrender,

Colonel." His eyes again became glazed, "but if the war is over - the cause is done - perhaps."

Colonel Ranna knew this man was truly of the Shinto caste, and the question he had wanted to ask since the Captain had erectly crossed the foot bridge into the camp came to his lips. "Why did you surrender, Captain?" he said softly and bent forward to get the answer.

Captain Hywisku rose and went to the open door which faced the China Sea. Hundreds of American ships dotted the horizon. Why indeed? It had been the only thing to do. After he had found the unorganized units who had tasted defeat and had their backs to the Pacific Ocean, he had known that the battle for the northern half of Okinawa had come to an end, if indeed the delaying tactics could have been classified as a battle. The real defense was to be waged in the South, he had known, and he and the other men to the 19th Imperial Division had been delayed and the troops in the south had fought behind their defenses well, he had known from the radios before they had been destroyed by the enemy.

When his own glorious company had been overcome, the word defeat had not come to his mind, he had fallen back to join the others. It had been all too obvious that if he was to join the battle again it would have to be in the south. But his efforts to penetrate the twenty miles of enemy held Okinawan soil had been useless. For weeks he had sought out methods to join the troops in the south, but then as the days went by the sounds of battle had moved further and further away until he had realized that it would be impossible to fight his way through. Then and only then, he had made up his mind! He would give himself up to the enemy. Once there he would find a way, he knew that the sentimental Americans would never shoot him down, to for a final time, cast a departing destruction for the Emperor. But who had known that the Emperor had deemed fit to surrender. He could not bring himself to believe it.

He turned to the Colonel who had been watching his back, "Why did I surrender?" He smiled, "I am a military man like you are Colonel. When the inevitable has happened - it is time to capitulate." The smile turned to a confused frown. He looked steadily at the colonel. "But why did the Emperor surrender? Had your troops invaded Japan?"

Colonel Ranna rolled the tip of the cigar around his mouth, and then dipped the edge into the ash tray. He didn't take his eyes from those of the Japanese. "Captain. We didn't invade Japan." He saw the doubt in the Japanese soldier's eyes, "This is too complex a matter for men like you and I, field commanders to understand, but," he drew a deep breath, "the American Air Force, one plane, dropped a bomb over one of your cities and destroyed it."

The incredibility of the words reflected in the Japanese eyes. His mouth opened unbelievingly, "One bomb?" Then he smiled, "Surely the Colonel cannot expect - "

Ranna got up from the commandeered chair. "It's a fact. One plane - one bomb. They call it an Atomic Bomb. It completely destroyed the city. Estimates of killed are over 100,000 people." Goddamn it! Ranna continued to himself. No wonder he doesn't believe it. I couldn't believe it myself.

Slowly Captain Hywisku sat down at the table. It was true he knew. It was apparent in the Colonel's face. 100,000 people killed - his people.

The officer's mess faded from the eyes of Captain Hywisku. He sat at the table, his hands at his side staring unseeingly at the Japanese brush painting which adorned the landward side of the wall. The bamboo painted there by an artistic and sensitive Eastern hand was limp, its leaves drooping beneath the weight of the heavy raindrops which so realistically adorned them. His spirit had sunk as low as this symbol of Japan.

Captain Hywisku felt the Colonel's eyes upon him. But the Marine officer's alone were looking to him. Almost demandingly he felt the need reaching out across the waters which lay between him and his beloved Japan. His lips moved slightly, the words almost inaudible. "What city felt the power of this," he hesitated finding the word strange, "atomic bomb?"

Colonel Ranna knew instinctively that his answer would cut deep into the very heart of the brave Japanese soldier. Hesitantly he answered, "Hiroshima."

Captain Hywisku seemed not to have heard his reply for he did not move a single muscle. But he had heard - though unconsciously he had known that his beautiful city was no more. Hiroshima.

"Did you have a family there?" Colonel Ranna cursed himself for asking the question and further berated himself for phrasing the question in the past tense.

Hywisku nodded and continued to look at the bamboo painting. "My wife and son." The words were spoken affectionately – and for the first time the professional soldier's voice was not evident.

"I'm sorry," Ranna mumbled, fuming at his inadequacy. He fought to find the correct thing to say and then blurted out, "Perhaps they were not killed!"

He was stopped by the smile which appeared on Captain Hywisku's lips. He turned his gaze away from the picture and looked at the Colonel. "Thank you for your kindness." Suddenly it was evident to Colonel Ranna that Captain Hywisku's wife and son were dead and that the Japanese had sensed it even before he had learned about the bombing of Hiroshima. "If I would be permitted to retire to a place of privacy, I would appreciate the thought." Captain Hywisku said as he rose from the table.

Once again the Marine Colonel was capable of action. He moved to the door and called in the sentry who was standing guard outside, "Peterson. Take Captain Hywisku to the house beyond the beach." Peterson stepped back to permit Hywisku to pass. Ranna added, "and Peterson, Captain Hywisku is not to be disturbed under any circumstance without a direct order from me."

Hywisku stopped as he reached the door and turning to Colonel Ranna, raised his hand in a formal salute, but informally his eyes gave their thanks.

A bewildered Peterson followed the Japanese down the company street which paralleled the beach. His prisoner drew the stares of the Marines who watched the pair disappear into officer's country. All eyes followed the rigidly held body of the Nip officer with a respect they had not thought possible.

"Cocky little bastard, ain't he?" Liverlip spat a mouthful of tobacco juice at an ant which was walking up the guide rope of the tent. He missed and quickly tried to work the chew into position for another try.

"Cocky, yeah!" Miss Blue offered "But that little man is a hell of a soldier." The words of tribute sounded strange even to his ears.

Liverlip's mouth opened in surprise, the dark fluid of the tobacco juice lying glisteningly on his broad tongue. "Since when have you become a Jap lover?" he thrust at Blue.

The Oklahoman wearily lifted his head to the sky which was beginning to darken in blueness as the sun reached far out in the west preparing to plunge into the ocean. He didn't answer Liverlip - though he felt he should. His feelings toward the yellow men had changed in the past month or so.

Malton looked from Blue to McPherson. Alex Blue sat on his sack, his frame suddenly heavy with age, an age which had not been so apparent a short while before. In direct contrast was Liverlip, who had continued to miss the ant from his perch on the outside edge of his cot across the tent - here was youth - careful, damnably inconsistent youth.

"Knock it off, Doug!" Malton used the given name of the short Marine. "The war's over - we've won. Why shouldn't we let it ride. It was a hell of a fight, but we won. You want to be a conquering hero? Save it for the dames back in the states." He rose and tapped his pipe on the center pole of the tent and then looked down on the squat Marine whose face showed incredibility. He jerked his head in the direction where Captain Hywisku had disappeared. "He lost, we won. So it's over. But I agree with Miss Blue. Just looking at that guy, with his straight back and straight face not asking for our sympathy or mercy either makes you begin to think." He gingerly placed tobacco in the bowl of the battered pipe, careful so not to drop any of the precious grains. "How would you react in his place - how would I?   I don't think I'd be half the man he is - would you?"

Liverlip spat the quid from his mouth and rose and left the tent, saying half under his breath, "You bastards have gone rock happy! Jap lovers yet! I'll be a son-of-a-bitch."

Cordyn Wagner III moved sideways through the open tent flap, looking down the company street to where Liverlip stormed, muttering to himself, "What's eating Liverlip?"

"He's upset at our feeling respect for the ---" Blue stopped, his eyes having caught the thread ends hanging empty on Wagner's right sleeve. "Where's your stripes?" he asked as the others became aware of the bareness of the khaki sleeves.

Cordyn Wagner grinned his eyes gleaming. "Don't rate them. I'm only a buck-ass private again." He sat down on Miss Blue's foot locker helping himself from the can of semi-fresh Chelsea cigarettes on the bunk.

Malton regained his voice first, "What the hell happened?" All ears tensed for the answer.

Wagner III lighted the cigarette carefully flexing his bulging muscle of his right hand as he did so. He blew a bluish cloud of smoke from his puckered lips and looked through it to Malton. "I took your advice, J.C. I punched the adjutant."

A stunned silence fell over the tent punctuated only by the grating of Malton's teeth on the bit of his pipe. Then Miss Blue started a laugh a small chuckle deep in his belly which grew until it rocked the tent. The others joined in rolling on their sacks! Only Cordyn Wagner alone remained unsmiling. He was flexing the forearm of his left arm thinking that now that he was any peon again, he'd have to do something about the slack muscle there. He didn't seem to hear the laughter.

Captain Hywisku knelt before the Buddhists shrine in the small ceremonial room of the deserted Okinawan hut. The shrine had been damaged in the sweep of the American attack, but save for a small piece of plaster which had fallen from the head as he had placed it back into its matted tabernacle, the Buddha showed no contamination from its contact with the Americans.

He knelt there now in his solitude, eyes intent on the God, his lips moving slightly in its incantations. He was oblivious to his surroundings and to the noise of a pick-up softball game which was in progress a hundred yards from the shelter. The house itself seemed alien to the noise of the American game. Sitting on the edge of the beach, the mat and thatch Japanese house was sheltered by large trees. The home of an itinerant farmer who had at one time farmed the very land which now served as the play area for the Marines, it contained but three rooms - a large all purpose room which at the desired time through the day served as the cooking and eating area, a play area for the farmer's children as evidenced by the quaint home fashioned toys which were neatly piled in one corner of the room as if waiting for their young masters to return; a smaller room which served the dual purpose of bedroom and bathroom as indicated by the rolled up sleeping mats and the prized bathing tub which bore the label of a United States firm; and the room in which Captain Hywisku knelt, the prayer and ceremonial room. It was tiny barely eight feet square, bare except for the shrine which was built into the wall.

Here were the true roots of Japanese teachings. The Okinawans had taken well to their conquerors of over a century, had indeed adopted their beliefs and way of life. The owner of this humble abode had embraced Buddha and was a believer in Shinto, it was evident. The years of occupation had not set heavily upon the Okinawans, and Hywisku felt that the loose hand of the Americans would not rest so comfortably and the day would come not so many years hence, when the Okinawans would yearn for the Japanese lordship.

Hywisku was dressed in a ceremonial gown and knelt upon the traditional ritual mat. His eyes were focused upon the Buddha and his ears shut out completely the exterior noise. He had no fear of being disturbed by Private Peterson who was standing outside watching the game. Colonel Ranna had been explicit in his orders.

Slowly his hands moved to the side of the pedestal until they found a loose panel. Gently he depressed the panel and knew instinctively that he had been correct in his assumption - that the master of the house was a believer in the Shinto tradition for a small opening appeared beneath his hand. Carefully he placed his hand within and drew out a pure silk wrapper. Almost religiously he placed it on the ritual mat before him and unrolled it.

His eyes rested upon the contents, a beautiful carved knife, its blade gleaming and free from all discoloration. Again he raised his eyes to the Buddha — his thoughts traversing the miles to Hiroshima! Once again he saw the beautiful doll face of his wife and the large unknowing eyes of his son. Slowly his lips moved, called each by name and declaring his love for them. Then he called to his mind the Emperor sitting majestically before the unfurled Rising Sun. Thus be dedicated his deed.

His hand, untrembling, fondled the knife and then cupped the hilt in both his hands the blade pointing to the center of his stomach. Gently, but deliberately, he leaned forward bringing his weight to the point. Slowly he doubled over and then swiftly as the blade pierced the organs.

His eyes remained open, unflinching as death rushed to join him with his loved ones.

Chapter 20

Although the hand which shook his shoulder was gentle, J.C. Malton started as he attained wakefulness. Instinctively he reached for his rifle beside him, but regained his bearings as his fingers brushed against the net finesse of the mosquito netting which encompassed the cot.

He swung his legs over the edge of the bunk and rubbed his eyes, and with difficulty saw that the other occupants of the tent had likewise been aroused. Squinting his eyes against the soft light cast by the Coleman lantern, Malton addressed the Corporal who was already leaving the tent, "What's the scoop?"

The Corporal, one of the headquarter's company clerks, jerked the list he held in his right hand. "You guys are shoving off." He disappeared before any other question could be asked, and moments later could be heard arousing the occupants in the next tent. Cursing hung heavy in the tepid night of the Rhy.

Liverlip yawned as he sat on his bunk, one pants leg drawn on, "It's just like this friggin Corps. Gotta move out at night, instead of daylight," he paused, then added speculatively as the thought occurred to him for the first time, "Where the hell we goin' anyhow?"

The words reacted around the tent. So disciplined were the occupants to obeying orders no matter how strange they seemed at the time, that the thought of destination had not as yet penetrated the thickness of sleep.

"China." Badger said authoritatively. "Got the straight scoop at the head yesterday. Whole outfit's going to China for occupation duty. Always wanted to see China."

"You're rock happy!" Liverlip said derisively. "China! That figures. The Raggedy Assed First! All the glory! First to fight, first to die - ," he spat furiously, "and first to stand guard over the yellow bastards."

A head poked in the tent. Battalion Adjutant Farnwell called, "Get a move on, men! Trucks pull out in five minutes. Just take your packs and sea bags." He was alone.

A moan followed the officer's exit, followed in turn by a hasty attack on the makeshift footlockers. Alex Blue drove his combat boot in the side of a reconditioned ammunition crate, "And I just finished building this thing." All treasures were taken from the boxes and forced into the sea bags, which bulged with gear. Cursing fiercely, Badger pulled out a moldy green topcoat and replaced it with several Japanese leather encased prints he had found on Peleliu.

"I've been carrying that foul smelling coat for two years. Now damn if I'm going to take it to China," Badger fumed.

J. C. dug about in his sea chest in the light of the Coleman lantern, selecting the objects of most importance. He chose carefully, remembering the day he had left for Okinawa and certain that the Division would return to Pavuvu, had left many objects he surely missed. Eliminating a shell casing he made into an ashtray, he picked up the envelopes which lay below. Shielding his actions with his back from any of the other tent occupants he placed the letters in his pack, the faint perfume which still clanged to the blue paper tingling his nostrils.

"Ready, J.C." Miss Blue stood behind him and Malton knew that the furtive placing of the letters in the pack had not escaped the wizened eyes of the hulking Oklahomian.

J.C. slipped the pack straps over his shoulder and accepted the positioning help preferred by Miss Blue. "Thanks," he grunted. "All set." He looked about the tent, now bare in the few minutes since the word to move out had been given. Hoisting the well rounded and firmly packed sea bag on his shoulder he moved to the center pole and turned off the Coleman lantern, a regret welling that they could find no space to take it with them.

"We'll borrow another one in China," Ben Badger, the South Carolinian said. The others smiled as they moved beneath the weights of the sea bags into the company street where other sleepy men had already began to form unconsciously into company ranks. The darkness of the night had been penetrated by a full moon which hung far out into the China Sea. Scurrying back and forth with roster lists were the headquarter's company office force. They waited there in line, in rank, in sleepy acceptance for three-quarters of an hour while the moon moved higher into the sky. The luminous dial of his watch showed that it was 0230.

The hoarse sound of six by six's motors signaled the approach of the transport trucks. "Climb in!" came a voice indistinguishable in the noise of the motors. Further invitation was not necessary as the troops quietly made their way up the slats of the truck and arranged themselves on the board seats which lined the two sides. The operation was not unique and did not call for any conversation. The men in the truck with J.C. were all familiar to him. All old timers, he thought. Miss Blue nudged him from his position alongside. J.C. strained his eyes in the semi-darkness and smiled. Chick Young had already fallen back to sleep, his head resting on Miss Blue's shoulder.

"We going to drive all the way to China?" Liverlip asked two hours later as the trucks continued to roar down the coast highway which had been put back into excellent condition by the Seabees.

"Won't be long now," Badger countered and pointed over the cab's roof to a cluster of lights on and off the land.

The lights of the docks and the ships in Buckner Bay grew larger as the convoy worked its way through the long rows of dispersed supplies which ringed the road. Here was the main post of Okinawa and would be until the docks at Naha had been cleared of the wreckage and destruction wrought by the bombs of the American bombers. Slowing, the convoy approached within a thousand yards of the beach and halted completely as the lead truck ground to a stop. From the cab of the first truck, Lt. Grayson, battalion executive, leapt and ran down the line of trucks yelling, "Everybody off. Fall out in companies - make ranks in alphabetical order. Move out - fall --" The voice trailed off behind Malton.

"Hurry up and wait," spat Liverlip. "We'll be on this friggin beach until late tomorrow.

Malton grinned in the darkness and looked up at the sky. Far off in the east he could see the first faint indication that dawn was on the way. Then strips of lighter sky filtered off the infinity which separated the sky from the sea. He glanced at his watch. It was 0500. Shifting the weight of his pack he climbed down from the truck and lined up in formation. The dark was as detriment - with practice comes methods of coping with the element of sightlessness.

Liverlip had been wrong. In fifteen minutes the battalion clerks had read off the names to check if all hands were accounted for and the men were crossing over and up a ladder to the deck of a fat transport ship. It was not yet fully light as the ship pulled out of Buckner Bay and headed out to sea.

Most of the troops crowded the gangway to catch a glimpse of the island which had been their home for seven months. Malton, Miss Blue and Ben Badger had found a spot on the fantail and their eyes followed the wake of the ship back to the now impersonal piece of real estate. Their thoughts were disturbed by the ship's public address.

"Now hear this! Now hear this! All Marine transient personal are to wear Mae West's at all times. We will be at sea approximately 16 days. Next stop - " The voice paused then roared, "San Diego, California."

A stunned silence followed the click as the switch of the public address system was shut off - then a growing roar which certainly must have traversed the mounting distance to Okinawa broke from the throats of the thousand men who had thought that China was to be the destination. Pandemonium broke loose as battle beaten Marines gleefully slapped each other on the backs and shook hands all around - the time which a large percentage of the troops certainly had never expected to see arrive had materialized - it added to but one word for them all - Home!

Alex Blue shook hands with J.C. Malton, a smile spreading more widely on his face than Malton had ever seen before. Home to Jessie and Alex, Jr.. J. C. clapped him fraternally on the back. Neither could speak - it would have been useless anyway - they would have not been able to hear each other in the noise which swept about them.

They stood there for a few minutes, reveling in unaltered happiness which abounded on board the ship. Then as the realization of their imminent arrival home began to settle heavily on their shoulders and the sound waifed out to sea J.C. turned once again to the wake of the ship, his eyes following the thinning foam as it disappeared into the greenness of Okinawa. Silently he looked at the arch made of white lumber atop a dimly visible hill, the sun gleaming on the white wood, the entrance to the cemetery which held the bodies of the slain Marines who gave their lives on Okinawa. There amidst the thousands of other bodies lay Cold Steel, his trusted knife sheathed in its leather case, turning slowly to rust.

Home - home from the wars came the Warriors! Heads held high - chests thrust forward to receive the accolades of those who had waited. But some were not going home - Cold Steel and the tens of thousands like him were destined always to silently guard the land - the foreign land for which they had given their lives. J.C. stared at the receding shore line - Okinawa! Here it had ended - the war between the yellow men of Asia and the assorted colors of the United States. On this island, more Asian than most - whose inhabitants bore the blood strains of the Japanese coursing through their veins - the war had ended for him - for Miss Blue and Cold Steel.

J.C. turned as the ship altered its course and the island slid from the stern of the ship and his view. Miss Blue turned and faced him and wordlessly they said goodbye to Cold Steel Fagan.

Chapter 21

The huge transport plodded heavily through the calm Pacific waters two days out of Okinawa. Aboard were 3,000 Marines, homeward bound. The war had been over a month and a half and rotation was in full swing. In October 1945, the nation had forgotten its pledge not to be caught napping again and Washington had been deluged with cries of "Bring the boys home!" The great strength of the services of the nation was again being dissipated by hurried discharges to reservists. A repetition of 1918 was in the offing, but no nation, no democratic nation, at least, could withstand the clamor of millions of women. For it was the women of the United States, wives and mothers, who had demanded the return to civilian status of their loved ones.

Corporal J.C. Malton, aged and yellow with atabrine tablets, stood quietly in the perpetual chow line. Shipboard feeding of thousands of troops was one problem that the high command had not been able to resolve. Men lined up for chow in the morning and after finishing the poor substitute for food served by the harassed ship's company, lined up again for noon chow. The procedure was repeated for the evening meal. Long queues of men were ever present, winding along the passageways, leaning against the bulkheads.

"Move up, mac," the voice of the man behind him stirred Malton into movement. He caught up with Richardson who turned to him.

"Fourteen more days," he said softly. "Fourteen more days and then home," his thoughts were on Mary.

Malton thumped him on the back. Fourteen more days! It had been almost two years since he had left the states – 21 months of hell. New Georgia, Peleliu, Guam and Okinawa - a lifetime of fear and death. He wouldn't forget those hell islands easily - nor would he forget easily the buddies who had stayed beneath the harsh coral rock.

Malton felt eyes upon him. He turned his eyes from Richardson, forward thirty yards where the chow line wound around an anti-aircraft gun mount, now secured. His eyes played along the line - then stopped as a familiar face crept into his vision. The features were drawn, the skin white under the yellow pallor. The trunk of the body was withered with the privations of combat-food. Recognition came to Malton.

It was Platoon Sergeant Carver, now Gunnery Sergeant. The same Sergeant Carver from New Caledonia he had battled with in his early days overseas and swore vengeance to. Malton stared at the man, who unbelievingly stared back. Fear was in the other Marine's eyes. Suddenly Carver bolted from the chow line, his place quickly swallowed up by the man behind. Stumbling frantically over a line of men he disappeared into the bowels of the ship. Malton watched him go, a broad grin on his face.

For days Malton watched for the sergeant, but he didn't appear. Finally his wonderment was answered one day when he was leaning over the rail. Two sergeants, neither known to him, were doing the same next to him.

"What's with Carver?" one was saying. "He hasn't come topside for a week. The son-of-a-bitch is nuts - must have cracked up."

The other answered, "He doesn't even come up for chow. He'd starve if the guys didn't bring slop to him!"

He thought a moment. "Come to think of it, he doesn't eat much of it anyway. He keeps mumbling something about it not being safe out in the open. He's rock happy."

Malton drew peacefully on his pipe, a smile on his lips as he envisioned the sergeant fearful to his bunk. So the guy is afraid - afraid of what? He answered himself and looked toward the wave thrown by the wake of the ship. The memory of his torment on New Caledonia had been forgotten long ago in the battles for survival he had been through. Ahead lay the states - the big, beautiful 48!

He tapped the ashes of his pipe on the rail. There was plenty of room for two enemies there. But the smile broadened as his thoughts formulated the picture of Carver always looking behind him for the man who swore he would kill him. He turned from the rail, sighed and joined the noon chow line.

Let the bastard suffer!!

Too young to vote
Too young to drink
But old enough
To Die!

Chapter 22

"How's Chick?" the voice was filled with anxiety. Its owner, a tall, huskily built Texan, joined the small group sitting idly on a hatch. They all waited for someone to offer an answer.

"Same." Fraley didn't look at McKean, the Texan as he answered, his thoughts were on the youngster below deck in the ship's sick bay.

"Christ," McKean fiercely cursed. "Can't those pill rolling bastards help him?" He paused, his sluggish mind working. "What's the matter with the kid anyway?" He dropped on the tarpaulin covered hatch, his long legs brushing Malton who was reading a paper bound book.

"Corpsman said it was Beriberi." Fraley, one arm crooked where a bullet had crushed a bone on Peleliu, didn't know what the word meant, but he took pride in his knowledge of it nevertheless.

Malton's eyes were still on the yellowed pages of the weather beaten paper book, but the lines of type were unread. Beriberi, a disease which was classified as Oriental, caused by a deficiency of vitamins, sometimes resulting in death. Inwardly he smiled as he remembered his college zoology course. His face creased as he thought of Chick Young lying painfully amidst the first sheets whose cleanness and whiteness he had not known for over two years.

"What's Beriberi?" Liverlip McPherson shifted the wad of tobacco to the left side of his jaw and inexpertly spit against the wind bringing a cursing complaint from McKean. Malton felt the eyes of the sorry looking group on him. Slowly he raised his eyes from the pages and faced them. God, how did he ever come to love such men, but love them he did.

"Well," he placed the book beside him, first dog-earing his page. "It's a disease which comes from not eating the right food, like fresh vegetables."

"That figgers," Fraley offered. "We ain't had fresh vegetables for a hell of a long time," the grunt of agreement came from the others. "But how come the rest of us ain't sick too?"

Malton gently patted the tobacco in his pipe, then held a match to the stained and crusted briar. "Lack of vitamins doesn't affect us all the same way. Chick's constitution just couldn't take it."

Couldn't take it - hell, the kid had no business being overseas, no business being in the service at all. Malton drew intently on his pipe, his eyes staring over the side of the ship to where the broad expanse of the Pacific disappeared into the horizon. Dimly in the vastness of the vista, the image of Chick Young appeared. Of medium height, he was slim, skinny was the word. His face was long and pointed, his cheeks hollow and sunken. Blonde hair, cut short and matted, was bleached white from the sun. Chick's shoulders were stooped and he looked much shorter than he actually was. His eyes - his eyes were what distinguished Chick Young! They were perpetually bewildered eyes - wonder, awe, sadness and fear crossed them frequently. The entire world perplexed Chick who remained bewildered always, uncertain it seemed, to the reality of all that had befallen him. No wonder, this October Day in 1945, he had four months to go before he reached his 18th birthday. Not yet 18 and the kid had been two years overseas - in three major battles. Malton cursed the stupidity of the Marine Corps. Not only was he young, but he looked young.

"Can it kill you?" McKean asked, concern evident in the squinted Texan eyes.

"Can what kill ya?" McPherson was lying on the hatch, gently pulling the small blonde goatee he had been growing for 6 months. He never could follow the trend of a conversation.

"Sometimes," Malton said softly, his teeth clamped tightly on the pipe, "sometimes it's fatal. It all depends on the ability of the body to recuperate." Young was weak, woefully deteriorated.

The men sat silently. About them other marines sat, killing the lonely, tiresome hours of the long shipboard day.

"When do we hit Frisco?" Liverlip's thoughts already had left the conversation. The words changed the attitude of the seven buddies.

"Scuttlebutt say November 6," Lohman said, raising his fatigue cap and scratching his black hair. "I've got the 5th on the pool."

"Frisco, man, oh, man!" McKean shouted. "That's the western part of Texas!" the men laughed at the typical boastfulness, the thought of home raising their spirits.

Malton smiled. Home! It had been a long time - too long! The 18 months he had been overseas had passed slowly, yet somehow as he sat aboard the transport plowing its way through the waves to the states, it didn't seem possible that it had been so long since he had watched Point Loma slip from sight. Yet here he was on his way home, the home he hadn't seen since the spring of 1943 - the parents who wrote daily and waited for their son to come back.

"Time to line up for chow." Lohman, the chow hound of the group called as he indicated the lengthening of the perpetual chow line. The Marines, all save Malton, stretched their stiff bones and moved toward the line.

"Coming, Malt?" Alex Blue asked, slowly limping off the hatch. Malton shook his head at the older man, his closest friend since Fagan had been killed.

"Later, think I'll drop in on Chick."

Blue nodded and moved away. Malton watched him go. The stupidity of the Corps - Young was not old enough, Blue too old. He tapped the tobacco from his pipe, put it in his breast pocket, and started for the passageway which led to the sick bay. The ship was overcrowded with men. So crowded in fact, that you couldn't take a step without either brushing or stepping over a green clad figure. He smiled as he thought of the lack of griping - these men were going home - nothing mattered but that fact.

Malton ducked his head as he entered the passageway. Climbing down two narrow ladders, he entered the ship's crew section of the vessel. The atmosphere was completely different down here. Clean and freshly painted, everything was neatly in place. He turned down a white passageway, a feeling of uncleanliness upon him. Stopping before a door he peered within. A white uniformed sailor sat at a desk. Looking up from his papers, a questioning look came into his eyes. Malton stepped into the cabin. "Could I see Chick Young?" he was surprised at the whispering quality of his voice.

The corpsman leafed through some papers, found the name and then said, "He's in Ward B. down the passageway, second door to your left." He looked into the eyes of Malton. "Don't stay too long. He's in bad pain."

Malton nodded and turning, left the cabin. Bad Pain! What a rotten deal. Two years overseas - through hell - and now that he's on his way home, Beriberi catches up with him.

Making his way down the passageway, Malton went from side to side as the ship rolled through the rough sea. An uneasiness came over him as he reached Ward B. Hesitating, he re-arranged his face and entered, searching the double row of beds for the sunken face of Young. The ward was almost filled with Marines, the majority suffering from an attack of Malaria - the Marines' sickness. Drawn and tired faces met his eyes. Half-way down the ward, a Marine was in the throes of an active attack.

A corpsman stood beside the bed, his strong and trained hands holding covers over the trembling and moaning man. Beyond was a white curtain which shut a bed off from the rest of the ward Malton slowly walked toward the curtain, conscious of the eyes of the sick Marines on him. The curtain was partially opened and Malton could make out the thin form lying on its back. Moving up the body, Malton's eyes found Chick Young's face. He was stunned at the pain twisted features of the youngster. The eyes were closed, clamped shut. Outside the sheet, yellowed fists frantically clenched and unclenched. Slowly the eyes opened and focused on the visitor. Recognition appeared and a hopelessly futile smile formed on the dry and cracked lips.

Malton moved to the side of the bed and instinctively touched the unmoving form. Instantly he cursed himself as he saw the pain react in the kid's face. Quickly he withdrew his hand and feebly smiled.

"How's it going, Chick?" Again he cursed his stupidity. The eyes looking up at him were those of a lost child in the woods. It wasn't fear, or hopelessness, but an inability to understand that those eyes clearly indicated.

The lips moved, "All right, Malt." His voice was pitched high and barely audible, "I guess!" He continued searching Malton's face for an answer to his condition. "I ache - ache all over. It's rough." Again the sad smile crossed his face.

Malton talked and talked, relating information about the men topside. Occasionally the boy on the bed asked a question, but most of the time he just lay there listening, content to nod. The words poured from Malton's lips, cheerful and amusing, but he didn't feel cheerful. His eyes searched the lad's face, trying to remember him as he had first seen him over a year before. Chick Young had joined the bloody First before Peleliu. Even before he had earned the respect of the company, he had been dubbed Chick. He may have deceived the recruiter about his age, Malton doubted that, but every man in the outfit knew he was just a kid. Unquestionably accepting all the orders of everyone, even fellow privates, he had soon become the companies' mascot. When he had been assigned to Malton's squad, he was accepted instantly and was looked upon as someone to watch over and protect.

Long before he had proven himself as a fighting man on Peleliu, he had come to be respected by the other Marines. He had latched on to Malton as someone to guide him, to instruct him, and quite unashamedly, to mother him.

Malton was astounded at the innocence of the youthful Marine. He would believe anything told him and accepted everything without hesitation. It didn't take the older Marine long to find out the short biography of the youngster.

Born in Tucson, Arizona he had been orphaned when three. His parents had been killed in an automobile accident. Shuttled between relatives, he had let a vagrant's existence, always unwanted. When he was fifteen he had tried to enlist in the army but had been told to go home and grow up first. But the Marine sergeant at the recruiting office was shy of his monthly quota and when Chick told him he was 17, he accepted the fact unblinkingly and enlisted him. For the first time in his life he felt he belonged, and Malton had also drawn from him that for the first time he had enough to eat. After boot camp he had tried for radio school, but his lack of education disqualified him. So he had been put in the Fleet Marine Force and soon found himself overseas.

Neither Malton nor Young saw the Naval Medical officer push aside the white curtain and enter, he moved so silently.

"You better leave, corporal," Dr. Benjamin Tyler softly said, smiling gently as the two looked up. "Don't want to tire our boy here."

Malton quickly rose, turned from the doctor to Chick, who was visibly saddened by the interruption. Catching himself as he reached to pat the boy, Malton said, "Take it easy Chick, I'll come back soon."

The withered lad on the white hospital bed smiled bravely and almost indistinguishly nodded his head. He closed his eyes and fought to hide the pain which racked his body.

The doctor followed Malton from the ward into the passageway. "How is he doing, Doctor?" The concern he felt for Chick was evident on his face and in his voice.

Doctor Tyler lighted a cigarette, the hand flicking on the lighter steady and sure. "The truth is, he's in bad shape. Don't know if we'll be able to pull him through or not." Gently he looked at the Marine, instinctively knowing that he could lay the facts on the line to this man. "It's not just the Beriberi. The boy has never been healthy, never been strong. The privations he's had to induce just wore what resistance he did possess down. We're doing all that the book prescribes, but - ," he stopped, shrugging his shoulders.

"Is he in much pain?" Malton asked the question whose answer he felt he already knew.

The doctor looked squarely in the Marine's eyes. "What he's going through, would make a strong man scream. Every bone in his body is affected, every bone throbs and aches, yet he hasn't as much as whimpered. I can't understand it. He's the strongest minded person I've ever cared for." The doctor shook his head, still not realizing what Malton had known for a long time. Chick never complained - about anything. He always accepted whatever his lot was - grateful for just the mere fact that he belonged.

"Can I do anything - anything?" Malton's voice was pleading.

Dr. Tyler dragged deeply on his cigarette, the smoke tently floating to the top bulkhead. He knew what this man felt - a buddy was suffering - he had seen it often before when casualties from an assault landing were brought on board ship. Men wounded always wanted to help more critically wounded friends. "Nothing now," he hesitated, "perhaps later. Young is going to need blood - lots of it."

Malton nodded and moved down the passageway. The doctor's eyes followed him. How he felt for these Marines. Tyler entered the sick bay office and slowly walked to the desk.

"Anything important, corpsman?" he asked tiredly. It had been a full day. A novice would have been surprised at the number of patients amongst the returning Marines, but not him. These men had been out in the Pacific a long time and the excitement of returning home, coupled with their weakened constitutions, took its toll.

"Nothing, sir," the corpsman checked over his patients roll.

"Good, I'm going topside for a while. Send for me if you need me." Tyler didn't see the nod of the corpsman, he was already heading for the hatchway.

Emerging topside, he adjusted his eyes to the already gathering gloom of dusk. He made his way to officer's country, crowded with the off-duty ship's complement. He nodded greetings to the salutations of his fellow officers as he moved to his favorite spot facing the stern of the ship. Dropping heavily into a deck chair he pulled a cigarette from his pocket, lighted it and watched the white wake of the ship. It was a clear night - the stars above were already twinkling faintly in the darkening sky. The sea was calm and a feeling of peace had settled over the ship.

Peace. It was a wonderful word. It hadn't been so long ago that the thought of peace had been merely a dream. Dr. Benjamin Tyler sighed, thinking of the days a few months before when he had been aboard the hospital ship Solace, off Okinawa. Most available surgeons had been pulled off the transports in the area and temporarily assigned to the hospital ship. Casualties in the north of the island had been heavy and the operating rooms had been full all night long.

He smiled as he remembered the young Marine who had been wheeled into the operating room, his helmet clutched tightly to his chest. Half delirious he had mumbled through his morphine stupor "good old helmet - good old helmet." The corpsmen had tried to take the helmet from him as he was transferred to the operating table, his bandaged head red with blood. It was no use. Tyler had gently unwrapped the bandage which had been so expertly applied at the beach casualty station. Moving the overhead light he had deftly examined the wound. Spreading the blood matted black hair, his fingers efficiently explored the crease that began inches beyond the front of the hairline and continued over the top of the head and stopped near the base of the skull.

Amazed at the injury, he had quickly treated the superficial bullet wound. Completing the treatment, he became aware that the Marine had become unconscious. He heard the corpsman whispering and looked up, surprised at the breach in operating room procedure. His two enlisted helpers had removed the helmet from the wounded man's chest and were examining it. He crossed the room and accepted the steel shell they offered him. His fingers traced the welt that crossed the top and he felt the smooth round hole that was prominent in the front. Turning the helmet over he held the interior to the light. The liner was split raggedly down the center, and wedged in the back, trapped between the fiber of the liner and steel of the helmet, was the crushed remains of a 31 caliber Japanese bullet. He looked up at the corpsman, his grin matching the smiles of their faces.

Tyler lighted another cigarette, the light of the match bright in the night's darkness. The smoking lamp outdoors was always lighted since hostilities had stopped. He burrowed deeper into the deck chair his thoughts still back on the Solace.

He recalled the night after the 5th Marines assault on Shuro. Casualties had been heavy, and the line of landing craft shuttling the wounded to the Solace was unending. He had been in the operating room for hours quickly patching gaping holes in the bodies of young Marines. He had been exhausted when the corpsmen had placed a seriously wounded older man on the operating table. The face was grimy from the mud of Okinawa, the eyes closed in unconsciousness. Quickly he examined the tag on the man. Multiple wounds. Dead tired he had probed the man's body. He counted seven bullet holes over the body, most in strategic places. He shook his head, the man had been evidently hit by a Nambu machine gun. He turned to a corpsman.

"Put this one aside. He hasn't a chance." The corpsman moved in and Tyler turned again to the wounded Marine.

The man's eyes were open, pain racked eyes. They were weak but determined. The mouth parted and Tyler bent over the operating table. "Doc," the marine whispered. "I've got a wife and four kids. You've got to save me." The eyes closed mercifully.

"Let him be," Tyler stopped the corpsmen. "If he wants to live that badly, we'll do our best to see that he does."

Dr. Tyler flipped the cigarette over the side. He wondered about the Marine. He had still been alive when the Solace had pulled out for the states, and he had been transferred back to the ship.

"Sir," Tyler hadn't heard the corpsman come up to him. He looked up, unable to make out the man's features in the darkness. "Yes," he said.

"You'd better come down, sir!" the corpsman said apologetically. "It's Young."

Tyler sighed again and tiredly pulled himself from the chair and followed the corpsman below deck. When his eyes became adjusted to the glare in the passageway, he glanced at his watch. It read 0200. He must have dozed off topside. He hadn't noticed the absence of others on deck.

The tension of expectation filled the air on November 5, 1945. The battle weary Marines on board could sense the nearness of home - home! The word had a warmth, a gentle savor as it crossed the lips. Tomorrow was the day - scuttlebutt had it that the giant transport would slip beneath the Golden Gate Bridge at dawn. Even the chow line griping was at a minimum, and the marine handy with the barber clippers was the objective of a long queue. Atop the hatches, men halfheartedly played cards, their minds not on the game, but floating over the few hundred miles of water to the mainland. All the restrained thoughts of the States and what the word implied to each, at last were permitted from the special niche in the brain to the forefront. No longer would it be dangerous for the thoughts to linger. All the demands they wrought would soon be a reality.

The unholy and heartsick seven were an exception to the rule. Though happy to be going home and to their loved ones, their joy was tempered by the thought of Chick. For days he had been lingering on the brink of death. When Malton had gone down to sick bay daily, the corpsman had sadly shook his head.

Dirty, unshaven, the group sat beneath a lifeboat high on the emergency launching dockets. They sat quietly, seeming oblivious to the preparation for debarkation of the rest of the Marines.

"Here comes the doc," McPherson sat with his back to the rail.

Dr. Tyler walked down the deck, his eyes darting right and left. Spotting the group in their semi-secluded refuge, he quickly made for them. Ducking beneath the lifeboat, he remained on his haunches.

"Malton," he began, his face lined with fatigue. "Young is worse, and needs blood, bad".

"I'm willing, sir," Malton quickly said, the others impulsively echoing his words.

"It's not so simple," the doctor shook his head. "The type is difficult." He paused brushing his hand over his eyes. "Check your tags, it's type 0."

The Marines hands were already digging inside their greasy dungarees. Quickly they scanned the dog tags which gave the name, serial number, branch of service, religion, and blood type.

"I've got it!" Malton cried. The others shook their heads, unhappy that they couldn't contribute to the cause which they all felt so deeply about.

"We'll need more than one transfusion," Dr. Tyler said, backing out and straightening his aching legs. "I'll call for volunteers over the P.A. system. Corporal Malton, report to the corpsmen at the sick bay."

Dr. Tyler's legs disappeared from view down the deck, and Malton quickly made his way to the sick bay.

"Now hear this! Now hear this!" the coarse voice sounded over the ship's communications system. "A Marine needs Type 0 blood! This is an emergency! Marine volunteers with Type 0 blood report to the sick bay at once."

Throughout the ship men quickly checked their dog tags. The story of Chick Young's fight with death had spread over the ship. From along the decks, Marines rose and quietly laid below to the sick bay.

Malton sat in the sick-bay orderly room. He watched as, one by one, other Marines checked into the corpsman at the desk and then found seats alongside the bulkheads. Malton counted eighteen. No conversation could be heard in the room. They waited, silently and thoughtfully. Ten minutes passed, every minute an eternity.

The quietness of the room was disturbed by the entrance of Dr. Tyler, dressed in the white surgical uniform symbolic of the profession. He nodded and smiled at the men as he moved to the corpsman's desk. The two conversed in muted tones, the corpsman nodding, and shaking his head in turn. The doctor turned to the staring men about the room.

"Men, we've sent for your permanent record folders from the transient office. They'll be here in a few minutes."

Looking over the seated men with pride in his eyes, Dr. Tyler felt the espirit-de-corps which was imbued in each of them. Tired with the fatigue of battle, they were still willing to part with the precious blood their weakened constitutions needed so badly.

A Marine Corporal entered the cabin, a pile of folders in his hands. Quickly he handed them to the doctor who, aided by the corpsman, carefully inspected each. One by one, the doctor called the men. Speaking softly, he indicated portions of the records to each. He ended the interview with a deep felt thank you. Slowly each man turned and left the cabin, a look of regret evident on his face.

"Corporal J. C. Malton," the doctor called.

Malton arose from his seat and went to the desk, apprehension on his face. "Corporal," Dr. Tyler began, "look at this record. Is it correct? Malaria,

Guadalcanal, April, 1944; Malaria, Peleliu, September, 1945, Malaria, Pavuvu, October, November, 1945 -" he stopped skimping over the many such inserts in the record with his finger.

Malton nodded his head, not grasping the point of the doctor's words.

Dr. Tyler put his hand on the corporal's shoulder, "Son, we can't take your blood." He hesitated, sadly observing the look which had come over Malton's face. "Malaria, we can't insert that malaria infested blood into Young. So much active malaria would do him more harm than good."

Malton felt useless. Remembering the others before him. "The others?"

Dr. Tyler nodded. He ached to comfort this Marine but words would not come.

Looking at the eight remaining Marines, Malton said, "I'll wait, sir."

Dr. Tyler nodded and called the next man. The emotionally spent Malton moved to the bulkhead near the door, watching the dwindling number of men in the room. As each was turned away and left the room, he looked into this friend of Young's eyes and silently offered a wordless apology.

Finally the room was void of Marines, save Malton. The corpsman quietly gathered the folders, not looking up. The corporal went to the doctor who was sitting on the edge of the desk, his thumb and forefinger rubbing his eyes.

"I don't understand, sir," Malton softly began, "I thought Type 0 was universal. Can't any type blood be given Chick?"

Dr. Tyler shook his head, "True, Type 0 is universal, but universal means that Type 0 blood can be administered to all the other types, but, a person with Type 0 blood can receive no other type." Tyler sighed and turned to the corpsman. "Call for volunteers from the ship's company."

The corpsman reached for the telephone on his desk and softly spoke into it.

"Don't worry, son," Dr. Tyler said, turning to the Marine. "There should be some sailors with that type. Want to wait?"

Malton nodded and again took a seat, the whiteness of the room beating a drum inside his head.

Malton opened his eyes, he must have dozed he thought as he looked at his watch. It was 2300. He hadn't had any chow and his stomach craved for food. About him in the cabin were a half dozen sailors waiting as the Marines before them had done.

His eyes moved to the corpsman who was smiling. Malton moved his cramped legs and strode to the desk. "I must have fallen asleep," he said self-consciously.

The corpsman nodded, "Not too long. It's going to be alright, I think." He indicated the sailors. "Some of these guys will be o.k. That is, if swabby blood won't contaminate a Marine," he laughed. The sound covered the room, breaking the tension all felt, "How about some chow? Dr. Tyler said for you to go to the duty mess when you awoke. They'll feed you there."

Malton was reluctant to leave, but he couldn't do any more than wait, and he was hungry. He muttered his thanks and left the cabin. The food didn't sit too well on his stomach, and the atmosphere in the cheery mess didn't correspond with his depression. Dutifully he ate the ham and potato dinner, realizing that this was not the usual fare served to transient troops.

Making his way back to the sick bay, he found the room empty. He sat down and waited, a prayer on his lips. His fingers counted the rosary beads in his dungaree pants pocket.

The corpsman re-entered. Malton didn't like the look on his face. Spotting the Marine he crossed the cabin to him. "Three of the donors were acceptable," he said. "It might not be enough."

Malton sat stunned, speechless. He watched the corpsman go about his work. The hours slipped by endlessly. He dozed again waking with a start, ashamed of his inability to remain awake. A hand gently shook Malton's shoulder. He opened his eyes and saw Dr. Tyler standing over him. He startled.

Dr. Tyler had watched the Marine several minutes before he awakened him, dreading what he must say to this friend of the dying boy.

"Son, I'm sorry," he hesitated at the pain in the Marine's eyes, "not enough blood. He's slipping fast." He stopped again, characteristically, rubbing his eyes. "If he can only hold out until we reach Frisco. I've radioed ahead for the blood he needs. It will be waiting for us."

Malton sat motionless, aware of the quickened motion of the ship. Please, God, Please. "Can I see Chick?" he asked, surprised by the loudness of his voice in the quiet room.

Dr. Tyler nodded and led the way through the ward. They passed the bed where Chick had lain and went into a tiny cabin at the end of the ward. A corpsman sat at each side of the bed. A dim, diverted light cast eerie shadows on the bulkhead. Young, lay still, his body incapable of reacting to the constant pain of the muscles. His face was ashen, twisted in pain. The bewildered eyes were closed to the scene about him,

"He's been unconscious since noon," Dr. Tyler softly said. He motioned to a chair in the corner of the cramped cabin, and Malton silently sat down. The doctor efficiently went about the task of administering to the slight form under the crisp white sheet.

Malton watched, no longer dozing. His eyes went to the face of Chick. His thoughts were angry, his heart bleeding for this young kid. The hours slowly passed, the vigil of four men, three professional medics, and the fourth a heart broken friend. Watching and praying went on.

One thought persisted in the brain of Malton. It's not fair! It's not fair! Why, Chick? A lonely kid, who had brought nothing but good into the world of all who knew him. An unquestioning friend, fighter - all that the damn world could ask of a man. He had wanted so little from life - just to belong. He had finally found a home in the service. Admired and respected by everyone he came in contact with, he finally belonged - and now - death.

Malton cursed the crazy world which was rejecting this kid from Arizona. Cursed the country which permitted the Youngs to suffer so - giving nothing and taking so much. This quiet body on the bed was too young to vote - too young to drink - too young to love - but not too young to die - and for what, who would remember him - save for the few who had known him in the service. Damn the world - damn the hypocrites who inhabited it.

Dr. Tyler bent over the form, taking a pulse count. Above, deck movement had begun. Marines were crowding the rails, cheers sounded dimly through the steel.

The doctor softly called the corpsman to the bedside. Quickly they conferred and then he left the cabin. Dr. Tyler turned slowly to the corporal sitting erect in the chair. Slowly he met his eyes and gently nodded.

Tears rolled down Malton's cheeks unashamedly, the tears welled and fell. He arose slowly, the rosary in his hand, and moved to the bedside. Gently he touched Chick's hand, a prayer on his lips. He raised his eyes from the body and looked through the porthole. The Golden Gate Bridge broke its majesty through the San Francisco fog.

Chick had come home!

John T. Maltese,
United States Marine Corps, 1943

John T. Maltese, in his 30s,
Steubenville, Ohio

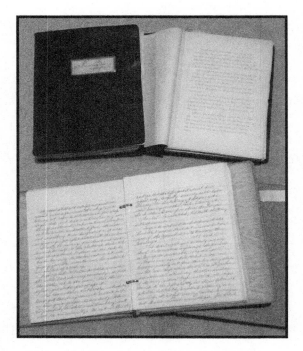

The original handwritten and typed manuscript.

CPSIA information can be obtained
at www.ICGtesting.com
Printed in the USA
BVOW08*0524130317

478250BV00001B/4/P